Books by Daniel Palmer

DELIRIOUS

HELPLESS

STOLEN

DESPERATE

CONSTANT FEAR

FORGIVE ME

Published by Kensington Publishing Corporation

CONSTANT FEAR

DANIEL PALMER

PINNACLE BOOKS
Kensington Publishing Corp.
www.kensingtonbooks.com

PINNACLE BOOKS are published by

Kensington Publishing Corp.
119 West 40th Street
New York, NY 10018

All Kensington titles, imprints, and distributed lines are available at special quantity discounts for bulk purchases for sales promotions, premiums, fund-raising, educational, or institutional use. Special book excerpts or customized printings can also be created to fit specific needs. For details, write or phone the office of the Kensington sales manager: Kensington Publishing Corp., 119 West 40th Street, New York, NY 10018, attn: Sales Department; phone 1-800-221-2647.

ISBN-13: 978-0-7860-3383-6
ISBN-10: 0-7860-3383-5

First mass market paperback printing: May 2016

10 9 8 7 6 5 4 3 2

Printed in the United States of America

First electronic edition: May 2016

ISBN-13: 978-0-7860-3384-3
ISBN-10: 0-7860-3384-3

For Clyde Terry and Susan Palmer Terry, who embody constant courage.

Chapter 1

"**D**eath doesn't schedule an appointment."

Jake Dent had said this on many occasions, but wasn't certain the mantra had stuck in his son's teenage brain. Still, it was the truth. Death could show up at any hour, on any day, uninvited, unwelcomed.

Jake was dressed for the cool March weather; and much like a hunter, he wore three layers to protect him from the elements. The windproof fabric of his camouflage jacket was a four-color woodland pattern, designed to blend with the widest variety of western Massachusetts foliage.

It would help him evade the enemy.

At three o'clock in the morning, his son would be sound asleep. Sure enough, Jake could hear heavy breathing through the hollow-core door to Andy's bedroom. Jake could have upgraded that door to a more substantial model, but it would have been an unnecessary expense. Jake opted to invest his limited resources in products that could help him and his son stay alive. *Priorities.* For this reason, Jake kept everything to only essentials in the double-wide trailer he and Andy called home.

To reach safety, Jake and Andy would have to traverse several miles of rugged woodland in complete darkness. If anything went wrong en route to their destination, they'd carry enough provisions to make the forest their new home until it was safe to move again. Everything Jake needed to survive was stored neatly inside his GOOD (Get Out of Dodge) pack. The nylon camouflage bags mounted to an ALICE frame, standard issue for the U.S. military for some years, offered plenty of storage. Two zippers on the front of the bag allowed rapid access to the contents within.

Inside the bags, Jake had packed three liters of water—one liter per day per person—as well as a four-liter water-filtration system. The other contents of his pack were equally vital. If they couldn't reach their destination, the meals and energy bars would provide enough nutrition for several days. Jake prepared for the "ifs" as *if* they were certainties.

He had packed enough clothing for a weekend camping trip. Sturdy boots, long pants, long underwear, two shirts (good for layering), two pairs of socks (wool, not cotton), two hats, and a bandanna. Bandanas had multitudes of uses, Jake had discovered over the years. A tent and ground tarp would provide some protection from the elements, and his down-filled sleeping bag was long and wide, perfect to cocoon his broad-shouldered, six-two frame. Jake had also packed three different ways to make fire, cooking gear, hygiene products, a first aid kit, and, perhaps the most important item of all, a .357-caliber SIG SAUER P226, carried by police officers and the military. Jake's SIG held fifteen 9mm rounds and was a durable weapon that could thrive in tough conditions.

Jake opened Andy's bedroom and sidestepped several piles of clothes strewn about like mini moguls. Standing beside Andy's bed, Jake gazed at his son and watched him sleep. They should be moving, and quickly, but he couldn't resist the urge to stop and stare. Even though Andy was sixteen—*Sixteen? How did that happen?*—Jake could see the little boy lurking inside the young man. This was his son, the one person in life Jake most wanted to protect.

With his ruffled mop of curly, dark hair and penetrating chocolate eyes, Andy would one day grow into a truly handsome man. But according to him, the girls at Pepperell Academy—popular, preppy, and loaded with cash—focused on Andy's braces, his nose (a bit too big for his face), a slight peppering of acne, and thin arms not yet muscular. While the awkward teenage years lingered, Andy would concentrate his energies on things other than dating.

Andy's cluttered room was typical of any teen. Posters on the walls showed characters from the hit television shows *Doctor Who, The Big Bang Theory,* and some cartoon that was apparently an Internet thing Jake didn't even pretend to understand. The most spectacular object in Andy's cramped but cozy bedroom was a desk he and his friends had built to look like a large-scale model of a TIE Fighter from the *Star Wars* movies. Andy and his pals from Pepperell Academy were self-proclaimed geeks, and damn proud of it.

Atop the TIE Fighter desk was the largest computer Jake had ever seen. Andy had built it piece by piece, and it looked to Jake like a sentient robot, with all the blinking lights and wires jutting out from the back. While Andy was a computer code maestro, writing apps that he and his buddies sold via iTunes, Jake's knowledge of the blasted machines was limited to e-mail, Google, and the occasional Microsoft Word document.

Jake shook Andy awake. The boy's bony shoulder fit inside his palm like a baseball, and Jake's thoughts flit back to days long gone. He closed his eyes and imagined the smell of fresh-cut grass, the feel, the texture of the pitcher's mound, and the roar of the crowd. How times had changed.

Andy's eyes fluttered open. He looked disoriented, but only for a moment.

"They're coming," Jake said, his voice calm and even. "We've got to go. Now. It's go time."

Andy swung his legs off the bed. A second later, he was on his feet, sturdy as if he'd been awake for hours. In the next instant, Andy had the accordion closet doors pulled open, grabbing the clothes he'd set aside for this very moment. They were the only clothes in his bedroom neatly folded and organized. His steel-toed hiking boots were intentionally unlaced, making them easy to slip on. Like his father, Andy dressed in layers, and wore a matching camouflage pattern.

Jake observed the rise and fall of Andy's chest. A push of adrenaline had turned his son's breathing visibly rapid. Adrenaline had its advantages. It would help Andy move faster through the woods, and might make him impervious to pain—should he fall or twist an ankle during the run. It had a downside, too. If stress and adrenaline induced insulin resistance, Andy could be in serious trouble, but his son knew best how to manage his diabetes.

Keeping Andy to a regular eating and sleeping schedule would have been ideal, but that was no longer an option. Andy must have shared his father's concern, because he took out his OneTouch UltraMini blood sugar monitor and a test strip. He held the lancing device against the side of his finger, pressed the release button, and didn't flinch when the needle broke the skin. A small drop of blood materialized with a slight squeeze of the finger. Andy placed the blood drop perfectly on the test strip. Practice, thousands of repetitions.

Andy didn't share the results with Jake. This was part of adolescence. Monitoring Andy's condition had been Jake's responsibility since his son was five. At some point, however, the baton had passed, and Andy took responsibility for his blood glucose levels without Jake's intervention. Like setting a curfew, Jake trusted that Andy would follow the rules and be diligent with his health. It was all part of building Andy's confidence and self-reliance.

When the levels weren't ideal, Jake had learned to avoid making accusations. As much as he wanted to shout, *"Why is your blood sugar so high? Did you eat something you weren't supposed to?"* he didn't. Jake believed in giving roots and wings, and he needed to show Andy that he trusted his judgment. He encouraged his son to make decisions for himself, offering praise whenever Andy made the right ones. It was what any parent of a teenager would do.

The glucose reading must have been fine, because no insulin injection followed. Andy slipped on his own GOOD pack. Inside were the same provisions Jake had brought, minus the SIG SAUER, as well as everything he needed to manage his diabetes.

Once his jacket was on, boots laced, pack secured, Andy got his night vision system in place. It was a tactical helmet, military issued, with an L4G30 mount from Wilcox. Secured to the swiveling J-arm was a PVS-14 night vision monocular, powered by a Gen 3 image intensifier. Jake had the same unit on his helmet.

For Andy's sixteenth birthday, Jake had bought his son an X-Bolt Micro Hunter rifle and helped him with the paperwork for his firearm identification card. It was a lighter-weight rifle with all the features of a full-sized X-Bolt. Jake had wanted Andy to have some way to protect himself for years, and now, legally, he could.

Andy slung his rifle over his shoulder and without a word headed for the trailer's back door. Jake fell into step behind his son, grabbed his own rifle by the door, and checked his watch. In five minutes, Andy had gone from being sound asleep to crunching dead leaves on his march through the woods.

His son was learning.

Through the night vision monocular, the world was an eerie shade of green, but the powerful optics made the forest come alive. They could see everything in pristine detail, from the smallest tree branches to the bumps and ridges on fallen leaves. The path they walked was a well-defined escape route that Jake meticulously maintained. It was far enough back from the road so they passed behind houses without being heard or seen, and wide enough in most places to let them walk side by side.

Both Jake and Andy were on the lookout for the slightest bit of movement that might betray the presence of the enemy. They refrained from talking, though Jake used preset hand signals to check in with Andy.

Andy kept his rifle slung over his shoulder, while Jake's was trained on the darkness. Both were on high alert, ready to pick up any noise—a snap of a twig or the rustle of some branches. Nothing. Not a sound. But that didn't mean they weren't out there somewhere. Eyes could be watching from the shadows. *Keep moving.* No other choice would do.

At some point, the path widened and became a road. Jake and Andy kept to the wood line and continued their march. Moonlight, which had powered the night vision optics, now provided enough illumination all by itself.

Eventually, the duo emerged from a copse and entered a vast hilly field, looking like a pair of soldiers returning from a scouting mission. They trekked another quarter mile before reaching a small fieldstone building situated directly behind the Groveland Gymnasium.

Built in the 1980s, the Groveland Gymnasium served the students and faculty of Pepperell Academy and housed an indoor hockey rink, squash and racquetball courts, swimming pool, basketball courts, weight-lifting area, and all manner of fitness amenities. It was best of breed, as was everything at "The Pep."

Jake lowered his night vision to scan the darkness once more. All clear. He took a moment to assess his son's condition anew. Sweat matted Andy's hair below the helmet, and his short, sharp breaths meant the adrenaline rush was still in effect. Through it all, Andy remained alert and focused. He was disciplined and well trained. Jake didn't like to brag, but he was proud that his son's body and mind were as strong as his character.

To the east of the fieldstone structure stood the

other campus buildings of Pepperell Academy, Andy's school and Jake's place of employment for the past ten years. While Andy looked on, Jake removed a loose stone affixed to the side of the field house to reveal a hidden key. Through the unlocked door, Jake and Andy entered a room crammed with supplies—bags of ice melt, sand, cones, all sorts of maintenance equipment.

In the center of the room, Jake moved a pile of lightweight mats to reveal the outline of a two-by-two square cut into the wood of the floor. One side of the square had two hinges, and a rusting metal ring lay in the center. Jake pulled open the trapdoor to reveal a ladder to the level below.

Nearly all of the buildings of Pepperell Academy were connected by a series of tunnels, some of which were rumored to date back a century. Forward-thinking architects, long before Jake's tenure, had designed the tunnels to hide the infrastructure belowground. They understood the value of distributing services (water, gas, power, heat, steam, telecommunication, and even coal) around campus without impeding the pedestrian traffic or having to maintain unsightly sewer lines and utility poles aboveground. The effort created a labyrinth of passageways few had ever seen.

As head custodian and grounds manager for Pepperell Academy, Jake was one of the few employees with access to these secret passages. The kids and faculty, even other maintenance personnel, were not permitted to use them. That was one reason it made a perfect bug-out location (BOL).

With their packs still on, rifles slung over their shoulders, Jake and Andy descended the ladder to the underground passageway below. The corridor they traveled was in an older portion of the tunnel system, and they followed it to another locked door. The passageway included several rooms—most, but not all, unoccupied.

An ADEL Trinity-788 Heavy-Duty Biometric Fingerprint Door Lock secured entry to one of the rooms. Jake put his finger on the biometric scanner, and the door opened with a click. They entered the room and Andy turned on the light.

The room was a massive larder, well stocked with canned and dry food, sacks of rice, water, fuel, portable heaters, gardening tools, guns, knives, and ammo. Jake lowered his weapon and took out a stopwatch. He pushed the stop button and the tension left his body in a long exhale. Andy relaxed as well.

"That's three minutes faster than the last time," Jake said to his son. "We're doing well, but we can still do better."

Andy slumped to the floor. He needed a moment to regain his composure. Jake could see the stress of the trek had taken a significant physical and mental toll. Andy's eyes flared with anger, but he mustered enough restraint to keep his emotions in check. His son hated these drills, and had been vocal about it for some time. However, whenever he protested, Jake would say, "Death doesn't schedule an appointment."

Chapter 2

Few things in life brought Fausto Garza more enjoyment than causing pain. Looking at Eduardo, the bruised and battered man in front of him, gave Fausto a rush of pure pleasure. Eduardo was sitting on the trash-strewn floor of an old, abandoned warehouse and was tied up with rusty chains secured to a radiator. His left eye was swollen shut, but he still had some vision out of the right. Jagged cuts from Fausto's many rings marred both of Eduardo's cheeks, and dried blood stained the front of his torn guayabera. For a time, the open wounds had poured blood, enough so Fausto had to apply dirty rags to the skin to keep Eduardo from bleeding out. He needed his prey conscious.

The unmistakable scent of urine filled Fausto's nostrils and fired up more pleasure centers in his brain. He relished the smell of fear like a fine perfume. It even got him aroused. He'd seek a release for his pent-up desires as soon as he disposed of Eduardo. But first, Eduardo had some information to share.

Fausto crouched to get eye level with Eduardo.

"¿Dónde están las drogas que te robaste?" ("Where are the drugs that you stole?")

Eduardo's eyes flared; but as he gazed into the face of death, his bravado retreated like a nervous paca vanishing into the forest underbrush.

"No le robé ningun drogas, Fausto," Eduardo said. *"Lo juro por la vida de mi madre."* ("I didn't steal any drugs, Fausto. I swear on my mother's life.")

Fausto, a natural-born skeptic, didn't believe him. "Where are the drugs you stole?"

"I took nothing from you. Please, you must believe me," Eduardo answered. His split lips could barely form the words and his speech came out slurred, as if he'd spent the night alone with a bottle of mescal.

"No es tan bravo el león como lo pintan." Fausto enjoyed taunting Eduardo. In most circles Eduardo *was* considered a fierce lion, but Durango, Eduardo's home, and home to a rival drug cartel, was more than six hundred kilometers from Chihuahua. Here, in Sangre Tierra territory, the man had no power.

"Sangre Tierra," or "blood earth." The cartel traced its origin and name to the day Arturo Bolivar Soto had ordered the execution of the leaders of the rival Torres cartel in a single, gruesome bloodbath. Ten bound and gagged men, all of them rich from drug money, had been tossed into a previously dug shallow grave near the Panteón La Colina. Standing at the edges of the pit were men from Soto's group, Fausto among them. They were armed with AK-47 assault rifles, and some even wielded Uzis.

"Be it known, today belongs to Soto."

Those were the last words those ten men ever heard.

Blood spilled from bullet-ravaged bodies, pooling beneath the corpses until the parched earth swallowed every last drop.

Sangre Tierra . . . Blood Earth.

Arturo Bolivar Soto was its first and only leader. From that moment on, a terror worse than the Torres cartel reigned. Already-dug graves became a trademark of Sangre Tierra, and mass shootings a favorite method of compliance and control. Soto's ambitions were far larger than the territory currently under his authority. The balance was soon to tip in his favor. Sangre Tierra already had a growing presence in the United States, and from there had plans to extend its area of dominance well beyond the boundaries the Torres Cartel once controlled.

Poor Eduardo had interfered with those ambitions. For that, he would pay.

"I don't have what you seek."

Fausto appraised Eduardo anew and suppressed the urge to bend back Eduardo's fingers with pliers.

"I'm going to tell you a story," Fausto said, standing and using his pants to brush away the grime collected on his palms. Fausto had a long face, a prominent nose, deep-set eyes, and hair like the mane of a stallion, which he pulled back into a long ponytail that swept across his broad shoulders. He was fit, narrow at the waist, muscled and in perfect proportion. Women were drawn to Fausto, but he preferred the whores, who asked for nothing and never complained of his sexual proclivities.

"When I was a young boy, no more than thirteen," Fausto began, "I lived in Ciudad Juárez. It was there I met Soto's cousin, Carlos Guzman, who gave me a gun and ordered me to shoot a man he had tied up and dumped on the ground. Carlos was so drunk he didn't think he could hit the man at point-blank range. I didn't know what to say. I had never killed before. But what captured my imagination was Carlos's diamond-studded watch, the fancy clothes he wore, the pearl inlay on the pistol's handle. You see I came from nothing, Eduardo. I was an orphan boy who escaped from an abusive master."

Here, Fausto could have elaborated on the sexual abuse he had endured, the endless rapes by the pervert who had taken him in under the auspices of hiring a young store clerk to stock shelves in his grocery store. *Store clerk!* His rapist wanted a victim, a plaything, and Fausto was too young, too inexperienced, too frightened, to find a way out.

"Why are you telling me this, Fausto?" Eduardo's voice snapped with fear.

"Shut up until I finish," Fausto barked.

Eduardo bowed his head sullenly.

"When I met Carlos Guzman," Fausto continued, "I had just recently escaped from my captor. I was living on the streets of Juárez, scrounging for food like an alley cat. I had experienced little but the darkest side of humanity for close to a decade. So when I pulled the trigger, blowing that helpless man's brains out his ears, I did so, hoping one day I, too, could have a pearl-inlaid pistol."

Fausto reached behind him. From the waistband of his jeans, he produced a pistol exactly like the one he had described. A pleased-with-himself grin creased the corners of his mouth as he put the gun away. The grin widened into a smile; for the first time since his abduction, Eduardo could see the ornately designed gold caps that covered each of Fausto's teeth. The caps were removable, but Fausto was considering having them affixed permanently. They sent a strong message of wealth and power, Fausto's two greatest loves.

"When Carlos sobered up and saw what I had done," Fausto continued, "he was so appreciative that he paid a visit to my so-called employer. The police found the grocery store owner's liver in one garbage can, his heart in another, and his head in another still. From that moment on, I became a part of something. Something I could believe in. Carlos raised me like a son. And Arturo Soto is a grandfather whom I treasure and adore. They trust me with the most important assignments. They respect me and my ability, and for that, I'm eternally grateful."

"Again, why are you telling me this, Fausto?"

"Why do I tell you this?" Fausto repeated. "Because you need to know that I view you like you're a rodent. Your life has that much meaning to me. I feel nothing for your suffering. And I would not be involved here unless this situation was indeed a very big deal."

Fausto went over to his toolbox, the only object on the warehouse floor aside from a busted wooden chair. He retrieved from within a cordless power drill, with a gleaming silver bit. With a push on the trigger, Fausto showed Eduardo that the drill's battery was fully charged.

"Now, then," Fausto said in a perfectly calm voice. "Let's talk again about the packages you took from us."

Fausto placed the drill on Eduardo's knee and squeezed

the trigger. Eduardo's eyes burst with panic at the loud whirring sound. The angry metallic whine quickly dampened as the tip of the drill bored through the fabric of his soiled pants and penetrated the first layer of skin. Blood erupted from the puncture wound; the scream that followed was symphonic to Fausto's ears.

Fausto prepared to drill again. He had bet himself he could bore nine holes before Eduardo passed out from pain. Fausto steadied Eduardo's shaking leg in a vise-like grip. He set the drill tip on the other knee when his phone rang. Fausto exhaled a loud sigh and returned his attention to the drill, but the persistent ringing proved too much of a distraction. He glanced at the caller ID and sighed once more. Eduardo did not seem certain how to feel. The anticipation of pain was its own form of torture.

Fausto answered the call.

"¿Que quieres?" Fausto said. ("What do you want?")

Fausto kept the drill bit against Eduardo's knee, but he waited to pull the trigger. He didn't want to listen to the caller over Eduardo's screaming. Eduardo's blubbering was bothersome enough.

"Soto te quiere ver ahora mismo, Fausto," a man said. ("Soto wants to see you right away, Fausto.")

"I'm a little busy right now," Fausto answered in Spanish.

"It's urgent," said the man. "There's big trouble in America, someplace in Massachusetts. You need to leave immediately."

Fausto ended the call and turned his attention back to Eduardo. "Always something, eh?"

Eduardo looked like a man who'd been given a new lease on life.

"I'll have to finish with you later. In the meantime, let me leave you with something to remember me by."

Fausto pulled the trigger on the drill and wished he had more time to make Eduardo scream.

Chapter 3

Ellie Barnes remembered how he stood.

Whenever she thought of the first time she laid eyes on Jake Dent, she remembered that the most.

Jake had drawn his weapon in a fluid motion, arm slightly bent—that little give so important for flexibility. Long, stiff arms create fatigue that can affect the shot. Jake knew this, and Ellie did, too.

Ellie was a police sergeant in the town of Winston, and one of the best shooters on the force. In ten years on the job, Ellie had stopped plenty of drunk drivers, burglaries, and domestic disputes, but never discharged her weapon in the line of duty. The police academy preached preparedness; so if the day ever came, she was practiced and would be ready.

She observed that the man to her left at the gun range, whom she'd later come to know as Jake, also shot one of her favorite pistols, a Ruger P95, the way William Tell could split apples. At some point, she caught his eye—or he caught hers, Ellie couldn't remember—but she did notice he was as fit as any guy on the SWAT team. She liked his boyish good looks and strong arms.

Ellie's colleagues at the Winston PD jokingly referred to her as "Pint-Sized Power." Few could match her reps in push-ups and pull-ups, despite her being only five-four. She had warm brown eyes and a pleasing smile that attracted plenty of interest from local men, including a lot of divorced dads, some of whom were intrigued by her chosen profession. Her smile must have attracted Jake, too. He had approached, introduced himself, and they made small talk about guns for a few minutes.

Ellie was taken by his knowledge of firearms. "Why do you like the Ruger so much?" she asked.

Jake didn't hesitate. "Dependability," he said. "May not be the easiest to hold, but you can always trust it."

For a second, Ellie wasn't sure if Jake was referring to himself or the gun. Either way, she fell into his blue eyes, and got lost there. It was as if Jake Dent had plugged into her brain and come up with two words that made him immeasurably more attractive: "trust" and "dependability."

Walter had those qualities when she married him, or so she had thought.

A week after their initial meeting, Jake invited Ellie out to dinner and she gladly accepted the invitation. He had selected a cozy Italian restaurant, with checkered tablecloths and dim lighting, a couple towns away from Winston. The maintenance guy from the local prep school and a cop from the same town out to dinner together would get some people talking. Jake was sensitive to this when he made the reservation, and that sensitivity intrigued Ellie.

For their first date, Ellie wore her chestnut hair down, so it fell across her shoulders, and a low-cut, curve-hugging yellow dress—a rarity for a woman who favored flannel and jeans. Jake had on an oxford shirt and something told Ellie it was the only one he owned.

"I wanted to have kids, but Walter didn't," Ellie said to Jake midway through the meal. She hadn't known she was going to talk about her ex—or herself—so much, but Jake had a way of bringing it out of her.

"I'm sorry," Jake said. "That must have been hard on you."

"It was."

"Is that why you got divorced?"

Ellie chuckled. "No. That would be the woman in his office he was sleeping with."

Jake kept a stolid expression. "Well, in that case, he's an asshole."

Ellie laughed again. "You don't know the half of it. According to Walter, the affair was just about the sex. Somehow this was supposed to make me feel better."

Jake showed an appropriate degree of disgust. "I'm guessing you two haven't stayed in touch."

"No," Ellie said. "But I did fill that kid void—well, sort of."

"You have children?" Jake asked.

The candlelight flickered and cast shadows that called attention to the deep creases on Jake's ruggedly handsome face. Every one of those lines had a story behind it, Ellie believed.

"Well, let's just say each of my kids weighs between seventy-seven to eighty-five pounds fully grown, and they're courageous, loyal, alert, and truly fearless."

Jake nodded. He understood right away, guessing correctly that Ellie had dogs.

Ellie explained how she'd started training German shepherds to help heal her broken heart, but what she'd discovered was a new passion and purpose in life. She had grown up around working dogs and was familiar with the breed. But it was not until Ellie trained her first service dog, and gave that dog to a new owner, that she fully appreciated her connectedness to these animals. It was love, pure and simple. Each dog she trained and subsequently gave away took a little piece of her heart along.

"What do you train the dogs to do?" Jake asked.

"They're for diabetics."

Jake gave her an inscrutable smile then. "We have more in common than a love for the Ruger, it seems," he said.

Jake told Ellie a little bit about his son, Andy, who had been diagnosed with type 1 diabetes as a toddler.

"My mom was a diabetic and died from the disease when I was fifteen," Ellie said, "and my dad was a K-9 officer. So in a way, training service dogs for insulin-dependent diabetics was a way of honoring both their memories."

"When did you lose your dad?"

Ellie pushed the remnants of her linguini dinner about her plate. "About five years ago," she said. Her eyes misted. "Heart attack. It was sudden, the way he wanted to go. Wish he could see my dogs. He'd be so proud. My dad always encouraged us to be of service to others."

Ellie explained how she trained her dogs to use their powerful sense of smell to detect changes in blood sugar levels. When those levels spiked too high, or dropped dangerously low, the dogs would go to work, barking a warning. The dogs were vigilant even through the night, as their owners slept.

Jake listened intently, but something about his expression was playful. Ellie eventually caught on. "You know all this, don't you?" she asked.

"I had looked into getting a dog for Andy, but he didn't want anything that would call so much attention to his condition. He refused to get an insulin pump, too, even when our insurance could finally cover the cost. By that point, he was used to managing his blood sugar levels with food and insulin injections as needed."

"From my experience, juveniles can be the most brittle," Ellie said.

"Your experience is spot-on," Jake said. "Andy's blood sugar can go from high to very low without much to tilt those scales. We've had more than a few emergency visits to the ER over the years. Now, in addition to glucose tablets and insulin, Andy carries a glucagon emergency kit everywhere he goes in case his blood sugar drops."

Ellie knew all about glucagon, a natural substance that raises blood sugar by forcing the body to release sugar stored in the liver. It was used in emergent hypoglycemic situations, when the body's blood sugar level dropped dangerously low. In those instances the body could not process glucose tablets, even foods like chocolate, quickly enough to get enough glucose into the bloodstream. If the low blood sugar condition persisted untreated, a diabetic could lose consciousness, slip into a coma, and ultimately die.

Dessert came. Ellie ordered chocolate mousse, wondering what something like that would do to Andy's blood sugar. Jake suggested they go out for a nightcap, but Ellie declined, with more than a hint of regret in her voice.

"I have to get home to Kibo," she said.

Jake shook his head in good-natured disappointment. "Is he a boyfriend you haven't told me about?"

"No, he's *my* dog."

Ellie had spent a year apprenticing before she trained her first dog on her own. She partnered with a reputable charity that helped place her dogs with people who could not afford the expense, but the time and effort that went into training made each donation a gut-wrenching experience. For this reason, Ellie got a puppy she knew would stay. She named her dog Kibo, for one of the three volcanic cones on Mount Kilimanjaro, which she had climbed in her twenties. After three years together, Kibo truly was woman's best friend.

"Will you go out with me again?" Jake said.

"I would have been supremely disappointed if you didn't ask."

At the end of their second date, Jake asked Ellie out again. And he asked her out again after that. Two months later, they'd ended up in bed after a bottle of wine and a bad movie on Netflix. Ellie always gravitated to the blue-collar types, the rough guys who were skilled with their hands. One night together and Ellie could attest to Jake's considerable skills.

More than a year had passed since that first date—a year of no big fights, no heartache, and no drama. That was just the way Ellie liked it. She liked the sex, too, but sex wasn't everything. Honesty was.

Ellie had something important to share with Jake,

something that could change their relationship drastically. He'd show up any minute, and Ellie would have to confront him.

Ellie gazed down at Winston from the hilly rise of the ten-acre plot of land her father had willed to his three daughters. As a matter of fairness, Ellie's father had divided his substantial assets equally among the three children, but only Ellie wanted to stay in Winston. She used her inheritance to buy out her city-dwelling siblings.

The home and land were special to Ellie, filled with cherished memories of playing hide-and-seek with her sisters, capturing fireflies, and roasting marshmallows in the big fire pit where her father frequently burned brush. No place on earth was quite like it, and Ellie felt lucky and grateful to have such a beautiful home. Over these last few months, Jake had come to know Ellie's home, and he, too, had fallen under its spell.

Ellie's property stood at the end of a long stretch of dirt road. It looked like something out of a fairy tale. A hilly landscape with breathtaking views of Winston cradled a gorgeous post-and-beam home, which her father had built by hand. Not far from the wide front porch was a large duck pond, which froze in the winter and made a perfect ice-skating rink. Neighborhood kids could always be counted on for a spirited game of hockey. The sounds of the children's shouts and laughter always made Ellie feel a little less lonely since the divorce.

Now she had Jake to cure those winter blues. Or did she?

Ellie had never been invited to Jake's home. She knew he lived in a double-wide trailer. That didn't bother her in the least, but maybe it bothered him. On the surface, Jake and Ellie seemed to have much in common—a love of dogs and guns, a history with a difficult disease—but a wall remained between them, and Ellie wasn't sure who was doing most of the construction. Initially she hadn't pushed the issue. Ellie still carried some of the wounds Walt left behind and she liked the relationship just the way it was. So Ellie let it go, and Jake didn't change. But she had fallen for Jake Dent and started to want something more. If she was going to be in a relationship, she had to believe it was going to grow and deepen. Ellie brought her walls down, but it was clear Jake had not. Ellie began to think there was more to Jake than just a supremely private guy.

Which was why she'd turned to Google. And how she found a whole lot more than she ever expected.

Chapter 4

Jake drove up Ellie's driveway in his Chevy Tahoe.
Kibo came running like his best buddy suddenly
materialized out of thin air. As Jake came to a stop, the
muscular German shepherd stood on hind legs, slipped
his nose under the front passenger-side door handle,
and lifted his head. No scratches left behind. The door
latch disengaged, and Kibo used his head to pry the
door open the rest of the way. He jumped inside and
gave Jake's face a proper licking.

Jake had seen Kibo do the door trick countless
times, but he never tired of it. Ellie's dad had trained
his dogs to open car doors, and Ellie did the same with
Kibo to honor her father's memory. As for Kibo, he
didn't care how he got to Jake. He was just glad they
were together. Jake grabbed Kibo's fur, gave him a
good petting, and laughed as the dog licked his face.

"You miss me, boy?" Jake asked in a high voice,
which always sent Kibo's tail wagging. "I missed you.
Yeah, I did."

Two years ago, Jake's much-beloved Rottweiler,
Cinnamon, had died from bone cancer. There were no

bad breeds, Jake believed, only misguided handlers, and Cinnamon was the sweetest, gentlest, most loving dog Jake had ever known until he met Kibo. Andy would be leaving for college soon, and Jake would think about getting a dog when the quiet really started to get to him. Who knows? Maybe he would help Ellie train a shepherd—apprentice with her, even.

Jake got out of the car, and Kibo did the same. Now that they could get closer, Jake ruffled Kibo's thick fur and gave him a hug, which turned into a wrestle. On the ground, Jake found a red rope bone, and soon the toy was locked in Kibo's powerful jaws. A game of tug-of-war ensued, in which Kibo growled his enjoyment and Jake marveled at the animal's natural strength. If *the day* ever came, Jake would want Kibo to come live with him—which meant he'd want Ellie to come along, too. But, of course, that meant confiding in Ellie about a part of his life he kept secret.

Ellie crossed the grassy lawn where Jake and Kibo were tussling. Kibo had probably just been with Ellie, but he sensed her coming and set off running as if she'd been gone for years.

Jake propped up on his elbows and took in everything about the moment. He had been in a few long-term relationships since his ex-wife, Laura, had left. All had ended amicably, but this felt different. Ellie was attractive, smart, tough, fun to be around, and maybe, just maybe, Jake had met *the one.*

Ellie came over to Jake, with Kibo heeling at her side. She gave him a kiss hello, but it felt different, guarded, cooler.

"We need to talk," Ellie said.

Five minutes later, Ellie sat on the sofa in her living

room, with three German shepherds lounging at her feet. To Jake's eyes, they looked like one big happy pack. Two of the dogs were being trained for future owners, but they still treated Ellie like the alpha she was.

"So, what's the big talk about?" Jake asked. He took the armchair across from the sofa so they could face each other. "I hope we're not breaking up." Jake's smile didn't lighten the mood any.

"I guess it depends on whether you want to start really opening up to me."

Jake felt a knot in his chest. His last two girlfriends had ended their relationship because of his lifestyle, and he was keeping Ellie at arm's length to prevent a number three.

"Well, what do you want to know?"

"I Googled you, Jake. I didn't before, because it felt kind of creepy. Like I didn't trust you. But something has been missing for me with us. So I did a quick search and, well, I know all about the accident."

Jake understood right away. This was the other part of his life he liked to keep secret for as long as possible. His baseball career was more than a decade in his past. He liked his new persona as the head of maintenance at a prep school, and he wanted Ellie to think of him as just that. Besides, opening up about baseball risked revealing the secret about his avocation. In many ways, baseball had turned Jake into a prepper. Of all the things Jake was prepared to deal with, the truth wasn't one of them.

"So, what do you know?"

"Everything," Ellie said. "But I want to hear it from you."

Jake looked resigned, but his deep, audible exhale made it known he was not entirely pleased.

"Where do you want me to start?" he asked.

"At the beginning," Ellie said.

"Guess we'll start in high school, then."

"I'm sure you were cute."

"Extremely," Jake said with a wink. "I was also in love with Laura, Andy's mom."

"I want to know more about her. And about you."

"She left us after the accident. Well, after the accident and after Andy got his diagnosis. Bad things come in threes, isn't that what people say? I crashed my Beemer while driving drunk and shattered my elbow, Andy got sick, and then the love of my life walked out on us."

Jake had made it a point to show Ellie the scars from his many surgeries. He had told her he had arm surgery, but intentionally had left out some critical details.

"Why didn't you ever tell me?"

Jake shrugged. "Because it's embarrassing," he said. "Because I was going to be a superstar major-league pitcher and I tossed it away so I could get drunk at a teammate's bachelor party. Not something I'm proud of. I keep that part of my life just where it belongs, in the past. I'm different now."

Ellie seemed to accept his explanation. "What does that have to do with high school?" she asked.

"I was a kid blessed with a golden arm," Jake said. "My high-school coaches ignored my grades because of my talent. I went to a two-year college, but didn't graduate because I was just there to showcase my skills to the big-league scouts. The Red Sox eventually took me and I did my time in the minors, but I was on my way to 'The Show.' That was a given, until I turned my elbow bones into confetti.

"Guess I could blame my buddies for not taking my keys that night, or the coaches, who made me think I was above it all, the golden boy with a golden arm—but in the end, who did I have to blame but myself?"

"You shouldn't be so hard on yourself," Ellie said. The coldness Jake had felt was all but gone from her eyes, replaced by a look of deep sympathy and genuine concern.

"My dad was a soft-spoken guy," Jake said. "Made a nice career for himself in the insurance industry. He tried to warn me about the dangers of believing the hype, but at that time I wasn't into hearing anything negative. I was twenty-two, had a lucrative contract with a big-league ball club, a step away from pitching in the majors, married to my high-school sweetheart, and now a father to a precocious three-year-old boy. I didn't think anything could touch me."

"The stories I read online weren't kind," Ellie said.

Jake laughed at the understatement. "Guess you uncovered old headlines from the *New York Post*."

"The Web is like faraway stars. It illuminates the past."

Jake smiled, thinking of those fall nights when he and Ellie had huddled on a blanket on her front lawn as new lovers, gazing up at the night sky.

"Let me see if I can remember what the *Post* had to say." Jake ruminated. "'You're Out,' right? They ran that headline above a picture of my crushed BMW.

And the *Daily News,* I think they wrote, 'Booze Ball,' but now that I think about it, maybe I have those two mixed up."

"The *Globe* was a lot nicer," Ellie said.

"Yeah, well, that's because the only person who got hurt in the accident was me."

"What happened after?" Ellie asked.

The more Jake revealed, the closer he felt to Ellie. For this reason, Jake was glad Ellie had forced the conversation, but parts of his life remained off-limits.

"After that, I sank into a depression," Jake said. "I missed everything about the game. The teammates, the camaraderie, the competition, everything—I loved it all. Then, about six months later, things got worse."

"Andy," Ellie said as if reading his thoughts.

"All the classic signs were there. His weight loss was especially alarming for a kid that skinny. Laura would say, 'How does that boy put away so much food, but we can't keep a pound on him?' Then one afternoon I put Andy in front of the TV and went to go make lunch. When I got back, he was conscious, but so lethargic. I panicked and rushed him to the hospital, where we got the diagnosis."

"That's a lot to handle in a short amount of time," Ellie said.

Kibo picked his head up and gazed at Jake with watery black eyes, as if to say he concurred. Ellie gave all three dogs some attention.

"There was some money set aside from baseball to help pay for Andy's care, but not a lot. Before the accident, Laura figured we were on easy street, and she spent money like that was our permanent address. But a hefty signing bonus only goes so far. I saw it all adding up, and I didn't do a thing about it. I let Laura handle the finances so I could concentrate all my energy on studying batters and working on my pitches. So when baseball ended and money got tight, Laura and I started fighting. One night, after a particularly long battle to get Andy's insulin levels just right, Laura left a good-bye note. That was the last I ever saw of her. I did my best to find her—my dad even paid for a private investigator—but she was gone. Vanished. Wasn't even in touch with her parents. I'm guessing she changed her name.

"Anyway, I got divorced by a motion to serve. Essentially, you just show a judge all your documented efforts to locate your spouse, and if a judge agrees you did your best"—Jake clapped his hands and rubbed them together—"you're divorced."

"How did Andy take it?"

"He was three. Hardly knew his mother at all. After Laura left, my depression got worse. Some days I couldn't get out of bed, and my parents had to help me take care of Andy."

"But you're not like that now," Ellie said.

"I guess I grew out of it," Jake said. "Sometimes you've got to look adversity right in the face and stick out your tongue." Jake did this and made Ellie smile while Kibo licked his chops.

"Eventually my brother saw I was getting better and helped me get a job at Pepperell Academy."

Ellie gave this some thought; then she said, "Don't get me wrong. I admire what you did and what you've overcome, but you could have stayed in baseball, couldn't you? What about becoming a pitching coach or something?"

Jake shrugged off the suggestion. "I thought about it," he said. "But I couldn't be close to the game without getting a hollow pit in my gut. I knew if I didn't leave the game completely, I'd live the rest of my life in the past. So I walked away and never looked back. That part of my life came to an end—and the rest, as the saying goes, is history."

Ellie got up from the couch and crossed the room with a kind of hip-swaying action Jake found hard to resist. She dropped into his lap and kissed him with passion.

"I like history," she breathed in his ear. "I feel closer to you. Much closer."

Ellie kissed Jake's neck as he ran his hands along the contours of her back. They were kissing again, but Jake saw Kibo looking at them and he stopped.

"Maybe this history lesson should continue in the bedroom," Jake said.

Ellie took Jake by the hand and led him down a narrow hallway. On the walk, Jake thought about what he hadn't told her. Maybe he would. Ellie seemed receptive to one part of his past. Would she embrace the other?

Back then, Jake had needed a new sense of purpose. He found it in the writings of Thomas Wiggins, the founder of a popular survivalist blog. Everything Wiggins said about the coming collapse resonated with Jake in ways he found surprising and inspiring. With Wiggins's guidance, Jake felt empowered to take control of his life once more. He devoted himself to becoming an expert survivalist. He learned how to use weapons—guns and knives. He improved his physical conditioning and built up strength in his injured arm. He learned about food storage, DIY fuel, gardening, raising livestock, medical supplies, and first aid. In essence, Jake became reborn: stronger in some ways, but weaker in others because for him, the future was always something to fear.

Chapter 5

Five boys and one girl, students at Pepperell Academy, gathered in the campus's main courtyard—The Quad, as it was officially known—for a meeting. In better times, the six would have been laughing and talking excitedly. They were the best of friends, and shared the same interests: watched the same movies and TV shows, visited the same websites, downloaded the same apps, ate most of their meals together, and hung out as a group whenever possible during their limited free time. They were, in fact, what other students labeled a clique. Their collective even had a special name—though no one but the members knew it. They called themselves "The Shire."

Andy Dent was dressed the same as the four boys with him. Each wore a nice button-down shirt and a solid-colored tie. The group's lone girl, Hilary Eichel, wore stylish white-rimmed eyeglasses, plaid skater skirt with dark leggings, and underneath her white button-down blouse—Hilary adhered to the school dress code as well—a fitted T-shirt that read: THINK LIKE A PROTON

AND STAY POSITIVE. The words on her T-shirt were barely legible through her overshirt's fabric. However, the near-frantic look on Hilary's face, and those of her friends, said nobody was in a particularly positive mood.

In the background, a sea of students, most carrying backpacks, ambled from one building to another. They chatted easily with friends, or buried their faces in their smartphones. It was a normal March scene at Pepperell Academy; but for The Shire, things were far from normal. They looked away from each other, as no one felt comfortable being the first to break the silence.

Rafa spoke up finally.

"We have to get this over with," he said. "I have track practice."

Two of the six members of The Shire were on school-sponsored sports teams. Rafael Dufoe, who had curly, black hair, olive skin, and the whisper of a mustache, could run an 800-meter race in two minutes, eight seconds, which was not the best in the state, or even at The Pep, but it did put him a few strides ahead of some other runners. "Rafa," the nickname his friends in The Shire gave him, was exceedingly thin. Some thought he had an eating disorder or digestive problem, but neither was true. Rafa simply had the metabolism of a hummingbird.

Andy seethed and his face went red. He addressed Rafa through gritted teeth. "Your track practice can wait," he said. "I think this is just a little bit more important."

Andy was the group's founder and *de facto* leader, and it was his text message that had brought them all together. "It's been over a week since it went missing.

One of us has it," Andy said, his voice shaky, "and one of us better fess up. Solomon?"

Solomon Burke was the other athlete in the group. As the captain of Pepperell Academy's bowling team, Solomon had led the school to a championship two years running. While few students at The Pep considered bowling a sport—most would call it a recreational activity—Solomon had a different opinion. He was a cranker, which meant he created as much spin as possible by using a cupped wrist with his delivery. Spin was what made the bowling ball hook, and it was also the reason Solomon had recorded two 300 games and bowled a 274, 258, and 279 at his last tournament. Somewhat fittingly, Solomon's physique matched the shape of the ball with which he had crushed the school's bowling record.

"I told you, I don't have it," Solomon snapped. "I don't."

Solomon looked close to tears.

They were all on the verge of tears. Pallid complexions. Bags under the eyes because there hadn't been a good night's sleep among them. Shoulders hunched, weighted down with dread.

Hilary Eichel gave Solomon a hard stare, but she couldn't tell if he was lying or not. Hilary often referred to her friends Rafa and Solomon as "Abbott and Costello." It was a joke few at The Pep could appreciate; most students knew nothing about Abbott and Costello, and would not understand the reference.

As a self-proclaimed geek, Hilary embraced the Geek Chic style with flair. An attractive girl, Hilary got a lot of attention from the boys because of her looks.

When they tried to flirt, she'd intentionally yawn. This usually sent them away. She had hazel eyes, long-layered brown hair, with ginger-colored strands, and a pert nose. She was in good shape, and could probably beat Rafa in a race if they ever went head to head, but Hilary was more mathlete than athlete. She already had taken two semesters of AP calculus and was currently acing her college-level statistics and probability course.

"We're all just going to deny it," Hilary said as if it were a matter of fact.

A cool wind kicked up and mussed Hilary's hair. She brushed the strands away from her face as her gaze retreated back to the dusty ground. March was not a particularly beautiful time of year at The Pep. Today the sun was a cool pale disc brushed upon a cloudless blue sky, but The Quad itself was an ugly shade of brown, and the tree branches were barren. In a few more weeks, nature would work its magic and everything would bloom and change and look like the pictures on the website and brochures, the ones that lured prospective students to the campus for a tour.

The brochures did a nice job of showcasing the western Massachusetts campus, but it wasn't the natural beauty and the historic buildings that inspired parents to fork over $45,000 a year for tuition and board. It was what they got for the money that had most students (and their parents) salivating.

A diploma from The Pep might not guarantee admission into an elite college, but it sure didn't hurt. A lot of graduates went on to prestigious schools and to do big things in life, which was exactly what The Pep counted on. While the average amount spent per pupil in Massachusetts hovered around $14,000 per year, The Pep blew that figure away by investing $52,000 annually to house and educate each of its twelve hundred students. To bridge the gap between tuition and costs, The Pep relied heavily on its endowment, which, thanks to a wealthy alumni base and shrewd investments, had topped $1 billion last year.

Some students depended on scholarships to cover their elite education, but most of The Shire came from privilege. Not Andy, though. He was in a special category. Because his father worked at the school, Andy got free tuition—tuition remission—and it came with some self-imposed pressure to do well. His GPA never drifted below 3.8, an impressive feat considering most of his classes were AP or high honors. Andy's father worked what Andy thought was a dead-end job to get him this education, which made Andy grateful for that sacrifice and determined to succeed.

At the moment, however, what mattered most to Andy wasn't his stellar academic record. It was an answer to his question.

"David, did you take it?"

Andy was glaring at David Townsend, who hailed from Chicago, and was the best (and only) bassoon player in the school's orchestra. David preferred to be called by his hacker name, "Dark Matter," and his eyes narrowed in displeasure when Andy used his given name. David was a tall, gangly boy, with a gap in his front teeth and freckled skin that reddened quickly in the sun. While not exactly handsome, David attracted a lot of attention because of his long hair, which descended well past his shoulders. David often wore his hair down, as if to invite ridicule from fellow students who would call him a girl and think they were being clever. Unlike Hilary, who ignored the attention of boys she found tiresome and juvenile, David embraced the taunts, maybe even trolled for them, as a way of proving they didn't really matter.

"I don't have it. I told you a million times. It's just gone."

Rafa began to pace. His breathing turned shallow.

"We're dead. We're *all* dead."

"Calm down," Andy said. His voice had a hard edge, almost scolding. "It's not going to do us any good to panic. We just need to get honest with each other and not be greedy. Nobody will be in trouble. But the money has to be given back."

Rafa put his hands on his knees and breathed as if he'd just run a race.

Andy looked up at the sky to clear his head and calm his nerves. He blinked away the sunspots and regarded Troy Cranston with suspicion. At fifteen, Troy, a sophomore, was the youngest member of The Shire. He also had the highest IQ of a group comprising high-IQ people.

Troy had on his favorite ratty, gray hooded sweatshirt over his school-mandated shirt and tie, and the dark sunglasses he wore anytime, day or night, outdoors or indoors. Troy didn't like it when people knew what he was looking at. He also didn't want anybody to see how scared he was. Troy shook his head back at Andy.

"We're really screwed, aren't we?" Troy said in a soft voice.

At some point, Troy's father, a senior-level investment banker with JPMorgan Chase and a former All-American quarterback for Notre Dame, had to face the fact that the jock name he'd bestowed upon his only son did not match the boy's physique or mental makeup in any way. The other Troys at Pepperell Academy were cool kids, muscular and athletic, probably closer to what Troy's dad had envisioned his son would be. This Troy, however, was a pixie-sized kid with a broad, flat nose, thin lips, and an oval face without much of a chin. His dark hair was cut close to his head, and always looked in need of a good washing. Troy would say he just had naturally oily hair.

He might not have been able to dribble a basketball with any dexterity, or catch a baseball, or master any of the skills his überathletic father dreamed about, but what he could do—and do better than anybody else at The Pep, including the professors in the computer science department—was hack. Troy, who went by his hacker handle, "Pixie," cracked codes as other people cracked eggs. As a requirement for acceptance into The Shire, all members had to demonstrate decent hacking prowess, but Pixie's gifts were something special. He was a digital Mozart, and probably the one most responsible for The Shire's dire situation.

It was the conspicuous consumption and egregious display of wealth at The Pep that had initially inspired Andy to found The Shire—well, that along with a viewing of the remake of *Robin Hood: Prince of Thieves,* starring Kevin Costner. Andy asked himself: *What if I robbed from the rich and gave to the poor, just like Robin Hood?*

Discussing this at school, Andy found among his peers others who shared a disdain for the gross display of wasteful spending. They'd never intended to hurt anybody. It was just for fun, and sure, the rush of doing something illegal and daring had its own appeal. The Shire stole small sums of money from the rich parents of students at Pepperell Academy and gave it anonymously to various worthwhile charities. They monitored the e-mails and text messages of their wealthy victims, and the few parents who even noticed the missing money simply changed their online banking passwords. The amounts taken were always negligible when compared to the size of the bank accounts that Troy had taught them how to access.

Always negligible, until now.

Andy took off his backpack and slammed it to the ground. "This isn't going anywhere," he growled. As group leader, Andy felt it was his mess to unravel, and he looked each member in the eyes: Rafa, Solomon, David, Hilary, and, once again, Pixie. "One of us has it, and that kind of money isn't going to just disappear without somebody taking notice. This isn't our usual small skim here. This is the big-time, people, and we need to put the money back where we got it. Now!"

David was about to respond when his gaze drifted to the girl coming up behind Andy. Andy turned to look, and upset as he was, he couldn't suppress a broad and almost silly grin. Every hormone in Andy's body came alive. He was so jacked up on teenage lust or love or whatever that the seriousness of the situation evaporated upon the arrival of Beth MacDonald.

To Andy, Beth MacDonald looked like every unattainable girlfriend in every '80s teen film he'd ever seen (and he'd streamed them all). She had a dynamite smile, wavy blond hair, full lips, and the most dazzling green eyes imaginable. Hilary noticed Andy noticing Beth, and frowned.

"Hey, Beth," Andy said, with that same toothy grin.

"Hi, Andy. Hi, guys and gal," Beth said, directing her last greeting at Hilary. Hilary smiled weakly and tried not to look like she was checking out how Beth wore her uniform. "What are you doing?"

"Just talking," Andy said. "What's up?"

"Nothing. I was hoping we could study for that trig test together."

Andy was thinking that he wanted nothing more in life than to spend every waking minute with Beth studying for that trig test. Beth was thinking that she really wanted a good grade. And she was thinking about Andy, too, at least sort of, in a strange way, because he really wasn't her type. Her type was supposed to be Ryan Coventry, the boy she'd broken up with last week. Ryan was all-American handsome, and could have been a stand-in for Thor if the Norse god ever sported a flat-top. In addition to his strong jawline, piercing blue eyes, and facial features all in proportion with the golden ratio of beauty, Ryan was captain of the football, wrestling, and lacrosse teams. He was also a champion debater, who, at the tender age of eleven, had made a list of life goals that included attending Harvard undergrad and Yale law school. Now a senior, Ryan could check at least one item off the list: along with four other students from The Pep, he had been accepted as an early decision into Harvard.

While Andy looked unblinking at Beth, Hilary made several short whistles, sounds of alarm. Andy followed Hilary's line of sight and immediately saw what was making her nervous. Ryan Coventry was marching toward the group from the direction of the Society Building, which housed classrooms for mathematics and humanities. He looked ready for a fight.

Chapter 6

Beth took a few steps back to get some distance from Andy and his friends. One glance told her that Ryan had her in his sights. From the red splotches creeping up Ryan's beefy neck, Beth knew the coming blowup was going to be a doozy. She contemplated running, but didn't want to make a scene.

Sure enough, Ryan skipped the snide remarks about David's long hair (a first) and didn't even bother elbowing Andy in the taunting way he often did when the two passed in the halls. His ire, his complete and total focus, was reserved for Beth MacDonald. He grabbed Beth's shoulder before she had a chance to pull away. Her upper arm seemed to vanish within Ryan's massive hand.

"We need to talk," Ryan said in a commanding voice.

Beth shrugged hard and freed herself from his hold, but the look on her face showed that it had hurt.

"Ryan, there's nothing to talk about," Beth said. She turned and tried to walk away, but Ryan accelerated, grabbed her once again, and forced her back around.

"There's plenty to talk about," he said in a low voice, almost a growl.

Afraid, Beth bent at the knees to try and break from his hold, but this time Ryan wouldn't let go. She squirmed, trying to get loose.

Andy's every impulse was to stop Ryan and help Beth. But would she welcome his involvement? It could turn into a thing between them. "Why did you interfere?" he imagined Beth might say. "This was between me and Ryan." He didn't want to upset her.

"You're hurting me, Ryan. I said there's nothing to talk about. Now leave me alone, you asshole!"

"No. Not until you talk to me, Beth."

Andy had enough. Ryan Coventry was way out of line, threatening even. Stepping forward, Andy tapped Ryan hard, several times, between his shoulder blades.

"Leave her alone, Ryan," Andy said. His voice came out a little weaker than he had intended; but then again, Ryan had four inches and seventy pounds on him.

Ryan whirled, catching Beth by surprise. She stumbled clumsily forward, and would have pitched face-first onto the grass, were it not for the pythonlike grip Ryan maintained around her wrist. For a time, Ryan said nothing as he glared at Andy with rabid eyes. A bull might have shuddered under his hostile gaze.

"What did you just say to me?" Ryan snarled.

"I said leave her alone, dickhead."

"No, no, you didn't," David said, correcting Andy. "You called him Ryan, not 'dickhead.' You added the 'dickhead' part after."

Pixie spoke up. "Good embellishment, though. Way

more effective. I bet that's what he wished he said the first time."

Ryan eyed David and Pixie with contempt before setting his sights once more on Andy. The splotch on Ryan's neck had grown to the size of Jupiter's great red spot.

All Andy cared about was that Ryan let go of Beth. The whole rapid-boil anger thing didn't seem to bother Andy in the least—until, moving with the speed of a lynx, Ryan lunged forward and seized Andy by his shirt, pulling him up on tiptoes as if he were a bag of feathers.

The four other boys in The Shire retreated a few steps, but Hilary held her ground. Beth leapt to Andy's defense, slamming her fists several times against Ryan's back.

"Leave him alone, Ryan. Stop being such a jerk," she said.

Ryan ignored her pleas just as he ignored the blows. Andy's shirt looked like a wrung-out dishrag within Ryan's meaty grasp.

"You better watch yourself, geek boy," Ryan growled. With his biceps straining, Ryan hoisted Andy up until the two were at eye level.

Andy fought to keep a serious expression, but a laugh escaped anyway, even though he had intentionally pulled his lips tight against his teeth.

"Are you freaking laughing at me?" Ryan was incredulous.

Andy tried to hold his laugh in, but it burst out once more in a loud *pfffftt*.

Ryan still couldn't believe his ears. "I thought I told you to watch yourself," he said.

Andy couldn't keep a straight face. "It's just that you sound like such a walking cliché, Ryan," Andy said. "I mean, look—you're the big, tough jock, trying to win back the affections of your beautiful girlfriend while you're holding one of the geekiest kids in the school by his shirt. You're kind of being Johnny Lawrence from *The Karate Kid* right now."

"The first *Karate Kid,* with Ralph Macchio, not the remake," Hilary said, feeling a need to clarify the reference.

Of course she'd know that, Solomon thought.

"Nah, I'd say he's more like Biff Tannen," Rafa said.

"From *Weird Science*?" Pixie asked.

"Back to the Future," Hilary said.

"I'd go with a blanket reference and say he's being totally Disney TV," Solomon said in a very matter-of-fact way.

The Shire desperately needed to release some tension, but none of this banter amused Ryan. He looked furious.

By now, some of the other students were taking notice of the commotion and began a swift trot over to the action. Jake Dent happened to be transporting a broken heater fan from Hillman Hall across campus to his workshop behind the Terry Science Center when he caught sight of the student migration. He followed the gaggle and was surprised to see his son in the center of the action. Jake knew the student who was holding Andy by his shirt, and it was obvious that these were mismatched opponents.

Rather than intervene, Jake took up position by the walkway abutting the Society Building—far enough back not to be noticed, but still close enough to see the action.

"You think you're really funny, huh?" Ryan said, pulling Andy up so high his shirt came untucked from his pants.

"I'm giving you a chance to let go of me," Andy said. His expression turned serious.

Hidden in the background, Jake Dent had to crane his neck to get a better look over the gathering crowd. He wanted Andy to take care of his own problems, but Jake worried the confrontation would be too one-sided. He didn't want anybody to get hurt.

"I'm going to give you one more chance to let go of me," Andy said.

Ryan's toothy grin suggested some devious thinking. Sure enough, he let one of his hands holding Andy's shirt go so that he could make a fist, which he cocked back behind his head in a quick and fluid motion.

At the same instant, Andy took a giant step backward and planted his left foot behind him. As he did this, Andy bent slightly at the knees and twisted his body to the right. To the untrained eye, Andy appeared to be off balance, but Jake could see that Andy already had the upper hand. Before Ryan could throw his first punch, Andy's right arm came up and over the arm holding onto his shirt and he twisted his body toward his left hip.

The move not only surprised Ryan, but it forced him to release his hold. Ryan was off balance, but he took a wild swing anyway. His punch connected with air.

Without missing a beat, Andy balled his hand into a

fist, bent his elbow, made what he thought to be a force-
ful yell, and uncoiled at the waist. Andy's elbow made
a solid strike against the side of Ryan's head. The blow
felled the larger student to his knees. For a moment, all
Ryan could do was rock back and forth in pain.

From his vantage point, Jake was impressed—not at
all surprised by the outcome, but not entirely satisfied,
either. He and Andy had worked on that move countless times. Breaking free from a front hold was one of
the most basic skills in hand-to-hand combat. Andy
was near perfect in executing his escape maneuver, but
his yell was more warble than war cry. Jake couldn't
count the number of times he had explained that the
purpose of the yell was not only to startle the assailant,
but also to focus the power of the strike. They'd go
over the maneuver tonight after Andy finished his
homework.

Beth MacDonald looked stunned, and also a bit
starstruck. Her eyes traveled back and forth between
Ryan, on his knees, and Andy, nonchalantly tucking in
his shirt. Andy's friends, Beth noted, didn't seem at all
surprised by the outcome of this David versus Goliath
battle.

"Andy, that was—that was amazing."

Ryan shakily got back to his feet. Embarrassed, he
lowered his head and charged off in the direction from
which he had come.

Andy smiled at Beth. "Meet me over at Tanner Hall
and we'll study together for that test. I've got enough
Red Bull in my backpack to guarantee us at least a B."

Beth nodded but looked dazed, still incredulous.
She turned and departed, heading toward Tanner Hall.

Andy watched her go and waited until she was out of earshot before he spoke. A glower materialized on his face. "One of us has taken two hundred million dollars' worth of bitcoins, and, trust me, that's more than enough money to get us all killed."

Chapter 7

Javier Martinez was in his home office, on the phone with the computer expert he hired. If he did not solve his problem soon, he was going to die. It was that simple.

When Javier first discovered the theft, he had tried to fix the problem without alerting Soto. The computer whiz, whom he'd found through a craigslist ad seeking a bitcoin guru, had given him hope. The man went only by his hacker handle—"L10n," or "The Lion," in its non-phonetic form—and he seemed well versed on the subject.

"But you told me you could find it, get it all back," Javier said.

His voice trembled and he felt on the verge of tears. Javier could not recall the last time he had really cried. It might have been at his father's funeral, ten years ago. So much had changed in those ten years, and Javier was grateful his father was not around to see his only son murdered by a Mexican drug cartel. This was not the life they had imagined for him when they left Mexico to come to America.

Javier's parents had grown up on the hardscrabble streets of Tepito, a barrio in Mexico City. Local residents called it *"Barrio Bravo,"* or fierce neighborhood, because of its reputation for crime—robbery and counterfeiting mostly. Having given their life savings—an amount equal to a few hours' work for Javier—to a man who claimed he could smuggle them into America, Javier's parents made it safely to California. They came to escape the violence. Evidently, they didn't travel far enough.

"I told you, Javier, I got into the kids' computers, all of them," The Lion said, "but the bitcoins aren't there."

"I don't understand," Javier said. "We know who took them."

Sure enough, The Lion had found proof of the theft on a certain piece of hardware, as well as the names of those he suspected of participating in the heist, but no actual bitcoins.

"Yes, that's true," The Lion said. "But I can't get the coins back if they're not in the wallet we thought they were in."

"But they're on the network!" Javier said. "I can see them."

The Lion couldn't see Javier tapping his finger against his computer monitor for emphasis. He was looking at blockchain.info, the public ledger website of all transactions in the bitcoin network. The ledger showed his bitcoins, but did not reveal who had them, or where they might be stored. All it told him was that the bitcoins existed somewhere in the Internet.

The Lion said, "Yes, you can see them. But that's

all you can do. Without the new key, you cannot get to them."

"So we get the key from the kids. It has to be one of them, it has to be," Javier said.

"Yes, I agree. It has to be one of them."

The main culprit, a boy who went by the handle of Dark Matter, had managed to fake the balance in Javier's digital wallet, making it appear that he had the bitcoins in his account when, in fact, they'd actually been transferred out. It took him weeks to even notice the theft.

"What can I do?" Javier asked.

"I'm afraid I've done all I can," The Lion said. "I'll expect payment immediately." The line went dead.

By now, Soto knew the money was missing, and the deadline for the bitcoins' return had passed. Javier hid his face in his hands. He contemplated suicide. He had brought this nightmare on himself. At no point in time had Javier planned to lose more than half of his clients' assets, but that was what had happened, and the ultimate reason for this catastrophe.

Fifteen years earlier, Javier had launched his boutique financial management firm, Asset Capital, with a small initial investment from a wealthy banking client who believed that the ambitious child of Mexican immigrants could generate big profits. He was right. Working with an independent broker-dealer, word spread of Javier's financial gifts; and until a few years ago, Asset Capital had been managing about $105 million.

Business, as his father often said, was like a relationship. If not properly cared for, it would sour.

After some bad picks put him in a hole, and some aggressive maneuvers only dug that hole deeper, Javier was in serious trouble. He spoke about his financial troubles to a cousin in Boston, and the next day got a phone call from a stranger inviting him to a meeting. What the meeting was about, the other party wouldn't say, but implied that he (whoever he was) could solve all of Javier's money problems.

The meeting took place in Javier's office in Newton. The man who showed up refused to give his name, but he was obviously Mexican and spoke Spanish with the same regional accent as his cousin. Javier suspected that the solution to his problem would somehow involve drug money. He should have told the man he wasn't interested, but desperation eclipsed his better judgment. He had so much at stake: a wife and son to support, a mortgage, bills, tuition, and car payments—not to mention the prison time he would face when his clients discovered the fraud.

"The Man with No Name" dangled the right carrot in front of Javier's face. According to him, if Javier made it into the organization, all his money problems would be gone. He wouldn't say more. At the end of the meeting, the man left with Javier's Social Security number and a promise to be in touch.

What followed was a series of phone calls, more meetings, and several business trips, all done under the radar by using burner phones, forged documents, encrypted messaging services, and even a couple dead drops. It was all very covert, but Javier went along blindly. He told the same story to each person with whom he met or spoke, and there were plenty.

They wanted to know about him as a person, what made him tick, the reason he got out of bed every morning. He had to be someone levelheaded and trust-worthy, and they seemed willing to overlook his current business troubles. People can learn from their mistakes, he was told.

They asked about his wife. Her name was Stacey. They seemed to like that he'd been married for seventeen years. It showed he was grounded. Javier had met Stacey at his thirtieth birthday party. She was the caterer, and although not Mexican, she made mouthwatering churros, delectable taquitos, and these amazing margarita cupcakes, which got most of the seventy guests completely wasted. Javier flirted with Stacey throughout the evening and scored her number as she was putting the last of the dishes inside her catering van.

They asked about his hometown of Winston and his son, Guzman Antonio Martinez—or "Gus," as his friends at The Pep called him. They liked that he was active in his community, his church. They smiled with him when he talked about coaching his son's Little League team, back when Gus was passionate about the sport.

"We all love baseball," one of the Mexicans had said.

They wanted to know everything they could learn about Javier's parents, specifically their life in Tepito, friends his mother still kept in touch with, enemies the family might have. He told them about growing up in New Bedford, Massachusetts, and detailed his résumé, including his work for Wells Fargo before going out on his own.

It was the most thorough interview Javier had in his life and he still didn't know what the job entailed.

Finally a man named Carlos, who spoke with him in a hotel room in Ciudad Juárez, told him what he had long suspected.

"We need a new money manager to help us expand our influence in America," Carlos had said. "There's a lot of money to be made, Javier . . . if you have a level head and a smart sense for business."

That was when the first girls showed up, long-legged and draped in silky negligees. It was a night Javier would never forget. What Javier later read about Sangre Tierra made his boyhood nightmares seem like fairy tales. But the allure of easy money, beautiful women, and the drugs—yes, he had sampled and enjoyed—proved too powerful to resist. The cash Javier made from laundering Sangre Tierra's drug money paid back the debt he had kept secret from his clients, and made him a millionaire many times over.

The money meant nothing to him now.

Javier's joints cracked as he got up from his desk. He used to be in better shape, but the women and drugs had turned him soft. They'd turned his mind soft, too. How had he not used better security to safeguard the bitcoins?

With his feet in slippers, Javier padded along the hallway of his spacious home; his robe flapped open. Beneath his robe, he wore boxer shorts over which his ample belly protruded. He had been to the office only a few times since the theft; in those days, his beard had grown thick.

At the entrance to his kitchen, Javier paused. Something wasn't right. He just had a feeling. He took a single step into the room and saw him.

A steely bolt of fear raced up Javier's spine. He thought of running, but his legs wouldn't move. He wanted to scream, but he had no voice.

Standing in front of the coffeemaker was a man Javier knew well. He had long, dark hair tied in a tight ponytail and wore a silken shirt decorated with a floral design, suitable for any of the nightclubs Javier frequented.

The man smiled, his grin twisted and wicked. Javier gazed in horror at the gold teeth, each ornately designed. He knew who this man was and, more frighteningly, what this man did. Fausto Garza whistled, summoning seven men into the kitchen. The men all had brown complexions, and they came in a variety of heights and sizes. One even had a shock of dyed bright red hair. Some were dressed casually, while others wore tactical clothing, but all of them carried rifles.

"Hello, Javier," Fausto Garza said to him in Spanish. *"Tenemos que hablar de negocios."* ("We've got business to discuss.")

Chapter 8

The soft, middle-aged flab of Javier's half-naked body sickened Fausto, who insisted his hostage get dressed. Minutes later, Javier stood inside his sizable bedroom closet, with Fausto and three of his sullen and silent minions keeping careful watch. Javier trembled putting on a dress shirt, and his hands shook too violently to do up the buttons, so he exchanged that outfit for an easy-to-slip-on black T-shirt and baggy gray sweatpants.

Fausto bristled at the final clothing choice. He preferred finer-looking fashions, but this was an American look through and through. Almost everything about the country displeased him—the women being the notable exceptions.

"¿Dices que eres mexicanoamericano?" Fausto said to Javier as he watched him fumble with his clothes. ("You call yourself Mexican American.") *"Pero, ¿qué es mexicano de ti? Nada. Eso."* ("But what is Mexican about you? Nothing. That's what.")

"I love Mexico, Fausto, and, believe me, I am committed to the cartel's mission. Please, you must know this."

Javier knew to speak only in Spanish.

"You are committed to nothing but your disgusting self," said Fausto. "If you loved Mexico so much, why not visit there? Why not live there? Oh, are you worried about the murders? The crime? Please, Javier, you of all people should know it is mostly just drug dealer against drug dealer. The finance types like you, they live a life of luxury. You listen too much to the media, my friend."

Once Javier was dressed, Fausto escorted him from the bedroom to the dining room, with the other men in tow. The dining-room chairs were heavy black lacquer over oak, and suitable for Fausto's purposes.

"Did you know," said Fausto, running a hand along the smooth finished surface of one of the chairs, "Cancun and Cabo San Lucas have murder rates lower than Arizona? *Lower!*" Javier did not seem impressed, and this made Fausto angry. "Washington, D.C.—four times the number of murders in Mexico City. Four times, Javier. But *you,* you're an American. You've lost touch with your people, your heritage." Fausto crowded Javier and gave his cheek several patronizing pats with his hand. "But your heritage is about to reach out and touch you real hard. Pick up that chair. Carry it downstairs for me. You can call it exercise."

Fausto would have two more chairs brought down in addition to the one Javier had carried. He would have three hostages here soon enough.

The unfinished side of the basement was nothing special, just a concrete room with a water tank, furnace, and a lot of ductwork. Javier kept his tools down here, however, and it was among them that Fausto had found the drill.

In a matter of minutes, two of Fausto's men had lashed both of Javier's ankles to the legs of the chair. Right away, the ankles began to swell. Javier's arms were wrenched behind his back and secured with rope.

Slapping the tip of a twelve-volt Black & Decker power drill against his meaty palm, Fausto hovered in front of Javier's chair and appraised his hostage thoughtfully. The drill had an orange plastic casing and a dull silver bit, which Fausto enjoyed spinning. The *whir* put a smile on his face and gave Javier a flash of the assassin's gold metal mouth.

Four armed men from Sangre Tierra accompanied Fausto in the basement. They had all crossed the border on false passports, along with Fausto, and had spent days together in a van. The van was the best way to transport the assault rifles the men had picked up in San Diego, along with other weapons concealed in various pockets and belts of their tactical clothing.

Upstairs, three other members of the cartel waited. They had come by plane, and they would greet Stacey when she arrived home from work and Gus when he returned from school.

Fausto had Javier's phone. He looked up Stacey's number in his contacts. "I'd have you send the message, but maybe you have a code word or something established for a situation just like this," Fausto said. "Who knows? You could be very well prepared. What do you call your wife, other than her name? Is it sweetie? Darling? Honey? Don't lie to me. Bad things happen to people who don't tell the truth."

"Honey," Javier said. "I'd say, 'honey.'"

"Oh, how sweet," said Fausto, sounding sincere.

To Stacey, Fausto typed in English: Come home honey! I've got a big surprise for you. We're taking a vacation. Bags are packed. We're leaving soon so hurry home!

Thirty seconds later, Stacey typed back: OMG!!! Are u serious?

There was some back and forth texting, half of it written by Fausto, but guided by Javier. Stacey needed a little cajoling to become convinced she could act so spontaneously. Eventually, she decided that she could.

Stacey's last message read: I'm so excited. Leaving work now. Love U!!!

Fausto sent a similar text message to his son and told him to take a cab home. Gus's reply came back quick: No WAAAAAAAYY so pumped!! Love you Pop!

Fausto showed the replies to Javier. Everything needed to hurt.

"Soto doesn't explain stuff to me," Fausto said. "He tells me to go get his money, but he doesn't tell me how. So you'll tell me everything I need to know, deal?"

Javier's chin was touching his chest in defeat.

Fausto lifted his head, using the tip of the drill. He wanted the eye contact. "Educate me."

"What do you want to know?" asked Javier.

"Everything," Fausto said.

Javier tried to speak, but an unexpected sob choked his voice. Fausto looked annoyed. To quiet the man down, Fausto slipped the drill bit into Javier's ear. Out of instinct, Javier pulled his head to one side to dislodge it, but Fausto grabbed hold of his chin and held him in place.

"Ssh, ssh, ssh, my friend," Fausto said. "Calm down or something messy could happen here. My finger could slip."

Javier stopped thrashing. The tears dried up enough for him to find his voice. Many years of experience had taught Fausto that terror was a special kind of motivator.

Javier explained everything. When he finished speaking, Fausto extracted the drill from Javier's ear canal. "These bitcoins," Fausto said. "They don't exist? They're not real?" His curiosity was earnest.

"No," Javier gasped, and spat. "They're . . . real."

"So I can buy things with them? Clothes? A car? That Dunkin' Donuts coffee you all drink?"

Javier tried to answer, but again the words got stuck in his throat. He shut his eyes tight. Then, like a free diver before making a descent, he took in several readying breaths.

"Just relax," Fausto said. "I won't hurt you if you help me."

Javier nodded several times. He'd be compliant. "You can buy things, yes," Javier said. "Or exchange them for other types of currency."

"And this kid you mention, he exchanged the bitcoins for real cash?"

"Not all," Javier said, his voice still shaky. "It was only a couple thousand dollars' worth, but it was a dumb thing to do."

"Why 'dumb'?"

"Because we could trace the coins to the new owner," Javier said. He stopped speaking to look once more at the empty chairs next to his. "The seller used this thing called a proxy server to mask his IP address, but my computer consultant said it was an 'unsophisticated means of tunneling.' Those were his exact words."

"Who is this consultant?"

"He calls himself The Lion. I can get you in touch with him."

"You will."

"Please, Fausto," Javier said. "Keep my family out of this. I'll help you. I promise. I'll do anything. Just leave them alone."

Instead of the ear, Fausto set the tip of the drill against Javier's leg, directly at midthigh. The leg began to buckle and shake in a grand mal seizure way, but Fausto kept the contact point.

"They are a part." Fausto indicated to the empty chairs. "You are a part." He motioned to Javier. "And we are a part." Fausto gestured to himself and his henchmen. "We're all in this mess together," he said, making a big circle with his hands, a big mess encompassing everyone.

"Okay. Okay. I got it. I got it," Javier said. He was close to hyperventilating. "What do you know about the bitcoin business?"

"I know nothing, except that I'm here to get the money back," Fausto said.

"It started when Soto had a lot of cash he wanted cleaned," Javier said. "More than I'd seen before. Instead of cleaning it through bank accounts like I'd been doing, I suggested we could use that money to make more money. I'd been reading about this currency, and I told him he could buy computers so we could mine for bitcoins."

Fausto looked puzzled. "Mine for them? Like dig-in-the-ground mine?"

"Not the ground," Javier said. "Computational mining. Very powerful computers solving complex problems."

"What kind of problems?"

"Computations that help to guarantee the integrity of bitcoins' general ledger."

"What does that mean?"

"Every bitcoin transaction has to be validated," Javier said.

"You're clear as fog," Fausto said.

"How do you prove somebody bought and sold something that you can't hold?" Javier said. "You can count dollars, weigh gold and silver, but how do I prove that I have as many bitcoins as I say I do? I could be faking it. Without proof, nobody would trust the system, and the currency would be worthless. The bitcoin ledger, that's the official accounting of all the bitcoins bought and sold. The computational mining we do validates that every transaction on the ledger is real. It's complex computing work, but anytime a bitcoin miner can confirm a block of transactions is real, they get bitcoins rewarded to them for the effort. Mining it is hard computing work. It's how they limit the number of bitcoins in circulation, which helps sustain value.

"So Soto bought a bunch of expensive computers with his money, and he's using those computers to mine for these bitcoins." A strange, almost excited look had replaced Javier's more terrified one. It was, after all, his idea; and with lots of highly educated but underpaid computer experts in Mexico, Soto had little trouble getting the operation off the ground.

"And that's how you collected two hundred million dollars' worth of these bitcoins? By mining them?"

"Not all," Javier said. "I also bought bitcoins on the exchange, but those transactions were anonymous. Nobody knows I bought them, unless I try to off-ramp the bitcoins."

"'Off-ramp'?"

"That's where you sell the bitcoins. Owners of the coins are anonymous until they sell their coins. When somebody sells, the transaction gets broadcast for the whole bitcoin community to see."

"So that's how you know this kid from the school took the money?" Fausto asked.

Javier nodded. "Yes, yes. The Lion traced the seller's IP address. I was shocked to see that the coins were sold from Pepperell Academy."

Fausto was beginning to understand, and it pleased him. "How do you know who at the school took the coins?" Fausto asked.

"The Lion worked his magic and somehow penetrated the school's computer network. From there, he got a name—David Townsend from Chicago."

"So then we go and get this David person to give us back our money."

"It's not that easy," Javier said.

"Why not?"

"The Lion hacked into David's computer at school. I figured we could get the money back before anybody even knew it was gone. My guy said it wasn't easy to do. I guess this David kid is a computer nut himself and he had all sorts of firewalls and protections, things I don't understand. Eventually he managed to get in, and that's when he showed me messages between David and his friends about the theft."

"Friends?"

"They call themselves The Shire."

Fausto creased his brow. "The Shire? What's that?"

"It's the name of their club," Javier said. "These kids are a group, a cartel of sorts. They're like cyber bank robbers or something. They steal from rich parents of kids who go to Pepperell Academy and give the money anonymously to different charities. My guy, he figured how to decrypt the group's charter and I read it. It details their methods. They use key loggers, different ways of getting pass codes to bank accounts, and then they transfer out small sums of cash."

"So they hacked into your computer here at your home. Is that it?" Fausto looked aggrieved.

"It's the only way they could have emptied my bit-coin wallet."

"And they took two hundred million dollars' worth of these coins?"

Javier nodded grimly.

"You kept that much money in one stupid wallet?" Fausto looked to his accomplice. "Efren, how much money do you have in your wallet?" he asked.

The stocky man reached into his back pocket, took out his brown leather wallet, and counted the bills within. "About six hundred pesos and a few hundred in dollars," he said.

Fausto, animated, pointed to Efren. "You see? That's a normal amount of money to have in a wallet. A few hundred dollars. Not *two hundred million, cabrón.*"

"It's different with bitcoins," Javier said.

A shadow crossed Fausto's face. He crouched to get eye level with Javier. "They emptied your big, fat wallet. It's no different," he said. "So we go find this David person and we get the money back. End of problem."

Javier shook his head. It wasn't the end of anything. "I've read the e-mails and text messages the kids have been sending to each other. They don't have the money. At least they say they don't."

This captured Fausto's attention.

"Or one of them is lying about not knowing," Fausto said. "Maybe they picked each other's pockets. Two hundred million dollars is a lot of reasons to betray a friend."

"What do you suggest we do, Fausto?" Efren asked.

"How many are in this group, this Shire?" Fausto asked.

Javier thought. "There are six," he said. "Five boys and one girl."

"Then we go door-to-door and take them," said Efren. "We make them talk."

Fausto frowned and gave Efren a cold, irritated look. "That's going to be a problem," he said. "We need to take them all at once. Do all these kids sleep at the school?"

Javier shook his head. He didn't know.

"Maybe they do, maybe they don't," said Fausto. "Either way, home or at school, we have too many doors to break down. Too many witnesses. Too much could go wrong and could bring a lot of police before we get back the money. We need to go in and get out without anybody knowing we're there. We need time to interrogate these kids all together, like the police would do. Get them to turn on each other until one gives up the money. We must make them talk. That's what we must do."

"The school is filled with kids," Efren said. "How do we do it?"

"I want to see a map of the area," said Fausto. His sphinxlike smile pricked goose bumps on Javier's skin.

"What are you thinking, Fausto?" Efren asked.

"A friend of ours works for BVC Environmental, a chemical trucking company. He's the reason we got this burro working for us in the first place." Fausto pointed to Javier. "I guess they are cousins or something."

"So?" Efren looked confused.

"I think with our friend's help we can empty out the school of every single student and teacher, but leave our friends from this so-called Shire behind."

The grin was back in full. Fausto's golden mouth reflected light from the overhead fluorescent bulbs, like a star going supernova.

Chapter 9

Winston, Massachusetts, was part of Berkshire County, a quintessential New England town with picturesque views that looked like something out of a bank calendar. It was a small community, only twelve thousand residents, but its downtown was thriving: several quality restaurants, a movie theater, drugstore, shoe store, various craft shops, and more mom-and-pop establishments than chain stores. If not for the dedicated efforts of the town's zoning commission, Winston might have turned to bigger companies for acquiring higher tax revenue. Instead, the commission made every effort to foster a traditional small-town atmosphere.

Pepperell Academy was only a few miles from downtown, surrounded by undeveloped woodland and farms. It was the perfect place for Jake and Andy's retreat. When "The Day" arrived, and the world collapsed as Jake so believed, Winston's town center would draw people seeking resources and shelter, leaving Pepperell Academy and the land around it mostly deserted.

Jake never envisioned that he'd be raising his son in a town like Winston. He thought he'd be living in the Back Bay, or maybe a sweet condominium in Cambridge during baseball season and somewhere warm in the off months. But life, like the sport Jake loved, could throw curveballs. Which was how he'd ended up in the western part of the state. It wasn't so bad. The community was supportive, the air clean, and the restaurants were more than halfway decent.

Jake and Andy liked to go out to eat at least once a week. Tonight they had settled on Lotus, the only Asian cuisine in town. Andy was busy checking over the menu and didn't notice his dad looking at him across the table.

"You know what you're getting?" Jake asked.

Andy studied the menu some more. "I might have the pad Thai and dumplings," Andy said with his face buried in the menu.

Jake appraised his menu anew. "That's what Uncle Lance usually gets."

Andy glanced up and looked around the restaurant. "Speaking of Uncle Lance, where is he?"

"You know if it's not school-related, your uncle is always fifteen minutes late. By my watch, we've got another minute or two to go."

Andy went back to studying his culinary choices, but with an odd look on his face. Jake had been noticing his dark mood, which was short-tempered and sullen, and wondered whether Andy was properly managing his blood glucose.

Andy noticed his dad's attention. "I'm at one hundred ten," Andy said with a roll of his eyes. "You've got to stop worrying."

Busted. "I'm your dad," he said. "It's burned into my DNA. Besides, I wasn't worried when I saw you in The Quad today."

Andy perked up. "You were there? Watching?" A spark of pride flared in his brown eyes.

"I felt bad for that Ryan boy from the get-go," Jake said, "but I wanted to see you in action."

"Yeah, well? How'd I look?"

Jake made a face. "The move was great," he said. "I saw it coming from a mile away, but he sure didn't. The yell when you made your strike, though—now, that needs some work."

"I thought I was loud."

"It sounded more like you got something caught in your throat."

"I could yell now."

"You'll have plenty of chances to practice your yell, where you won't scare the waitstaff. I thought maybe we'd toss some Muay Thai training into the mix, or even Krav Maga. I think there are instructional DVDs in the library."

"Krav Maga's pretty badass," Andy said.

"When The Day comes, you might have to pull some of those moves on tougher opponents than Ryan Coventry."

Andy looked seriously annoyed, and then he just looked away. "I'm glad you're teaching me self-defense because I think it's cool," Andy said in a soft voice, as if anything louder might trigger an avalanche of emotion. He locked eyes with his father once more. "But enough talk about The Day, Dad. Serious. I want to enjoy my meal."

Jake respected Andy's wishes. He only wanted

what was best for his son, but the parent and the child didn't always agree on what that entailed. He felt the years were slipping by too quickly, and he worried about the time remaining to prepare his son properly for the bleak future they most likely faced. At first, Jake thought Andy's constant complaining about the drills was due to pressures at school, or maybe a temporary dip in enthusiasm, but lately he'd begun to see that it was something much more serious and involved.

Nevertheless, the drills weren't stopping anytime soon. Drilling meant survival. He could still vividly recall the first time Andy wasn't prepared for catastrophe. Jake hadn't been, either.

Andy was only three when he strolled into the kitchen, pulling Draggy by its purple tail. Jake had won the stuffed dragon at the Deerfield Fair; it had been Andy's inseparable buddy ever since.

"Where's Mama?" Andy asked.

Jake slid Laura's note into the kitchen drawer so Andy wouldn't see what had made his father cry.

Jake wiped his eyes. "She's not here, little buddy."

Andy made a face. His dad's voice sounded funny. He looked around. "Where is she?" he asked.

Andy's doleful eyes put a hole in Jake's chest, and he had a hell of a time getting air past the lump in his throat.

"She's not here, champ," Jake said, sweeping his son into his arms. Laura had bought Andy's fleece dinosaur footy pajamas last Christmas, but already they were a little snug.

"Why you crying, Daddy?" Andy asked.

His genuine concern cleaved Jake's heart. The boy

kicked to get down, and then he trotted off to explore every room in the house, with Draggy in tow.

A few minutes later, Andy reappeared in the kitchen. He was holding something other than Draggy in his hand. Jake could see it was a photograph of Laura.

"Mama left a picture of her on my bed," Andy said. "Why'd she do that?"

Again, Jake took his son into his arms. He clutched Andy tight to his chest and stroked the silky hair on the back of his son's head. He wanted his voice to be strong, but it had come out trembling then.

"Because she loves you so very much," Jake said.

Andy didn't appear to understand.

"I want my mommy," he said, sniffling, his eyes going moist. "I want my mommy," he repeated.

"Me too," Jake said as he rocked Andy in his arms. "Me too."

The bells above the front door chimed a sweet set of notes and pulled Jake out of that painful memory. Lance Dent entered. Jake and Andy stood to greet Lance and the three exchanged quick hugs.

Lance had a thick head of raven hair, while Jake's was ash blond and close cropped, but it was obvious to any stranger that these two were brothers. Lance was Jake's fraternal twin, eight minutes the elder, but the rigors of his job—the alumni dinners, social functions, committee meetings, parent conferences, fund-raising events, and school-sponsored activities—meant he didn't have time to take a fifteen-minute jog, let alone practice Krav Maga. Over the years, Lance, once married but now a committed bachelor, had packed on twenty or so extra pounds compared to Jake, who maintained his pro athlete physique. Even today, Jake could still fire off a ninety-mile-an-hour fastball, but only because he'd spent years rehabilitating his pitching arm.

Lance took a seat next to his nephew.

"Thinking about trying something new this time," Lance said as he perused the menu. "What else is good here?"

Andy looked incredulous. "Good at Lotus?" he said. "Heck, Uncle Lance, just close your eyes and point. You can't miss here."

Jake gave Lance a cautious shake of the head. "You're a creature of habit, bro," he said. "Just get the pad Thai and dumplings and be happy about it."

Lance put the menu away and smiled at his brother. In all the years Lance had been coming here, he'd never ordered anything other than the pad Thai. Jake knew he'd be disappointed with any other choice.

Jake and his brother were close growing up, but their bond had strengthened since Jake joined the staff at Pepperell Academy. For a time, the brothers' paths had diverged widely. While Jake battled to make it out of the minor leagues and into The Show, Lance Dent got a B.A. in education from Tufts and took a job as a math teacher at Pepperell Academy.

Then came the crash and burn, and the next thing Jake battled was depression. Though he was busy with work, Lance never lost touch with his brother or his struggles. He returned to the family home in New Hampshire every Sunday for dinner, and he and Jake would spend hours talking about life and how Jake might find his footing once more. After Lance's short marriage ended (he was childless, and vowed to remain that way), the brothers had even more in common.

Little by little, Jake got stronger as he dedicated more time and effort to learning survival skills. Lance might not have agreed with his brother's beliefs, but he noticed the physical and emotional turnaround. Without reservation, Lance had offered to help get Jake a job as a custodian at his school.

After a lengthy interview process, Jake had accepted a position, but not Lance's offer of financial help. Committed to the survivalist ethos of self-reliance, Jake and Andy moved to the double-wide trailer, all they could afford, a few miles from campus.

Lance's only request had been that Jake would keep his beliefs private. Nobody needed to know that the school custodian was a dedicated survivalist and what some would term a doomsday prepper. Jake had no trouble honoring Lance's wishes. He would keep lots of things secret, including his use of those underground passageways and chambers that would eventually function as his and Andy's retreat, their BOL. Even Lance didn't know about those.

After they ordered, Lance turned to Andy. "I had an interesting conversation with the dean of students about you today, Andy, my boy." He ruffled Andy's hair.

"What'd you hear?" Andy asked. He reddened and looked down at his lap. In three years at Pepperell Academy, Andy, now a junior with Carnegie Mellon at the top of his college choice list, had never violated the school's disciplinary policies.

"Easy, honcho," Lance said with a fractured smile. "She apparently spoke to Ryan, and he insisted you two were just roughhousing."

The three looked at each other.

"Thank goodness for Ryan's ego, eh?" Lance said with a wink and a smile.

"That guy is a major-league A-hole," Andy announced.

"Well, that may be the case," Lance said, his smile fading, "but his parents are major-league benefactors of the school. I'd advise you to try other approaches in dealing with any future confrontations. Understood?"

Andy said nothing.

"Understood?" Lance repeated, more sternly.

"Understood," Andy finally agreed. "But he's still an asshole."

Jake was trying to hold down his grin, but the corners of his mouth lifted up anyway.

Andy gave a shrug as if to say, *"Why should money make anybody special?"*

While Jake was learning a new trade as the head custodian of the school, Lance had spent several years enhancing his credentials. He'd earned an Ed.D. from Amherst College through an accelerated doctorate program for working professionals. By the time Andy was old enough to enroll in Pepperell Academy, Lance had taken the job as head of school. In that role, Lance assumed responsibility for managing daily operations, overseeing curriculum, hiring and supervising the faculty, and implementing the operational mandates of the school's board.

His biggest responsibility, however, was not included in any job description. A good head of school was a beacon for wealthy donors; and in some ways, Lance likened himself to a gold miner. Many parents could not afford the pricey tuition, some could just cover the cost, but plenty—well over 50 percent, Ryan

Coventry's folks among them—could lay out the cash for a year of schooling and not even notice they'd spent the money. Those were the parents Lance spent a great deal of time courting.

The three chatted like poker buddies while waiting for their meals. They talked about cars, the latest viral videos—Andy showed one on his phone that was essentially two people acting out the biological processes of the human digestive system. They talked of the teachers, as always, and Andy felt like a useful spy giving Lance the inside skinny on which classes were guts, which professors were dull, and which teachers were hot (as ranked by the students).

"How are things going with your computer club?" Lance asked.

A shadow crossed Andy's face and he seemed to retreat into himself. "It's fine," he said.

Jake was well versed on the many meanings of the phrase "It's fine." Judging by his son's response—eyes to the floor, and arms folded—he interpreted Andy's reply as *"Something's not fine, but don't ask about it."*

Diabetes had taught Jake to respect Andy's boundaries. He trusted his son to come to him if a particular situation needed his counsel.

The food came; and for a while, nobody spoke—it was all about eating. But Lance wasn't finished clearing the air.

"Look, buddy, about this Ryan Coventry thing—I get it, I really do," he said. "Some of the students here have a pretty warped perspective on the world. They've never wanted for anything at any point in their lives."

"Some of them? It's most of them. Uncle Lance, in case you haven't figured it out yet, I don't really fit in here. Everyone has so much money—it's like they don't get it. Not everybody can have the latest-model iPhone." Andy made a show of showing Jake his Samsung Galaxy Star, one of the cheapest brand-name Android smartphones currently on the market.

"And some of us could look at the school's job board and earn some extra money for the things they want," Jake said.

Lance nodded. "It's not always easy for me, either, buddy," he said. "I spend a lot of my time trying to get money from people who make more in a day than I do in a year. I see how they view money. It's warped. They just don't seem to appreciate their good fortune."

"Yeah," Andy agreed. "It's like they have tons of money, but it's still not enough."

"All I'm saying is that I can appreciate that it gets frustrating to be surrounded by so much wealth, and, well—not have so much of your own."

"Thanks for understanding, Uncle Lance."

"Sure, but don't take that as a license to start hosting mixed martial arts fights with the upper crust. I may be your uncle, and I love you like a son, but I'll still expel your sorry ass if you violate the school's disciplinary code. *Capisce?*"

"Yeah," Andy answered, inhaling a mouthful of food. *"Capisce."*

Chapter 10

All three chairs were occupied.

Stacey Hoyle Martinez and Gus Martinez were not tied up, but a man wielding an AR-15 proved to be as good as any rope. They were both easy to take down. No troubles there. Stacey had gotten home from her job as an administrator at a nearby culinary school an hour earlier than usual and entered her front door with an expression of someone about to take a surprise vacation. She was dressed nicely, and Fausto appreciated the way her clothes hugged her body in all the right places. He liked curvy women.

Her bright and excited smile dimmed with confusion as two armed men moved from either side of the front door to grab her from behind. One yanked her hair back; the other clutched her arm. Stacey's eyes bugged in their sockets and she had tried to scream, but Efren flexed his muscled arm as he slapped a hand over her mouth. He pressed a retracted stiletto against her lower back.

"Gritas y mueres," Efren said.

"Scream and you die." Fausto emerged from the

shadows to translate. She did not understand the order, he saw. Fausto was disgusted. Javier hadn't taught his American wife how to speak Spanish.

From the photos of Stacey Martinez displayed throughout the home, Fausto had expected a decent prize. He was not disappointed. Stacey had wavy, light-blond hair, exotic to a man accustomed to darker colors. Her nose fit her face—no work done there—but the breasts were certainly enhanced, and supremely enticing. She had slender shoulders and what Fausto imagined were toned legs hidden beneath dark slacks. He would have enjoyed sampling this one, all his senses working on overdrive, but he was here on assignment. The job required complete discipline and a devotion to the mission, nothing more. Seven men were currently under his command; and if Fausto's plan developed as he expected, that figure would grow substantially.

The boy's arrival was more of the same. They waited for the cab to drive off before taking him down. This time, Armando, a thin man whose many scars made his face into a relief map, did the honors.

Even though Gus was a young boy, Fausto felt no compunction to treat him with special kindness. Fausto had murdered his first man when he was four years younger than Gus. In Fausto's world, Gus Martinez was an adult. Fausto would treat the boy the same as Gus's father and mother. If he made any trouble, he would bleed.

Taking three hostages required some planning. They needed provisions, and three people could hardly live on chairs for what might turn into a multi-day affair. As far as others would know, Javier's family was taking an impromptu vacation. The house would need to look vacant. Anything cooked would be prepared on hot plates down in the basement.

The basement itself was converted into a makeshift prison. Fausto's men cleared space by moving boxes from the unfinished side, which had only a couple of small hopper windows, to the finished side, which had much more natural light and ways to escape. They brought mattresses down to function as beds. There's a saying, *"A buen sueño no hay mala cama"*—"a tired person can sleep anywhere"—even with armed men always posted on guard duty.

While Armando went to the supermarket, Fausto took on the task of providing clear instructions to the hostages. There would be no misinterpretation. The three sat with forlorn expressions on the hard dining-room chairs in the dimly lit basement.

Gus, wearing a shirt from the Levi's store and jeans, looked like a combination of his mother and father. He had Stacey's more delicate face, but Javier's darker coloring. He was tall, strong, and fit, and he might have been a bigger threat if he weren't so terrified. Fausto suspected he might pass out. If he did, that would be fine.

Standing before his captives, bookended by two of his armed guards, Fausto appraised his hostages thoughtfully.

"This is obviously a difficult situation for you," Fausto began. His English was very good. Soto had insisted he learn, but he spoke with an accent and paused often to translate the right word from his native tongue to this foreign one. "We may have a good result here, but only if you cooperate. So I'm going to explain the rules. Are you ready?"

Javier said yes, because he was more accustomed to Fausto and his people, but Stacey couldn't muster a single word. Her silence did not sit well with Fausto. With his drill head, he lifted Stacey's chin and forced her to make eye contact. Gus's dark eyes went wide with horror. He looked ready to spring to his mother's defense, but the boy's bravery withered with a single flash of Fausto's golden smile.

"I know you are scared," Fausto said, addressing both mother and son. "I would be scared, too. But I don't want to hurt you. This is a promise. We just need to get what is ours and we'll be gone."

Stacey's shock eased, and she gave Javier an angry look. Her eyes said, *"What did you do?"*

"We d-didn't d-do anything to you," Gus said in a stammering voice. "Let us go."

Fausto smiled wryly. "You can take that up later with your father."

Gus leaned forward in his chair so he could glare over at his dad. "Jesus, Dad," he said. "Are you working for a Mexican drug cartel?"

Fausto was impressed. "You just figured that out from what I said? Smart kid." He turned his attention from Gus to Javier. "That school you send your boy to? It's worth the money."

The twinkle in Fausto's eyes darkened into something more sinister. "Now, then, here are the rules. They are simple. If you try to escape, warn somebody, or fight back, you will be hurt. I don't know how badly. Depends, perhaps, on our mood." Fausto paused to let this information sink in. The hostages looked ready for the next instruction. "That's it," Fausto said with a shrug. "That's pretty much it. There are no other rules. You are all prisoners, and this will be your prison until we get back what is ours. Understood?"

The three nodded silently.

Fausto clapped his hands together—*that's settled.* "Okay, then. I'm glad to have your cooperation."

Fausto put his arm around one of his guards. The man had a thin build and the whisper of a mustache. His near unibrow stretched across dark brown eyes. He kept his long hair pulled back into a ponytail, which gave prominence to a broad forehead. A scowl seemed to be his only facial expression.

"This is 'Odio,'" Fausto said. "Translated, that means 'hate' in your language. There is good reason for this name, and you do not want to learn what it is." Fausto held up a finger and pointed it at each hostage in an admonishing way. "He will be in charge of you three. If you need something, you will ask him."

"How long are you going to keep us down here?" Stacey asked.

"Until this is done," Fausto said with finality. "Now, we need to let the people who matter know you won't be around for a while. We'll start with your work, Javier."

Javier handwrote an e-mail to his staff, informing them of his plan to be gone for the week. Fausto read the message over carefully for any hidden meaning. "If you have a code word and the police show up here, I will gut your wife like a fish and bathe your son in her blood while you watch," he said.

Stacey had already told her boss of her vacation plans, but she needed to let friends and family know about their secret getaway. For that, Facebook was the best tool for the job. Stacey also handwrote her post and Fausto typed it into the computer upstairs. Next she called the cleaning people to cancel, as well as a local handyman who was going to install a new vanity in the upstairs bathroom. Gus posted to his Facebook account. With a few messages broadcast to the world, the Martinez family disappeared.

Fausto left Odio and two other guards to watch over the clan while he and Efren went upstairs to plan. Armando would be back soon with the food. They would have fresh produce, rice and beans, so nutrition was no problem. With a bathroom downstairs, the family could live in the basement eternally. Perhaps he would bring down a TV to help pass the time. At least he'd bring down some books. An idle mind was more likely to be restless, and that could lead to trouble.

Fausto and Efren retreated to the master bathroom, where they could speak and not be heard or seen. The bathroom was tiled with high-quality marble and the fixtures were the best money could buy. As a man of privilege back home, well paid by Soto, Fausto was not unaccustomed to great wealth. But America was something entirely different. Javier's neighborhood, with its huge houses and wide lawns, gave the impression that everyone here lived like a king. No wonder so many of his friends had tried to make a new life across the border. The lure of money was an enticing scent, difficult to resist.

"I say we go after those kids, one by one." Efren was good on muscle, but he lacked imagination.

"I told you that would be complicated. There are other ways."

"What do you have in mind?"

"I have heard back from this cousin of Javier's, the one who works for the trucking company."

"And?"

"Let me ask you this first. If we had all the kids in a room and nobody around to bother us, how long do you think we'd need before we broke them?"

Efren considered the question. His dark eyes seemed to reflect on past interrogations, calculating the time it had taken from initial threat to full cooperation. "Hours. A day at most," he said.

Fausto nodded. "With a margin for error, I say a day. I agree. And to get back the money is not a long process, at least not according to Javier."

"Agreed," Efren said. "What are you thinking, Fausto?"

Fausto sat on the edge of the massive tub. "We need to get these kids together in a single place where they can disappear for some time without being noticed," Fausto said. "Vanish within a cloud of chaos and confusion. No alarms would be raised, at least not over any missing students. Not if there's a big enough distraction. It would allow us to operate without intervention and do what we do best."

"And what is it that we do best?"

"Get results for Soto. There is no other line in our job descriptions."

Fausto and Efren exchanged smiles.

"So, what is it you're thinking?" Efren asked.

"Do you believe this Lion person Javier told us about could get access to the students' class schedules? Time, room, building, that sort of thing?"

"I'm sure he could."

"Then I say, 'Look out, Winston, Massachusetts, because a devil wind is coming,' and it's going to blow their town down."

"Tell me your plan."

Fausto did just that. When he was finished, Efren looked shell-shocked.

"But, Fausto," Efren said, "what if the police find out before we get what we came for?"

"I have a plan in mind for that, too," Fausto said. He stood and patted Efren's shoulder. *There, there. We'll be fine. Trust me on this.* "A good employee of Soto's," Fausto added, "is always prepared."

Chapter 11

Every year, on the third weekend in March, Jake brought Andy to the Self-Reliance Be Ready Expo and Convention held in Syracuse, New York. Better known by its acronym, SRBR, it was the trade show for the latest and greatest in survivalist gear, training, and the best prepper paraphernalia.

Jake and Andy left after school on Friday and stayed until Sunday. They attended discussions and seminars during the day at the Expo center. They returned at night to their tent at the local campground, where they stayed with other like-minded individuals. Real preppers doing the SRBR never booked a hotel room.

Jake always looked forward to the annual convention. It was a time to bond with his son. These moments weren't going to last forever, and soon enough Andy was going to move on with his life, as he should. For now, being here with Andy meant the world to Jake, and he tried his best not to think too far down the road.

As they walked the conference floor, Jake and Andy did what they always did at the SRBR: talked about gear, clocked the latest trends, shopped for deals, and did some networking. Most kids got to do fun things with both their parents, but not Andy. The loss of his mother remained a raw spot etched on Andy's heart. Jake had done all he could to support his son over the years, even compiling a nice photo album—a memory book, he called it—filled with pictures of Andy's mother from her high-school days and happier times as a family.

For many years, Jake had been distraught and angry with Laura for leaving him, but he made it a point to craft something positive out of heartbreak for the sake of his son. The pain had an upside, and he and Andy might not have been as close as they were, had his mother stayed.

In his small campus office, Jake had taped a Mark Twain quote to his wall:

Anger is an acid that can do more harm to the vessel in which it is stored than to anything on which it is poured.

As time passed, Jake lost a lot of the anger, but not all of the emotion. Even Ellie, strong and loyal, couldn't completely replace Laura in his heart. On occasion, Jake would sneak into Andy's bedroom to leaf through the memory book on his own. Every picture of Laura was so clear to him: the day it was taken, where they were, how he was feeling. Some of the shots were so darn beautiful it was difficult to look at them without feeling the ache of missing her.

Perhaps the only way to vanquish Laura was to let Ellie in. But there was the small problem of his lifestyle.

Many people had the wrong image of a prepper, but they'd have to come to the SRBR or a similar expo to debunk the myths. Images of a deluded, rootin'-tootin', gun-obsessed nut job were far from the reality. People who prepped were just average consumers who happened to be deeply concerned about the fragility of the "system," and growing numbers were fueling an emerging lifestyle trend. If anything, Jake was on the low end of the economic spectrum, as many SRBR attendees were financially more solvent, with deeper pockets to make them better prepared.

Andy paused at a booth Jake would have preferred to ignore. "Check this out." He pointed to one weapon in particular, enclosed in a locked glass case.

"That's a grenade launcher, son," Jake said.

"Yeah, and?"

"And we're not here for weaponry, especially something like that. This is about having skills and knowing how to do things for yourself when nobody is there to do it for you. We're not at a gun show." Jake actually bristled around the gun show crowd. He needed to know how to defend himself, and was highly competent with many weapons, but he wasn't interested in building up a massive arsenal. "Come on," Jake said. "There's a lecture I want to sit in on that's starting soon."

Andy groaned and rolled his eyes. He looked back at the grenade launcher as if it were a million times cooler than his dad. "I don't know if I can take this anymore," he muttered.

Jake heard him. "What did you say?"

The words hurt, so Jake wanted to make sure he didn't misunderstand. Andy might as well have said, *"I don't want to fish with you anymore, or go camping, or go hiking, or go skiing,"* or any number of other things fathers and sons did together. The SRBR was their thing. It meant a great deal to Jake to share the experience with his son.

"Seriously, do you not want to be here?"

Andy gave Jake a sidelong glance.

He doesn't want to hurt my feelings, Jake thought.

"I'm fine. Let's go, Dad. I don't want you to miss anything."

Jake slipped his arm around Andy's shoulder. Andy didn't seem to mind, which lifted Jake's spirits in ways Andy would only understand once he was a dad.

"Thanks, buddy," Jake said. "That means a lot."

The lecture hall was a large conference room, which had folding chairs set out in rows. Richard Weismann was an internationally recognized authority on self-reliance, and for months Jake had been looking forward to hearing him speak. Seats near the stage were filling up fast. Making a dash to the front, Jake nabbed two empty chairs together in the first row, just to the left of the podium on the stage. He turned to see that Andy had staked out his claim in the very back of the hall. He was already engrossed in his smartphone, eyes glued to the screen.

Jake saved the seats with his coat and walked to the back of the hall. "What's up, buddy?" he asked. "You don't seem as into it this year. You've always loved coming to the SRBR. We look forward to it all year."

"No, Dad. You always loved coming here. I just go."

Ouch!

"Stop slinging arrows, okay? I'm your father, and I love you very much," Jake said. "And this lecture is important to me, but I want to be with you, too. So come on up front. I've got us two seats. So, how about you humor your papa for a bit? Okay, kiddo? It means a lot to me to have you here." Jake gave Andy a playful punch on the arm.

It was enough to wheedle him from the back up to the front. A few minutes later, Richard Weismann took the stage to a round of rousing applause. Andy didn't clap once, and kept his face glued to his phone's display.

"Hey," Jake whispered, "put that thing away, buddy. Let's be respectful."

Weismann was in his early sixties, and looked like anybody you might see at a business convention. He wasn't too tall, had a bit of a belly, and not much hair left on a splendidly round head. He didn't look anything like those characters on *Duck Dynasty,* an image that often came to people's minds when they thought about preppers.

"Good afternoon, friends," Weismann began. His microphone kicked feedback, so he adjusted the height until it was gone. "It's great to be back here at the SRBR. I always look forward to the chance to speak, and this is one of my favorite expos on the circuit. Today I'm here to talk about self-reliance. When the power goes out and the grid goes down, how will you stay warm? When the supermarket shelves go bare, how will you feed your family?"

Weismann paused for dramatic effect. He was an eloquent speaker. In a few sentences, he had captivated his audience and could have held their attention indefinitely.

"I'm going to tell you a little story to get the conversation started. The folks at NORAD go from a quiet morning, sipping coffee and observing the world from the comfort of their computer monitors, when chaos erupts. A ballistic missile has been launched from a cargo ship off the U.S. coast. The weapon is designed to release EMP, an electromagnetic pulse capable of destroying the U.S. power grid. A single explosion over the Midwest produces electronic waves a million times more powerful than any radio signal on earth. The current and voltage surges that follow will literally cook the semiconductor chips of critical electronic devices. In an instant, communications will fail. Computers will lose power. Car batteries will no longer function, and transportation will come to a complete and grinding halt. Telecommunications are down everywhere. You can't get a cell phone signal, let alone make a call.

"The power grid will be out, and probably out for months. Every bit of electronics we use—medical devices, gasoline pumps, phones, cars, water pumps—will no longer function. Of course the stock market crashes, since all trading has abruptly ceased. Bank accounts are gone, lost in a black hole of the crippled electrical grid. A single blast, if detonated high enough over the middle of the country, will be enough to plunge us all into total darkness. Food stocks will run out quickly. Everything about our current way of life will end in the sizzle of burnt-out circuitry, and we'll be plunged back to a preindustrialized society.

"Who could possess such a weapon? China, Russia, North Korea, and even Iran or Hezbollah, that's who. It's been estimated that a year after an EMP strike, between seventy-five and ninety percent of the U.S. population will perish from disease, starvation, and overall societal collapse. Imagine it. You wake up one morning and nothing works. No running water. No food in the stores. No money in your bank accounts. No hospitals. No transportation. Nothing works the way it once did. Cities in darkness. How will you live? How will your family live? We are lying to ourselves when we say we are prepared for this attack. We are not prepared as a country. But you can be prepared as individuals."

"Oh, give me a freakin' break."

The dissenting voice, meant to be spoken as an undertone, came out loud and attracted a great deal of attention. The murmurs rippled from front to back and grew in volume until Weismann could no longer be heard.

Jake looked at Andy with what, at first, was a bemused expression. Andy had retreated to the safety of his smartphone screen; he did not take notice of Jake's now-angry stare.

"Young man, it would appear you disagree with the scenario I've outlined here." Richard Weismann, accustomed to confronting his critics, did not seem the least bit perturbed by the interruption.

Andy looked up and realized Weismann was addressing him directly. Andy turned to his father for guidance.

"Your bed—you made it, you deal with it," Jake said, a little gruffness evident in his voice.

Andy stood, looked around at the sizable crowd, and pocketed his phone with a confident air.

"Look, I'm not denying the science behind EMP, Mr. Weismann," Andy began, speaking respectfully and earnestly. "What we're really talking about is the Compton effect. In 1925, the physicist Arthur Compton asserted that photons of electromagnetic energy would loosen electrons from atoms with low atomic numbers. This would create fluctuating electric currents and induce a powerful magnetic field capable of knocking out electronic circuitry. I get that. It's real. But do you honestly believe a country like North Korea or Iran, or some terrorist organization like Hezbollah or, say, ISIS, could develop a warhead sophisticated enough to deliver a really damaging EMP blast? Have you honestly studied the technology required to make an EMP-optimized warhead?"

"Determined foes can overcome even the most challenging hurdles," Weismann said.

"Yeah, well, dedicating my life to a technically implausible scenario makes no sense to me. Oh, wait—a rogue nation could launch a weapon from a freighter off the U.S. coast. You said that. So maybe it's not so farfetched. Let's see, Iran's Shahab-3 is the only medium-range missile small enough to be launched from one of those boats. But it has a payload capacity of maybe one thousand kilograms, which doesn't come close to the devastation that you describe. And any terrorist cell that miraculously gets a nuclear-type weapon is going to blow up a city, not risk wasting their crown jewel on a complex EMP strike that's likely to fail."

Hushed conversation passed through the crowd. Jake was wide-eyed and astonished. *Where did he learn all this?*

"You're forgetting our other enemies, young man," Weismann said.

"That's right. But let me ask you, why would Russia do it? Or China? I'll tell you the answer. They wouldn't. The trace-back would result in catastrophic nuclear war. We've had nuclear weapons for decades, and nobody is using them in wartime for a reason. Besides, our economies are joined at the hip. There's a major economic deterrent here nobody is talking about."

Weismann no longer appeared amused. "Since you seem so well versed on the topic, young man, what would you suggest we do?"

Andy turned to Jake. His body language was that of a child having to confess an uncomfortable truth.

"I'd stop living my life in constant fear," he said. "I'd learn how to do things for myself—things like gardening, mechanical repairs, self-defense, and whatnot—simply because it was interesting to me. I wouldn't come to these conferences anymore. I wouldn't prepare for the future at the expense of enjoying my present."

"So, why are you here?" Weismann asked.

Jake's eyes held Andy's in a head-on stare.

"Because I love my dad more than anything," Andy said. "But I can't do this anymore."

Andy walked across the room, heading for the exit. And Jake watched him go.

Chapter 12

Jake bought his 2007 Chevy Tahoe because of the aggressive tires, towing capacity, and ability to traverse most terrains. He didn't know how he'd get to his bug-out location when TEOTWAWKI (The End of the World As We Know It) came, so the car offered an option if the woods behind his trailer were impassable.

Jake saved all year for the expo. Normally, he would have stocked up on supplies—freeze-dried foods, seed, communication equipment, medical kits, and homeopathic medicine—and the Tahoe was a good way of hauling it all home. But Andy had demanded they leave the expo early. Jake didn't argue, so the back of the car contained only the camping gear they'd brought and some clothes.

For the first hundred miles of the trip home, Andy had been silent. Jake did his best to coax some words out of his son, but Andy retreated into himself, with his thousand-yard stare fixed firmly on the scenery rolling past his window.

Jake wasn't angry with Andy. His son's passion and

conviction had impressed him and he'd said as much, but something was still bothering Andy. Whatever it was, he was keeping tight-lipped about it.

They were about an hour outside Winston when Andy finally broke the quiet.

"I'm going to stop, Dad," Andy said. "I can't drill anymore. I can't prep, either. I'm done. And I mean done for good. I'm out."

Jake took his eyes off the road to give Andy a measured stare. This wasn't a complete surprise. Jake had felt Andy pulling away for the past year. But something about the way Andy had announced his intentions felt final, nonnegotiable. The words hurt.

Jake bit his tongue to hold back what he really wanted to say. "You've got to do what you think is right for you, I guess," he managed.

If he got angry with Andy, or tried to scare him the way Richard Weismann had tried with his EMP scenario, it would only push his son farther away. But to Jake, this was like hearing his son announce plans to go skating on thin ice. The end of civilization was as real to Jake as if he'd seen an army of advancing soldiers. It was coming; and if they were not prepared, it would level everything in its path—including his son, the most precious person in his life.

"There's more," Andy said.

Jake appraised Andy anew. "More than deciding to give up every advantage you can have when The Day comes? That's what the drills are for, son."

"No. This 'more' is about you."

"Look, no matter what, I'm not going to leave you behind. But you're going to make it a lot harder than it needs to be. We're a team here, and if you don't drill, your skills will rust. You know that, don't you?"

"I want your skills to rust, Dad," Andy said.

Jake jerked the wheel. The car veered a little to the left, but he quickly recovered the steering.

"Last I checked, I was the parent here and you were the kid. I can tell you what to do, but it doesn't work the other way around." Jake did a poor job of tempering the anger in his voice.

Andy retreated to his view out the window. When he turned around again, his face was red and he was on the verge of tears. Jake knew from experience how difficult it could be to confront a parent. Andy's emotions had welled up, and they needed a place to escape.

"You know, Dad, just because you think the world is going to end, it doesn't mean that I do. I'm tired of living your fear. It's yours, not mine. Don't you get that?"

"It's not science fiction. It's all proven fact."

"Maybe so, but I happen to think the world is going to be just fine," Andy said in a tone he'd never used before with his father. "I don't think there's going to be an EMP attack, or a solar flare, or a super volcano, or a biological agent, or freaking all-out nuclear war. It's not going to happen in my lifetime. If it does, fine, but I don't want to live like it is, because it's *not normal.*"

"We are *not* abnormal," Jake protested. "We're prepared. There's a difference."

"Growing up, I had more gas masks than toys," Andy said. "That's not normal, Dad. Not by a long shot."

They had just driven over a hilly rise. On the descent, the Tahoe picked up speed, going eighty-five before Jake noticed. He eased up on the accelerator.

"This is about Pepperell Academy, isn't it?"

"No, Dad, it's not."

"It's your friends, isn't it?"

"No."

"I bet it's Hilary. Are you two dating? Because sometimes love can skew your thinking."

"No, Dad. We're not dating. And Hilary didn't put me up to this. Neither did David, Rafa, Pixie, or Solomon. They know I can hold my own in a fight, but they think it's because I took karate lessons. I don't talk about us, because I'm honestly embarrassed by it."

"You're embarrassed?" Jake said. The shake of his head was meant to show his incredulity. "Were you *embarrassed* when you kicked Ryan Coventry's ass all over The Quad?"

Andy shrugged. "That's different. I'm glad you taught me self-defense. But it's the reason you're teaching me that's got me all bugged out."

"Damn girls," Jake muttered under his breath, but it was loud enough for Andy to hear.

"Don't blame Hilary!" Andy snapped. "She's done nothing to influence me. Nothing. If anything, you should be blaming Mom for making you the way you are."

Jake sneered and cocked an eyebrow while glancing over at his son.

"What's that supposed to mean?"

"It means you became this way because Mom left you."

Jake looked at the road once more. "You're psycho-analyzing your dad now, is that it?"

Andy folded his arms across his chest. The posture was part defensive and part frustrated. "It's not that hard," Andy said. "I took Psych 101 with Professor Cooper."

Andy exchanged looks with his dad and unfolded his arms when he saw the hint of a smile.

"Okay, boy genius," Jake said, but in a challenging way. "You think you know me so well? Go for it. Analyze me."

Andy shook his head. "You're baiting me. You're just going to get mad."

"I'm not going to get mad. I'm being honest here. If you think you know me so well, go for it. Analyze me. Why do I prep?"

Andy didn't respond.

"I'll tell you why. Because of all those reasons you listed. EMP, solar flare, bioterrorism—it's the law of probability. Something major is going to happen, and when it does, we'll be prepared to deal with it. It's not complicated."

"That's not why, Dad," Andy said.

"Well, enlighten me."

"You promise you won't get mad?"

Jake waited until he passed a car on his left before meeting Andy's stare.

"I already promised. Analyze away."

Andy nodded. *Game on.* "Okay, let's start with your life after high school," he began. "You're a hot prospect for the Boston Red Sox. Then what happens? Instead of going to the majors, your arm gets crushed in an accident."

"Because I was drinking and driving." Jake pointed

at Andy. "And if I ever catch you doing the same, the only thing you'll be driving will have pedals and no motor."

"I don't even drink."

"Okay. Let's keep it that way."

"Then what happens after the accident? You can't pitch. The dream is gone."

"I thought you were going to analyze me. This sounds more like history to me."

Andy drummed his hands against his thighs. He was enjoying this opportunity. "Give me a chance," he said. "So after your baseball career comes to a crashing halt, what happens next? You find out your little boy has a serious medical condition. Now you've got two things going against you, but there's a third headed your way. Mom leaves. She can't take it anymore. She was dreaming of a big ballplayer's salary and now she has a sick kid and a broken husband."

Jake lifted his hands off the wheel for just a second. *You got me.* He wasn't going to offer any defense. Andy knew his facts, and it was what it was.

"Well, that explains why I believe the EMP threat is real and you don't," Jake said sarcastically. "Come on, Andy. What's your point? Why are you revisiting the past? I've always been open with you about Mom and what happened to us."

"It's not just about Mom. It's where all your fear comes from, Dad."

Jake furrowed his brow. His son was making as much sense as he'd expect from someone who had decided to stop prepping for the inevitable.

"Sorry, I'm not following."

"Think about it," Andy said. "One minute your life is headed in one direction and then it takes a U-turn, but not to backtrack. Instead, you're on these unfamiliar roads, navigating in the dark. Everything that was secure to you is suddenly insecure. In Freudian psychology, it's known as the displacement theory. It's the unconscious redirecting of emotions from one thing to another. You lost your sense of security, so you replaced it with prepping. Now you feel secure again. It's pretty simple when you think about it."

And Jake did think. He thought a lot, falling silent, gazing out the window, but not really seeing the traffic. Everything Andy had just said hit him square in the heart—right where it counted.

"They taught you all that at school?" Jake said.

"And some."

"We're sure getting our money's worth."

"It's free tuition, Dad."

"Well, aren't we lucky, then?" Jake held a serious expression, but soon it slipped into a wry grin. Andy relaxed enough to allow the corner of his mouth to lift a little as well. When it did, Jake slugged Andy's shoulder in a loving, guylike way.

"Why are you telling me this now?"

Andy started to laugh. "Dad, I've been trying to tell you this for ages. You just haven't been listening."

"That's not true. I listen to everything you say."

"No, Dad, you want just to teach me about communication equipment, gardening, and self-defense—which, by the way, is the only thing I really like."

"It's not just about what you like to do," Jake said. "It's about having the skill set you need to survive."

"You see? You see? You're doing it again! You're not hearing me."

Jake held up his hands to show he wasn't going to be defensive. "I'm hearing you! I'm hearing you! So you don't want to drill anymore?"

"That's right. No more three A.M. wake-up calls. It's affecting me in a negative way."

"Did you learn that in Professor Cooper's psych class as well?"

Andy chuckled. "No, that's my own personal observation. If you love me, and I know you do, we're going to stop being preppers."

"What do you mean 'we'?"

"I want you to dismantle the bug-out location," Andy said.

The mood turned sour in the time it took Jake to change lanes. Jake fell silent for several miles, and Andy let him think.

"You may want to hamper our ability to get out of Dodge, but that doesn't mean I'm going to do the same. Stop the drills if that's your desire, but the BOL stays. And I'm not going to stop doing what I have to do to protect us."

Andy pondered the offer; then he extended his hand. "Yeah, I guess it's a deal, Dad."

Jake shook on it.

"But I want you to do something for me," Andy said.

"Anything, but what I said I wouldn't do."

"I want you to *think* about dismantling the bug-out location. I'm not asking you to do it. I'm just asking you to give it some real serious consideration."

"It's not happening, son."

"Just think about it, Dad. That's all I'm asking."

Jake gazed out the window and said nothing. Andy gripped his father's arm.

He's trying to reach you. . . . Listen to him. . . .

"Please," Andy pleaded.

Jake saw the desperation in his son's eyes.

"Yeah, buddy," he said. "I'll think it over. Promise."

The rest of the drive back to Winston was uneventful. They stopped at McDonald's for a couple of shakes and some burgers, and made excellent time the rest of the way home. Jake kept the conversation light. They talked about music and TV shows, Andy's classes and college, and Vines that his son found endlessly amusing. Little by little, Jake would goad Andy back into the life. He felt hopeful, because Andy's decision put them both at risk.

The sun had nearly set when Jake turned onto the dirt road that led to the trailer a quarter mile away. The tough winter had left deep ruts in the road, and Jake imagined making a midnight dash to his bug-out location, driving right over those divots using his truck the way he intended when he bought it.

As Jake pulled into his driveway, the Tahoe's headlights illuminated the figure of a woman sitting on the stairs at the trailer's front door. Jake came to an abrupt stop and cut the engine, but he kept the headlights on so he could see the person clearly.

His jaw dropped.

"You've got to be kidding me," he said.

Andy followed his father's gaze, and his eyes went wide as well.

The woman sitting on the front steps smoking a cigarette didn't look all that different from her pictures—the pictures in the memory book, the pictures seared into his consciousness. The years hadn't aged her beyond recognition. Andy knew his mother.

He'd know her anywhere.

Chapter 13

L aura.

Jake shut off the Tahoe's headlamps, but the spot over the front door shone down on Laura as if she were the focus of some play.

On the pitching mound, feelings didn't matter, actions did. After baseball, Jake had continued to use actions to dampen his feelings. In this instant, all that changed. Emotions came at Jake so hard and so fast, he had to sit in the truck a moment to get his bearings.

Eventually Jake got out, but Andy didn't budge. He looked weak, stunned, and could only stare open-mouthed at his mother.

Jake approached Laura with caution, as if fast footsteps or a sudden movement might scare her off. The pounding of his heart drowned out all sound. Jake stopped a few feet from the front stairs and tried to relax his jaw muscles.

Laura took a drag from her cigarette and blew the smoke out the side of her mouth. Her head was tilted to the right, and her long, blond hair cascaded across her shoulders in a way Jake remembered and adored. It was brisk outside, and Laura was dressed for the weather in a thick green parka, jeans, and hiking boots.

Laura's car was parked off to the side in the little pullout used to make a three-point turn. It made Jake sort of sad to see Laura driving a Chevy, a beat-up Impala, because she was always so proud of her fancy cars. Laura had left them with hope of having a better life. Up close, it was clear she had been chasing that dream ever since, and the years had been harder on her than they had been on Jake.

While Laura had smoked some in high school, she'd shelved the habit after they married, occasionally having a cigarette or two when they went out for drinks. It appeared that Laura had made it a habit once more. Jake could see where her skin had wrinkled and puffiness marred the underside of her eyes. But nothing truly dampened her beauty; and while Laura's hair was less lustrous than he remembered, her mouth was the same as ever.

"Hi, Jake. You look good."

Jake scratched at his head, trying to make sense of it all. His emotions went wild. He was exhilarated, dazed, and angry. He'd never experienced anything like this before. He could only imagine how Andy was feeling.

"What are you doing here, Laura?"

Laura stood and took a few steps toward him. Her eyes were like two warm pools, inviting him inside, pleading to forgive and forget.

"I've been thinking about you, about us," Laura said.

She came closer. Every move—the dip of her shoulder, that playful upturn of her mouth, a slight list of her head to one side—it was all so Laura, so familiar to Jake. He could tell right away she was flirting, acting coy, and gauging his reaction to see if he, too, could pretend she had never walked away.

But he couldn't play along. Jake folded his arms across his chest, closing himself off. Laura took another step toward him, and Jake turned his head to look back at Andy. His son was sitting inside the truck, eyes lowered. He couldn't watch, and Jake couldn't blame him.

"This isn't right, Laura," Jake said. "You shouldn't have come around here like this. Better if you had called. Given us some warning."

Laura was close enough to reach out and touch Jake's shoulder. When she did, he didn't flinch. He didn't feel a spark, either, like he had when they first started to date in high school. Still, something was there, a little echo from the love they once had shared.

Laura said, "I didn't want you to say no."

It was exactly how Laura would think.

Laura peered over Jake's shoulder at the Tahoe. "Is he in there? Is that Andy?"

Jake nodded. "He's in there, but I'm not calling for him. If he wants to talk to you, he'll open the door himself."

Laura looked surprised. "He knows it's me?" she asked.

The hopefulness in Laura's voice again made Jake feel sorry for her. She'd missed so much of the good stuff. Andy had given Jake's life shape and purpose, and Laura had spurned it all to chase down the hope of a better tomorrow. But what was she really chasing? An easier life? More money? Jake had never thought Laura stopped loving her son, but she did stop loving her life. For that, Andy had paid the heaviest price.

"I gave him a book of pictures," Jake said. "You haven't changed much, Laura. It's still you."

Laura gave an indifferent shrug, but her act didn't fool Jake. She was clearly pleased by the compliment. "Has he talked about me much?" she asked.

"Your name has come up a few times."

Laura smiled, and Jake broke away from her gaze. He couldn't stare at her for long without seeing the past. Plenty of good memories offset the bad. Of course there were the fights, the blame and shame for the accident, dishes shattered against the kitchen wall, but time brushed clean the intensity of those memories—the good feelings that came from being in Laura's presence were easy for Jake to recall.

At the stadium, she had been a fixture in the stands— always cheering him on, her voice carrying above the others, filling him with encouragement. In bed, Laura had been inventive and uninhibited, and her touch was not easily forgotten. In a way, Laura's sudden arrival made Jake fully aware of his growing feelings for Ellie. Laura was the past, whereas Ellie could very well be his future.

Laura reached for another smoke, but something made her put the pack away. "How'd you know I was here?" Jake asked.

"Facebook," Laura said.

"Facebook?"

"I'm friends with Andy."

"Oh, shit, Laura."

"Of course I didn't tell him it was me. I used a picture of a girl I . . . I know."

From the way Laura paused, Jake suspected the picture was the daughter of a man she'd been with. Maybe her own daughter—what did he know?

"You're going to have to tell him about the Facebook account."

"I will," Laura said.

There was a moment of silence that Jake wanted to fill, but he couldn't find the words.

"Where have you been?" he finally asked.

"Around," Laura said. "A lot of time in California. The last couple of years I've been living with my mom. She died a few months ago."

Jake's eyes became downcast. He'd always been fond of Laura's mom and dad. However, after Laura left, they withdrew from Jake and from Andy, feeling it wouldn't be fair to Andy to be a part of his life. He was too young to know them, and their presence would have been confusing and a reminder of his mother's abandonment. Jake didn't agree. Why deprive a child of his grandparents? But the decision was made and final. Laura didn't just remove herself from the family; she took all the relationships tethered to her as well.

"I'm so sorry, Laura. Your mom was a wonderful woman."

"My dad's been doing okay, but he misses her."

"Is that why you came looking for me? For us?"

Laura got a faraway look in her eyes. "I guess Mom's passing put things in a different light."

"Yeah, I guess."

The silence returned.

"What do you want, Laura?"

Laura tried to swallow a sob, but her tight lips couldn't hold it in. "I want to see my son. I want to see Andy. I want so much." Tears pooled in her eyelids and fell freely, and her body convulsed as she gasped while weeping. "I'm so sorry. I've messed so much up."

Jake took a step toward her. The instinct to comfort had not abated with the years. But he stopped and turned at the sound of a car door opening. He saw Andy approaching, hands stuffed into the pocket of his sweat-shirt, eyes cast down.

Andy stopped a few feet away from Laura. "You think you can just show up here and start to cry and make me feel sorry for you? How about my tears? I don't think you felt sorry for a single one."

Laura brushed her eyes clear with the back of her hand.

"Please, Andy. Let's talk."

"There's nothing to talk about."

Andy sprinted for the woods. Laura got ready to pursue him, but Jake lowered his arm like a barricade and held her in place.

"Where's he's going?" she asked.

"He wants to be alone," Jake said.

"In the woods by himself? Aren't you going to go after him?"

Jake couldn't suppress a smile. "Trust me, Laura, he'll be more than all right on his own out there. Where are you staying?"

Laura craned her neck to look back at the trailer.

"Any extra room here?"

Jake chortled. "You're really something," he said. "If the circumstances were different, I'd honestly be tempted. I won't lie to you. I've always cared for you, and I've missed you. I want to know where you've been all these years, what happened to you. I want to know it all. But this is Andy's home, too, and we've got to respect him."

"You're seeing somebody, aren't you?" Laura asked.

"I am."

"Do you love her?"

Jake thought a beat. "I do."

And maybe soon, I'll even tell her that myself.

Jake fished sixty dollars out of his wallet. "There's a Motel 6 a couple miles down Route 120. I'll give you my number. You can check in with me in the morning and we'll see about getting you and Andy together. But it's going to be up to him, not me, to make it happen."

Laura nodded. She obviously wasn't thrilled, but she took the proffered cash anyway. "Thanks, Jake. You always were a sweetheart."

"Yeah, maybe so," Jake said. "But you're going to do something for me."

"What's that?"

"You're going to unfriend Andy. Tonight. Find a computer and get it done. If you're going to come back into our son's life, you're going to do it with honesty."

Again Jake thought of Ellie, and he knew she deserved the same.

Chapter 14

Given the number of student organizations on campus and the limited amount of available space, the CB-B10 conference room, in the basement of the Cargill Building, should have been booked constantly, but it was no longer in the system. Pixie had hacked the online reservation system and deleted the windowless room from the available inventory, essentially making it disappear. Because students could no longer reserve CB-B10, and because the administrative folks knew it was not to be commissioned for classroom use, it was available to The Shire as a dedicated meeting spot. They had renamed it "Sherwood Forest," in deference to the theme of their operation.

Cargill was not centrally located on campus. Sometimes the distance made it more practical to meet in The Quad or at one of the school's many lunchrooms between classes. For this particular gathering, though, Andy wanted to use Sherwood Forest. The mood of the six young people seated around the solid oak conference table was somber and tense.

"This meeting will come to order," Andy began. "Let's take roll call."

Solomon groaned. "Dude, you sound like such an anus when you get all formal. Can't we skip this part and just get on with it?"

"It's important," Hilary said. Solomon rolled his eyes, because Hilary was always coming to Andy's defense. "Roll call, minutes of our meetings, our charter—these things are what give our group structure," Hilary added.

"Even French club doesn't have roll call, and they're uptight about everything," Rafa said.

Andy slammed his palm hard against the table. The sound got everyone's attention. "Hey, people, wake up! I mean it! We're in deep shit here, if you haven't figured it out yet. If you don't want to do roll call, don't do it. I don't care. Let's move on."

Roll call and other formalities aside, all six members were present: Pixie (aka Troy), David (aka Dark Matter), Rafa, Solomon, Andy, and Hilary. The Shire.

"What have you got, Pixie?" Andy asked.

"Let's start with the obvious." Pixie pushed his sunglasses up the bridge of his nose. He was wearing his usual Western-style plaid shirt, dark jeans, and well-worn Doc Martens originals. "How many people had the private cryptographic key to unlock our specific address on the bitcoin block chain?"

Andy nodded. It was a fine question to ask. A bitcoin private key was nothing but a long string of numbers and letters; with digital currency, that was ultimately what defined ownership. You couldn't stuff a bitcoin in your wallet, but you could use the private key to unlock the cash. Stealing the money only required getting that key.

"We all had access," David said. In a fluid and practiced motion, he pulled his thick hair into a ponytail and tied it off with a rubber band. "Isn't that the problem?"

"Did we all have access?" Pixie asked. "Who here actually used the key to look at the block chain? I didn't."

"Can you prove that?" Solomon asked. He popped a Twix bar into his mouth as if it were a cigar; then he fixed Pixie with a skeptical glance. "Let's be honest here. We can't trust each other anymore. We all had access in some way because we all knew where the key was. It's as simple as that. Everyone here is a suspect." He leaned back in his chair with a satisfied grin, as though he'd just gotten to the heart of the matter—without roll call.

"I told you the wallet would never be safe on a computer connected to the Internet!" Rafa snapped. Never one to sit still, Rafa bounded to his feet and began to bounce on his heels, leaning on the back of his chair for support. He pointed at Andy. "I told you," he repeated.

"It *was* protected," David said. "I had the best firewall running."

"But did you set up a cloud backup service, David?" Pixie asked. "Or use Ubuntu on a machine with zero connections and zero blocks to generate the wallet-dot-dat file? Or any of the other thirteen steps I told you to follow?"

David/Dark Matter leapt from his chair and pointed his own accusatory finger at Pixie. "Maybe you took it. Maybe you did it just to teach me a lesson."

Pixie pushed his chair back and puffed his chest as much as he could. If his dad had been there, he'd have seen a Troy who was worthy of the tough-guy name. "You really think I have the money? Is that what you think?"

Hilary banged her fist against the conference table. It was hot and stuffy in the cramped room. She had taken off her button-down shirt to reveal the black T-shirt underneath: a graphic of the evolution of man, going from ape to biped and concluding with a modern-day human walking and texting.

"Enough! You guys are like a couple of squabbling kids. This isn't going to help anybody," she said.

David and Pixie held their stare-down confrontation a couple more seconds before they retreated to their respective chairs.

"The good news is that we can see the bitcoins in the ledger," said Hilary.

"I can also *see* Jupiter through my telescope," Solomon said, "but that doesn't mean I can go there."

"I've never seen you use that telescope to scope out anything except the girls in Hamilton Hall," Rafa said.

"Hey, numbnuts, *I* live in Hamilton Hall," Hilary said.

Rafa and Solomon broke eye contact and fell silent. Their body language suggested the lens of Solomon's telescope might have once fallen on her.

"Really, guys?" Hilary said with a slightly amused expression.

"Hil, it was an accident, I swear," Solomon said.

"Guys, can we focus here?" Andy asked. "Hilary is right. We can still see the coins on the ledger. That means we can tap the address if the owner tries to sell them."

"Not necessarily," Pixie countered. "If somebody tumbles the bitcoins to a clean address that we don't know, those coins will vanish."

"And they can do it, too," Rafa said. "They'll sip the coins ten or so at a time, and there's no way to spot the transaction, especially if the tumblers split the payouts. The bitcoins will end up somewhere on the block chain that we won't know about. Then they'll be gone, and gone for good."

Pixie nodded vigorously and had to push his sunglasses up the bridge of his nose once more.

"Is it possible that Gus's dad took the bitcoins back?" Hilary asked.

"Possible," David said. "But that would mean he had somehow traced the theft back to us, and I know we covered our tracks."

"Just like you safeguarded the bitcoins," Solomon said in a snippy tone.

"Hey, it's an extra sixty bucks to you if you're going to ride me like that!" David shot back.

Solomon slipped the second Twix bar into his mouth before he had finished chomping down on the first. "Speaking of Gus Martinez, did any of you see his Facebook post?"

Andy looked alarmed. "No," he said. "What did he post?"

Solomon shrugged. "Nothing, just that his dad was taking him and his mom on some surprise vacation. No wireless, but he wrote he'd post pics when he got back."

"A vacation three weeks before spring break?" Andy sounded dubious.

"I didn't think it was a big deal."

"Yeah, well, it could be a huge deal," Andy said. "Everybody listen up. Until we know what happened to the bitcoins, we have got to pull our heads out of our collective assess and start thinking. Anything out of the ordinary, anything at all, could be trouble. You got that?"

Silence.

"Got it?" Andy repeated.

This time, everyone nodded.

"As of right now, The Shire is finished. We're done. No more meetings. If we want to talk, we do it by encrypted messaging or in person out in the open. I don't know who is watching us or what's going to happen, but Gus going on a sudden vacation should make us all nervous."

"Good idea," Pixie said. "I'll set us up with Whispernet."

Andy's dark eyes smoldered. "One of us has the bitcoins," he said as he got to his feet. "I know it and whoever took them knows it, and if you don't return the money, it's going to end up being the biggest mistake you'll ever make in your life." Andy spun on his heels. Without so much as a glance to the others, he stormed out of the conference room, slamming the door behind him.

For almost a minute, the remainder of The Shire sat at the conference table, silenced by the heavy pall that had settled over the room. Solomon finally broke the spell.

"Look, I know things are tough, but what's really eating Gilbert Grape there?" he asked, pointing at the closed door.

"His mother showed up in town," Rafa said. "I guess she came to his house, and he kind of freaked out."

Solomon's eyes went wide. "Whoa," he said. "That'd do it."

"He's supposed to meet her tomorrow for lunch or something," Hilary said. "That's what he told me, at least."

"Long-lost mom comes back and the bitcoins are missing," Solomon said. "Is there some sort of connection here, people, we should be looking at?"

"Yeah," Pixie said, "the one from your brain to your mouth."

"I love you, too, Pixie," Solomon said. "In fact, I love all of you guys, even if you did steal the money."

Everyone got up to leave. Nothing more could be said. In a way, Solomon had said it all.

Chapter 15

The tanker truck barreled down Route 120 three miles inside the Winston town line. A 350-horsepower engine hummed in perfect working order, and the Bridgestone tires spun fast enough to go five miles above the speed limit. It drove like brand-new because the truck mechanics at BVC Environmental, who maintained the vast fleet, took great pride in their work.

For years, BVC was the go-to company for transporting nitroglycerin, explosives, flammable products, and compressed gases. On the heels of the Hazardous Material Transportation Act of 1975, BVC Environmental was responsible for many safety innovations accepted as standard practice today. But a truck was still a truck; and even if the cargo was properly secured, operator failure or negligence was the most cited reason for traffic accidents and chemical spills.

In his seven years working for BVC, Pedro Sanchez, a married father of two, consistently scored high on his driver-performance evaluation, which meant he had received the largest possible pay raise when it came time for his annual review. He knew how to use the two-way radio, had received only two traffic violations (an impressive feat, considering the miles he had logged), kept his vehicles impeccably clean, was always punctual and cooperative, and demonstrated superior safe-driving habits. He had never been in an accident. Only a handful of drivers could make such a claim.

On this day, the clouds were puffy white cotton balls painted on a pale blue sky, and the buds on the tree branches seemed bursting to get out. The winter had been typical for New England—brutal—and the road was marred with numerous frost heaves. Sanchez had to be careful. He was hauling a small ocean of chemicals in his tanker, and sudden movement was not advisable.

At one particularly scenic spot, with views of a wide field and a large white farmhouse with an adjacent red barn, Sanchez shifted his truck into a lower gear to help climb a hilly rise. He had never driven these roads before, so he was careful to take the turns at a slow speed. Flipping a tanker truck was not all that hard. It was even easier when the tank was filled with four thousand gallons of aluminum sulfide. The yellow crystalline solid dissolved in a water solution and gave off a strong, rotten-egg, ammonia-like odor; but as long as it was secured inside the tank, Sanchez could smell nothing.

Sanchez whistled to the fast beat of an Enrique Iglesias tune while navigating a series of sharp turns. The aluminum sulfide shifted and sloshed inside the massive tank, forming waves with each tap on the brakes or turn of the wheels. Sixteen tons of chemical waves could make for treacherous driving, but Sanchez was a pro. He knew how to drive *with* the waves, and intentionally kept them small so the truck stayed in control. Baffles subdivided the interior of the tank into several mini-compartments. While they reduced the overall wave effect by eliminating the space needed to build momentum, by no means did they provide total stability.

At the point where the road forked, Sanchez should have gone straight; that was where the plant was located. Instead, he checked his map and went to the right. There weren't many textile plants in the state anymore, but the recent trend to move manufacturing back to America had given a jolt of life to a sector of the economy once thought headed for extinction. This trend benefited BVC as well as drivers like Sanchez, who had seen an uptick in shipments of hazardous materials like aluminum sulfide, used in textile manufacturing.

Dispatch had no idea he'd taken a different route to the plant, but they would find out soon enough. Trying alternate routes wasn't enough of an infraction to get him fired, but Sanchez didn't care either way. He was done with the job, and would make more money from this one trip than he could earn in a lifetime.

The truck lumbered past a small blue sign for Pepperell Academy. Three-tenths of a mile later, Sanchez spied the black pickup truck pulled over to the side of the road. The truck was where he expected it to be, but Sanchez checked his notes anyway and confirmed the license plate was a match. He steered the truck onto the shoulder and applied the brakes with care. They made a loud screeching sound, followed by a hiss of air before the tanker came to a juddering stop.

Sanchez climbed down from the truck's cab at the same time that three men got out of the pickup.

"Primo, Javier me ha contado mucho de ti. Qué gusto conocerte por fin en persona," the man with the long ponytail said. ("Cousin, Javier has told me much about you. It's good to finally meet you in person.") He opened his arms and the two men embraced. Also in Spanish, Fausto said, "These are my associates Efren and Armando."

Sanchez was related to Javier, not Fausto, but membership in Sangre Tierra blurred the bloodlines. Fausto shivered. "I am not used to this weather."

Fausto wore aviator sunglasses and a fine-looking brown leather jacket. Sanchez did not know these items belonged to his cousin Javier Martinez. Efren and Armando were also dressed for the chilly March weather in Javier's expensive clothes.

Sanchez shivered as well, but his was the chill of fear. He had felt in control while inside his truck, but now he had second thoughts. A spike of anxiety put a tight band around Sanchez's chest. He looked past Fausto to a point down the road.

"What about other cars?" Sanchez asked as he bounced on his feet to help calm his nerves.

"You worry too much, my friend," Fausto replied. "Have you seen any other vehicles on the road? No, you have not. Why? Because we have set up a detour, that's why. One of our associates has connections to a road crew, and he brought us some very authentic-looking detour signs and little orange vests. We are on our own for now."

"How many others are involved?" Sanchez asked.

"Now you ask questions that don't concern you."

"I'm sorry, Fausto, but I'm nervous. I want to make sure I brought enough of what you asked for."

"Worry not. I came here with a handful of men, but Soto's contacts are many and he got me the rest of what I needed. Including me, there are twelve of us to take out six kids. I like our chances." Fausto's smile showcased his precious-metal mouth.

Sanchez had never met the famed assassin in person, but he had heard plenty of stories, and the man's golden smile filled him with dread. After Soto had called, Sanchez thought only of the money. Seeing Fausto in person made it all seem real, and he was burdened with second thoughts. Fausto's smile said there was no going back.

"Let's get this over with," Sanchez said as he exhaled a weighty breath. "The chemical suits are in the cab."

Fausto whistled and pointed to the truck. As if a starter pistol had gone off, Efren and Armando rushed over to the tanker, climbed up, and removed a messy pile of chemical suits from within. Sanchez had no problem stealing from his company. Nobody ever guarded the locker room where those suits were kept.

Fausto checked his watch. "We need to report this accident soon if we're to keep to schedule," he said. "So please hurry."

Sanchez got the feeling Fausto wasn't being entirely truthful, and he suspected there was much more to this plan than what he had been told. Efren snatched the tanker's ignition key from Sanchez's outstretched hand. Sanchez was impressed by Efren's strong build and repulsed by Armando's many facial scars.

"I know how to drive," Efren said, as though reading Sanchez's thoughts.

Armando and Fausto helped Sanchez load the chemical suits into the back of the pickup truck, while Efren climbed into the tanker's cab. Efren turned the ignition key and Sanchez stopped his work to listen to the tanker's engine rumble back to life.

"Let's move! Let's move!" Fausto ordered as he pulled Sanchez toward the pickup.

Sanchez held his ground. His gaze sharpened on the tanker. All it took to say good-bye to one life for another was a phone call from Mexico. He thought of everything this day would bring him—money for his children, for his wife, Maria, for the things he saw on television but only dreamed of owning. Sanchez shelved his apprehension. It would be worth it in the end, Sanchez assured himself.

Efren depressed the gas pedal with the brakes still engaged, and the tanker's engine revved like a bull readying to charge. Sanchez was already in the pickup, sandwiched between Fausto in the driver's seat and Armando to his right. The tanker's engine revved up once more. Sanchez could tell Efren was trying to put the truck in gear. A horrible grinding sound, metal on metal, rattled Sanchez's fillings. The tanker lurched ahead several feet but stopped abruptly; then it bucked forward again. Sanchez grimaced at Efren's apparent incompetence.

Fausto took notice and set a comforting hand on Sanchez's shoulder. "Fear not, friend. Efren is a fine driver. And besides, the quality of those gears won't matter a few moments from now."

The tanker lunged forward again, this time without

the sudden stops and starts. Fausto hit the gas on the pickup. After a spray of loose dirt as the tires fought for traction, Fausto was keeping pace alongside the rumbling tanker. Sanchez gripped the seat hard enough to turn his knuckles white. The road was not wide enough for a car driving in the opposite direction to pass safely.

"Are you sure about those detours?" Sanchez asked.

"Cousin, you worry too much." Fausto pushed on the gas some more as the tanker picked up speed.

Sanchez watched the speedometer's needle rise. *Fifteen . . . twenty . . . twenty-five . . .*

The pickup pulled slightly ahead of the tanker, until the truck bed containing a cushion of chemical suits was even with the tanker's driver's-side door. With the truck still in motion, Efren took his foot off the gas pedal, but the truck kept most of its speed, partially propelled by a gradual downhill slope. Efren's eyes showed no fear as he opened the door and gave Fausto a big thumbs-up sign. Without hesitating, Efren leapt from the truck traveling thirty miles an hour and made a bull's-eye landing in the middle of the pickup truck bed, using the chemical suits to cushion his fall.

As soon as Efren landed, Fausto slammed on the brakes. The driverless truck plunged ahead just as the road bent sharply to the left. Sanchez reflexively pantomimed slamming on the brake pedal, as though he were able to prevent a collision with the fast-approaching tree line.

A moment later, the air vibrated with a thunderous crash that sent clusters of birds into frantic flight. The engine compartment folded around a thick oak tree, which swayed from the violent impact. The sides of the cabin crumpled until the glass windshield shattered and the metal twisted like origami.

A contained tsunami of chemicals jackknifed the tanker. The massive steel drum spun sideways and sliced through a thicket of pines, snapping trees like blades of grass. Another series of chemical waves pushed the tanker off balance until it teetered on the uneven ground and eventually tipped over, with an earsplitting crunch of metal and snapping branches. Large gashes opened up in the metal wall, spilling gallons of poisonous liquid by the second. The air was fouled with the stench of rotten eggs and ammonia.

Sanchez buried his face in his hands. "Oh, sweet Lord, what have I done? Forgive me. Please forgive me."

Fausto shot Sanchez a disapproving look tempered with a hint of sympathy. Maneuvering within the pickup truck's cramped quarters, Fausto put his knees on the seat as he placed his hands over Sanchez's ears. It was a gesture meant to comfort a distraught man. He appraised Sanchez once more, looking deeply in his eyes, and seemed satisfied by what he saw.

"I forgive you," Fausto said as he twisted hard in one direction, while pulling his arms the opposite way. The spin generated enough torque to snap Sanchez's neck like a tree branch crushed beneath a tanker truck. Instantly Sanchez's body went limp. Fausto released his grip and Sanchez's head slammed against the dashboard and lolled to one side at a ghastly, unnatural angle. "I am truly sorry, my friend," Fausto said. "But this was Soto's desire."

Efren didn't waste a single second. Without prompting, he hopped out of the truck and dragged the body outside. From the back of the pickup, he grabbed a chemical suit for himself and one for Armando. Armando assisted Efren with the zippers before he put on his own suit. They both wore respirators underneath a yellow hood, and the front visor shielded the rest of the face from chemical exposure. The suits were banana yellow and covered every inch of their bodies. They were challenging to walk in, and it took a lot of effort to drag Sanchez twenty feet beyond the mangled truck. They dropped him faceup on the hard earth. When Armando let go, he was breathing heavily, but Efren was stronger and not at all winded. Both men appraised Sanchez thoughtfully.

"He looks like he came shooting out the window," Efren said in Spanish. The respirator altered his voice, but his words were intelligible enough.

"Let's make it look a little more authentic anyway," Armando said. "Just to be sure."

Efren returned to the wrecked truck and grabbed some shards of shattered glass from inside the cab. All the while, liquid poured out from various breaches in the tanker walls and formed poisonous lakes in the saturated earth. Efren sprinkled the glass shards over Sanchez's face, hair, and clothes. Then the two men, both dressed in bright yellow chemical suits, took turns beating a dead man's face with thick tree branches.

And they had only just begun.

Chapter 16

Four miles from the tanker crash, Officer Ellie Barnes didn't know anything terrible had happened. She was sitting in her patrol car, hoping to snag unsuspecting motorists. She wasn't going to ticket all the speeders, only the frequent violators. Essentially, she was a mobile-radar-speed display, there to inspire motorists to adopt slower driving habits on a stretch of road notorious for speeding.

Ellie glanced in her rearview mirror and saw an SUV slowing down as it approached. Normally, she would have been on guard, but Ellie recognized Jake's Tahoe from a signature dent in the front fender. Jake pulled up alongside Ellie's cruiser and lowered his window.

"Morning, Officer. I thought you might be thirsty, or sleepy, or both."

Jake slid over to the passenger side so Ellie could reach the Dunkin' Donuts coffee he bought for her. One cream, two sugars, just the way she liked it. Ellie took a sip and made a delighted *hmmmm* sound.

"You free for dinner tonight?" Ellie asked.

Jake shook his head. "I need to be there for Andy right now."

Ellie returned a nod.

Two nights ago, Jake had called with the bombshell news that Laura had shown up at his house. Ellie was caught off guard both by the news and a sudden flash of jealousy. It wasn't entirely logical; Jake had never expressed any lingering feelings for Laura, but they still had a long history.

"I wish I could see you," Ellie said. She tried to sound more understanding than disappointed. She was both.

"Next week, I'm all yours," Jake said. "Monday, dinner at your place?"

"Always at my place," Ellie said, sounding a bit doleful.

Jake gave this some thought. "How about dinner at my place?"

Ellie's face broke into a bright smile. "I've been waiting for that invitation a very long time, Mr. Dent."

A cryptic expression came over Jake's face, one Ellie found both curious and endearing.

Jake blew Ellie a kiss. "Seven P.M., sharp," he said. "And bring your handcuffs."

He drove off with his arm out the window, waving good-bye.

Ellie's mind wasn't 100 percent on speeders. When Ellie saw the Chevy Impala crest over the hill, she had been thinking about Laura and wondering what it was like to be with Jake back when he played baseball. Laura and Jake had just started their life together when it all came crashing down. In a way, Ellie could understand Laura's motives, but that didn't justify abandoning her son.

The Chevy blew by Ellie as if her cruiser were hidden behind shrubs, not out in the open. She checked her computer to make sure no calls needed her attention.

This would be fun.

Ellie put on her flashers and got right up on the Chevy's bumper. Although this was a routine traffic stop, Ellie's training kicked in. She didn't know what she didn't know. Was this driver high on drugs and potentially dangerous, or just late for work?

She picked up her radio mike and announced her intentions to dispatch. "644 Traffic."

"Go ahead, 644."

"Minnesota plate GTL732 at Wade and South Merrimack."

"Minnesota GTL732 at Wade and South Merrimack, copy."

The name came back Laura Collins, not Dent, but Ellie was wondering if this was Jake's Laura. She approached the Chevy steadily, but carefully. She checked to make sure the trunk was latched, satisfied nobody would pop out to surprise her. The driver had her window down.

"Hi, I'm Officer Barnes. The reason I stopped you is because you were going eighteen miles over the speed limit. May I see your driver's license and registration?"

Jake hadn't described Laura in detail, but Ellie was increasingly suspicious. With documents in hand, Ellie returned to her cruiser. Using the computer, Ellie ran the plate and saw that the car belonged to the driver. When Ellie returned, Laura looked sheepish and embarrassed.

"I'm so sorry I was speeding, Officer," Laura said.

"What brings you from Minnesota to Winston?" Ellie asked.

"I'm here to see my son," Laura said. "He goes to the prep school in town."

Confirmation. "Well, Mrs. Collins, I'm afraid I do have to issue you a citation today. Watch your speed and have a nice day." Ellie's face showed a stern expression as she handed Laura her citation, but inside she was beaming. It was petty for sure, but Laura deserved a lot more payback for what she had done to the man who now shared Ellie's bed.

At quarter past nine, Ellie pulled up stakes and set off for Pepperell Academy. The access road was notorious for speeders who were running late for class. Minutes later, Ellie made the right turn off 120 and drove another mile when she saw the accident. Her instinct was to put on the strobes and rush over to help, but she could see from a distance that it was a tanker truck that had crashed. Ellie instinctively applied the brakes. This was a hazmat response. She'd been trained to proceed with caution. Until Ellie knew what that tanker was hauling, she would stay back, even if the driver were in distress.

Stepping out of the car, Ellie made sure she was upwind before retrieving her department-issued binoculars. The air was definitely foul. Whatever was leaking out smelled poisonous. Through the binoculars, Ellie searched for the hazmat placard posted in several locations on the tanker. This would identify the material without exposing her to any deadly fumes. Ellie saw what she was looking for. She had also observed the condition of the cabin. If the driver of the truck were alive, it would be a miracle to rival the turning of water into wine.

The mobile data terminal in her patrol car gave access to the material data sheet, and Ellie entered, "aluminum sulfide." The MDS returned a plethora of data: *The material with a chemical formula, Al2S3, causes irritation to the respiratory tract, skin, and eyes. Harmful if swallowed. The hydrogen sulfide gas, if formed, is poisonous. Victims who suffer from inhalation exposure need to be closely monitored for signs of respiratory distress.* There was no data on explosion limits or auto-ignition temperature, but firefighters were advised to be equipped with a NIOSH-approved, positive-pressure, self-contained breathing apparatus and full protective clothing.

Police procedures required Ellie to stay back and put in a call to the fire department. They had the expertise to handle the spill, and would take command of the situation. It wasn't long before fire and ambulance arrived on scene. Ellie coordinated the roadblocks, rerouted traffic, and kept the area clear of pedestrians, while Captain Steve Singer assumed incident command.

Steve Singer was a fifteen-year vet of the Winston FD. He had at his disposal a 2005 Smeal engine, a newer Spartan truck, a Tower truck, two ambulances, and a Hackney heavy-duty rescue truck. Singer dispatched them all. He called in support from two neighboring towns as well.

The first task was driver rescue. To ensure their safety, the first responders donned respirators. Singer could see the body of a man—the driver, presumably—thrown about twenty feet from impact. The man, heavy-set and in his midfifties, wasn't moving. It appeared his neck had been broken. *Poor guy,* Singer thought. Some of the EMT folks might have grown accustomed to seeing horrible things, but Singer would never be numb to the sight of a dead body.

Minutes later, Singer's suspicions were confirmed. The fatality was placed on a stretcher and loaded into an ambulance. Singer had dealt with plenty of blazes over his career, but a chemical spill of this massive proportion was a nightmare scenario for all involved. Singer's team had already been overexposed to the noxious fumes, and they needed proper chemical suits before doing anything more. Somebody would need to remove all sources of ignition and make sure they did not contaminate the air by raising dust levels.

Morning dew clung to the tall grasses and reflected the many lights from the dozen or so emergency response vehicles on the scene. Singer returned to his car and dialed a number he had called maybe a total of three times during his tenure with the Winston FD.

"This is Jackson."

Jackson West was the field coordinator for Clean Air Environmental (CAE) Services, one of the largest private environmental and hazardous-waste management services in the country. Singer had worked with West in the past, so the two were familiar with each other. Clean Air dealt with incidents as small as bottle mercury and as large as an oil spill. This disaster was probably a Level B or A, closer to the oil spill category.

"Hey, Jackson. This is Steve Singer with Winston Fire Department."

"Steve, how are you? What can I do for you?"

"We have a major incident here," he said. "A tanker carrying what has to be thousands of gallons of aluminum sulfide tipped over on the access road to Pepperell Academy by Route 120."

"Aluminum sulfide, you said?"

"That's right."

West groaned, confirming Singer's suspicion that this would indeed be an ugly mess.

"Okay, I'll dispatch a team right away. We can assist with the evacuation effort as needed."

Clean Air had a network of emergency-response service centers. With a phone call, it could deploy hundreds of experienced and certified workers to tackle any level of incident.

"What's the recommended radius?" Singer asked.

"For safety, I'd give it a half mile."

Singer checked his map. "Okay, so that's two businesses and about a dozen residential properties. We have four chemical suits. That will be our evacuation team for now."

"Again, we can help with that once we get on-site. I'll bring in extra crew."

"That would be great," Singer said. "We could use all the help we can get here."

"Is there any immediate risk of fire?"

"No," Singer said. "We've got one fatality. That's it. I'll put in a call to the trucking company and see what we learn about the driver."

"Okay," West replied. "For now, I'd advise that you keep your crew a safe distance away and make sure everyone outside has on a respirator. We'll be there soon."

"Will do," Singer said.

Twenty minutes later, the first emergency trucks from Clean Air Environmental Services arrived on the scene. Singer led the Winston FD on evacuations. A team leader from CAE greeted Captain Singer with a quick, perfunctory hello. They had work to do. The first task was absorption, and for that, Clean Air had brought along their tanker truck. Clad in yellow protective suits, five workers set to the task of applying a mix of vermiculite, sodium carbonate, and other dry noncombustible adsorbents. Soon enough, the scene was swarming with workers in bright yellow chemical suits. They worked efficiently and without direction from the Winston Fire Department, even though Captain Singer remained in command of the entire operation.

Captain Singer checked in with Ellie Barnes to make sure the roads were still blocked.

"Hey, I just heard on the radio that somebody over at Pepperell Academy called the station to report an ammonia smell in the air," Ellie said.

Shit.

Singer got West on the phone and told him the bad news.

"We're going to have to expand the evacuation radius," West said. "I'd say two miles, just to be safe."

Singer checked his map. "That includes another three businesses, a whole bunch of residences, and Pepperell Academy."

"I guess the prevailing winds decided not to cooperate," West said.

Singer sighed loudly. He didn't have enough manpower to manage something this large, and West knew it.

"Don't worry, Steve," West continued. "We'll help you out with the evacuations. I can even get buses there if you'd like us to deal with the school."

"That would be great," Singer said. "We can transport the students and faculty to Winston Regional High School until this gets sorted out."

"Might want to have the Red Cross help with shelter."

"Can you take care of that, too?"

"Of course," West said. "I'll dispatch a crew over to the school right now. I bet we can get buses there in about twenty minutes."

"Sounds pricey," Singer said.

"I'm sure your taxpayers aren't going to love it, but what can you do? You'll be able to recoup some of the cost from the trucking company, I'm sure."

Singer chuckled. He could already imagine who at the upcoming town-budget meeting would be most vocal about the bill.

Singer agreed with West's plan and dispatched police and fire to Pepperell Academy. Hopefully, with CAE's help, the chaos would be kept to a minimum.

Hidden in the trees on a hilly rise overlooking the school, Fausto Garza waited in a parked white cargo van until he saw the blue and red strobe lights of the emergency responders racing down the access road before he radioed his crew. He took a moment to check his phone again. The photo Carlos had sent him was perfect. He had followed Fausto's instructions to the letter. The image showed four large oil drums each linked together by thick wires. The wires terminated into a brass box affixed to the side of a fifty-five-gallon lime-green metal drum. Lining the top of the lime-green drum was a special seal that was secured in place with a five-inch bolt. A metal tag bolted onto the drum beneath that seal would mean something very significant to the right people. He was glad to have the photo, even though Fausto hoped he would not have to use it. If he did, it would mean their mission here had been compromised. This operation had many variables, many moving parts, and Soto who understood the necessity for such a contingency plan arranged with Carlos to have the contraption created, photographed, and sent to Fausto without delay.

Through high-powered binoculars, Fausto studied the unfolding emergency response. Sanchez had been right. The evacuation-zone radius would not initially include the school. This gave his team time to get into position. The members of the police and fire departments scurried about like ants on a chaotic but controlled march.

Patience . . . patience . . .

He had waited until the hazmat crew had shown up at the tanker crash before phoning the police to report an ammonia smell at the school. He could wait a little bit longer before he blended his crew in with the actual emergency responders.

Chapter 17

Trust in God, but have a deep larder.

Prepping wasn't about having a supply of food to last a few days. It was about how to survive for the rest of your life. Jake believed that when The Day came, society would cease to function, and he'd have to hunker down for the long haul. It was as simple as that. The larder in his bug-out location, and the other provisions he stockpiled, were the means by which he would endure the coming collapse.

Now Andy wanted it gone, and Jake had to give this serious consideration. He made a promise. Jake was prepared for everything, except to say good-bye to this part of his life. It was like ripping a security blanket from the hands of a young child or taking a teenager's cell phone. He'd feel naked without it, lost, alone—and, worst of all, vulnerable.

Jake slumped down on a stack of bags filled with brown rice. He had come down here not just to check on his supplies, but also to connect with the space, to think. He'd built this from nothing, and the sweat equity made this more than just a storage area.

When Jake first discovered this underground room, it was filthy, in complete disrepair, covered in cobwebs and infested with rodents, as were most of the abandoned tunnels. It took hours of work to clean it up, and countless lost weekends to get the rooms suitable for storing his supplies.

The rooms and tunnels were still connected to the school's power supply, so getting light down here was as simple as replacing and reconnecting lots of forgotten wiring. Jake thoughtfully selected natural daylight fluorescent bulbs to bring a bit of artificial sunshine down below. Now the space was lit, clean, and organized as any general store. It was massive like a store, too: almost seven hundred square feet with eight-foot-high ceilings. Thick, concrete brick walls and a lack of windows made the room a bit dungeon-like, but posters of the outdoors—mountains, lakes, and forests—lightened the dreariness.

Jake looked at the freestanding shelves and could recall loading and stocking each item there. The twenty pounds of salt, bags of brown sugar, and raw honey would give the food some needed flavoring. He'd thought about keeping flour down here, anticipating that Andy would want his famed pancakes, but the grain stored poorly and rotating it was more than a bit cumbersome. Andy would get used to wheat berries, and it was a more nutritious breakfast anyway.

In addition to other grains, like buckwheat, dry corn, and quinoa, he had plenty of canned fruit and vegetables, beans (stored, like the grains, in pails certified for food), peanut butter, coffee, tea, powdered milk (nitrogen-packed from Walton Feed), as well as tins of olive oil. He had cans of meat and tuna and other supplies such as toilet paper, soaps, lighter fluid, and bottled water.

The temperature never got much above sixty-five degrees in the summer, and Jake siphoned off heat from the preexisting ductwork so nothing ever froze in the winter. In the event of a power failure, kerosene heaters would keep the larder and sleeping quarters toasty warm. Jake kept careful records of his inventory, and any food item close to expiring would be moved from the larder and brought to his home so nothing went to waste.

How to dismantle it all?

If it came to it, most of the equipment could be sold, Jake supposed. Items like his hand-cranked grain mill, home dehydrator, and the vacuum-packing machine (great for sealing plastic bags and evacuating the air from mason jars) would probably sell for close to what he paid on sites like craigslist.

The real money would be in the guns and ammo. Jake had chosen his weapons carefully for their versatility. No single firearm could be counted on to do every job, plus he had to limit the cartridges to what was readily stocked in most places that sold ammo. If he needed to go scrounging for bullets, it would be better to look for .22 LR ammunition, by far the most common in the world.

For hunting small game, Jake had a Ruger 10/22 with a ten-round rotary magazine. The recoil and noise were minimal, making it a good gun for Andy to shoot as well. Newer shooters, afraid of noise and kickback, often developed bad habits such as poor shooting posture and flinching when firing a higher-caliber weapon. Jake had recently added an AK-47 to his arsenal. The AK-47

shot a 7.62x39mm round, and Jake would use that gun for
hunting larger game as well as defense. When the collapse came, he'd need to be able to fight force with force.

The long guns had better velocity and a longer sight-
ing radius, but they were not always practical to carry,
which was why Jake had pistols down here as well. The
SIG SAUER he kept at home, but here Jake's Glock 19
served him well. It was a reliable gun, and the 9mm
round was a popular choice, useful to have on hand
when bartering with others who survived the coming
collapse. Jake also had a Smith & Wesson .22 LR rimfire pistol, with a ten-round capacity, and a Ruger LC9
in his arsenal. The Ruger was an easily carried backup
pistol, and at one pound fully loaded could be worn
day and night without second thought.

For mobility, Jake used a Condor H-Harness chest
rig with a battle belt. He could carry plenty of mags on
the move. If he had to, Jake could slip a mag into his
back pocket, just in case. Even though he had refin-
ished the rifles using Cerakote H-Series materials finish, Jake still stocked plenty of RIG (rust-inhibitive
grease), and he maintained his guns with the same
thoroughness as he rotated his inventory.

If the larder went, though, the guns would go, too.
Jake knew he couldn't keep a window to this part of
his life open even a sliver. Just like with baseball, it
would be too tempting to open it all the way and climb
right back in.

The brown rice shifted and made a rhythmic sound
as Jake stood. He walked to the back of the larder,
where a thick metal door opened into a smaller adjacent room. Jake flicked the light switch and made a
quick inspection of his fuel and power supplies. The

storage room, half the size of the larder, locked from the inside and doubled as a safe room, but Jake wouldn't want to stay in there for long. He had a stockpile of rechargeable batteries for various electronic devices, including his communication equipment, and rechargers for each type. Two solar-powered rechargers would serve as backup, should the electricity go out. The underground tunnels and many of the rooms were wired to run off the school's generator; and if the grid went down, Jake had a fuel-transfer pump to keep that generator humming. The pump ran off a 12v motor that could siphon ten gallons of gas per minute. He could get gas from abandoned cars, or even dig up a tank at a gas station if necessary.

In here, Jake kept his water-treatment filtration system, medical supplies, and bags of seed. How could he let it all go? Laura showing up the way she did was another reminder that uncertainty was life's only certainty. Since seeing her, Jake had thought of little else. Every detail of the encounter had been etched upon his mind. How could he still have feelings for her? It was illogical, nonsensical, and yet undeniable.

A thought struck him. Was it really Laura he wanted, or just the idea of Laura? Was his bug-out location a way for Jake to cling to a time in his life when he felt most secure? Was all this planning and prepping just a means to find a safe haven after all his losses? Displacement, Andy had called it. All these years, Jake simply accepted what he did without truly understanding where the behavior came from.

He wondered if now was the right time to step off the path. Maybe Laura was like a cool breeze, telling Jake it was time to close that window to his past once and for all. He knew Ellie well enough to know she'd never embrace his ways. It was foolish for him to think otherwise. Perhaps letting go of Laura, Jake could find it in himself to dismantle his bug-out location. The possibility intrigued him.

Andy had gotten Jake thinking. He'd achieved that much with the promise he'd extracted.

Laura had been in town only a couple of days, and the urge to see her felt sometimes overpowering. They had met for coffee the day after her arrival and enjoyed a pleasant conversation, albeit one tinged with sadness. Jake didn't offer any details about Andy because his son should have the prerogative to choose what information to share. What he did talk about was his life after she had left, and she of hers, but for the most part the conversation didn't dip below surface level.

Either way, Jake would see Laura again, but first Andy had to meet his mother. Jake had offered to be there, but Andy wanted to confront her on his own. Confused as Jake was, he could only imagine how his son was processing everything. Jake had tried to get Andy to open up, but that conversation had gone nowhere. Jake only knew that Andy and Laura were going out to a late lunch.

Poor kid. His head must be spinning, unsure what to feel.

Jake snagged the clipboard he kept tacked to the wall, thinking he'd do some work on the inventory, when he heard the fire alarm. Usually, the alarms were nothing and Jake was inclined to ignore them, but he had a Uniden scanner and figured he might as well check. Sometimes he turned on the scanner while he worked, and would smile when he heard Ellie's voice.

The Winston PD was already preset. With a push of a button, Jake dialed the scanner to that channel. Between bursts of static, Jake listened to the chatter.

"How many ambulances can you get there?" The male voice was professionally calm.

"We got three en route, but I'm looking for more."

"There is a big team from Clean Air here. They're going to help with the evac."

Jake's head began buzzing. What were they talking about?

"Buses are already at Pepperell Academy. We can load them and move out quickly. We'll take them to the regional high school."

"I'm not smelling the ammonia." This was a new voice. The people communicating knew each other, but Jake didn't know any of them. *What ammonia? Ambulances? Buses? What the hell is going on?*

Jake shut off the radio and raced for the tunnel. Something big was happening at the school. Like any father would feel, his concern was for his son.

Chapter 18

The upper hallway of the Terry Science Center was jammed with kids making an orderly exit. Andy was somewhere in the middle of the pack. Students shielded their ears from the piercing alarm while blinking strobes cast everything in a light of urgency. *Is this a drill or the real thing?* Andy overheard someone say something about a shooter, but he looked and saw it was that kid who was always talking trash. This was probably just another drill. With the recent rash of school shootings, they had drills every few weeks, or so it seemed.

Andy was walking behind Beth MacDonald. It was impossible to ignore the sway of her hips. Some girls wore the uniform especially well, and nobody could rock a pleated skirt and red cardigan like Beth Mac-Donald. Andy was completely inexperienced in the ways of women, and he had no idea how to make something happen with Beth that didn't involve a quadratic equation.

As it happened, Lydia Dyer said something funny, which made Beth throw her head back with a hearty laugh. Of course Andy noticed everything about the moment—the perfect lines of Beth's arched back and neck, her dancer's physique, the *swoosh* of her long ponytail sliding from shoulder to shoulder, the sweet timbre of her voice. For a fleeting instant, Beth unwittingly helped Andy forget about his troubles.

Of the two brontosaurus-sized issues confronting him, the missing bitcoins and Laura, it was Andy's mother who occupied most of his waking thoughts. What would he say to her? Would he even speak? Could he? Should he have let his dad come along, like Jake had wanted? Andy contemplated canceling; but in his heart, he wanted to meet her, get to know her, and maybe even come to know more about himself. He wasn't even angry that she had created a bogus profile to reach him.

The messages exchanged with Andy when Laura wasn't being Laura were innocuous, limited mostly to talk about cool bands and interesting or funny websites. Ironically, it was the effort that went into pulling off the ruse that made Andy feel as if his mother cared. The same night Laura showed up at Andy's house she sent a new friend request that also confessed to her deceit. The Facebook messages she sent him as Laura were cordial, but nothing more. Unless they met in person, a hole in Andy's history would remain, and what he wanted was a complete picture.

Beth turned and saw Andy walking behind her, which brightened her smile even more. The hormone soup swimming about Andy's body made him momentarily clumsy. He stumbled in the stairwell and had to grab a railing to regain his balance. Instead of tumbling down the stairs and into the throngs of students marching below him, Andy's fast footwork put him in lockstep with Beth. She reached out and touched his arm. The contact sent bolts of electricity shooting through his veins.

Lydia rolled her eyes. Like a lot of the students making their way to the exit, she turned her attention to her smartphone. Andy figured Vine was probably already full of posts about the fire drill, with captions like, *Here we go again.*

"Do you think Mr. Forbes will notice if I don't come back to class?" Beth said. The stairwell amplified the noise level, and Beth shouted to be heard over the persistent din. Andy didn't mind leaning in close to hear her more clearly. He was thinking about a joke he could make that would get her to laugh again, when he caught a flash of something yellow at the bottom of the stairwell.

It took a moment to register, and even after the yellow-clad figures came in full view, he still wasn't quite sure what to make of it.

"I don't think we are going back to class." Andy pointed at the three figures encased in chemical suits stationed at the bottom of the stairs, urging the students to hurry. A fresh surge behind Andy came like a tide picking up speed as more students saw what he did, and the realization set in that this might not be a drill.

Andy was glad to have his backpack with his insulin, glucose tablets, and emergency glucagon kit with him and not in the classroom. In the fracas, Andy became separated from Beth. He was looking for her when a strong tug on his arm refocused his attention. Andy turned to see who had pulled on him. His eyes narrowed on Ryan Coventry's snarling face.

Ryan gave another hard yank. There was no resisting. The only direction Andy could travel was the one Ryan wanted him to go: up. Like a salmon fighting a steady current, Ryan shoved students aside to make a space large enough to drag Andy up the stairs with him. Andy fought for a foothold, but Ryan exploited his advantage and Andy could do nothing but stumble along behind him.

The bodies thinned at the second-floor landing. Ryan tossed Andy through the stairwell's open double doors. Andy's arms spun for balance as his legs kicked out like a boy on ice skates for the first time, but there was no stopping his fall.

Ryan charged as Andy, still a bit dazed, staggered to his feet. Lowering his shoulder like a battering ram, Ryan plowed into Andy's exposed right side with the full force of his two-hundred-pound frame. The blow flattened Andy against the unforgiving wall. He made a loud wheezing sound when the breath left him.

"Bet you're not feeling like a big shot now," Ryan said, standing over Andy's crumpled body.

"Ryan, what the hell?" Andy said, still gasping for breath. "We've got to get out of here. There's some chemical spill or something and we're all being evacuated."

Ryan's expression suggested a different plan. "Yeah, that's why I'm leaving and you're not."

Concealed inside a bright yellow chemical suit, Efren moved freely among the real employees from Clean Air Environmental Services. As Fausto had predicted, all it took to look like a person of authority were the proper uniforms and attitudes.

Efren had come to the Terry Science Center, knowing which exit was closest to Andy Dent's classroom. Fausto had given his team everything they would need to accomplish their mission. They had building plans and, thanks to the help from a man called The Lion, they also had class schedules of all six targets. Efren had memorized Andy's face, and it was easy to spot the boy on the stairwell behind a pretty blond girl with a long ponytail. Fausto was right, as usual. The chaos was ideal for concealing the abduction; the smile beneath his faceplate was not so easy to hide.

Efren directed a mob of students to the nearest exit, but mostly he was mindful of the classroom down the hall, its door intentionally left open. As Andy passed, Efren would follow. Within a second, he would have his target trapped inside that room, where they would wait for the evacuation to conclude.

That was the plan, until another student had intervened.

Students asked questions as they flooded down the stairs.

"What's going on?"

"Are we in danger?"

Efren didn't respond. Instead, he tapped the suits of the two men stationed with him. They were contract employees of Clean Air, and each thought Efren was the same. Efren pantomimed his intention to go upstairs to have a look around. The other men nodded their understanding and consent. Soon Efren was on the move. Students alarmed at the sight of a man in a yellow chemical suit parted to make room for him to pass. Efren found it cumbersome to walk in the suit, and the guns and knives he carried didn't make it any easier.

Hilary followed the herd, walking with her head bent and eyes fixed on the marble floor. She had barely been paying attention to her French teacher; the break could not have come at a better time. Her thinking was addled, and she worried about her upcoming midterms.

Before joining The Shire, Hilary had been a straight-A student who had no clue where the dean of students' office was even located. Now she was a felon, several times over. *Stupid! Stupid! Stupid!* Hilary couldn't believe how quickly her life had come undone. She was the third and youngest daughter of Sam and Renee Eichel, of Westport, Connecticut. Nothing in her background even hinted at a future life of crime. No abuse. No neglect. Hilary's parents were pillars of the community, and both loving and devoted to their daughters.

By any measure, Hilary had enjoyed an enviable childhood. She got along well with her two sisters and partook in lavish family vacations, including trips out west to ski and April vacations spent under the Caribbean sun. Her mother was a big corporate attorney and her father ran a hedge fund, so she had grown up knowing nothing of financial hardship.

All that changed in middle school. In some ways, Hilary had Mrs. Lewis, her seventh-grade social studies teacher, to blame for her recent criminal behavior.

Each year, Mrs. Lewis taught a segment on poverty. For her class project, Hilary pretended to be an unemployed single parent. She was given a fictional mini-mum-wage job and each day scrounged the Internet looking for an apartment she could afford, a car, day care for her fictional kids, and, of course, a better-paying job. Hilary had found it impossible to get by on such meager earnings. During the project, she learned about various federal-assistance programs; but even with those, her imaginary kids went hungry most of the time. In a few months, Hilary had come to know a good deal about affordable housing, welfare reform, and, most devas-tating of all, poverty's heart-wrenching effect on chil-dren.

While her sisters seemed bent on following Mom and Dad's footsteps into the world of law and finance, Hilary had visions of using her passion for technology to cure global poverty. She had been ignoring her class assignment, looking on the Web at internship opportu-nities with socially conscious companies, nonprofits mostly, when Andy Dent sent her a Facebook message that ultimately changed her life.

The first line of Andy's message had been intrigu-ing: Your Test. Somehow he'd known that would be an irresistible lure. Hilary read the rest of the message without knowing much about the sender. Andy was in her computer science class, but they hadn't spoken often. They were friends on Facebook, but didn't hang in the same circles in real life.

You have been kidnapped by an alien, the message continued. Hilary read on.

To be released, you must send an e-mail to Help@AlienPrisoner.com from Mr. Rubin's e-mail account. You have fifteen minutes to accomplish

your mission. Go! Glory awaits those who escape from this grave peril.

Hilary tried to get Andy's attention, but he refused
to look her way. He was sending a message: *Either do
it, or don't.* He had nothing more to say on the matter.

The computer lab was crowded as usual and most
everyone had headphones on, gazes fixed to the monitors in front of them. Hilary smiled and thought only of
winning. She wanted to prove herself. Impressing
Andy meant nothing to her, but perhaps he knew she
wasn't the type to back down from a direct challenge.
All that mattered now was that she accomplished the
task.

Ten minutes later, Hilary sent Mr. Rubin an e-mail
that contained an embedded link. She approached his
desk and asked him to check her code. Mr. Rubin
clicked the link in Hilary's e-mail and frowned when
the requested webpage came up blank.

"You've got to do better than that, Hilary," he had
said.

Hilary did not agree. She had done perfectly well,
but for a different assignment. Returning to her desk,
Hilary opened a Web browser and from there launched
the remote access tool she had just secretly installed on
Mr. Rubin's computer via the link he had clicked. The
tool gave Hilary control of Mr. Rubin's desktop from
her workstation without her teacher's knowledge. It
was a matter of Hilary making a few clicks of her own
before Andy started to laugh.

When he turned and smiled at her, Hilary felt a rush
like never before. She had gone bungee jumping, para-
sailed, and skied double-black-diamond runs, but this

was an entirely different sort of thrill. It was utterly intoxicating. She didn't give boys much attention or thought, but suddenly Andy was quite attractive to her. Later, she would fall in love with him. But that moment was the start of Hilary seeing Andy in a different light.

They talked after class. As it turned out, they had English together, and that was how he'd learned of Hilary's passion to fight global poverty. She'd shared an essay with the class that had stuck with him. Andy made her an offer, a secret club he wanted her to join. Hilary was intrigued.

After they pulled off their first theft—$1,000 from a kid's dad who ran a shipping company—Hilary was hooked. It was like Mr. Rubin's e-mail trick, but on steroids. This was a street drug of a different variety. She justified her actions by convincing herself she was making a real difference in the world, but the thrill of the hack was never too far behind. Besides, her victims were wealthy.

They didn't notice what was missing. It was all harmless fun, until they took those bitcoins. Now Andy believed someone would notice, and Hilary did not disagree.

As the students marched along, Hilary thought about Andy and his never-ending fascination with Beth MacDonald. Why didn't he notice her the way he did Beth? She was pretty in her own way. Maybe she and Andy were destined to be the dreaded "friends," Hilary thought glumly. But perhaps there was another way to Andy's heart.

If those missing bitcoins were suddenly found, and if *she* were the one to find them, maybe then Andy would notice her. These were Hilary's thoughts as she headed toward the rear stairwell of Richmond Hall. Ahead, Hilary heard several loud gasps. Over the din, she heard someone shout, "Chemical spill!"

It was then Hilary saw a man in a bright yellow chemical suit emerge from the stairwell to help direct traffic. There was a crush of bodies as students rushed to be first down the stairs. What had been an ambling march turned into more of a sprint. Whoever was co-cooned inside the yellow suit helped the students maintain some order.

Hilary fell into step behind a group of girls she didn't know. The man in the yellow suit followed close behind her. More kids were coming down the hallway, and Hilary wondered why this suited man didn't stay up on the landing to help direct them.

Pixie was alone in his dorm room, dressed in his work uniform—Ray-Bans and a plaid cowboy shirt. He sat at his cluttered desk with his headphones on, hunched over a computer keyboard like a maestro caught up in a burst of inspiration. Within arm's reach was a two-liter bottle of Mountain Dew, which he kept uncapped. He also had a big bag of M&Ms, in case the Mountain Dew didn't charge him up enough.

Pixie was working in SketchUp, his preferred 3D-modeling software. His template was a simple rectangle of the exact length and width of the iPhone. He had extruded the depth and then added fillets around the four edges of the rectangular prism and around the top and bottom faces. From this basic template, he could print just about any design.

His noise-canceling headphones blocked out all sound except for the electronic music from Cash Cash's latest release. He was in the zone, and might not have heard the fire alarm even if the music hadn't been blaring. His roommate, a heavyset boy named Garth, from a suburb in Chicago, was in class and not around to alert Pixie to the alarm. Pixie should have been in class as well. But he ran a business and needed to fill orders for his custom iPhone cases. He'd decided to skip biology to work.

3D printing had come a long way since Pixie first learned of the technology. Because of fire concerns and energy consumption—it used fifty to one hundred times more electricity than injection molding—Pixie was not allowed to have a 3D printer in his dorm room. But Pixie was never much for rules. The PLA filament used to heat the plastic emitted a burning smell, like cooking on a gas stove. He used fans and an open window to help mask the odor.

Pixie had a couple more design tweaks to make on the iPhone case for a Japanese student who loved death metal and wanted angry symbolism printed into the plastic. Pixie didn't care for that sort of music, but the design was intricate, hard to pull off. It was a challenge.

When Pixie wasn't hacking into bank accounts or printing iPhone cases, he was writing apps for smartphones. Taped to the concrete wall in front of his desk were pictures of Pixie's heroes: Steve Jobs, Steve Wozniak, Mark Zuckerberg, Larry Page, Sergey Brin, and a few other Internet entrepreneur titans. At times, Pixie would gaze at the wall and call to these men for inspiration and guidance as if they were his gods.

Maybe someday a kid will put my *picture up on a wall.*
Whenever Pixie let his mind wander into fantasy, he'd
imagine what his father would think of him after he became a millionaire—or even a billionaire.

"How do you like me now?" he'd say one day.

But that day hadn't yet come. So Pixie was alone in
his dorm room, skipping class again, working toward his
future. Since he couldn't hear the alarm, it was under-
standable that he didn't answer the persistent knocking
on his door.

The door opened anyway.

The entrance to the secret stairwell was at the end of
a long tunnel and up a flight of well-worn metal stairs.
At the top of those stairs was a thick metal door that
opened into a locked maintenance closet. Many of the
tunnel entrances were concealed in the back of maintenance closets. Inside that particular closet was a mess
of mops, buckets, and cleaning supplies. Jake came up
those metal stairs, navigated an obstacle course of
paraphernalia in the dark, opened the locked closet
door from the inside, and then emerged, feeling a bit
like Superman stepping from a phone booth in his
Clark Kent disguise.

He entered into chaos. Students were scrambling down
the hallways, being ushered outside by men dressed in
yellow chemical suits. Panic had overtaken civility, and a
mash of bodies was trying to squeeze through the double
doors of the Society Building. The marble floor and
walls intensified the sound, and the noise of the students
and faculty reverberated as indiscriminate chatter.

What the hell is happening?

Jake saw a police officer wearing a gas mask and directing traffic. He approached and asked, "What's going on?"

The officer took off his mask, but looked nervous in doing it. "Big chemical spill near the access road to the school," he said. "As a precaution, we're evacuating everyone to the regional high school. We have buses out front to get folks out of here, and we're asking everyone to leave their vehicles in the lot so we can expedite the evacuation."

So that was it, then. Chemical spill. Evacuation. Instead of ordering Jake to the exit, the officer put his gas mask back on and resumed his directing duties. It was a Get Out of Dodge scenario, but for a different reason. Andy was fine. He was probably on one of the buses already.

Jake merged into the flow of bodies, but halfway down the hall he skirted off to one side. He seldom worried about folks venturing into the labyrinth, but a chemical spill might necessitate an exhaustive search of the property. Someone could have architectural plans and mandate every square inch be checked for contamination. If so, his sophisticated biometric door lock would certainly attract some attention. Jake could replace the mechanism with a rusty old lock, but it would take a bit of time. Good thing he had all the tools to do the job in the storage room adjacent to the larder.

It might be an unnecessary precaution, but Jake wasn't a man who left much to chance.

David, Rafa, and Solomon had been together in chemistry class when the alarm went off. They filed out of the classroom along with the others, thinking nothing of it. Another drill, or perhaps some kid who wanted to get out of a test had pulled a fire alarm on his way to the bathroom. Those things happened. At the far end of the hallway, Rafa spotted a man wearing a yellow chemical suit and pointed him out to his friends.

"What the heck?" David said as he brushed a thick band of hair off his face. David was always brushing hair from his face. Solomon and Rafa never tired of imitating him, but they were too preoccupied with the man in protective gear to have noticed.

"Figures we're at the back of the pack when something really shitty happens." Solomon's comment referred to the location of their classroom, which was at the end of a long hallway of classrooms. They would be the last to reach safety.

Meanwhile, the man in the yellow suit moved against the flow of traffic, perhaps headed to one of those classrooms.

"This is the chemistry wing," Rafa said, loud enough to be heard above the piercing alarm. "Maybe a freshman tried some advanced mixology and screwed up royally."

The man continued to force his way through the crowd. As he moved, he scanned in all directions. Only occasionally did he motion for students and faculty to hurry to the exit. Rafa and David picked up the pace, but Solomon lagged behind. They slowed to wait for their friend.

"We're not going anywhere fast," Solomon shouted while he huffed for breath. He pointed to the traffic jam at the stairwell. "Why rush it?"

Rafa looked disapprovingly at Solomon. "You may

be the most out-of-shape human being I know," he said, only half joking.

Solomon poked Rafa's sternum hard. "You have insulted my honor, and I challenge thee to a bowl-off."

David surveyed the pedestrian backup and frowned. "Hey, if this is a real problem, we could be in big trouble waiting to get out. We might be inhaling deadly fumes right now."

Rafa sniffed the air. "Doesn't smell bad," he said.

"You just came from chemistry, dinkus," Solomon snapped. "Does everything deadly have a smell?"

"I know from your farts it doesn't always have a sound."

"Har, har, har," Solomon said.

David turned to survey the empty hallway behind him. His eyes narrowed as an idea set in. "Guys, let's go out the fire escape," he said. "It'll be faster and way more fun."

Several corridors branched off the main hallway, and at the end of one of them was window access to a fire escape. Rafa and Solomon nodded their agreement. Better than twiddling thumbs while waiting to get down those stairs.

Rafa pointed to the man in the yellow suit, who continued to march their way. "We better go now before 'Banana Man' sees us and makes us wait with the others."

The three turned and began a fast walk to where the corridor branched. Halfway there, Rafa turned and noticed the man in the yellow suit had quickened his strides. He seemed to be shoving kids aside to get where he needed to go. But where could that be? There was nothing down this hallway except for empty classrooms and . . . well, the three of them.

Rafa tugged on David's arm and pulled him to a stop. The suited man no longer showed any concern for people's safety. He did not point to any exit or corral folks into a more orderly line. No, this individual was dead set on getting to something—or someone— in front of him. Even in the glare of overhead lights, it was easy to see the man's dark eyes were fixed on the three boys.

The boys retreated a few steps, but they never turned their backs to the approaching man. Dressed in bright yellow, he looked something like a lion on the hunt, salivating over targets that had separated from the herd. He moved. They backed up. He advanced some more. They backed up some more.

"Maybe we should just wait with the others," Rafa suggested. His voice quavered, because his gut told him something was very wrong.

"Fuck that," Solomon said. "I'm getting out of here."

David turned and broke into a trot as Rafa sprinted ahead of him. Solomon's all-out run was more like the others' jog, and he immediately fell into third place. A few strides into his all-out dash, Rafa risked a quick glance behind him. The man in the yellow suit pushed harder through the crowd. He was definitely coming for them.

"Faster!" Rafa could barely hear himself over the piercing alarm.

David heard him, though. He found a new gear, falling into step right behind Rafa. Solomon picked up speed as well, but his friends had already disappeared down the hallway up ahead. By the time Solomon reached the corridor, Rafa and David were already at work on the shuttered window. It appeared to be stuck, and they struggled to pry it open.

Solomon went from a run to an amble. He wanted to rest his hands on his knees to catch his breath, but a long, thin shadow materialized on the floor in front of him. He looked back and saw the man in the yellow suit, blocking the only way to the main corridor—his only way out, unless David and Rafa could get that window open. The man's dark eyes appeared as venomous as a cobra's bite. He raised his arm, and Solomon cowered in response to the gun in his hand. A suppressor stuck out from the pistol's barrel like a long, black finger.

Instinct took over. Solomon dove to the floor—duck and cover—and shouted to Rafa and David to look out, but the boys were too preoccupied or didn't hear. The window, for whatever reason, wasn't going to budge without some tools. But Rafa and David worked aggressively to force it open.

The screech of the alarm masked the pop of gunfire. A bright flash erupted from the barrel of the gun. Almost simultaneously the wood near Rafa's hands splintered and sprayed his face. Rafa fell back and landed on his bottom. David dropped to the floor and covered his head with his hands.

A sound rose above the alarm, a high-pitched squeal. The man in the yellow suit dragged a screaming Solomon down the corridor by the boy's shirt. Solomon kicked and struggled to get free, but the man's gloved hand was locked on tight. He kept his gun aimed at

Rafa and David, and used the weapon as a pointer to direct them into the classroom adjacent to the window.

Frozen with fear, neither boy could move. In response, the man shot again. This time, the bullet slammed into the concrete just below the window, blasting fragments of chipped debris like shrapnel. Rafa and David covered their heads and scurried into the classroom, where they'd been directed.

The man in the yellow suit materialized in the open doorway. He tossed Solomon into the classroom like a bag of laundry. Solomon landed face-first on the grimy linoleum floor and he cried out in pain. The three boys cowered together, arms around each other, while the man in the yellow suit removed his head covering. He smiled at the boys. They shrank at the sight of his gold-metal mouth.

"Hello, kids," the man said in a thick accent. "You have taken something of mine, and I am here to get it back."

Chapter 19

It was bedlam at Winston Regional High School. By the time Jake had changed the lock and driven into town, students from Pepperell Academy had already taken up residence in the newly renovated school and turned it into squalor. Body heat made the gymnasium humid as a jungle and there was little space to move about. The noise level rattled Jake's ears. Students spilled out into hallways and stairwells. Those who weren't bantering held out smartphones to document the mayhem on social media.

The high school was a good distance from the quarantine zone, so parents of students who lived close by showed up in droves with boxes of food, blankets, and other items they thought would be helpful to those students who called Pepperell Academy home. Several local restaurants pitched in to shuttle over food to the students, who had taken to calling themselves refugees. Nobody knew how long the school would be inaccessible.

Jake lost track of the time pitching in to help.

"This place is like the Superdome after Katrina,"

Jake heard a teacher say. It was hardly an exaggeration. Bodies were everywhere, and trash accumulated like breeding rabbits. The local high-school kids who resided in designated safe areas had all been dismissed because the school's facilities could not accommodate such a large influx of people.

If things weren't repellant enough, the outside temperature had dropped precipitously in just the last hour and a cool misty rain had begun to fall. Nobody wanted to go outside, and no one wanted to be inside, either.

Jake walked the perimeter of the gymnasium and again hunted for Andy, but he was tough to spot among the masses of bodies. Jake had called Andy's cell phone twice, but each time it went right to voice mail. Poor kid probably ran out of juice and didn't carry a charger in his backpack. Jake hoped he had all his medications with him.

Jake made a second pass around the gym before he bumped into Lance. His brother looked like the embattled sheriff of Amity Island right after a shark attack forced him to close the beaches.

"Hey, Jake," Lance said. "Well, this is unexpected."

"You just never know what's going to happen."

Lance returned a knowing glance. "Is the school secure?"

"We have procedures in place for everything," Jake answered with a wry grin.

Lance knew most doors to the school were intentionally left open in the event emergency responders needed access.

"Have you seen Andy?" Jake asked.

Lance surveyed the chaos. "He's probably here somewhere, but I haven't seen him."

"What time you got?" Jake asked.

Lance showed Jake his wristwatch so he could check the time for himself.

Their father was a big wristwatch aficionado and Jake noticed the brand and his eyes went wide.

"Wow, bro, Patek Philippe?"

Lance shrugged it off.

"Gift from a grateful parent. This job doesn't pay that well, but sometimes you get nice perks."

"If you see Andy, tell him to call me," Jake said.

Lance excused himself to go deal with the crisis of the moment. Jake was going outside for some fresh air when he felt a tap on his shoulder.

He turned to see Laura. She had her hair pulled back into a ponytail, no makeup on, but damn she still looked beautiful. She had on a green sweater, with a white shirt underneath, and jeans; she looked pretty much like any of the harried moms who had come to look after the kids.

"Laura," Jake said, sounding enthused to see her. "Enjoying everything Winston has to offer?"

Laura didn't smile at Jake's sarcasm.

"If by 'everything,' you mean chemical spills and speeding tickets, yeah, it's been great so far."

Jake said, "Who gave you a ticket?"

"Some woman cop," Laura grumbled.

Jake knew right away who it was and he fought to suppress a smile.

"Have you seen Andy?" Laura asked. The alarm in her voice was audible.

"No," Jake said, "but I'm sure he's here some-where."

Laura checked her phone.

"It's past two o'clock. I was supposed to meet him downtown an hour ago."

Jake almost laughed. He directed Laura's attention to the chaos around them. "I think there's plenty going on here to distract him. And, besides, I don't think he's supposed to be wandering around downtown right now. He's here somewhere with his friends."

Laura observed the pandemonium, but did not look convinced.

"Downtown isn't quarantined," Laura said. "I was just there. People are out—shopping, eating, all that. Even if he couldn't meet me, at least he would have called."

"I didn't even know you two were meeting." It stung a bit that Andy hadn't shared with him, but Jake tried not to let it show.

Laura looked away and said, "We've been communicating on Facebook."

"As the real you?"

Laura flashed an angry look. "Yes, as the real me," she snapped. "You might not believe it, Jake, but I'm trying here. I'm really trying."

"Easy. I believe you."

Quick as Laura's temper flared, it fell away and her face showed her anxiety. Jake marveled at how seamlessly both of them had slipped into familiar roles: the worried mom and the lackadaisical dad. It had been like this when Andy was an infant and a toddler. "You worry too much," Jake would often say. But Laura would still check to see if Andy was breathing, years after the danger of SIDS had passed. Andy was more than capable of taking care of himself, which was why Jake limited his worrying to things like an EMP and global pandemics.

"I'm really worried something has happened to him," Laura said.

"Laura, I think you're overreacting here."

"There's been a massive chemical spill. What if he got sick from the fumes or something? Maybe he passed out."

"The spill was pretty far from campus," Jake said. "They evacuated the school only as a precaution."

"What about Andy's friends? Do you see any of them around?"

Jake gave the gym another quick scan. No, he didn't see any of them, but there were a lot of bodies here.

"Maybe they all went out together. You know how kids can be. Maybe they snuck out to go goof around or something. It's not hard to slip away, with all this chaos."

This did not sit well with Laura. She pursed her lips together. Her head shook slightly. "This isn't right. Something is wrong. I know something is wrong."

"Why do you say that?"

"A feeling I have. If he couldn't come to meet me, he would have called. You didn't read his messages. This was really important to him, Jake. He wouldn't just blow me off like that."

For the first time, Jake felt annoyed with Laura. Who was she to act so parental? It felt like a dismissal of all Jake's hard work. He alone had raised Andy while she went gallivanting about the country in search of—who knew what? She hadn't earned the right to assert herself in this way.

"Laura, I'm glad you and Andy are talking. You're taking steps, and that's good. I want you to have a relationship with your son. It's important for him. But this isn't your responsibility. It's mine. I've been looking out for Andy on my own for a lot of years now, and I think I have a good handle on when to worry and when not to worry. The fact that I'm not seeing any of his friends suggests to me they're all together somewhere. And this isn't a time to be panicked."

Laura bit at her lower lip. The mannerism was so familiar to Jake. "I don't know what to say. I just have a feeling."

Jake's eyes flared. "So you're telling me you have mother's intuition now? You haven't been in our lives for the last twelve years, you show up out of the blue, and suddenly you've got a *feeling* about my son? Come on, Laura. Let's get real here."

"He's *our* son," Laura said defensively.

"You get my point."

"I don't know. I don't know how to explain it," Laura said. "Maybe the intuition never really went away. Maybe it went dormant or something until I got close again. Now it's here, and I can't deny how I'm feeling. He would have called me. It was important to him. It was important."

"Maybe," Jake said, softening his stance, "but you might be overstating that importance. Look, Laura, you may be Andy's mother, but you're essentially a stranger to him. Maybe he changed his mind. Maybe he's pissed at you. Maybe he's just being a normal teenage boy and not doing what you expected him to do. Or maybe, just maybe, he's leaving you hanging the way you left him."

Jake regretted the words as soon as they came out of his mouth. They were hurtful and unnecessary.

"I'm sorry. I shouldn't have said that."

Laura didn't answer, but nodded, and Jake knew she accepted his apology. What she didn't seem ready to accept, however, were any of the possibilities he had listed.

Chapter 20

The darkness was total. Whoever had blindfolded Andy had done a fine job of it. He couldn't move his arms or his legs except to wiggle them back and forth a little. He still had circulation in his limbs, but those were starting to throb. The fear became something Andy could actually taste: sour, acidic, all-consuming.

Where he was, Andy couldn't say. He was seated on a hard-plastic chair somewhere in the school. Even if he'd had the forethought to count his steps, Andy didn't know which direction they had walked, or the precise distance between the Terry Science Center and any of the surrounding buildings.

The speed at which everything had happened bent Andy's mind. Space and time seemed to fold in on each other. One moment, Andy and Ryan were squared off, ready to go at it, and the next he was tied to a chair.

He called out for help, but a gag in his mouth silenced those cries. The blindfold covered his ears, and Andy could hear his own muted grunts as if they were coming from inside a seashell.

Andy thought back to the moments before his abduction.

When the man wearing protective chemical gear appeared in the abandoned second-floor hallway, Andy figured the fight with Ryan was over. He lowered his arms. Ryan, with his back to the stairs, kept a fighting stance. The man tapped Ryan several times on the back and pointed to the stairs. Maybe he couldn't be heard through the protective hood covering.

Get out, his gestures conveyed. *Get out now.*

Ryan hesitated, but the man pointed at the stairs with added urgency. Ryan held his ground. He wanted to be left alone to finish what he had started. The man stepped into the hallway, spun Ryan around, and shoved him hard from behind. Ryan stumbled toward the stairs. The man took a few threatening steps toward Ryan, who turned—no hesitation now—and bolted down the stairs as though the hallway were on fire.

What got Ryan so spooked? Andy wondered.

Andy went to join Ryan, but the man in the suit reached out and seized him by the shoulder as he passed. He held Andy in place, watching the stairs. Waiting. What was he looking for? No one was there. They were alone in the hallway. Andy tried to pull away, but the man held on.

Without provocation, the man unleashed several quick jabs into Andy's gut. Andy's mouth opened wide. His face writhed in pain, but the screeching alarm swallowed every bit of his scream.

The attacker shoved Andy down the hall in the opposite direction of the stairwell. Andy regained his balance and whirled around, thinking only of escape. He juked left and went right, but the man wasn't fooled.

Inside a breath, he clinched Andy in a crushing embrace. Instinctively, Andy pushed his hips back to try and create some space from his attacker. The key, he knew, was not to panic, but Andy was caught by surprise and reeling from those punches to his gut. He executed the move properly, giving a little bend at the legs before he unleashed a powerful strike to the face. The blow struck hard against the man's face shield and caused no damage. Panic had got to Andy after all. He had done exactly as his dad taught him, but failed to account for all of the variables. A fight with Ryan Coventry was one thing, but a real life and death struggle proved to be something else entirely. A second later, the man had his hand wrapped around Andy's throat.

The pressure on Andy's windpipe was excruciating. He kicked his legs frantically, but had no leverage. The man pushed him back into a wall.

"No te muevas o mueres."

Andy wasn't entirely sure what that meant. He'd studied Latin in school, and while it helped with translation, the gun pressed under Andy's chin made the order terrifyingly clear. The weapon seemed to have materialized out of the ether. With quick, fluid motions, the man wrenched Andy's cell phone from his back pocket and shoved him into a nearby classroom. The man slammed the door shut.

Andy went to the windows. From there he could see students piling into waiting buses. Andy was about to open a window to scream for help when the man returned.

"Aléjate de la ventana," the man said.

The man spoke Spanish. *Who was this man? Where*

had he come from? What did he want? The hood made it hard to hear his attacker's voice, but Andy understood the man's gestures just fine. He moved away from the window.

The attacker removed Andy's backpack; then he wrapped rope around Andy's wrists. How could he say "too tight" in Spanish? Instead, Andy said it in English. No adjustments were made. The man knotted a blindfold over Andy's eyes and slipped a gag into his mouth. Pressure on Andy's shoulders settled him to the floor where he waited perhaps thirty minutes, maybe more. He didn't dare try to escape. He couldn't tell if the man was still in the room or not. He was helpless to do anything but wait. Then he was on the move. Escorted down a flight of stairs.

He felt cool air against his skin and figured they had gone outside. He had never heard the campus so quiet. Even weekends had some commotion, but now it was just birdsong and distant sirens.

Soon he was inside again. He was led down a hallway and into a room, up a short flight of stairs, where a chair was waiting for him.

Andy pounded his feet against the floor. It made a hollow sound. He thought the floor was made of wood. Hard to tell. He concentrated. He had nothing to focus on but his fear. The tightness in his chest could snap his ribs. His heart rattled about as if it had broken free.

Andy hollered and again made only unintelligible grunts. The gag made breathing difficult, and his lungs felt like they couldn't get enough air. Andy inhaled a bit more oxygen through his nose, but the ache in his chest remained. He fought against his restraints, but managed only to chafe the skin. So Andy settled into his seat and he waited. If they wanted him dead, he would already be dead, Andy told himself. Something would happen.

It did.

Laura didn't know these woods at all, but she wasn't concerned about getting lost. The kid she spoke with at the regional high school told her about the path. According to him, it was a couple miles long, easy to follow. It had been easy to find, just as he promised. She was told the cross-country team used the path to train, and it was the fastest way from The Pep into town for anybody riding a bike.

The entrance to the path was nothing but a weed-strangled pullout on the side of a single-lane road several miles from where the chemical truck had crashed and spilled. Laura had seen where police had blocked off the access roads to the school and surrounding area, but a path through the woods was not worth guarding.

After she parked, Laura locked the car doors and set off on foot. The flat ground made it possible to walk quickly, but she was badly out of shape and could not keep a pace. Almost immediately Laura's lungs began to ache. She regretted every stupid cigarette she'd ever smoked. She also regretted every major life decision she had made. She had left her home, her husband, and her son in search of a better life, only to find broken promises, lies, and missteps all along the way.

There were men, slick charmers or even worse, abusive men. There were hangovers, no shortage of those. And plenty of highs—coke, pot, Ecstasy, magic mushrooms. For Laura, avoiding heroin and meth had felt like a commendable display of willpower. When she got clean, she got clear and she could finally taste the ruin of her life. Her friends were people of convenience who went to the same parties, hung out at the same bars, and screwed the same guys. Take away the drugs and booze, and everybody in her life had the staying power of a lit cigarette.

She'd come east looking for Andy and Jake, ready to embrace them in whatever shape that took. She had no grand vision of a happy family reunion. In this way, Laura was not naïve. Maybe in time she could establish a meaningful relationship with Andy. It would start there, with her son. And there was no denying her feelings for Jake. Even so, it made her sad to be with him, causing her to focus on all the "what-ifs" of her life. It was a dangerous game to play. *What if I didn't leave? What if I weren't so angry with Jake?*

That was what had pushed her away. He had been selfish. He drank away their future. Her answer was to make a clean break from it all. Start over. And so she left on a multiyear walkabout, and was now on an unfamiliar path based solely on a hunch that her son was still at the school.

I'm looking forward to seeing you.

That was what he wrote in his last Facebook message to her, sent yesterday. I'm looking forward to seeing you. Those few words meant so much to Laura. Men had told her they loved her. Friends had confided in her. But their words, which at the time had seemed so personal and intimate, paled in comparison to Andy's simple six-word message. Andy's words brought meaning to her life. Real meaning. She'd turned her back on her son. She vowed never to do it again.

The path narrowed. The clear and crisp morning had given way to afternoon cloud cover, and a misty rain fell and thickened the muddied earth. Her footing slipped as she quickened her strides.

Laura's imagination dictated her pace. In one scenario, Andy was facedown in a hallway. He had inhaled too much of the chemical and was frothing at the mouth. Nobody was there to save him. His heartbeat was fading. But Laura would come to him. To protect against the chemicals in the air, Laura would wear the painter's mask she bought at the hardware store. Perhaps it wouldn't fully safeguard her from the fumes, but she could at least get Andy to safety. Her cell phone worked. She could call for an ambulance.

In another version, Andy was roaming the empty school with his pals like a pack of wolves. It wasn't like he forgot about his meeting with her, more like he had to take advantage of the opportunity. No faculty. No other students. He and his friends would have the run of the place. Andy would be playing Frisbee on a quad, Laura imagined. Laughing with his friends. Laura would be able to hear him from the woods. She would emerge from the forest path, and Andy would see her. She'd be dirty, soaking wet, looking like a lost hiker.

She wouldn't be upset with him. No, this was a demonstration of her commitment to their nascent relationship. She and Andy had made a plan to meet and she was damn well determined to keep it. And Andy would smile at her. At least in her mind, he would. He'd come to her, and they would actually hug. And he'd say, "Laura, what are you doing here?" Of course he'd say, "Laura," not "Mom"—not yet . . . anyway.

And she'd shrug and tell him nothing was more important to her than being with him.

"How'd you figure out where I was?" Andy would ask.

"I thought about what I would do when I was in high school," Laura would say.

And then they would share a laugh.

At least in her mind they would.

The path widened, and Laura entered a wide clearing. The grass was dewy from the rain. In the distance, Laura could see the brick buildings of Pepperell Academy. She could see The Quad, too.

Nobody was outside playing Frisbee.

Chapter 21

Powerful hands gripped Andy's shoulder, but he couldn't tell if the person—a man, it had to be a man—stood in front or behind him. Perhaps not long ago those same hands had been wrapped around his throat. A moment later, someone escorted Andy down a short flight of stairs.

Completely blindfolded, Andy could see nothing. He was led to a cushioned seat, and Andy thought he knew where he was. He couldn't ask because the gag was still in place. Andy heard a door open somewhere to his left. His ragged breathing drowned out most every sound, but he might have heard footsteps, many sets of them. Shuffling feet mixed in with grunts and dulled cries.

Andy slowed his breathing. Now he heard it distinctly. Scraping sounds. Chairs being pushed around perhaps?

"No te muevas. No te muevas," a man's voice said. He repeated that command several times.

Andy focused. With concentration, he could pick

out the sound of footsteps. They seemed to come from the same short set of stairs Andy had just descended.

He felt a sudden and strong tug on the back of his head. Someone loosened his blindfold. The fabric fell away and light flooded Andy's eyes. He blinked to clear his vision. Shapes came into sharp focus. He recognized the Feldman Auditorium, located on the first floor of the Academy Building. The Academy Building was the largest on campus, a gateway to The Quad and surrounding dormitories and classrooms. It was used mostly for history, art, anthropology, and religious studies.

The auditorium, named for one of the school's most prominent benefactors, seated three hundred people and provided a stately environment for performances and assemblies. It was a modern theater with balcony seating. Andy sat in the center of the front row, facing the stage.

Onstage, lit as though they were part of a school production, were his five closest friends: David, Pixie, Hilary, Solomon, and Rafa. Each was seated on a classroom chair. Their wrists were restrained with rope. Their school uniforms were wrinkled, torn in places, dirty in others. They wore blindfolds and had gags made of the same thick cloth that was stuffed in Andy's mouth.

Fear poured out from the five as sweat. Andy called out to them, but that gag—that damn gag.

More horrifying were the men who stood in a line onstage behind his friends. There looked to be a dozen of them, but Andy was too rattled to count. These men were armed to the hilt with shotguns, pistols, assault rifles, and large knives. They flashed their weapons like peacocks showing off feathers.

They came in all shapes and sizes: tall men and thin men, some with long, dark hair and some who kept it short. Some of them had bushy mustaches; others had scruff; a few displayed beards; the minority were clean-shaven. One had red hair and stood next to a man with a prosthetic hand and a claw attachment. They looked relaxed, and why not? Andy was nothing but an unarmed sixteen-year-old boy.

In front of the stage, Andy saw his backpack among some of his friends' belongings. *Thank God!* Andy had to have access to his glucose tablets if his blood sugar dropped. He had some food in his system, so the danger wasn't imminent.

Andy felt a hot breath against the back of his neck.

"I don't speak English perfectly," a man said into Andy's ear. He spoke in a thick Mexican accent. "But I will do my best. Nod if you understand me."

Andy's body heated as if ravaged by fever. The man stepped over the second-row seats to confront Andy directly.

He expected to see a monster, but this was not the case. The man had a handsome face and long hair like David's, which he tied into a thick ponytail. He wore a fancy silk shirt decorated in a paisley pattern, jeans, and polished work boots. It was not the most threatening attire, but he smiled and Andy recoiled. The man's golden mouth horrified him. The intricate designs cut into the metal were reminiscent of crop circles.

"My name is Fausto," the man with the metal mouth said. "You must think of me as a friend. I am here to help you. If you do as I say, you may live. It's simple. Do you understand me?"

Andy nodded.

"Good. I'm going to take away the gag," Fausto said. "If you scream, I will hurt you. Not that anybody will hear you. The school is empty. No people. We know this for certain. The campus will stay this way for some time. The roads are blocked. We hear things on the radio. But my ears are very sensitive to noise, so I don't want to have them hurt. Again, nod if you understand. Damn my English, huh? Should have studied more. You study hard in school? I hope so. Very important."

Andy nodded several times, all in quick succession, and the gag came free. He would have agreed to anything to get that gag out of his mouth. His throat was dry and raw.

As if he could read his mind, Fausto produced a bottle of water. Andy drank thirstily.

"Now here is the deal," Fausto said. "You are going to describe what you see to your five friends onstage. I keep the gags on them, and the blindfolds, too. Now talk."

Andy started to hyperventilate. It was difficult to get out any words.

"*Cálmate,*" Fausto said. "*Tranquilo, hijo.* You're not dead yet."

Not . . . dead . . . yet . . .

Slowly Andy began to piece this together. These men spoke Spanish. They had stolen bitcoins from Javier Martinez, and Andy knew from Gus that the Martinez family had come to the United States from Mexico. He didn't have to solve complex math equations to understand the significance. This was all about the money. Whoever had come for the money had probably orchestrated the evacuation of the school. It was a smoke screen of epic proportions. In the chaos, their targets would be easy prey. Somehow they knew Andy was involved, which is how they knew about the others as well.

Andy tried to settle. He needed to be brave for his friends.

"Guys, it's Andy." His voice came out in a warble. "You're onstage in the Feldman Auditorium. You're all here. You know who you are. It's all of us."

Andy didn't want to say their names out loud. There was a good chance these men already knew everything about them, but it still felt like a significant reveal. Andy would hold on to every piece of information until he was forced to share it.

"Tell them more," the man said.

"There are many men in here with us. Standing behind you. They're all heavily armed."

"Good!" Fausto shouted. His booming voice reverberated up to the balcony level. "You've done well. By now, you must know or suspect why we are here. Can you tell your friends why we are here?"

Andy didn't respond.

"Andy, I speak to you. You tell them."

A shiver cut through Andy. Fausto had said his name.

"You . . . you want the money back?"

Fausto's face brightened. His smile was broad and authentic. The gold-metal mouth caught the reflection of some overhead lights and glinted for a moment like paparazzi flashbulbs.

"You got it! You know! Good! We get someplace quick."

Onstage, Hilary started to sob. At first, just her

shoulders heaved up and down, but it quickly became a whole-body shake. The noises she made sank into the gag, but were loud enough to be heard by the others who joined her onstage.

Contagious as a yawn, everyone began to cry. Bodies convulsed. Andy had never felt so desperate, so afraid.

"Now, Andy, we know you have our money," Fausto said. "So let's make this easy. Okay? Easy. Give it back now. Right now. If you don't, I kill one of your friends. Ready? Seriously, are you ready? Because here we go."

"I—don't have it. I swear."

"Armando, coge el cuchillo más grande que tengas y ven al frente del escenario," Fausto said.

The man with many facial scars produced a twelve-inch carbon-steel hunting knife from a sheath latched to his ankle and came to the front of the stage.

"Efren, anda con él."

Efren came forward and stood beside Armando. He had short hair and a long knife, just like Armando, but he was built like a pro wrestler.

"Tornado, por favor, ven después. Todos los demás retrocedan cinco pasos."

A man with a head of untamed long, frizzy hair, appropriate for any metal band, and these wild, hate-filled eyes came forward with a knife dangling by his side. A dark presence swirled about him like a funnel cloud. The rest of the men took five steps back.

"Each of you go and pick a kid to stand behind," Fausto said. "I don't care which one. You decide."

The English was for Andy's benefit, but the men understood and they did as ordered. Efren stood behind Pixie, Armando took up position behind Solomon, and "El Tornado," called so because of his wild hair and temper, went up behind Rafa.

"Pónganles los cuchillos en la garganta," Fausto said.

Up came the hunting knives, each big enough to bushwhack through a field of sugarcane. One at a time, the men leaned forward and set the razor-sharp blades against the throats of the three who were chosen.

"Now, don't move, kiddies," Fausto called out. "You don't want to cut yourselves."

Armando put Solomon's head into an arm lock just to hold it still.

Fausto pulled a case from underneath an auditorium seat and withdrew a PC laptop. He flipped open the cover and set the computer on the floor in front of Andy. The computer was already booted up.

Fausto said, "Now, here's what happens. I give you five minutes to transfer the money to someplace we can get it. I don't know how to do this, but you do. You took it—you can give it back. So go. Give us the money. After five minutes, if I don't have the money, I will point to one of your friends, and one of my friends will slice open his throat and spill blood all over this stage. Is that clear? Do I make sense?" Fausto seemed genuinely concerned that he might not have been well understood.

"Please, no," Andy said. His voice shook like Solomon's body. "You don't understand."

Fausto fiddled with his watch. "Time has started—now!"

"I can't!" Andy shouted.

Fausto touched his ear. "Careful, young one. Remember my ears are sensitive to sound. I might do something to cause blood, out of frustration."

Andy sank to his knees with the computer in front of him. "You don't understand. We don't have it."

"Ticktock . . . ticktock . . . ticktock," Fausto said, pointing at his watch.

The computer had automatically connected to the school's Wi-Fi network. Andy looked to the stage. The men behind his three friends stood like trained Dobermans ignoring a slab of meat while awaiting their master's order.

"I can't give you the money," Andy pleaded. "We don't have it! I swear. I'll show you. The money is on the bitcoin exchange. It's out there. Somewhere. But we don't have the key to access it. It was taken from *us*! Someone stole it from us, same as we took it from you!"

"That's one minute down. Four to go."

Andy's fingers shook so violently he could barely type, but somehow he managed to access the website blockchain.info. In another browser window, Andy opened his e-mail and with a few clicks found the bitcoin address. It was a long string of letters, a mix of capital and lower case, and numbers.

Andy copied the address from his e-mail and pasted it into the search box on the block chain website. Another webpage loaded. This one had summary information, transaction history, and entry upon entry of meaningless-looking numbers. He turned the laptop so Fausto could see the screen.

"The private key is connected to a bitcoin address," Andy said in a rushed and panicked voice. "Gus's dad didn't safeguard the key, and it was easy for us to steal.

But then somebody took the key from us. We can only see the money, but we can't get it back without the new key that accesses it. Do you understand?"

Fausto seemed to be contemplating what Andy had told him. The silence was interminable.

"So you're telling me we're going to kill you all?"

Tears pricked the corners of Andy's eyes. "No, please . . . please."

"Please what?" Fausto said, sounding frustrated more than angry. "'Please' means nothing to me. We are here for one thing only. So if what you say is true, then you will all die."

Fausto turned to the stage and dramatically extended his arm. *"De tin marín de dos pingüé,"* he said. With each word Fausto uttered, he pointed to one of the three being held at knifepoint. The cadence of his voice reminded Andy of "eeny, meeny, miny, moe," and he guessed this was the Mexican version of the children's rhyme.

"No!" Andy screamed. "Don't!"

Fausto snapped his arm like a whip and cracked Andy's face, using the back of his hand. Knuckles hard as lead shot slammed into the orbital bone of Andy's eye socket. The searing pain dropped Andy to the floor.

"My ears, *idiota*!" Fausto scolded. "I told you to be quiet. Now, where was I? Oh yes, I remember now. *Cúcara, mácara, títere fue.*"

From his perch on the floor, Andy said, "Wait." His voice came out soft as the flapping of a butterfly's wing.

Fausto opted to ignore him. Instead, he spoke as he pointed: *"Yo no fui, fue Teté."*

"One of them might have the key," Andy said, whimpering. He'd all but given up hope, but he got the words out anyway. A chance. Just a chance. "Maybe one of them stole it from the rest of us."

"Pégale . . . pégale," Fausto slowed down his rhythm. Each word came out elongated and he appeared to take notice of what Andy said.

Andy locked eyes with Fausto. He had found a way in. It might only prolong their misery, or worse, but it was a glimmer of hope. "One of them might have the key," Andy repeated, breathing hard. "If you kill whoever has it, you'll never get the money."

Fausto fell silent as he took it in. Andy filled the void by repeating what he had said. "If you kill whoever has the key, you'll never get the money."

Fausto faced the stage as though directing a performance from the audience. *"Al . . ."*

He pointed at Solomon.

"Quien . . ."

He pointed at Rafa.

"Fue."

He pointed to the floor.

Curled into a fetal position, Andy gasped for air. The five on the stage looked to be doing the same.

"This, I'm afraid, complicates things," Fausto said. "Now we must find out which of you has this magical key. Is that right?"

From the floor, Andy nodded.

"Pity," Fausto said. "I think you'll find death would have been preferable."

From just beyond the auditorium door, Andy heard a loud clatter. It rolled and echoed as if a metal trash can had fallen over. Fausto looked as surprised as everyone. He pointed to four men standing onstage closest to the door and shouted, *"Vayan a averiguar quién mierda hizo ruido. Si es alguien, ¡mátenlo! Pero no dejen que los capturen."*

If Andy spoke Spanish, he would have understood the men had been ordered to track down whoever had made that noise and kill him.

Chapter 22

Laura didn't have plans to do a lot of exploring. The campus was completely deserted, and she suspected Andy wasn't even there. Jake was probably right. Andy had gone off with his buddies and had forgotten all about her.

Laura chided herself for thinking Andy would embrace her with open arms. She had been foolish to expect it could have been so easy. She contemplated turning around, but felt even more foolish to abandon her quest after coming so far to find him. She was wet, muddy, and discouraged. But the air around campus didn't smell like poison. It was worth taking a minute to look around.

If anything, Laura was curious about the school. This is where Andy spent most of his time. She felt connected to him just by being here. The possibility of having a relationship with her son was foremost on Laura's mind when she ambled across The Quad and entered the Academy Building through the massive front doors. She thought the building would have been secured, but people had left in a rush, or maybe these doors were never locked.

Either way, the door was open. Laura entered an elegant marble foyer, which featured impressive columns and a magnificent high ceiling. She had dreamed of having the kind of home that people would gawk at, and her fantasy always included a marble foyer. She knew it was grandiose, but what the hell.

Inside the massive foyer, Laura heard noises, odd muted sounds that seemed to be coming from a doorway to her right. The closer she got to that door, the louder the sounds became. The wooden doors were closed; Laura pressed her ear against them and listened. She could hear one man doing most of the talking, and it sounded to her as if he spoke with an accent. Perhaps he was part of a work crew assigned to check the air quality or test for chemical contaminants.

Curiosity got the better of her. Laura pried the door open a crack. All she wanted was to take a quick little peek inside. She peered into a darkened auditorium.

Her thoughts froze as an icy fear settled into her chest. From her vantage point, Laura could see five kids seated on classroom chairs onstage. Their wrists were bound with rope and all were gagged. Onstage loomed three savage-looking men, each holding a massive knife to the throats of three of the kids. Behind them was a second row of men, each more brutal-looking than the next, armed with an array of assault weapons she'd seen only in the movies.

Recoiling from fright, Laura inhaled with a gasp and fell sideways. She stumbled into a trash can pushed up against the wall next to the door. The auditorium door slammed shut with a hard bang as the trash can toppled, making its own thunderous crash. One thought immediately dominated all others: *Run!*

Laura dashed across the foyer and slammed into the front door, using her hip to push against the crash bar. The door swung open and she toppled outside. Momentum carried her across the top landing and in a flash the stairs loomed before her like rocks materializing out of a fog.

The misty rain turned those same stairs dangerously slick, and Laura was going too fast to navigate them safely. She misjudged the first step and her arms flailed wildly as she fought for balance. She tripped down a few more stairs, but somehow managed to stay on her feet.

At the bottom step, Laura lost her footing completely. She teetered and then toppled over. It happened so fast that she couldn't get her hands out in time to brace her fall; she slammed face-first onto a cement patio. The intense impact felt as if it had compressed her brain against the back of her skull. Blood poured from a gash on her forehead and oozed thick goo into her eyes.

Wiping the blood away with the back of her hand, Laura labored to get to her knees, still dazed. She heard a sound. A door opening. They were coming. Men with guns, with knives.

Get up! Run! Run!

Fear choked her breathing.

Laura staggered to her feet and broke into a frantic sprint. She was impervious to the pain in her knees and head. Blood gushed from the wound in her scalp, blinding one eye, but she could still see The Quad in front of her, maybe ten, twenty feet away. It was a massive expanse of brown and green grass. No place could have left her more vulnerable, but her mind wasn't clear. Her only thought was to run ahead, and as fast as possible.

Weaving awkwardly, Laura lurched onto The Quad. Her feet slipped on the dewy grass. Her arms spun for balance, but this time she kept upright. Blood seeped into her mouth. The taste of it on her tongue and down her throat nauseated her, but still she ran.

With wind battering her face, Laura risked a glance over her shoulder. Four men were coming down the stairs. They had no trouble navigating the slick surface. Two of them were leveling rifles. Laura diverted from a straight course into a zigzag pattern, thinking it would make her a harder target to hit. She had seen the tactic used on television, and somehow the reference came to her at the moment she needed it most.

Beyond The Quad, beyond another brick building, stood a thick patch of woods. Somewhere within that thicket was the path she had used to reach the school, but the woods would be fine if she couldn't find the path. Probably better. Laura could lose them in the woods.

From behind, Laura heard a loud crack and boom that rolled off into the distance. The hum of a bullet sliced through the heavy air. There was another crack. Another bullet zipped past. This time Laura saw where the ground erupted from the impact. The tree line was just ahead. Laura tried to lengthen her strides.

Keep running . . . keep running . . .

She heard another boom and felt the air part. The forest was in front of her. Not too far. She could make it. The burn in her legs became intense, and an agonizing stitch developed in her side. From somewhere within, she dug deep and found another gear that actually quickened her pace.

Almost there . . . almost . . .

Another rolling boom came, followed by a *pfft* sound. That was when Laura felt the sting. It didn't hurt at first. It was more like an odd and strange sensation—a breeze traveling through her that shouldn't have been there. But then came the fire. A wickedly sharp pain radiated up from her right side. Laura tumbled to the ground and rolled several times. Blood continued to pour from the gash in her scalp; but now, it was pouring from this new wound as well.

From the ground, she touched her side. Her hands came away slick and red. She staggered to her feet. Adrenaline was all that kept her moving as it also held the shock at bay.

Glancing behind her, Laura saw the men readying to fire again. She darted into the woods just as a bullet splintered a tree by her head.

Laura sank into the dark. She could hear men's voices behind her, coming at her. The trees offered some cover, but the forest still had the bare and brown look of winter. Still running, Laura peeled back the jacket she wore and lifted her sweater to inspect her side. A massive red stain spread across much of her midsection and traveled partway up her armpit. Her light cotton shirt was drenched with blood. Pain more intense with each breath came at her with the force of a hurricane.

Laura plunged on ahead. Was her vision dimming, or had a cloud darkened the sky? Voices cried out.

They were searching for her, but she had vanished inside the gloom and was still on the move. With each stride, Laura felt weaker.

Five minutes on the move became ten. Ignoring the painful burn, Laura kept one hand on the cut to her head, and the other pressed against her side, but her life force seeped between her fingers.

She was wobbly on her feet, moving in whatever direction she managed to stagger. The men's voices receded into the distance like the fading forest light. Soon Laura's frantic, haphazard run downshifted into a trot, and then it became something of a drunken stumble, until she slowed almost completely and ping-ponged from one tree to the next without direction or purpose.

The men's voices were gone, gone like the feeling in her leg and the pain in her side. Oh, the bliss—it was such pure bliss to have no more pain in her side. It had been like a hot poker squeezed through a tight hole in her skin. Now everything was cast in a delirious haze. The world had a glow, and Laura felt connected to the trees and muddy earth as never before. Droplets of water clinging to the tree branches and moss shone like spinning diamonds. Was she even moving? No, she was floating. She sensed her body moving as if the wind itself carried her.

Off in the distance, Laura saw twinkling lights. She went toward them. Walking, or flying, or pulled by some invisible force, she couldn't tell. *Just follow the shine. It's right there. Just reach for it.* The twinkle came in alternating colors. Red. Blue. Red. Blue. It flashed and whirled and summoned her with its own gravitational force.

Laura emerged from a shroud of trees and reached

for the lights, but she couldn't take hold. She sank to her knees and felt hands descend upon her. Many hands. Touched by angels. The touch made her spirit rise, and she lifted her arms up to the heavens to beckon for more. The colors that drew her here danced before her eyes. *Red. Blue. Red. Blue.*

Laura fell to the wet earth, and she understood there were no angels by her side. These were police officers. They knelt and talked to her in loud voices. Laura opened her mouth, but did the word come out?

Can you hear me? Did I say it?

Their lips moved, but Laura couldn't make out what was said. Her ears were filled with a deafening roar like powerful ocean waves crashing against massive rocks. She felt the life leaving her body. Peace coming to her. Finally she had found it. What she had been searching for since she had left Jake and Andy. But one thing had to be said. That word. Had she spoken it?

Laura tried once more. Her blood-splattered lips were so dry. She was so thirsty. If she closed her eyes, the thirst would go away. And the cold, too. But a memory came back and Laura marshaled one final effort. She put the word in her throat and spat it out through red-stained teeth.

"Hostages."

Then, finally, she was at peace.

Chapter 23

Jake hadn't found Andy and it tugged at him. Bothered him a lot, but he kept fear out of his voice as he asked around for his son. Nobody had seen him. He kept his eyes out for Andy's friends, but they weren't around, either. The kids were together, like he told Laura: goofing off, doing what kids do. He wasn't going to panic. Not yet, anyway.

Andy would turn up soon.

In the meantime, Jake busied himself with the post-evacuation chaos, doing his part to pitch in and help. He fetched enough bottles of water to fill a swimming pool and was instrumental in organizing food distribution.

As Jake spoke informally with a representative from the Red Cross about contingency plans for longer-term shelter, Lance Dent ran by. Lance was clearly alarmed and frightened. Something horrible must have happened. Jake thought of Andy. He excused himself and went chasing after Lance, apologizing as he pushed through the crowd. He caught up to Lance at the gymnasium exit and seized his shoulder from behind.

"What's going on, brother?" Jake asked.

It looked to Jake as though leeches had drained the blood from Lance's pale face.

"There's been a murder on Route 111, near the school," Lance said.

"Holy hell. A murder?"

The murder rate in Winston hovered just north of zilch. Jake couldn't think of one such crime in the recent past.

"It's worse." Lance leaned in close and whispered, "Somebody may have taken hostages at The Pep. Maybe kids."

Jake's eyes went wide as a surge of adrenaline coursed through his body. Several thoughts came to him in staccato bursts.

You're never safe. The bad things can happen at any time, anywhere, even little towns like Winston. It's good to be prepared. Andy.

Jake blocked out all other thoughts the way he could on the pitcher's mound. The task was to get more information from Lance. He had his reason. His son still hadn't been seen.

"What do you know?"

"If people find out, we'll have a mass panic on our hands."

"They're going to find out." Jake reached for his phone even though he had tried Andy fifteen minutes ago.

"Are you calling Andy?"

"Have you seen him?"

Lance shook his head.

"What about his friends? You know them. Hilary. A kid named Troy, goes by Pixie. David Townsend. Have you seen them around?"

Again it was a no from Lance.

Jake had been so determined to be the parent here, the guy who understood how kids behaved because he actually raised one, that he had dismissed Laura's concern. Maybe his pride had gotten in the way and had blinded him to an actual crisis.

Lance headed for the exit.

"Where are you going?" Jake asked.

"I'm going to meet with the police chief and lieutenant. What about you?"

"I'm going home," Jake said.

Jake was scrounging through Andy's bedroom, looking for the phone numbers of his friends. Just maybe, he had something written down. It was old school, of course. He also figured Andy's contacts were synced between his smartphone and tablet, but Jake couldn't find the device in his room. He called Laura to see if she'd found Andy, but his call went right to voice mail, the way it did when a phone was shut off.

While searching Andy's room, Jake listened to the police scanner. It would not be long before the news traveled throughout the community. In a town like Winston, with everyone connected to Facebook, word of a murder and a hostage situation at the elite prep school would spread faster than a cold in a day care.

Andy's pals boarded at the school, so Jake saw no reason to try and track their parents down. Soon enough, those parents would be calling, trying to reach somebody in charge if they couldn't reach their kids.

Jake checked under the bed. To his delight, he saw the flat rectangular shape of Andy's iPad hidden within a crumpled pile of dirty laundry. As a house rule, Andy had to give Jake the pass code for all his electronic devices. Jake never checked the devices for inappropriate content, but the threat alone was enough of a deterrent. He entered 0121, which was Laura's birth month and day, and all of Andy's downloaded apps soon appeared on-screen.

Quickly Jake checked the contacts and found three names he recognized: Hilary, Troy, and Solomon. He called all three numbers. No response. He sent each a text message, waited five minutes, and then sent another. No answer.

The bottom line was that Jake didn't know where his son was, and he couldn't reach any of Andy's friends. Laura's worries no longer seemed overblown.

Jake ran into a massive police barricade miles from the school. He parked his car on the side of the road and joined a growing crowd that also had come as far as the police would allow. There were several fire trucks, ambulances, police cars, and men in chemical suits, as well as others in official-looking uniforms, swarming the area. A sea of flashing lights and strobes turned the landscape into an undulating dance floor.

A misty rain peppered Jake's cotton T-shirt. He scanned the faces of the police and fire teams, searching for Ellie or somebody familiar. He kept calm. No reason to do otherwise. A good pitcher was well disciplined. Running around creating a spectacle wasn't going to help anybody or anything. Finding someone to give him some information would.

Jake saw a cluster of cops, some of whom he recognized by face but not name. He wanted to get one of them alone. Jake was about to approach when he felt a hand on his shoulder. He turned and met Ellie's sympathetic gaze. Something about the way she looked at him made Jake uneasy.

"Come with me," Ellie said.

Taking Jake by the arm, Ellie escorted them to a more private location. Jake reached for Ellie's hand, but she pulled away. Dressed in her blues, Ellie was on the clock and it was not permissible to be affectionate with a civilian. But Jake sensed Ellie's distress. She wanted to embrace him, to comfort him. But why? One thought flashed through his mind.

Andy!

"What's going on here, Ellie? Talk to me."

Ellie got close to Jake so she could speak without being overheard. "Something has gone down at Pepperell Academy," Ellie said.

Jake's insides went cold. The scene behind Ellie—a sea of bodies, lights, and trucks—blended together into a singular blur of motion.

"What is it? Is Andy all right?"

"Have you heard from him?" Ellie asked.

Jake picked up on the vibration in Ellie's voice— genuine concern.

"No. And I haven't been able to get in touch with Andy's friends, either."

Ellie grimaced as if the information physically hurt to hear. Jake seized Ellie's shoulders. At that moment, she wasn't his girlfriend or the police. She had the answers. She was holding back on him, and Jake needed to know everything.

"Listen, Jake," Ellie said. She didn't pull away, even though a civilian had no business touching a cop. "A woman has been killed. Shot." Ellie broke from Jake's gaze and looked around to make sure nobody was listening. This information could not be shared freely. "She said one word before she died. 'Hostages.' That was it. She came from the direction of the school. We have SWAT teams being mobilized right now. The state police is already on the scene, and the FBI may be called in."

Jake's heart sank. He closed his eyes and felt Ellie's hands on his arms to comfort him. Laura had been right all along.

"Is Andy one of them?"

"We don't know anything at this time. Trust me, Jake, if I knew something, I would tell you."

Jake's head spun with horrible thoughts of the physical and mental abuse his son might be enduring at the hands of his possible captors. But he also had it in his head that a hostage situation meant a protracted negotiation. Time was adversary of a different sort. "If Andy's blood sugar gets too low, he could die," Jake said.

"Right now, we don't know if he's a hostage or not. We don't even have confirmation that the woman was right."

"Who was it?" Jake asked. "The woman who was killed. Do I know her?" Winston was a small town, and there was a good chance he knew the victim at least by name.

Ellie bowed her head and spoke in a low, somber tone. "Jake, I don't know how to tell you this, but I think the victim is your ex-wife, Laura."

Jake's jaw dropped. He set his hands on his knees to catch his breath.

"Describe her," Jake said.

"I pulled her over this morning and gave her a speeding ticket," Ellie said. "If you talked to her, she probably told you about it."

Jake turned his back to Ellie, his hands clenched into fists, and for a moment he focused only on the feeling of the misty rain as it bathed his face. It made even more sense now. Laura had gone looking for Andy; and when she couldn't find him around town, she headed to the school. How she got past the block-ades . . . he couldn't say. Maybe she took the path to avoid the main roads. One thing he knew was that Laura saw something she wasn't supposed to see.

Jake turned back around. "How did she die?" he asked.

"Gunshot. Can't tell you more than that because I don't know."

With his peripheral vision, Jake saw someone approaching. He turned his head and recognized Ryan Coventry. The boy looked anxious about something, unsettled. He was with a lot of other teenagers who had gotten as close as they were going to get to all the action.

"Mr. Dent," Ryan said, "have you seen Andy around?" He seemed sincere, truly worried.

"No," Jake said. "Why? Do you know where he is?"

With his arms folded across his chest, Ryan looked to the ground and kicked at the muddy earth. This was a different Ryan. This Ryan was meek and docile, and unsure.

"Not exactly," Ryan said. "We were—uh—we were on the second floor of the Science Center getting out together, you know. There was some guy in a chemical suit pushing us along. Trying to hurry things up."

"So, where is he? Did he leave with you?"

Again, Ryan appeared uncomfortable, and Jake knew more was coming.

"It was pretty chaotic," Ryan said.

Jake's eyes flared. "No bullshit, Ryan, talk to me. Where is Andy?"

As a pitcher, Jake was always a keen observer of body language. Ryan was bothered, but Jake didn't need years in baseball to see the obvious.

"I may have seen something weird," Ryan said.

Ellie stepped forward to address Ryan. "What was it?"

Guilt. That was the feeling Jake was getting. The boy was feeling guilty about something.

"Well, I turned around as I was heading down the stairs. And the guy in the chemical suit kind of stepped in front of Andy, like he wanted him to stay behind. I was going to go up and, you know, make sure Andy left with me, but I thought I saw something in the guy's hand."

"What did you see?" Ellie asked.

"Honestly, for a second, I thought it was a gun. It was crazy chaotic, you know? It was just a flash. Anyway, I freaked a bit and I just bolted down the stairs. When I got to the buses, I was laughing, because I was sure it was just my imagination."

"No, it wasn't your imagination," Jake said. There was a dose of asperity in his voice. "You saw what you saw and you just got scared. Why did you wait so long to say something?"

Ryan shrugged. "I dunno," he said. "I figured it was nothing, but I saw you here, so I guess I just thought to ask if Andy was around."

Jake's jaw set. "Can you tell me anything about the man you saw?" he asked.

Ryan shook his head. "You could barely see the guy's face. He was in a suit, you know?"

Jake pawed the ground with his foot, summoning all the restraint he could manage. "Go back to your friends," Jake said. "If anybody you know hears from Andy, you get in touch with me. What's your number? I'll call you."

Jake called the number and watched Ryan enter the contact information into his smartphone. When the boy was gone, he turned his attention back to Ellie.

"Andy is inside that school," Jake said.

"You don't know that for certain."

"I called three cell phones, three, and I got no answer. These kids have their phones glued to their hands. And now Ryan thinks he saw a gun? It's my boy, Ellie. It's Andy. He's in there."

"Even if he is, you have to let the police handle this."

"Yeah? When are you going in? How long?"

"I don't know. These things take time. We have to assess the situation first."

Jake's face went hot. "We may not have time!" he said, and regretted the outburst.

Ellie didn't flinch. She was accustomed to dealing with belligerent drunks. She took hold of Jake's arm, but he yanked it away.

"What are you thinking, Jake?"

"I'm thinking my son needs to get his blood sugar up before your guys get their act together."

"If that's the case, Andy will tell whoever is holding him hostage."

"And what if they just let my son die?"

"You have to trust the police to handle this."

Jake shook his head. "I'm sorry, Ellie. You, I care about. The police, SWAT, the FBI, not high on my list."

Ellie looked offended and genuinely confused. *Where is this mistrust toward law enforcement coming from?*

If she had seen Jake's larder, his storage room, his cache of weapons and ammunition, she would have known.

Jake backed away.

"What are you going to do?"

"I'm not going to do anything, Ellie," Jake said. "Don't worry. I'm going to let you handle it, just like you asked."

Ellie reached for her belt. He knew she was thinking

about taking out the cuffs and putting a stop to whatever plans he had just concocted. He took another step back.

"Jake, let us handle this."

"I'm not going to let my son die."

"You don't even know if he's in there."

Jake said nothing.

"He's my son, Ellie."

Jake turned and ran for his car. Ellie watched him go.

Chapter 24

Inside the Feldman Auditorium, Fausto Garza had changed things up. The six members of The Shire occupied the auditorium's front row. Behind each of them sat one cartel enforcer. They were there to keep watch, even though the kids weren't going anywhere. The teens had their hands and feet bound with rope, but the gags were out and blindfolds off so their eyes could take in the full spectacle.

Onstage, in a perfect line, bodies rigid as if at attention, stood four members of Sangre Tierra:

The redheaded one.

A fat one.

And two tall ones, thin like Rafa.

They were the four who, per Fausto's orders, had chased after a woman who had seen too much. Fausto was on the stage with them. He stood in front of the men and paced back and forth, eyeing each contemptuously, a cross between an irate stage director and a drill sergeant.

Minutes ago, in a fierce rage, Fausto had ripped off the arm of one of the auditorium chairs. He wielded the lacquered piece of rounded wood like a club. He slapped the armrest against his meaty palm with steady taps. Whimpers of the teens and the slapping of wood against skin were the only sounds inside the hall.

Fausto stopped pacing to glower once more at the men onstage with him. He turned around slowly, apparently ready to address his audience, those he had kidnapped and those he had employed. He spoke in English for the benefit of The Shire. This show was to be something for all of them to see and understand.

"Okay—okay—okay," Fausto began. "We are here now to have a discussion about what happened."

Hilary gasped for a breath and spat out a choked sob. In his cushy seat beside her, Solomon shook violently, as did David. Pixie, Andy, and Rafa might have been the most stoic of the bunch, but their eyes were wide and swimming with fright.

Fausto held up his hands theatrically and hoisted the makeshift club high as his head. He turned back around to communicate with the men onstage.

"So, who would like to tell me what *they* think has now happened?"

Nobody spoke up.

"Nobody has an idea?" he asked, his voice lengthened by an echo. Fausto paced in front of the four men, but stopped to address specifically the man with red hair. "You really have no idea what has just happened?"

"Perseguimos a la mujer, pero se nos escapó," the redheaded man said.

Fausto's expression turned fierce as he sidestepped to his left to stand in front of the man who spoke. Without uttering a word, Fausto spat into the man's face.

"In English, Gallo. *¡Idiota!*" Fausto screamed. "In English. Not all of your audience can understand you!"

"El Gallo" wiped the long trail of bubbly spittle from his face before it dribbled into his mouth. His nickname fit his appearance: his body type was squat, like that of a rooster, and his bright shock of dyed red hair looked like plumage. He took several ragged, readying breaths and said in a weak voice and very thick accent, "We run after a woman, but she get away."

"'We run after a woman,'" Fausto said mockingly, "'but she get away.'" He felt the need to repeat himself, even louder and more unrestrained. "'We run after a woman, but she get away!'"

"But we shot her," El Gallo added. "I made the bullet. Or how you say, I did the shoot. We followed her to the woods and lost her there."

Fausto turned to face his audience once more and raised his arms over his head almost triumphantly, as if all the answers to all the questions in the universe had just been revealed.

"'Lost her there,'" Fausto repeated slowly, in a low, dramatic voice.

Without any shift in his expression, Fausto spun on his heels as he lowered the wooden armrest level with El Gallo's head. With as much force as he could generate, Fausto connected the head of the club squarely with El Gallo's ear. The blow instantly dropped the plump man to the stage floor.

Without a pause, Fausto pounced on the fallen man, straddling his round belly, and lifted the club over his head. He brought the weapon down in a wide arc. This time, it smashed in El Gallo's nose. There was a horrible crunch, followed by a scream, and a gush of blood that seemed to defy gravity.

Fausto raised the club once more and brought it down again on El Gallo's battered nose. And again. And again. With each strike, El Gallo's face vanished more and more beneath a wash of red. The fifth strike completely destroyed El Gallo's skull. For a few seconds, El Gallo's legs kicked about spastically, but those movements soon abated and his legs went perfectly still. Even so, Fausto struck the man three more times, seemingly just for good measure.

Still straddling the dead man, Fausto slowly lifted his head to show the others onstage his blood-splattered face. El Gallo's blood had turned Fausto's fine silk shirt into a gruesome imitation of a Jackson Pollock. The killer's eyes glowed in a satisfied way, like an animal having feasted on a carcass.

The other men onstage kept perfectly still. Not one stole a single glance at the pulpy remains of El Gallo's face.

Breathing hard, Fausto climbed off El Gallo and again turned to face the audience. He tossed the bloody club onto the floor at Andy's feet. It landed with a loud thud. Fausto gave a fractured smile that put his metal mouth on prominent display.

Solomon started to sob. "I want to go home," he muttered. "I want my mom. I just want to go home."

This caused a chain reaction of sorts and soon all of the kids were openly crying. Fausto ignored their terror.

"Correction," he announced, holding up one of his blood-covered fingers for all to see. "We did not just shoot a woman and then lose her in the woods. We have lost *everything.* Our advantage now is gone. Do you know what this means?"

Fausto drew a pistol with a pearl-inlaid handle from the waistband of his jeans and spun around again. This time, he marched over to the man standing closest to the remains of El Gallo. Fausto put his arm around the frightened man as if to suggest they were close friends, bosom buddies. Fausto summoned a flat smile, while the man appeared utterly terrified.

"This is Tony, 'El Cortador,'" Fausto proclaimed in a booming voice. "*El Cortador* means 'cutter' in Spanish, because Tony loves to work slowly and he uses many sharp objects. Tony, can you please—for the benefit of everyone, but especially our new young friends here—explain the significance of what has happened?"

Tony's mouth opened. For a moment, no sound came out. He managed to expel a wheezing breath, which eventually gave way to actual words. *"Podría estar viva,"* Tony said.

Fausto's face turned crimson. "In English!" he screamed.

Tony cowered. "She could be alive!" he shouted, using his arms and hands reflexively to shield his head. "She could still be alive!"

Fausto stepped to the side and nodded approvingly. His expression darkened again as he seized El Cortador by the shoulder and shoved him forward hard. As El Cortador stumbled, Fausto raised his pistol and fired. The bullet exploded the skull of the man standing to the left of El Cortador. But as that bullet exited one skull, it entered another; and thus two men dropped to the floor. Looking jubilant, and more than a little surprised, Fausto raised his arms in triumph.

Sprawled on the floor, El Cortador crawled to the edge of the stage like a commando going under razor wire. Fausto ambled over to him and placed his boot on his back to hold him in place. El Cortador began to weep inconsolably.

"You see, now it is possible the police will be coming. If this woman lived long enough to say anything, then you must believe that we soon will have company. And this, my friends, is a very big problem. They will have more men and more guns and smoke bombs and many tricks to kill us and save you."

Fausto pointed at all six hostages with his pistol, indicating the "you" to whom he had referred. El Cortador convulsed and squirmed with Fausto's foot on the small of his back.

Fausto placed his gun against El Cortador's head and pulled the trigger. There was an audible *click*, but no bang, no flash, and no blood except the few drops belonging to El Gallo that dribbled from Fausto's hand onto El Cortador's neck.

Tony sobbed louder. Fausto examined the gun, nonplussed, as if something was wrong with its mechanics. He shrugged and his expression was slightly bemused.

"Pensé que tenía otra bala. ¡Qué suerte la tuya!" Fausto said.

Fausto made eye contact with the six panic-stricken teenagers seated in the front row. "I said to him, 'I thought I had another bullet left. Looks like it was El Cortador's lucky day.'"

Efren stood, towering over Pixie, and showed genuine concern. *"Pero usted dijo que la policía va a venir por nosotros ahora. ¿Qué hacemos?"*

Fausto nodded, seeming unbothered by the Spanish spoken. "It's true," he said in English, "we assume we are known and the police will come. We assume this. Okay, that's fine. Well, not fine, but it is what it is. But your pal Fausto has a plan for everything, including the mess these four have caused us."

The barrel of Fausto's gun pointed out three dead men and El Cortador. "So, from this moment on, my friends, we are no longer drug dealers. We are something else, and that something is going to change the game for everyone."

Chapter 25

Jake did some reconnaissance work, checking police barricades and access roads, getting a sense of how the command and control operation was established. Then he drove home to get ready.

About halfway to his house, he picked up the tail. The car was a nondescript silver Ford Focus, but he got the feeling its two occupants were involved in some manner of law enforcement. Jake took a left down a dirt road that any local would know looped back to the main road, and the Focus followed. It was a sure bet they had at least one oscillating colored light that could be mounted on top of the vehicle.

For a moment, Jake bristled with fury at Ellie. How dare she put the cops on him! But quick as it came, Jake's anger left him. Ellie was just doing her job. Jake had given her every reason not to trust him. She cared for him, and this was probably her way of showing it. He would have done the same, had their roles been reversed.

On the pitcher's mound, Jake had excelled at keeping an even keel. His highs never got too high, and his lows never too low. He tried to present an image of steadiness that often unnerved opponents who would rather see him rattled. Regrettably, Jake had broadcast his intentions to Ellie in high definition. He would not make the same mistake again. Communication between them was over for now. Jake would be on his own.

The rest of the way home, Jake drove the speed limit. He glanced in the rearview mirror after turning down the access road to his trailer home. The Ford Focus was still there.

In his driveway, Jake pulled the car to a quick stop, cut the engine, and strolled over to the silver car, which was parked on the side of the public road. The driver lowered his window as Jake approached. He was younger, maybe thirty, with nut-brown hair cut short, a well-scrubbed and clean-shaven face. Five more years at this job and he'd look fifteen years older, but he'd probably have on the same suit, still wear the same sunglasses, even on cloudy days like this one. His partner, also wearing shades and a suit, could have passed for a brother.

"Can I help you guys?" Jake asked in a friendly voice.

"No," the man said.

Jake backed away. "You always follow people?"

The man's sullen expression conveyed much to Jake, but he said nothing. Guess he had nothing to say. It was obvious to Jake that this guy did not want to be tailing anybody to a trailer home. All of the action was happening by the school, not watching over some anxious dad who might try to do something ill-advised.

"Can you at least show me your badges?" Jake asked. "If you're going to stake out my home, it seems only fair."

The man in the driver's seat held up a billfold with a silver badge, about three inches by three inches. Jake could make out the words "Mass State Police" spelled out across the top of the badge. These two were detectives, not troopers.

Jake shrugged. What else would he do? "I'm just going inside to wait until I hear from my son or the police," Jake said. "It's been an eventful day. Look, you fellas have fun staking out my home. I'm sure this is what you dreamed of doing when you signed up for the academy."

Jake was distraught, but tried not to let it show. Better to downplay his grieving and terror than give the police real cause for concern. Inside his home, Jake lowered the window shades. It made sense he'd want some privacy.

Pacing, Jake went from room to room dialing Andy's cell phone. When he got no answer, he dialed the numbers of his friends. He rubbed his hands nervously together, until he became aware of what he was doing.

After he drank some water, Jake went to the living-room window, pried back the shade a speck, and watched the detectives watching him. That was the job. If Jake drove off, they would follow. Which meant he had the woods all to himself. But he still had much to prepare.

To vanish inside a forest, Jake had to become his surroundings. He retrieved his camouflage paint from a box he kept underneath his bed and retreated to the bathroom. He took out a tube of the dark green paint first and used that to color the high points on his face: nose, cheeks, and forehead. He mixed in some darker tan, but was careful in the application not to make any patterns. Objects in the background tended to show shadows, while those in the foreground were generally lighter. The goal of camouflage was simply to trick the eye and reverse the optics. Jake did up the sides of his face and neck in lighter colors, but he kept everything irregular. The approach was not to be fancy, but just knock down the shine. The Marine Corps had camo figured out.

Every part of him had to be hidden. That meant his hands, neck, and ears as well. Eventually his skin oil would wash away the paint, but by then Jake would be inside the school.

Examining himself in the mirror, Jake put on a hunting shirt and pants. The tan-and-green color scheme formed irregular patterns that worked well with the woods at this time of year. The barren trees offered little protection, so Jake's best bet was to blend in with the dead leaves and other vegetation closer to the forest floor. Jake's boots matched the rest of his attire. Inside, he looked a hunter; outside, he would look like the wild.

Jake went to the kitchen and filled his canteen. He glanced over at his GOOD pack, thought about grabbing it, but decided to leave it behind. Everything he needed was already at the bug-out location. Jake's weapons weren't necessary, at least for now. This mission was about evasion, not stalking.

With nothing left to do, Jake opened the back door and got on the path he and Andy could have navigated blindfolded. Jake made it about fifteen feet when he heard a car door slam shut. The agents had probably gotten tired of waiting. Maybe one of them had to take a leak.

A nearby patch of ferns offered Jake the best cover. He sank into the vegetation and maneuvered to where the shadows were the deepest. If they came looking, their eyes would tire quickly, trying to see through so many layers of masking vegetation. Jake kept his body still and waited patiently. Movement of any kind, even while camouflaged, attracted the most attention. Snapping twigs, rustling leaves—those things might as well be a bullhorn in the quiet woodland. He was going to wait it out, a few minutes at most. If nobody showed, he'd get back on the move.

It was not long before Jake heard footsteps. Seconds later, a detective came into view. He walked cautiously, as if he were an uninvited guest. Jake in full camouflage would certainly give cause to detain him for questioning. Getting through the woods and into the school was going to take long enough. Who knew what the hostage takers might be doing to his son and the others? Jake could hardly fathom the possibilities. But hours being questioned by the police would be a death sentence for Andy if his son's blood sugar levels dropped.

Jake moved his leg to stave off a cramp. The leaves underneath him made a slight rustling sound. Jake went rigid. The detective turned to face the noise and his gaze fell directly on Jake. He took one step toward Jake's hiding place, and then another. He stopped and listened. The only sound was the pitter-patter of the misty rain falling on dead leaves. The detective took another step in Jake's direction. If it came to it, Jake would try to lose the agent in a footrace.

The detective scanned the area once more and his entire demeanor changed. Instead of encountering a threat situation, he looked frustrated for chasing a squirrel or something similar. Jake exhaled as the detective worked his way back to the front of the house. Soon he'd be telling his partner nothing was going on, and they'd go back to complaining about getting a bunk assignment in what could be the biggest case of the year.

Jake got to his feet and set off for the school. His walk became a trot, which soon quickened into a jog. Cloud cover lengthened the shadows and would have helped conceal him, had anybody been in these woods. But the chemical spill and the rain were good deterrents and kept folks indoors. There was a chance the detectives might get bored enough to go knock on Jake's door. If so, they would either break it down, or call it in. Either way, by the time they noticed Jake had snuck away, he'd already be inside the school.

When the path became a road, Jake slipped into the wood line and continued his march north. He could hear sirens in the distance; and if he walked about two thousand yards from his current location, Jake would probably run into Ellie and her friends on the Winston PD.

Jake arrived, undetected, at the hilly field behind the school. Here he used his binoculars to scope the campus for any guards or safety workers. It appeared deserted. Any plans to send air-quality testers to the area were probably dashed when the situation turned to a potential hostage crisis. The campus was utterly deserted. Jake sniffed the air, but picked up no foul odor.

Maybe the call about the ammonia-like smell at the school was part of somebody's plan. But who was somebody?

For a few gut-wrenching moments, Jake envisioned Laura's frantic sprint across The Quad as she fled for her life. *Did they shoot her before she got to the woods or after?* He didn't know. *What do these people want, anyway? Who are they? And why would they take kids as hostages?* The answers, Jake believed, would be revealed soon as he got inside the school.

Jake was about to make his final push when he noticed movement in the tree line to his right. Focusing his binoculars on that particular patch of woods, Jake got a clear visual of a SWAT team member in tactical gear. He was motioning to someone nearby, and sure enough another member came out of the shadows to take up position behind a massive tree. The woods probably held a dozen SWAT forces, if not more, but Jake had the advantage. They were looking for people coming out of the school, not anybody trying to get in.

Jake took to the tall grasses. Forest animals moved without causing a stir by keeping close to the ground and walking with a steady rhythm. Random sounds were more noticeable. After he got into a crouch, Jake used his knees to absorb the weight of his body as he crawled forward. Every muscle was engaged. The shortest path to the door was a straight line, but Jake needed the cover of the field, so he took time to reach his destination. On the way, he kept a lookout for any puddles, sticks, and gravel—anything that could make a sound.

He controlled his breathing. Hyperventilation negatively affected most every critical function, but most especially motion, balance, and coordination. This was something Jake had perfected on the mound. A pitcher had to pay attention to the "when" of breathing and the "where." It was easy to forget proper breathing in the heat of battle. It took mindfulness to maintain focus, inning after inning. Jake never lost the skill.

At the fieldstone structure, Jake took cover behind the building to observe the woods, which were now fairly far away. This section of school grounds was not where SWAT or the local police would concentrate manpower, so Jake felt relatively confident he could enter the building unseen.

After he removed the loose stone, Jake retrieved the hidden key, unlocked the door, and was soon descending into the tunnels, which were his home away from home. He marched right past his retreat, remembering he had changed the locks so the bug-out location wouldn't stand out if the tunnels had to be tested for air quality. Jake dug out the new key and was ready to go exploring fifteen minutes later.

"Ready" included an AK-47 and a chest rig with a battle belt. Jake stuffed the rig with as many 7.62x39 mags as he could fit: three on his chest, two on his belt, and two pistol mags as well. He slipped another mag in his back pocket, just in case. Beneath the chest rig, Jake's Kevlar vest felt heavy, but he'd rather the discomfort than the alternative. He grabbed a syringe and several vials of insulin from the refrigerator, which he kept at a constant forty-two degrees Fahrenheit. He also took the spare glucagon emergency kit and glucose tablets. If the hostage takers gave Andy food, his insulin would help balance out his blood sugar. If they denied him nourishment, the glucagon injection might save his life. Jake's Peltor tactical hearing protection, compatible with his tactical helmet, reduced the hazardous impulse noise from amplified sounds, such as firearms, to harmless levels. Built-in stereo microphones would equip Jake with enhanced sound detection. Jake had water, binoculars, his Glock, two Bushman Series knives, with ten-inch blades made of SK-5 high-carbon steel, a portable Bearcat handheld scanner, and a map of the school's numerous tunnels and passageways.

He was ready to go looking for his son.

Chapter 26

The six teenagers had been separated. Each occupied a different room in the main building, far enough away from each other, Fausto hoped, that they couldn't hear any screams.

The interrogation would soon begin, and Fausto felt confident he could retrieve Soto's money. Getting out would be another matter entirely. But first things first, Soto always preached. One of these kids had the digital key to access the missing $200 million. All it would take to get it was the proper incentive. And that had nothing to do with money.

Fausto would personally oversee the process, but he assigned a man to each kid. Efren would be with Andy—the strongest with the leader. Armando, with the many scars on his face, got the girl, Hilary, but with strict orders she was not to be violated. Not yet, anyway. El Cortador got a second chance and was assigned to the fat one, Solomon. Poor Solomon. That left Joaquin, "El Mata Padres"—which meant "The Father Killer," so-named for good reason—to take the long-haired one, David. El Tornado, whose real name was Emmanuel, would interrogate the thin boy called Rafa, and Miguel, "Una Mano"—which meant "One Hand"—had the little one who went by the name of Pixie. Miguel had lost his right hand to a machete, and the substitute, an ugly hook, made a fearsome weapon.

Having a handle in a cartel was a sign of respect. It was like a personal brand. It meant that you mattered, you were someone of importance. The two men not assigned an interrogation had no handle. These were foot soldiers, as were two of the three men Fausto had murdered onstage. El Gallo was someone of importance, but incompetence trumped status in Fausto's world.

Fausto's handle had been given to him by Soto himself: "El Dorado"—"The Golden." In keeping with tradition, Fausto had named his two chief lieutenants. Efren was called "El Toro" because of his size, and Armando, for obvious reasons, was "Scar Face"—the only nickname in English.

These computer types had taken up the naming practice, like The Lion, who'd helped Javier first and Fausto second. It amused Fausto that these kids also had handles. They had their own hierarchy, it seemed. He knew two of their handles so far—Pixie and Dark Matter—but soon he would learn the others. He would discover everything he needed to know about these kids, and they, in turn, would learn many things they didn't know about themselves.

But first, Fausto had business to address. For now, the situation at Javier's home was under control. It was one thing Fausto did not have to worry about. The Martinez family would live until Javier was no longer of any use to the cartel. Fausto spoke by phone with the man in charge of the Javier situation, the one he called Odio. The conversation had turned tense; one of the men Fausto murdered onstage was Odio's cousin. But Odio's anger came and quickly passed. No tears were shed. Life in the cartel was notoriously hard, and no one dared grieve the dead openly, lest he suffer the same fate.

Fausto was using the auditorium as his war room. It was there he summoned Efren to his side. The contingency plan he had mapped out was about to be put into action. It was time to make those who mattered aware of the stakes.

Efren had taken off his shirt and entered the auditorium wearing only his white cotton tank top. His massive arms were adorned with tattoos, many as intricate as the delicate designs cut into Fausto's gold teeth.

"The boy Andy is being watched," Efren said in Spanish. "I sent Pancho out to patrol the grounds and check for anybody in the surrounding buildings."

"Good thinking, Efren," Fausto said. "But why do you look concerned?"

"It's the boy. He doesn't look well to me. He tells me he's diabetic."

"And you believe him?" Fausto asked.

"I don't think he's faking."

"If he has the key, he must not die."

"You think I don't know this? I brought his backpack to the room, but haven't searched it. I wanted to check with you what to do."

"We break him first. If he says he doesn't have the key and you believe him, kill him and let's move on."

"Understood," Efren said. "Now about our problem. You said at Javier's house you had a plan if something went wrong. Well, I'd say something has gone very wrong."

"I am prepared," Fausto said. "But first, listen to me. This situation may not go well for us. I am telling this only to you because you, my friend, like me, are not afraid to die. I am not wrong, am I?"

Efren shrugged his indifference. "If I'm dead, will I even care?"

Fausto chuckled and put his arm around Efren's broad shoulders. "You are a good man. We have two goals now. First, get the money to Soto. He will make sure some of it, a fair amount, goes to our families."

"Do you think there's any chance of getting out alive?"

"I think we will buy ourselves time. But if it looks like we are cornered here, our chances are not so good. Understand? For now, our objectives remain the same. Retrieve the money, and return to Mexico."

"How do we buy time?" Efren asked.

"We are going to have to play a little game of chicken. And we'll see who wins." Fausto took out his cell phone, looked up a number on the Internet, and dialed.

A ring.

"Winston Police, Dispatcher Gavin, this call is being recorded," a male voice said. "How can I help you?"

"Yes, I am calling to report a situation at Pepperell Academy," Fausto said in English.

Fausto heard the sound of clicking.

"The school has been evacuated. Are you calling about the odor or something else?"

"Well, I am the one who caused all of the problem," Fausto said calmly. "Including a woman we shot. Have you met her? Seen her? Did she live? Just curious. It doesn't matter now anyway."

"Excuse me?"

"You heard me. I have *caused* the problem—the truck, the spill, the chemical—and now the hostages. All of it is me. Please now, listen very carefully."

"Who is this?"

"My English is not perfect, but I do not believe what you are doing is listening. I think that is talking, no? We try again, okay? Listen to me. Just to be clear, you may respond you understood."

"Okay—okay. I'm listening."

"Good. My name does not matter. What does is that I am in possession of a weapon of great destruction. I will send you a picture. What is your e-mail address?"

"My e-mail?"

"You want to see this device, no?"

"Yeah. Yeah," the man said.

Fausto enjoyed the man's hard breathing as he spelled out his e-mail address. From his photo library, Fausto accessed all the pictures of the oil drums hooked together with wires that Carlos had sent to him from Mexico. Carlos knew enough to strip the images of GPS location information, so Fausto was free to send whichever pictures he wanted. He selected the image that best displayed the lime-green drum, the one with the special tags, and sent it as an e-mail attachment through a wireless network.

"Did you get it?" Fausto asked.

After a pause, "Yeah, I got it. It's here."

"Do you know what this is?" Fausto asked.

"No," said the dispatcher.

"This is a very ugly bomb," Fausto said. "It's what you call a dirty bomb."

"Who is this? What is it you want?"

Fausto ignored the question. "There was a theft in Mexico not long ago, five months or so. A truck transporting cobalt-60 taken from an old—how do you say in English?—*aparato de rayos x,* X-ray machine, was hijacked. We did this. And we used the stolen material in the bomb."

This was partially true. One of Soto's affiliates had hijacked the truck and discovered inside the cargo hold several of these radioactive containers. Soto was not sure what to do with the cargo, but he kept it hidden because the theft had caused quite the stir in both Mexico and the United States. Both governments worried about such material ending up in the hands of a terrorist. Soto figured the cobalt-60 could be of value to the right buyer, but at the time these pictures were taken, a buyer had yet to come forward. The oil drums had been mostly forgotten, with their radioactive material sealed inside.

Fausto had personally coordinated the transport of the cobalt-60 to an abandoned airfield some fifty kilometers outside Ciudad Juárez. Those oil drums were still fresh in Fausto's memory when he thought to use them as part of his contingency plan. He had foreseen the need to have a significant threat that would hold any potential rescue team at bay.

Fausto knew the plan would not guarantee his escape. He'd make a demand for transport back to Mex-

ico; but if that plan failed, Fausto was fully prepared to
die and he'd gladly take others down with him. If it
succeeded, Efren and Armando would thank him for
his foresight once the three friends were enjoying mar-
garitas and women on the beaches of Cabo San Lucas
again.

"There's a tag on one of the oil drums. Read it,"
Fausto told the dispatcher. "It will be a match for the
stolen material. This is not a bluff. The other drums in
the picture are filled with a high-powered explosive,
and the vehicle holding the device is parked where
there are many people. I can set off this bomb with a
phone call. The explosion will mix cobalt-60 pellets
and make a very big problem wherever the boom may
be. If anybody comes near this school, I detonate the
device."

"What is it you want? Your demands."

"You heard them already!" Fausto snapped. "What
is it with you people and listening? I said fall back. Retreat. Give me the space I want. Two kilometers. If I
see so much as a single police officer, SWAT, FBI,
any chemical cleanup people, a *maldito* janitor, I detonate the device. Ask somebody who knows what happens then."

Chapter 27

A series of hanging lights illuminated the tunnel like the shaft of some forgotten coal mine. The numerous ways into the tunnel system were well hidden. Jake didn't worry about anybody being down here with him. All his thoughts were centered on what was happening aboveground.

The FBI was mobilizing its big guns—the Hostage Rescue Team, or HRT—but there was no indication of an imminent assault. Jake kept the volume on his portable police scanner low as he listened. There was some discussion of a new threat, but all related conversation was directed to a secure channel Jake couldn't access. The mission was now clearly defined: ensure his son was here, alive, and get him his medication. If Jake could extract Andy and the others safely, he would do so. Otherwise, he could relay critical information back to the FBI as needed.

The tunnel between the field house and the Society Building went straight for about a hundred yards and terminated at a set of crumbling cement stairs. Jake climbed those stairs, pulled his hearing protection to one side, and placed his ear to the rust-speckled door at the top of the landing. He listened. All was quiet. He powered down the scanner and turned the doorknob with caution.

Jake entered a dark closet, about eight feet by eight feet, with a ceiling high enough for him to stand upright. Buckets, mops, and cleaning supplies were in his way, but Jake got to the front of the closet without knocking anything over.

Holding his assault rifle with one hand, Jake reached for the knob and turned it slowly. The worst mistake he could make would be to move too quickly. He had to maintain a pace that would allow him to shoot with accuracy. He opened the closet door and stepped quickly to the side.

He trained the barrel of his AK-47 into the sliver of hallway he could see. His head, cocooned inside his tactical helmet, heated up. Jake took small steps as he worked his way incrementally from the closet wall to stand in front of the open door. He brought the weapon up to nose level, but knew not to get so focused looking down the barrel that he'd forget to scan the space in front of him, floor to the ceiling. Hiding places could be anywhere.

Self-discipline had always been one of Jake's strengths, and pitching had bolstered that innate ability. There was a right way to do things and a wrong way, and practice and repetitions locked methods into memory. After seeing how long it took just to open a closet door, however, Jake debated trading caution for speed. Andy's condition could be deteriorating by the minute.

Slow it down. Do it right.

Jake stepped out into the hallway, committed, and aimed the gun to cover only what his eyes could see. Mounted to his rifle was a SureFire light, activated by a hand switch. The light didn't eliminate all shadows, but it did a damn fine job illuminating the dim corridor.

Jake assessed his environment. Classroom doors ran along both sides of the hall. Some of the doors were closed, but others had been left open. As he cleared each room, Jake would have an increasingly difficult time keeping an eye down the hall. But he needed to get to the stairwell at the far end of the corridor to go up a level.

From higher ground, Jake would be able to see the Academy Building and he'd also have a partial view of the Terry Science Center. He'd have limited sight lines to Gibson Hall or the library, but one thing at a time.

Jake imagined a scenario in which Laura encountered hostage takers inside the Academy Building. From there, she would have sprinted across The Quad, run right past the Society Building, where he now was, and made it to the woods. Probably bleeding. Probably dying. Or maybe she'd found her killers in this very building. The campus had always felt small to Jake, but now it seemed vast as an ocean.

Jake had done several room-clearing exercises before. Clearing a house alone was an absolute worst-case scenario, so practicing it was an important part of his preparedness training. He had no backup—nobody to take a zone for him. The situation stank. No other way to put it. His enemy had every conceivable advantage. Jake needed to commit to each room, and he would have to clear them all.

After one final check down the hall, Jake moved quickly into the adjacent classroom to his right and swept it. His gun barrel canvassed every corner of the room, moving high to low and covering everything in between. Nothing. Jake ventured into the hall once again, with his rifle ready: nose level, eye looking right down the barrel, finger hovering over the trigger. His pulse accelerated, but his breathing stayed steady. At one time, with ice in his veins, he had stared down plenty of batters facing a three-two count.

The classroom across from him was next. He crossed the hallway as if he were walking a tightrope, each step careful, quiet. His ears were attuned to any sound. The slightest scrape could mean a gunman, a burst of gunfire.

Fortunately for Jake, half the classrooms put him on the strong side of the door. He could reach over, open the door, and step back without exposing himself to any threat inside. Jake cleared the next classroom, same as the other. The desks were all in neat rows, suggesting the students had evacuated in an orderly fashion.

At the classroom door, Jake paused to collect his thoughts and refocus. Stress decreased situational awareness and could result in tunnel vision. A few deep breaths and Jake's mind felt sharp again, except for the constant pangs about Andy. Those wouldn't go away.

Jake slipped back into the hallway, keeping his eyes peeled for signs of danger. He cleared the next classroom, and the next, until he had done them all. Eleven classrooms in total, and not a single threat encountered. No moving doors. No unusual shadows. No signs of life. The effort took seven minutes. Seven minutes for Andy to get sicker. Seven minutes for whoever took his son to do something dreadful.

At the end of the hall stood the door to the stairwell. Jake stopped and listened. He might have heard something. A scraping sound? He tossed open the door and leveled his weapon into the darkness. It was a mistake. He had moved too quickly, but he wanted an answer. He wanted Andy. The stairwell was concrete and sound traveled. But the door had opened silently; and if somebody was above or below, they probably heard nothing.

Jake listened. Nothing at first, but then, his ears picked up the faint click of a door closing shut. Not his door, of course. It came from the door above him. One floor up. The floor where Jake was headed. Jake hesitated, waiting for footsteps, his gun trained on the spot where a body could appear. Nothing. He checked his weapon and undid the snap, securing his Bushman knife to his ankle holster.

After one readying breath, Jake headed up the stairs.

Chapter 28

Andy was in trouble when his vision blurred. It was a sign, and he knew them all. The effects of low blood sugar could be sudden and disastrous.

A moment earlier, Efren had been in sharp focus. Andy could see the huge man's many tattoos clearly. Then the bull of a man went fuzzy, and it became an effort for Andy to refocus. Andy needed his backpack. Efren had left it within Andy's view on the large oval table that took up much of what he thought was a history classroom. Andy begged Efren to give him his glucose tablets. In response, Efren tightened Andy's rope restraints and held up the backpack as a taunt.

At some point, Efren left the room and a different monster came to guard Andy. This one had a hint of a mustache over mocha-colored skin, short, coarse hair, and dark, nervous eyes that darted about like a ferret's. One moment, the Latin Thor was here; the next, Andy had this whippet of a man watching over him. When did that happen? Andy had known he was losing his concentration, but the extent was alarming.

Sign number three happened a few minutes later, when Andy's mouth went cottony dry. It was only a matter of time before these symptoms got worse and new ones arose.

Andy watched "Whippet" pace anxiously in front of the classroom. The thin man said nothing. Did nothing. He just paced, armed with an assault rifle, an AR-15, a gun Andy knew well. Fired one at the range with his dad. *Dad.* The thought of his father ripped Andy's heart and brought tears to his eyes.

Whippet made frequent checks of the hallway. He seemed eager for a changing of the guard. Inevitably, nobody would be outside, and Whippet would resume his pacing. Whippet's dark eyes would occasionally fall on Andy, which sent shivers of fear through his body. Andy still wore his school uniform, but the button-down shirt was soaked with sweat and his tie hung askew. The sweat gave off a musty, somewhat rancid odor. Who knew terror had its unique scent?

Andy's vision blurred once more, in and out of focus, like the camera in his phone.

He thought of his father. Tough as things had been between them lately, Andy was more grateful than ever for the long hours of prepping that gave him skills to survive and had toughened his exterior. But no amount of training could keep his body from shutting down.

Again, Andy's eyes went to the backpack on the Harkness table. He never had a class that used the Harkness method, but it was part of Pepperell Academy's teaching philosophy. The large oval table replaced traditional desks, and was thought to encourage a more open and informal exchange of ideas with instructors. Andy suspected there would be no free-flowing exchange of ideas with Whippet.

"Do you speak English?" Andy asked. His voice came at him like an echo scattered in the darkness. His body thrummed out a warning: *not enough sugar.* He needed food. Or his tablets. If things got really bad, he'd need the injection. How long did he have? Andy couldn't say. But a storm was brewing inside him.

"English?" Andy asked again. He tried to control the tremor in his voice, but it was no use. He was more afraid of his body than these men.

Whippet approached, eyes blazing. A snarl creased his top lip, showcasing yellowing teeth that looked like fangs. *"¡Cállate!"* the man ordered. His voice was as coarse as sandpaper.

Up close, Andy could smell the cigarettes, and he saw the nicotine stains marking Whippet's fingers.

"Please," Andy said, croaking out the word. The moisture in his mouth had retreated like water in the desert heat.

He wanted to reach for the man, grab hold and fight the way his dad had taught him, but his arms were wrenched behind his back, and his hands lashed together with rope. Andy's legs had gone numb from sitting. Or was something else causing him to lose the feeling in his feet, in his limbs?

The man got close and knelt before Andy. His penetrating gaze forced Andy to shut his eyes and look away. The smell of cigarettes overpowered his senses.

"Cállate," the man said again, drawing out the command. It was clear he took pleasure in Andy's suffering. Whippet stood and clamped a strong hand around

Andy's shoulder. Andy braced himself for the blow—
a strike to the face, perhaps.

Instead, the classroom door swung open and two
men entered: the one who called himself Fausto and
the bull of a man who had guarded Andy before. Seeing Fausto, Whippet removed his hand from Andy's
shoulder. Fausto gave Whippet a displeased, hard
stare. The look said that nobody was supposed to lay a
hand on the hostages without his direct order.

Fausto came around behind Andy and undid the
rope restraints. The relief was instant. Andy rubbed at
his sore and aching wrists.

A second later, Andy had the oddest thought. *Who
undid the rope? Fausto? Efren? Whippet? When did it
happen?* One minute he was bound, and the next he
was free. It all took place in blackout time. The gale
forming inside him had blossomed into a hurricane and
was moving past Category 1. Soon it would strengthen,
and it would rage on until it swallowed him whole.

"I need food," Andy said. "I'm diabetic and my
blood sugar is getting low."

"I need two hundred million dollars," Fausto replied
matter-of-factly. "We trade. Money for food. Deal?"

Andy recoiled at the sight of the man's metal mouth,
his bloodstained shirt, and the dried blood knotting his
dark hair. Rippled with sinewy muscle and crowned
with long, flowing hair, Fausto looked to Andy like a
stallion that had trotted through a slaughterhouse.

"I told you, I don't have your money."

Fausto shook his head in exasperation and eyed
Andy contemptuously. "Now I show you something."

Andy expected to see a gun, but instead Fausto produced a Galaxy smartphone with a large screen dis-

play. Next, Andy heard the distinct sound of a video chat request. Fausto was calling somebody, but who? Andy rubbed at his sore wrists and peeled his sweat-soaked shirt from his skin. He loosened his tie. Efren stared coldly at Andy. He was imagining doing things—terrible things, Andy suspected.

The next sound Andy heard was the audio cue indicating somebody had answered Fausto's call. A pleased expression overtook Fausto's face. The killer's smile could freeze the sun. Fausto pulled up a chair and sat facing Andy. Instead of cigarettes, Andy smelled cologne mixed with the coppery scent of blood. From the phone's small speaker Andy heard indistinguishable noises.

"Ponte frente al teléfono. Quiero que el niño te vea la cara," Fausto said.

Andy did not know what that meant, but Fausto repositioned his chair so they could both look at the phone's display. A man's face filled much of the screen. He had a broad forehead, wide and flat nose, and disturbed, deeply set eyes.

"This is my friend. I call him Odio. That means 'hate' in your language," Fausto explained. *"Odio, muéstrale al niño que están allí."*

The phone panned away from Odio's face. The movement turned everything into a blur. But as the motion settled, Andy could make out the shape of a person—no, *persons*—tied to chairs, with gags in their mouths.

Andy recognized the boy right away, even with the blindfold that the boy wore. Gus. A classmate. A chum. The woman he didn't know, but he assumed she was

Gus's mother. The man he'd never seen, though Andy knew he and his friends had robbed him of millions.

Javier Martinez.

Oh, God, what have we done? Andy thought. *What have we done?* It was supposed to be thrills mixed with a message. The Shire never meant to hurt anybody. It was a statement about society, about income inequality. Yes, they all enjoyed the rush of hacking—it was addicting, for sure—but they were also taking a stand for something important, much like the group Anonymous, which used the Internet for justice. Andy founded The Shire on those very principles. He had wanted to send a message, but not this one.

A choice, a terrible misbegotten choice, a break in protocol. Stealing more than the paltry sums the group's charter allowed had spawned a nightmare that stretched far beyond the boundaries of the school. One woman might have been killed. Who she was, Andy couldn't say. A cop? A teacher? He had seen a man bludgeoned to death before his eyes. Two others shot. Andy had no doubt more death was to come.

"Odio, muéstrales a Javier."

The camera went to the man who could move only his head and see only darkness.

"Quítate la venda."

The camera spun erratically, distorting the view until it eventually came to a stop. When it did, the blindfold had come off. Andy could see panic in Javier Martinez's wide eyes. That seemed to please Fausto to no end.

"Busca un taladro."

The camera jiggled again. A few seconds later,

Odio held the camera out at arm's length to show that he had in his possession a power drill.

"Good," Fausto said, now directing his attention to Andy. "Let me explain something. I want to hurt *you* to get my money. But I'm afraid." Fausto chuckled. "Let me explain—I'm not afraid of hurting you. My English, what can I do? I'm afraid you would die, and maybe it's you who has the key."

Andy's ragged breathing made it hard to speak. "Don't you think I'd give it to you if I had it?"

Fausto shrugged. "I do not know. Until I get the money, I must assume any of you could have it. So you have a chance right now to prevent this man—this man who you robbed—from suffering greatly. I don't think you want to hear a man screaming. Do you?"

What did he just say? Andy's world had slipped into the black again. He tried to recall the last few seconds, but they had been erased from time. His blood buzzed. Bit by bit, he felt himself weakening. It came in waves, and would keep lapping against him, until like a sand castle, the whole structure would collapse.

"Here's the deal," Fausto said. "Give me the money. And I don't have Odio drill this man's legs."

Tears gathered in Andy's lower eyelids, distorting his vision even more. "I don't have it. Please don't hurt anyone. Please. We didn't mean for this to happen. We'd give it back to you if we could. Honest."

Fausto shrugged again and looked somewhat annoyed. "'Honest,'" he said, chuckling. "We are *all* thieves, my friend."

Fausto turned the phone so Odio could see him. He nodded. Then Fausto put the phone up to Andy's face. Efren came around behind Andy. He grabbed the sides of Andy's head and forced him to look at the phone. Whippet also came over and made sure Andy wouldn't try to stand. Andy closed his eyes.

"Open your eyes," Fausto said. "Or I will kill them all."

Andy did as he was ordered.

The sound of the drill whirring to life rattled the phone's speaker, distorting the audio.

"One last chance. My money."

"I don't have it," Andy said, whimpering.

The hurricane inside him surged and roiled to Category 2. His arms felt too heavy to lift. His heartbeat came fast. The room slipped in and out of focus. Still, he heard the scream. It was visceral, animal-like—nothing like the scary movies Andy and his friends liked to watch. This sound was also human. It was honest. Andy's blurred world sharpened.

"Open your eyes!" Fausto shouted. "Open them and see what you have done!"

Andy did as he was told.

And he saw.

Chapter 29

Jake stopped at the door of the stairwell and listened. Anybody near the door—or on the opposite side—would hear it open. Patience was key. Slower was better. Excruciatingly slow.

As the head custodian, Jake had made it a point to keep door hinges well oiled and frequently treated them with WD-40. A carryover from his pitching days, where a millimeter adjustment on the laces could mean a strike, Jake paid attention to the little things, the minutiae as well as the big picture.

Satisfied nobody was near, he moved the knob slowly, turning it only as much as necessary. He pried the door open with a gentle tug, holding the knob in place, knowing that the release might make a sound. With the AK-47 in his left hand, Jake only let go of the knob when the door was back in its original position.

He paused. Listened again. Had he given himself away? Hard to be sure. Dim light at this end of the hallway filtered in through a series of windows that overlooked the main quad. Farther down, shadows loomed to create excellent hiding places. Jake was exposed out here, a deer standing in a field of short grass.

The floor above was a mirror of the one below, minus the windows. Classrooms lined both sides of this long corridor. Jake glanced out the window. The grounds were quiet, the campus deserted. But that was misleading. The enemy was here, somewhere in the school, but hidden.

Jake moved out. He entered the classroom closest to him, using the stealth techniques he had practiced into muscle memory. From down the hall came a whistling sound, low tones haunting in the stillness. The whistling morphed into singing. The voice was tuneless, almost drunken. It sounded to Jake like Spanish. He wasn't sure. Hard to tell with the echo. The sound took an irregular route, bouncing off the floor, walls, and ceiling. It was foreign, no doubt. And it was only one person. Good for Jake, bad for the other guy.

Jake poked his head out of the classroom far enough to get a visual. A lone figure, tall and lanky, with short hair, canvas sneakers, dressed in jeans and a green golf shirt, which was sliced with white horizontal stripes, strolled the hallway with his back to Jake. He kept his rifle, an AR-15, slung over his right shoulder as he poked his head in and out of a couple classrooms. He gave each room a cursory inspection at most. Jake got the sense he was here on orders to check out the different floors. Maybe he was looking for stragglers, students who hadn't taken the evacuation order seriously. He probably started at the top and was working his way down. Didn't seem like *he* was taking the job too seriously. He ambled from classroom to classroom, opening doors without caution, poking his head inside, and moving on to the next room. He never raised his weapon. He didn't expect to encounter any threats.

The pattern of movement changed. The man went into one room smack in the middle of the hallway and stayed there. Jake knew exactly which room the guy had gone into, and what he was going to do in there. The time to strike was now.

Hugging the wall, Jake sidled down the hallway. He kept his AK-47 trained on a spot where the man would appear. A lot depended on how long this guy took to go to the bathroom. Jake tried to recall the Spanish words for "drop your weapon." He thought it might be *"baja la pistola,"* but that could be meaningless if the guy spoke Portuguese or Italian.

At the bathroom door, Jake paused. He heard whistling coming from inside, and the sound of a toilet flushing. A surprise attack would give Jake the edge, but should he charge in or ambush the guy in the hallway when he came out? The bathroom might muffle sounds of struggle. Others could be nearby.

Weapon versus weapon—the other guy held the edge. Jake's AK-47 might have been the most common rifle in the world, but the AR-15, best selling in the States, was no slouch. It was longer, weighed less, and could fire off more rounds in a minute than Jake's assault rifle; it came at a cost about double what Jake had paid for his. It was easily 30 percent more accurate at a distance, too, but the advantage was negligible inside a building. It was the kind of weapon used by the ATF in Fast and Furious, the infamous "gunwalking" operation to Mexican drug cartels.

Jake made a couple quick associations. The man's

coloring could make him Latino, and the gun was the weapon of choice with Mexican drug gangs. This guy could be from some cartel. What business a drug cartel could have with a prep school in the middle of nowhere Massachusetts was a question for another time.

Jake put his shoulder to the door and gave it a push. No backing out now. A smart man would have left, given up the mission, retreated, and let the pros do the job. But this was not a question of smarts. It was about living and dying. It was about his son. On the mound, Jake had to be dominant, an alpha male fueled by confidence. *Commit to the pitch.* The door swung open. As it did, Jake, more or less, fell into the second-floor boys' bathroom.

Jake aimed his gun at the first blur of movement he saw. It was the man. He stood at the sink with the water running. Nice. Jake had wanted him occupied. The man whirled in Jake's direction; and as he pivoted, the strap of his AR-15 functioned as a slingshot to propel the weapon right into his waiting hands. He wasn't going to aim. He was going to fire. Spray the walls with bullets. If the AR was converted to fully automatic, it would fire more than nine hundred rounds per minute. He'd hit something, all right—5.56x45 NATO-caliber bullets could shred concrete at this range.

Jake forgot all his Spanish as he squeezed the trigger of his rifle. He exchanged no words, no *"Freeze"* command or *"Drop the weapon"* in any language. No demand to put hands in the air. It was either act or die.

Jake had not converted his AK-47 to fully automatic. He had to pull the trigger separately to get off each round. Long ago, he'd learned not to bump fire;

that was for the movies. While he could leverage the recoil of his semiautomatic to fire multiple shots in rapid succession, accuracy would suffer.

Jake squeezed the trigger. The bang made that characteristic whip-cracking sound, dampened by his earmuffs. Anything traveling faster than 1,100 feet per second at sea level breaks the sound barrier, and the AK-47 fired its bullets at 2,330 fps.

The first bullet from Jake's gun struck the man in the neck, and the second entered the skull through the forehead. Pink mist sprayed out the back of his head. A thick gush of arterial blood spurted sideways from the neck wound like a horizontal geyser.

The man got off a shot, all right—one bullet that smacked into the wall to Jake's right. Poor guy had no brain function to pull the trigger again. Bits of gray matter and bone, mixed with blood, speckled the bathroom floor, which Jake had personally mopped countless times. Somebody else would do this cleanup job.

The man fell backward to the floor. With nothing to brace his fall, the crack when his head hit the floor was profound.

Jake got clear of the door and spun around to engage other threats. Nobody came in. Nobody fired. He backed up a few steps, managing to avoid contact with the dead man, but his feet slipped a little on all the blood. He waited a minute, breathing heavily. Either nobody had heard the shots, or this guy came here alone. Jake relaxed some, and that was when his stomach gave it up. He managed to get to the toilet before all the contents emptied out.

Jake staggered out of the stall and gazed down at the only person he had ever killed. Dead eyes layered with a milky film gazed up at Jake from the floor. The man's neck was pretty much shredded. Jake couldn't see the back of his skull, but that was probably for the best. Blood covered a wide swath of the tiled floor, and the smell was enough to make Jake queasy again. His face felt hot. Skin clammy. He had murdered a man who would have killed him, but that didn't make it an easy thing to do.

Keeping watch over the door, Jake searched for a wallet, lifting the man's body to check each pocket for an ID. Nothing. What Jake did find was a square sheet of paper in the man's front right pocket, folded several times over. Jake's hands trembled as he unfolded the paper, and his eyes went wide when he saw the contents.

It was a map of the school campus. Someone had drawn lines through the Terry Science Center and the library, and Gibson Hall. This man had checked those buildings, Jake believed. And he was here in the Society Building doing the same. He was working counterclockwise, going from building to building. After the Society Building, he'd have to clear the dormitories and dining hall. Smaller buildings were dotted around, too. None of those buildings had any markings on them. Dead guy hadn't cleared them yet. The campus could become confusing, but the man made sure he would have no trouble getting back to his colleagues. Around the image of the Academy Building, somebody had drawn a big circle. It might as well have been an *x* to mark the spot.

Jake knew where to look for his son.

Chapter 30

Leo Haggar, the FBI's special agent in charge of the hostage crisis, commandeered the largest conference room at the Winston PD for his team's tactical-operations center. Lining the walls were maps of Winston and Pepperell Academy, adorned with pushpins to denote the location and type of assets deployed. More than a hundred feet were on the ground, and that number would grow. Haggar's Red Unit mobilized to this sleepy little hamlet in excellent time.

The Red, Blue, and Gold Units comprised the three tactical teams that formed the FBI's HRT. These units were part of the tactical-support branch of the FBI's Critical Incident Response Group (CIRG). They were the elite of the elite, a national SWAT team that trained for the most dangerous missions.

Even at fifty-five, Haggar could blend in just fine with the supremely well-conditioned men under his command. He had close-cropped salt-and-pepper hair, broad shoulders, and a thick waist to support his powerful legs. If Haggar had a spirit animal, it would most certainly be a silverback gorilla, which also shared his fierce disposition. His face was square, with creases that ran the length of his forehead. A pair of frosty blue eyes gave the distinct impression that Agent Haggar was never truly pleased, which was often the case. Two long lines framed a dimpled chin and seemed to pull his mouth into a permanent scowl. No doubt about it: Leo Haggar was an intimidating presence even when he wasn't wearing his bulletproof FBI tactical gear.

Haggar had been at home, helping his teenage son with pitching mechanics, when his boss called to report a hostage crisis at a prep school.

There was a threat of a dirty bomb, and Haggar knew he'd soon initiate deployment protocols of his Red Unit.

His son's coaching would have to wait.

The motto of HRT was *"Servare Vitas"* ("To Save Lives") and Haggar focused on the most pressing challenge: how to neutralize the threat and retrieve the hostages unharmed. No simple task—but if anybody could do it, it would be HRT.

The elite force had evolved from a simple observation made in the late 1970s, after then-FBI Director William Webster watched a demonstration of the capabilities of the U.S. Army's Delta Force. Webster asked why the men didn't carry any restraints.

"The dead don't need handcuffs," a Delta operator had replied.

The two dozen or so highly trained hostage-rescue specialists included fearsome assault and sniper teams. Two helicopters from the Tactical Helicopter Unit (THU), a Bell 412EP and UH-60M Black Hawk, were parked at the same private airfield where the transport plane carrying the HRT forces had landed. From there, it was only a short drive to Winston, and the state police used a convoy of tactical-response vehicles to help get the Red Unit into position.

Jurisdiction was no longer a question. The state and local police were on hand to lend support, but this was the FBI's show. The HRT's credentials were unchallenged. Only a handful of special agents made it through the rigorous selection process, which included eight months of intensive training before their first mission deployment. They were skilled in tactics, firearms, and, most important, teamwork. This mission, it seemed, would tax every one of those disciplines to the extreme.

So far, Agent Haggar was not about to take any chances. He commandeered forces already deployed; and following the hostage taker's instructions, he established a perimeter two kilometers from the school. It was not an impossible distance for a highly skilled sniper equipped with a long-range rifle. But the sight lines were terrible unless they moved closer, which risked exposure. And even if they took out one of the targets, there was no telling how many others were holed up inside the school. The campus had at least thirty buildings. The targets could be spread out in different buildings, and any of them could possess the ability to trigger the bomb.

Specially equipped aircraft were already scanning the nearby area for radioactive signatures, but that process was a bit like finding the haystack so they could then go looking for a needle. They needed more information. Who were these people? Terrorists? If so, why did they take students as hostages? And which students did they take?

A roll call was in process to account for all of the students, but the effort was proving cumbersome. Some of the students were legitimately away; others might have gone home rather than to the designated evacuation zone; still, others might have taken advantage of the free time to roam and play. It was a sloppy evacuation process from Haggar's point of view, and it could be hours before they had a definitive list of hostages.

At least for the moment, nobody was going near the school until Haggar had more information. He had been involved in several lengthy hostage barricades, and understood they could be physically and mentally challenging. Haggar knew they were in for the long haul.

A knock on the door drew Haggar's attention. Ellie Barnes entered in her police uniform, while Haggar was dressed for war. Haggar had been expecting this visit. Ellie's boss, William Bladd, the chief of police for the Town of Winston, had arranged the meeting. He told Haggar that Ellie was one of his best cops, and she evidently had some vital information to share.

Haggar shook Ellie's hand and invited her to sit down. Ellie spent a moment standing, gawking at the array of maps and intel wallpapering the room.

"It doesn't mean shit," Haggar said. "Looks impressive, but it's nothing. This is the first minutes. When we're done, all that will matter are the results. Freed hostages, a defused bomb, and no dead except maybe for the assholes who did this."

"Understood," Ellie said. "Do we have any idea who these people are?"

Haggar's mouth dipped into a sour frown. "No clue. We have a team at Quantico analyzing the voice recordings. All I can tell you right now is the guy who called in the threat sounded Mexican. So what do you got for me?"

Haggar moved a chair so Ellie could take a seat.

"I called in a concern I had about the ex-husband of the woman who was shot."

Haggar glanced down at his notes. "Laura Collins, is that right?"

"Yes. I'm—I'm friends with Jake Dent, Laura's ex."

"And you were concerned because why?"

"Because I thought Jake might do something in retaliation for what happened to Laura. He was also worried that his son was missing, and he couldn't get in touch with several of his son's friends."

"Does he think his son is a hostage?"

"It's definitely a concern."

"Have you given those names over to our team? The son's friends, I mean."

Ellie nodded. "Yes, of course. I told my lieutenant and he said he'd relay the information to the FBI."

That intel hadn't made it to Haggar. A clog in the pipeline he'd clear by ripping somebody a new asshole.

"Jake Dent—do you know where he is now?"

"That's the thing," Ellie said. "I can't get in touch with him. Before your team got here, I brought up my concern about Jake to the state police and they sent two detectives to follow him."

Haggar scowled. He should have been briefed. The size of the asshole he was going to rip just grew. "Did they find anything?"

"Not to my knowledge," Ellie said.

Haggar got on his phone and within minutes got an earful from a detective about being left on a lengthy stakeout for what was certainly a dead end. Jake Dent had gone into his home hours ago and nobody had come out. They even canvassed the woods behind his house. The car was there, TV was on, and the shades were drawn. Haggar didn't like that one bit. He knew nothing about Jake Dent, but he did know something about being a dad.

"Try to coax him out for a chat. Hell, see if he's even there for goodness sake," Haggar barked into the phone. There was a pause while Haggar listened to some response. "Call me back when you get some useful information," Haggar said before ending the call.

"We can go in other ways," Ellie suggested. She was tiptoeing on a line that wasn't frequently crossed. The FBI was a stickler for rules and procedures—in part because the organization operated under the microscope of media scrutiny, but also because they were tasked with upholding the law, not breaking it.

"I'll get a warrant if it comes to it," Haggar said. "In the meantime, I'm going to learn everything about Jake Dent that's possible to know."

Chapter 31

Fausto brought the teens back to the auditorium. His expression had changed. The playful glint in his eyes was gone. The cat that had been toying with a cornered mouse seemed to have grown tired of its game. Fausto sat all six members of The Shire in the front row. The kids were no longer tied up, gagged, or blindfolded. Fausto had terrorized them enough so they wouldn't attempt anything foolish, he believed. The dead bodies were off the stage; the lifeless forms of El Gallo and the two other cartel members had been dumped through a trapdoor. Normally, the door was used for theatrical productions, but in this case it functioned as a quick disposal mechanism.

Andy sat at the end of the row, next to Hilary. Beside Hilary sat Solomon, followed by Rafa, then David, and last Pixie. Fausto, Efren, and Armando, whose scars were more apparent under the harsh glare of the theater lights, clustered onstage, talking in Spanish. Four of the cartel sat in the row behind the teens with their weapons resting on their laps. One guard was posted at the door. There would be no tolerating another surprise visitor.

Andy's legs bounced up and down continuously, and the rest of him—arms, neck, head—had trouble keeping still. He sweated as if he were hot, but shook as if he were freezing. Hilary took hold of Andy's hand, linking her fingers with his, making an effort to settle him. Andy ripped his hand away and flashed Hilary an angry look.

"Don't touch me," he whispered in a harsh, scolding tone. "I don't want to be touched."

His speech came out thick, the words a bit slurred. At first, Hilary was offended, but almost as quickly she understood. She saw all the symptoms. Andy had educated The Shire, his closest friends, about what to look for in the event he hadn't managed his blood sugar properly. He was irritable, sweating profusely, and not speaking clearly. There were progressive stages of hypoglycemia, and Hilary believed Andy was past the point where food would work fast enough. He needed his glucose tablets, more likely an injection of glucagon. She knew he kept an emergency kit in his backpack at all times. Andy clutched his stomach as though he was going to be sick, and he couldn't quiet the shaking in his arms and legs.

"What's your blood sugar level?" Hilary whispered to Andy.

"Gonna kill Whippet. Gonna kill him," Andy breathed out the words.

Hilary saw that Andy's gaze was locked on an exceedingly thin man with just a trace of a mustache, guarding the door and brandishing a gun sleek as he was. To her eyes, he did, in fact, resemble a whippet—lean and muscular.

"Calla la boca," Tornado, with the frizzy hair, scolded.

Hilary ignored him. Same as she had ignored the scar-faced man who had interrogated her, groped her, insulted her, and threatened her. There was nothing else she could do. Every answer was the same: "I don't have the money," even when they showed her the video feed of poor Javier.

"Your backpack with your medicine, Andy. Where is it?"

"Backpack," Andy managed.

El Tornado yanked on Hilary's hair hard, wrenching her head back and snapping her neck so hard she yowled.

"¡Cállate!" he said. "Shut up!"

Fausto, drawn to the commotion, looked displeased. He stepped to the front of the stage and spread his arms in a dramatic gesture.

"We have spoken to each of you individually," he said in a booming voice. "You have all seen the pain you caused Javier Martinez, father of your classmate. I cannot drill another hole without killing him, and, sadly, I need him alive. I showed you the horror of me and yet you still do not cooperate. I take this as a personal failing. I am deeply disappointed in myself. I admit this. But I do not give up easily. So I try something new to inspire you."

Fausto exited to his right, leaving Efren and Armando alone on the stage. The enforcers chattered among themselves, and Hilary used the distraction to lean into

Andy. "Your medicine," she whispered. "Where is your backpack?"

Andy's head rolled onto his chest. Hilary could tell it was an effort for him just to lift it. His blinking turned rapid. Reaching across her body, Hilary touched Andy's chest and could feel his heart mimicking the pace of his fluttering eyes.

Fausto returned to the stage, brandishing a massive knife, more like a machete. "Who here has been to a pig roast before?" he asked.

One of the enforcers raised his hand.

Fausto glowered at him from the stage. *"¡No, pendejo!"* he barked. "Not you, the kids. *Los malditos.* Who here has been to a pig roast before?"

No hands went up this time. Fausto came to the front of the stage.

"Please, Andy, you're sick," Hilary whispered again. "Where is your backpack?"

Andy strained to make eye contact. His head bobbed up and down as if he were going for an apple inside an invisible tub of water.

Fausto hesitated, scanning the front row. His gaze settled on Solomon. "You, fat one. Come up here."

Solomon shrank in his seat. He looked to his left and right as if perhaps a different Solomon had entered the room. Fausto brushed the hair off his face so his eyes could be seen and his intent understood. He was in no mood for delay tactics.

"Bring the fat one to me," Fausto commanded.

Two of the enforcers, Una Mano and El Cortador, rose from their seats and came around to the front row. Each took one of Solomon's arms and with effort hoisted him to his feet. They dragged him to the stage and up a short flight of stairs, with Solomon whimpering the whole way. Once they got him onstage, the pair shoved Solomon hard from behind. He stumbled as he lurched forward, arms whirling for balance before he dropped to his knees.

Fausto seized a clump of Solomon's hair and hoisted him back to his feet. Next he set the sharp edge of the machete's blade against Solomon's meaty throat.

"I explain now how I gut a pig," Fausto said. "Again, my English, I'm sorry. But my machete speak a different language. One I think you all understand."

Terror flooded Solomon's eyes. His breathing turned shallow and he began to make strangled noises from deep in his throat as his whole body shook.

Hilary's attention vacillated between poor Solomon and the boy she loved. "Please, Andy, answer me," she said.

The man with angry eyes, the one she'd heard Fausto call El Mata Padres—Father Killer—leaned over and bathed her face with his hot and sour breath.

"Quiet and listen," he said.

From the stage, Fausto continued with his demonstration. "First," he said, "you must put the pig on its back."

With a sweep of his leg, Fausto knocked Solomon off his feet. Solomon hit the stage floor and let out a cry of complete surprise. He opened his mouth to gasp for air, flopping about like a fish tossed on a dock. Annoyed, Fausto stepped on Solomon's chest to hold him still, but his writhing continued. David and Rafa lowered their heads. They could not bear to watch. But Pixie fixed his gaze on Fausto. If Fausto's men took notice, they would have seen something change inside the smallest member of The Shire. Hatred now—not fear.

"With the pig on the ground," Fausto said, "you clean off the hair using a knife." Fausto directed his attention to Solomon. "Now don't move, piggy, or you will get hurt." Fausto pulled up Solomon's shirt and exposed a fleshy midsection dimpled with fat. Efren pinned Solomon's arms over his head. Working slowly, Fausto scraped the blade of the machete against Solomon's stomach, using a long stroke in a languid, fluid motion. There was no blood. Fausto applied no real pressure, but the machete produced the same scraping sound a shaving razor makes as it glides over the skin.

Solomon began to whimper. "I want my mom," he said in a strangled voice. "I want my mom."

Fausto ignored him. "When that is done, you hang the piggy upside down." He motioned for Efren and Armando to hoist Solomon up.

Solomon might have weighed 225 pounds, but those two lifted him as if he were filled with feathers. They had an equally easy time flipping him upside down to hold him by his legs. Solomon's face turned beet red as blood flooded his brain. Strands of hair gently kissed the stage floor like the bristles of a broom. Coins and gum wrappers tumbled out of his pants pockets, and Solomon's shirt fell down to cover part of his face.

Solomon's whimpers turned to sobs. "Please let me go," he begged. "Please let me go." Each word blended into the next, in one long and desperate plea.

Fausto stood to the side, not wanting to block the

view of those in the audience. He turned his attention back to Solomon and set the machete blade between the boy's trembling legs.

"Don't kick too much, young one," Fausto warned in a soft voice, which grew louder as he again addressed his audience. "Next you cut the ass—how do you say, *el ano*—ah, yes, the anus. You make a big hole here to rip out the insides. And this you tie off with string."

During the grisly demonstration, Andy appeared dazed and had almost no reaction to anything taking place. He rolled his head forward and yanked it back like he was trying to stay awake. Forward. Back. Repeat.

With growing alarm, Hilary put her fingers under Andy's chin and turned his head to face her. His clammy skin felt slick and unpleasantly cool to the touch. His eyes held a vacant and empty stare.

"I'll get my homework done," Andy muttered to himself. "Just stop bugging me, Dad."

"Andy, you're not at home. You're here at school," Hilary whispered. "You've got to tell me where your backpack is. What room did they bring you to?"

He needed the glucagon injection, not food. Hilary was certain of it.

"Darkness," Andy mumbled. "Darkness."

Hilary let go and Andy's head flopped down until his chin rested on his chest. This time, when Andy tried to lift his head, he lacked strength. So he closed his eyes and rested.

"Don't go to sleep, Andy," Hilary pleaded. "Stay awake. Tell me which room."

Hilary thought maybe she could talk Fausto into giving her Andy's backpack. Perhaps use the same tactic Andy had used before. If Andy had the key, he could not die. It was that simple. But it was increasingly clear to Hilary that nobody had the key. If that was true, the one bit of leverage they had would be gone, and soon they all would be dead.

Hilary looked right and saw tears streaming down David's face. While Rafa hid his face in his hands, his body convulsed, and it was obvious his tears were falling as well. But Hilary had other concerns that trumped poor Solomon's torture, a need far more pressing.

"You've got to help him," Hilary cried out. "He needs his medicine or he'll die."

Fausto stopped his demonstration and redirected his smoldering gaze onto Hilary. He pointed his machete at Andy as if it were an extension of his hand. "That one, I believe, does not have the key," he said. "He is your leader. I know all about leaders. They are not selfish. They sacrifice for the good. If he had the key, he would have given it to us. So now he's expendable. And if you interrupt me again, *hija,* you become expendable, too.

"Listen to me, all. Your time here is running very, very short. Is it clear? Because what I'm doing to this pig now, I do for real on each of you. You will feel it all. Every bit of pain I can make happen. And I will take my time. Now, where were we?" Fausto put the tip of the blade against Solomon's belly. "Yes," he said. "You have to cut the belly and chest." Fausto traveled the tip of the blade from Solomon's navel up to his throat. He kept his eyes on David and Rafa the entire time. "You must be careful not to puncture the intestines, but once the little piggy is opened up, you pull all the muck out into a bucket."

Fausto raised the machete over his head like an executioner. Solomon saw this and squirmed to get away, but Efren and Armando held him in place. Generating incredible force, Fausto brought the blade down toward Solomon's head.

David rose to his feet and screamed, "Nooooo!" The timbre of his voice shook the room. But instead of flesh and bone, the tip of Fausto's blade sank harmlessly into the floor inches from Solomon's ear. David bowed his head and again sobbed.

Rafa stood and pointed at David. "He's got it! He has the key!"

Hilary let her attention drift from Andy to David; if this were true, it changed everything.

"No, I don't," David said. David's shirt was untucked, tie dangling, but he pushed back his long hair as if trying to look more dignified.

"You do! You do!" Rafa insisted. "Give it to them now. I don't want to die. Just do it, David."

At last, a smile crested on Fausto's face. "Bring them both to me," he said, pointing to the teen boys.

El Mata Padres and Tornado rose from their seats and came around to escort Rafa and David onto the stage. The boys went willingly, heads bowed, like death row inmates en route to the gas chamber, each resigned to his fate. One guard remained at the door— the thin one Andy called Whippet—while the rest of them came onstage.

Hilary took notice. The odds of sneaking out of the

auditorium to go on a hunting expedition had greatly improved. Still, she did not know where to go looking.

Andy muttered the word "darkness" over and over to himself. The word came out slurred. Hilary thought maybe he'd said "parkness" or "markness." Neither word meant anything. And yet it was important because Andy kept repeating it.

Hilary tried to decipher what Andy might be saying by trying to form words that sounded like "darkness." She started with *A—"arkness," B—"barkness," C— "carkness,"* and so on. She did this effortlessly and quickly until she got to *H,* when she stopped the mental exercise altogether.

H—"Harkness."

And Hilary knew exactly where to look.

Chapter 32

Pepperell Academy's extensive tunnel system connected most campus buildings. Some of the tunnels were extremely narrow and hot, while others offered enough space to walk side by side.

Jake made his way through one of the narrow sections beneath the library, not his favorite by any stretch. His boots scuffed noisily against the rough concrete, the tap of his heels amplified by damp stone. Creatures scurried in the darkness. Rats, probably, but mice and moles lived down here, too. Jake was in charge of extermination and he kept the pests mostly under control, but not entirely. The clicks and scrapes of their clawed feet came at him from all directions. It was impossible to pinpoint a location in the dark.

Cables running above Jake's head served as conduits for electrical and communication systems. Pipes of various thicknesses affixed to the walls with rusted metal brackets carried water and heat throughout the campus, and emitted a steady hum that became background noise. Some of the pipes leaked water that rhythmically punctured the eerie stillness in this other-worldly darkness.

At the spot where Jake could turn right or backtrack, he went right. The low ceiling forced him to stoop, but he kept a steady pace. Here the mildew smell was most intense, but it couldn't make him forget the stench of fresh blood from the bathroom homicide. That smell overpowered all present odors, and those vacant eyes seemed to watch his every step.

To see in the dark, Jake used a headlamp secured to the front of his tactical helmet by an adjustable piece of stretchable nylon. He had left the PVS-14 with the J-arm attachment back in the larder. Night vision worked by magnifying existing light, and down here there was none. Jake could have turned on the overheads, but the fuse boxes were decentralized and mostly aboveground. He didn't want to risk exposure by going to the surface. The headlamp worked fine. He could shut it off easily, and it freed his hands to let him traverse obstacles while wielding a weapon.

He kept his AK-47 slung over his right shoulder. In the cramped confines of the tunnels, it was far easier to maneuver his Glock than a long rifle.

The jouncing white light of the headlamp formed a portal in the gloom through which Jake could make his way. The way could be confusing. Enthusiasts circulated maps around campus to try and illustrate the various entrances to tunnels, but Jake found most renderings woefully incomplete. The real tunnels looked more like the schematic for a complicated piece of circuitry than a bunch of straight lines between buildings. Tunnels went in straight, curved, and diagonal lines. Some terminated in dead ends; others looped back like snakes consuming their own tails. This was a maze belowground, and it was easy to become disoriented and lost.

Jake crawled over a series of corroded pipes that looked like a pile of giant pickup sticks blocking the archway ahead. His guns and gear restricted his movement, and Jake needed to compensate for the extra weight. As he climbed down, Jake's footing slipped and he staggered forward a few steps. His face bristled with stickiness: cobwebs. With his left hand, Jake cleared the webbing from his mouth and eyes, and brushed off a large spider, which had crawled across the nape of his neck.

He was accustomed to the tactile sensations down here. There was always something new to discover, to observe. This section of tunnel looked to him like the innards of a dying machine. Everything here was sagging, corroded, or rusty. Wires barely clung to decaying fasteners and dangled perilously close to pools of brown water. Jake kept his eye out for markers—spray-painted letter and number codes on the walls that served as trail guides. His predecessors had put them there and it helped with navigation if you knew what they meant.

School officials downplayed the extent of the tunnel system to keep interest in them to a minimum. Nobody wanted kids underground getting wasted or having sex around dangerous electrical equipment, hot pipes, or chemicals.

Students caught lurking in the bowels of The Pep faced immediate expulsion. That was generally deterrent enough to keep them out. But from time to time,

Jake would come across wrappers and beer cans, even fresh graffiti scrawled on the cement walls. Denying access invited plenty of brazen daredevils. Over the years, various communities of underground explorers had sprung up with the expressed goal of getting in and roaming about just for kicks. It was Jake's responsibility to keep them out.

The truth was, nobody came down here much anymore. A lot of effort went into making the maintenance work accessible aboveground—at fuse boxes, AVC controllers, boilers, and various circuits. Sections of the tunnel system had once served as pedestrian thoroughfares, but those had been shut down ages ago. The important thing now was that Jake could travel from building to building without ever seeing daylight. Without ever being seen.

At the end of a particularly claustrophobic stretch, Jake came to a stop at another arched passageway. His headlamp lit up a wider and higher section of tunnel beyond. *Good thing.*

The tunnels reminded Jake of the ball fields. The transition from corridor to dugout always put a smile on his face. It was the feeling a butterfly must have after crawling through its hard shell to take flight at last. Emerging from the darkness to catch that first glimpse of an emerald-green field was a joy like no other. Tunnels were a means to that end; and for this reason, Jake took to them just fine. But these narrower passageways, with the low ceilings and compressed walls, were as pleasant as giving up five runs in the second inning.

Jake had a sudden recollection about baseball that

involved Andy. His son was eleven at the time, maybe twelve, and Jake was teaching him how to throw left-handed.

The ball had sailed in every direction but the one Andy had intended, with little velocity, either.

"This is a stupid waste of time," Andy said.

"Throwing with your nondominant arm is good for building a balanced body," Jake said. "Besides, you've got a better chance of going pro if you're a southpaw."

Jake was naturally bilateral, but he threw right and rarely worked his other arm.

"I'm never going to make the pros," Andy said.

"You can do anything you set your mind to, son," Jake said, almost reflexively.

Andy had guffawed. "That's a load of horse crap, Dad, and you know it," he said. "But I should clarify. I don't *want* to be a pro baseball player."

Andy had gone into his windup and threw the base-ball left-handed, hard, using all the proper mechanics this time. The ball had sailed straight and had gone fast enough to make a pleasing slap, once it hit the leather of Jake's glove.

Even then, his kid had attitude.

"So, what are you going to be when you grow up?" Jake asked, tossing the ball back to Andy.

"I dunno. Guess we'll just have to wait and find out."

"Wait and find out."

Andy's diabetes made that statement a lot less certain. It was especially true given the wild swings Andy's blood sugar could take. But Jake never believed the disease would claim his son. And that belief carried over into today.

After passing through the archway, Jake stood, giving some relief to his cramped leg muscles. Fifteen feet farther, the tunnel branched to his right. That way would bring him to a staircase. From there, Jake could gain entry to the basement boiler room in the Terry Science Center.

He wanted to call Ellie, and probably could get a signal there, but decided to wait. He was close to the Academy Building, close to Andy, his purpose for being here. He pressed on ahead. Somewhere behind him, the rats began to scurry.

At one point, Jake had to crawl again. To get from one section of tunnel to another, he had to pass through a square opening at the bottom of a concrete wall. The fit was very narrow, and Jake squeezed through on his belly. He emerged into a new section of tunnel, with high ceilings and updated electrical and data cables. And then, the stairs. A lot of the yellow paint had chipped away, but the railings were sturdy and the steps safe to climb.

At the top landing, using his master key, Jake unlocked a steel door painted gunmetal gray. He pushed the door open and stepped into a janitor's closet in the basement of the Academy Building. He had his AK-47 ready to do the talking for him, just in case.

No need. The closet was empty. He pushed a bucket and mop out of the way, clearing a path to the closet's front door. He stopped and listened. Not a sound. Fine. Just to be sure, Jake put an ear against the bottom of the door to give another listen. Each cup on his Peltor earmuffs had a built-in microphone, receiver, and amplifier that provided an adjustable 19dBA sound gain. All was silent. The tunnels were louder than this. Jake opened the door and exited the closet.

He worked his way out of the basement and up to the first floor of the Academy Building. The school was weekend quiet. No people. No lights. No sound. The tunnel ran directly below the stage in the Feldman Auditorium and went the length of the building. If he had to, Jake would go outside and scope the building's perimeter to try and pinpoint the enemy's location.

He returned to the closet. Without several feet of stone in the way, Jake could get a signal there. He didn't want to risk being overheard in the hallways. Ellie's number was stored in Jake's list of favorites, where she belonged.

His mind clicked over and Jake thought for a moment of something other than Andy. He thought of Ellie. It happened in a flash, but the message his brain was sending had come in, loud and clear. Once this was over, things between him and Ellie would be different.

It was an odd time for these thoughts, but Jake didn't fight it. He had messed up with Ellie, kept too many secrets, but he could make amends. He'd tell her everything about his life, about his fears. He'd open up to her in ways he never could with Laura. He'd grieve for Laura openly; and in Ellie's presence, he'd find comfort.

On the mound, Jake believed that most everything was within his control. *Throw strikes. Keep the ball away from a hitter's sweet spot. Do your job and get the out.* It was away from baseball that things became more complex. But Jake was going to tell Ellie who he was and how he felt, regardless of the consequences. All he could do was throw the best pitch possible.

He slipped the ear protectors to one side. Ellie answered on the first ring. He heard panic in her voice. "Jake, where are you?"

"Trying to find my son."

"But where?"

"I need to make sure Andy is all right. And after I do, I'm going to need your help."

"Jake, it's not that simple."

"I'm going to tell you where these guys are, and you're going to send in the troops."

"Jake, what is going on? Where are you?"

"I'll call you back," he said. "I'm not going to have a signal where I'm headed."

"Jake, please," Ellie said. "If you're where I think you are, you need to get out of there right away. Jake, are you hearing me? *Jake?* Are you there?"

Jake headed down the stairs with the phone pressed to his ear. He would let the rock walls disconnect the call, as he couldn't bring himself to do it.

As he descended back into the darkness, Jake's mind conjured up the smell of Ellie's hair and Kibo's fur. They brought feelings of home and belonging, and finally something took away the scent of blood.

Chapter 33

Ellie put away her phone and set her gaze once again on Jake's trailer home. A sizable contingent from the Winston Police Department was there, along with vehicles from the FBI, and the state police, too. From the number of strobes flashing, anyone would think Jake was a fugitive killer and the target of an unprecedented manhunt.

Leo Haggar came over to Ellie with a hostile look she knew was not directed toward her. It was just Haggar's natural mystique.

"That was him," Ellie said.

Haggar's eyes narrowed. "Did he give his location?"

"No," Ellie said. "But I think he's in the school."

Haggar whistled and one of his agents, a fit woman in a blue uniform and body armor, came running over.

"Everyone is in position to enter the premises. Are we still waiting for a warrant?"

"Forget the warrant," Haggar barked. "Get in there ASAP. It's my call, and I'm saying this guy will further endanger the hostages. I want to know everything there is to know about him. What he reads when he's taking a dump. Where he shops. Who he's screwing. Everything. And have forensics in there with you to secure all of the electronics. I don't want a single byte of data lost. Got it?"

"Yes, sir."

The agent turned on her heels to go, but Haggar whistled her back around. "And I want to see the blueprints to the school again. Hell, I think I have them memorized by this point, but have somebody get them to me anyway," Haggar said.

The agent acknowledged the order with a nod and was off again.

"I'll try to call him back," Ellie said. Her voice came out too soft, too weak, too damn emotional.

Haggar's ears must have been tuned to a different frequency, one that picked up subtext like it was amplified, because he gave Ellie a knowing glance.

"You might not know what he's reading on the can," Haggar said, "but I think you can tell me who Jake is screwing."

Ellie's face reddened. The twinkle in Haggar's eyes surprised her.

"It's okay," Haggar said. "I already figured. But now you can tell me more."

Ellie set her hands on her hips, pursed her lips, and looked to the sky. A constricting lump blocked her throat, and everything about Jake hit her at once: the blue of his eyes, the swagger in his smile, a scent sweet as his personality, a touch aware of her needs, the firmness of his body when he lay on top of her, the feel of him inside when she was on top. She loved Jake, but those words had never left her lips. Instead, they had tumbled about in her head, ready to spill out the moment he said it first.

If he'd opened up to her more fully, those three magical words would have come out faster than Kibo could chase down a stick. But Jake Dent had more secrets than he had shared with her the night of their big talk. And Ellie had a sinking feeling whatever they were would be found inside that trailer.

"Talk to me, Ellie," Haggar said. "This guy is a real threat to our operation. We're talking thousands of people potentially getting sick here from radioactive fallout if that bomb goes off. Not to mention the number of would-be terrorists an incident like that would embolden. Your guy is a match to that bomb's fuse and I'm going to snuff it out, one way or another. Help me do it without spilling any blood."

Ellie took a breath and told Haggar the story, beginning with her meeting Jake at the gun range and concluding with the details she had only recently learned.

Haggar listened with rapt attention. Despite the crisis unfolding around him, he had a remarkable ability to tune out the world and focus on whatever he deemed most important. Jake Dent was evidently very important to Haggar.

"Can you talk him out of there?" Haggar asked.

"I sure as hell can try," Ellie said.

"I have seasoned hostage negotiators on hand who can help," Haggar said. "Will you be willing to do whatever it takes?"

"Anything," Ellie said.

The FBI agent Haggar had sent off to retrieve the school blueprints came running over with them in hand.

She had an electric look in her eyes; Ellie guessed they had dug up something of vital importance.

"Sir, you should come inside right away. I think we have a serious problem on our hands."

Someone handed Ellie a pair of gloves. She put them on as she followed Haggar into Jake's trailer. This was not how she'd imagined being invited into his home, but here she was.

Ellie looked around and saw only a devoted dad doing his best to provide for his son, to create a home— but the light was dim and rather depressing, the walls were paneled wood and dark, the quarters cramped, and the furniture all looked secondhand.

Despite this, Ellie had to admire Jake for his effort. Being a single parent under any circumstance was not easy; and in addition to the worry over Andy's diabetes, Jake's salary could not have been very much. The trailer was not the ideal place to raise a child, but Jake had spruced it up by filling the home with photographs of a father and a son, memories of good times together, two people making a go of it best they could.

Seven or so gloved agents began tearing the place apart and their combined body heat turned the trailer sauna hot. For Ellie, it was as difficult to breathe as it was to move. A special agent, tall and dark-haired, greeted Haggar in the living room and led him and Ellie down a narrow hallway. Ellie excused herself to push by the crush of agents engaged in a carefully orchestrated demolition of Jake's life.

The agent escorted Ellie and Haggar to Jake's bedroom. He had the same excited look as the woman who had summoned them into the trailer.

"What do we got?" Haggar asked.

"Guns and a whole lot of crazy," the agent said.

He opened a closet and cleared away some clothes to reveal a gun rack with five secured rifles, only two of which Ellie recognized as a Browning and a Remington.

"So he's a hunter," Haggar said. "These weapons all look properly secured to me. And they're not on his person, so that's another plus."

"That's what I said, until we found this."

From within the closet, the agent removed a large backpack secured to an ALICE frame and brought it over to the bed. He opened the pack, tipped it over, and dumped out the contents. He took more stuff from various zipped-up pouches.

Ellie studied the items with growing unease. On the bed were several liters of water, a filtration system, clothing, a tent, a tarp, a sleeping bag, cooking gear, and a hygiene kit. It would have all made sense to her, except Jake had never mentioned a love of camping. Somebody who loved camping enough to own this kind of gear would have talked about it, she believed.

He unzipped another pouch. What he pulled out made Ellie shiver: a SIG SAUER P226, with ammo to go with it. Most campers Ellie knew carried a whistle to scare away the bears, not a high-caliber pistol.

Haggar eyed the items. "So he's an outdoorsman who doesn't want to be mugged in the woods," he said. "I'm still not concerned."

The agent said, "Yeah? Just wait."

The agent removed from the closet a twenty-gallon plastic tote with an attached lid. He set the tote on the floor by the bed and took off the lid. The agent pulled out from the tote a tactical helmet with a J-arm attachment, which Ellie suspected accommodated a night vision optical. They took more items out of the container and piled them on the bed: ammo, laminated maps, several large knives, a compass, green Kevlar line, wire, duct tape, magnifying glasses, handcuffs, body armor, satellite phone, batons, and lots of books.

Their titles made Ellie's stomach sink. She focused on a few of the meatier tomes: *Surviving the End of the World*, *After the Fall: How Doomsday Preppers Will Look Like Prophets*, *The A–Z of Prepping*, and *Get Ready for the End of the World*, whose title left little doubt about its contents.

"I'm not a profiler, sir," the agent said with a gleam in his eyes. "But it seems we've got a loose cannon. This guy thinks the world is coming to an end, and I suspect he's armed to do battle."

Ellie watched the color drain from Haggar's face and guessed hers had done the same. Heartbreaking as it was, without a doubt, Ellie knew this was the real secret Jake had been guarding.

Haggar unfolded the blueprints and spread them out on the bed, covering Jake's survival gear like a blanket. He studied the plans thoughtfully; then he looked to Ellie.

"Does Jake Dent know how to access all the tunnels at the school?"

Ellie said, "He never said anything to me, but he's in charge of maintenance, so I suspect there's a good chance he does."

Haggar whistled long and low. "If that's the case, our problem just got a whole lot bigger."

Chapter 34

David and Rafa squared off onstage like martial arts combatants gearing up for battle. Their heads were bowed, eyes to the floor. Fausto stood behind the pair with one hand perched on each boy's trembling shoulder. He looked supremely satisfied.

"So," Fausto said, eyeing Rafa, "your friend here has the key, you say?"

David lifted his head and pulled his long hair back from his face to fix Rafa with a furious stare.

"He has it," Rafa said. "I know it's him."

"I do not," David said through gritted teeth. "How do I know you didn't take it?"

Rafa bellowed, "Because I didn't!"

David craned his neck to look at Solomon, who cowered on the floor, shaking like the last leaf of autumn. "I just want to go home," Solomon said. "I just want to go home."

Without warning, Rafa leaned forward and shoved David hard in the chest. David tried to hold his ground, but staggered a few steps back.

"Don't be a coward," Rafa said, panting out the

words. His sweat-drenched face crinkled with a look of utter contempt. "They're going to kill us if you don't give it to them. So give it up now."

"I told you, I don't have it!" David screamed back. He lunged forward and gave Rafa an equally hard shove.

The attack took Rafa by surprise, and he lurched backward before regaining his footing. David and Rafa went at each other simultaneously, clinched, and began to wrestle with neither gaining much advantage over the other. They gripped each other's shirts as they spun around haplessly.

Fausto could not have looked more pleased. He pulled the machete out of the stage floor and raised the blade level with his shoulders as he lifted his arms. For a moment, he looked like a crazed conductor about to guide a symphony with a brutish, oversized wand. His mouth parted into a twisted grin and the metal inside caught the stage lights.

"Boys, boys," Fausto said, lowering his weapon. "I say you fix this problem like men."

Rafa ignored Fausto. His determination to get David's confession had become its own presence in the room. "You're a liar, David. A big, fat liar!"

"He's not fat, really," Fausto said in a semi-serious tone while he appraised David, his fingers rubbing against his chin. "But I do get your point."

The boys were focused exclusively on each other. David shouted back, "You know what I think? I think you have it!"

Rafa's face contorted with rage as he lunged at David, arms outstretched. David stepped back, but Rafa continued his advance. He fired punch after punch, all of them coming fast and furious. David tried to fend off the blows as best he could by spinning his arms like a windmill, but he had no adequate defense. David dropped to his knees and used his arms to shield his head from Rafa's unrelenting blows.

Fausto crouched down to David's level. "Why don't you fight for yourself?" he screamed into David's face, like a boxer's trainer. "You let him beat you like this? Like a dog? It makes me think he's right. You are guilty. Hiding something. Maybe I torture you until you talk. Maybe I focus my steel on you."

"Tell him!" Rafa screamed. "Give him the key! Give it to him!"

David picked up his head just in time to see more fists coming his way. He reached up at exactly the right moment and took hold of Rafa's right wrist. Without letting go, David leapt to his feet, clenched Rafa in a tight embrace, and hurled his friend hard to the stage floor. David went down to the ground, his hair exploding around him, and the wrestling continued.

The two rolled around on the stage floor exchanging punches, much to the delight and cheers of Fausto's men, who had circled the entwined pair like a group watching a schoolyard brawl.

Rafa went for David's eyes with a clawed hand. David blocked the strike with his forearm, but Rafa managed to grab hold of a clump of David's thick hair and gave it a hard yank. David howled in pain as he fought to raise his head high enough to sink his teeth into the exposed flesh of Rafa's delicate wrist. It was a vicious bite, like that of an angry dog.

Now it was Rafa's turn to cry out, and he let go of

David's hair as he ripped his hand away. Rafa favored his wounded left hand as he scrambled back to his feet. David clawed his way back to his feet and cleared Rafa's blood from his mouth with the back of his hand.

The two squared off again.

Solomon slid over to the far corner of the stage, away from the commotion, and huddled into a fetal position, traumatized. Pixie didn't budge. He just sat in his chair and watched the chaos unfold as if it were a feature film.

Fausto waved to the guard at the door, the one Andy called Whippet, to join everybody onstage. In his hand, Fausto clutched a stack of colorful bills and he held them up over his head and shouted something in Spanish. The rest of the men took the cue and went looking for bills in their pockets. Soon they were shouting indecipherable commands and money began to exchange hands.

"Cuarenta por El Flaco," Una Mano said, pointing to Rafa. Fausto ripped the bills from Una Mano's hand.

David stepped forward and unleashed a vicious punch to Rafa's gut. The blow landed hard enough to double Rafa over. This was followed by a rapid exchange of money. The men were laughing and clapping; and though they spoke only Spanish, it was obvious they were betting on the outcome.

Hilary saw Whippet leave his post by the door to join his comrades onstage. Andy was slipping in and out of consciousness, sweaty, mumbling, glassy-eyed. Hilary knew he was dying.

Everyone was so focused on David and Rafa's battle that nobody noticed Hilary leave her seat and sneak

over to the unguarded auditorium door. She glanced
back at Andy. Even from a distance, she could see his
lips moving, and it was easy to imagine him saying,
"Harkness, Harkness, Harkness," over and over again.

Hilary engaged the push bar and cringed at the
sound it made. It was probably just a soft click, and
most likely drowned out by the shouting men, but to
Hilary it rang out like a gunshot. She froze in place and
looked to the stage. All attention was on the boys.

Hilary opened the door enough to let in a sliver of
light, enough for her to slip out. She stepped into the
empty hallway directly outside the auditorium and
kept pressure on the door to make sure it closed as
silently as possible.

To her left, Hilary saw the building's exit. Gray
light filtered in through two tall picture windows on either side of the front door. Beyond those windows was
a wide expanse of green and brown lawn—The Quad.
She could run for it. By the time they noticed she was
gone, it would be too late. She would lose them in the
woods. She could get help. But then how long would it
take to get someone back inside? Get Andy his medicine? Andy would never last that long. Never. Or worse,
maybe there would be dire consequences because of
her escape, and Fausto would slaughter her friends in
retribution. What kind of survival would that be? Instead of being their savior, she would contribute to their
execution. Her mind flashed on the image of Fausto
bludgeoning El Gallo to death all because someone
might have alerted the police. What would he do if the
police tried to get inside the school for real?

Hilary took one more wistful look outside. *They
will negotiate for our release,* she thought as a single

tear slid out from her eye and snaked down her face. She thought of her mother and father. Her sisters. The life she might never get a chance to live. Her stomach cramped from the weight of her decision.

Inside, the shouts of the men grew louder. It was the sound of laughter and joy, pure revelry. Hilary turned from the door and sprinted down the hall headed for the stairs. She had taken history with Mr. Langford last year.

She knew which basement classroom had a Harkness table.

Chapter 35

The tunnel ran straight as a razor's edge, and Jake had choices about which way to go. East would take him the rest of the way underneath the Academy Building. West would bring him back the way he came. He headed east.

Surges of adrenaline kept his mind sharp and body tense. His heart thudded like the steady beat of a war drum. There was enough headroom to stand upright, and plenty of space for Jake's Glock. He kept the pistol out in front of him as he walked. Five years ago, this section of tunnel had received a much-needed face-lift, and a lot of the wiring was fairly new. But it wasn't pristine, by any stretch. It still smelled dank, and the walls were slippery to the touch. Jake could hear dripping water anytime he stopped walking.

As he made it another twenty yards or so, Jake picked up a different sound. Not dripping water. Not rats. Nothing mechanical.

It was the sound of laughter.

The laughter resolved itself into something else—shouting that became indiscriminant chatter. The noises were muffled but distinct. Jake paused to listen. He thought he heard somebody shout, "Give it," but the long corridor and thick walls distorted the sound.

Those noises became yelling. The tumult roused Jake and drove him to a quicker pace. He let his mind go blank. His pistol aimed at nothing. He ignored all the precautions he should have been taking. The voices were coming from aboveground, and he knew only one place where that could be—the stage in the Feldman Auditorium.

The tunnel ran right underneath it. There were two locked doors on either side of the pit below the stage. The pit was nothing but a crawl space about six feet high, taking up roughly the same area as the stage. Theater productions used the pit for all sorts of things, mostly set changes, but a movable staircase down there allowed actors to make quick entrances or exits if required. Running along the back of the pit wall were utility pipes that came through holes bored into the concrete, as well as a sizable fuse box, tapped into the main power supply, which controlled electrical currents for the auditorium. The pit was otherwise empty, with no way out unless somebody had the keys to the tunnel entrances.

Closer to the pit doors, Jake forced himself to slow down. The voices bellowed even louder. Jake could not make any sense of what was being said, or how many people might be involved. Was it a mix of hostages and hostage takers, and was Andy among those present?

Jake shut off his headlamp and let the darkness take over. He got onto his stomach and peered through the sill of the green metal door, which secured access to the pit, looking for any trace of light. If the trapdoor happened to be open when Jake went inside, he'd be spotted for sure. He couldn't see anything, but his nose picked up a definite smell. It was the musty, metallic odor of the blood-splattered bathroom, only on steroids.

He put his nose against the doorsill, took a big whiff. Something horrible was behind the door, the smell of death. Jake took off his headlamp, turned it on, and shone the light through the crack, trying to see what lay beyond.

He saw shapes, shadows on top of shadows, but couldn't make out what they were. Then Jake's light caught a flash of something bright, something gold—a watch, maybe. He brought the beam back and soon had it fixed on a discolored hand. The fingers were knotted into a claw.

He realized it was a man's hand. A teacher, perhaps? Jake couldn't say for sure, and the way the body was positioned kept him from seeing the head. Jake could make out only one disfigured hand, but other shapes, probably other people, were in that crawl space. The pit made an ideal place to dispose of a dead body.

Jake pictured the scene unfolding on the stage, and assumed hostages were in the auditorium somewhere, maybe on the stage, maybe in the seats. Jake powered the headlamp back on and fished out the master key from the pocket on his chest rig. It was tucked inside the pouch, next to the one where he kept Andy's emergency glucagon kit. Jake slipped the key into the lock and gave it a turn.

He powered off the headlamp and darkness came once more. Jake would be almost impossible to see in the darkness, in his camouflage. He opened the door with his left hand, while the right hand was ready to shoot anything that came at him.

The smell of blood hit Jake like a tidal wave. He looked all around. No light filtered down, which meant no light could filter up. The chatter coming from the stage was louder and clearer. Jake heard thumps and bumps and heavy feet stomping about the stage. He could make out some words, but most of what he heard was in Spanish, or at least he thought it was Spanish. He heard grunts and a loud thud, as if somebody had fallen to the stage floor. This seemed to please some of those above him, because a series of delighted cheers broke out. A few choice words came to him.

"¡Lucha! ¡Lucha!"

No idea what that meant.

"Mátalo!"

Not that one, either.

Jake shifted his attention from the noises above to what was inside the pit below. He turned his headlamp back on and skulked into the pit area. He shone his light on the lumpy object closest to him and saw it was a body. The man's face was covered in purple welts; below a shock of red hair, Jake saw cracks in the skull. The mysterious shapes Jake had seen under the door turned out to be two other bodies, tossed down into the pit, along with "Big Red."

Those two had clearly been shot in the head. Big Red might have been as well, but he was badly beaten and it was harder to tell. Of the three, Big Red was the lightest colored, but the other two had the same skin tone as the guy Jake had ventilated with lead inside the bathroom. All four could certainly be a part of the same crew. They were a team, and none of them taught at this school.

Jake assumed these guys were involved in Laura's murder, and were probably hostage takers. So, why were they dead? Who had killed them?

Jake's first thought was Andy. His son had the skills to kill, and access to weapons. Maybe he was down in these very tunnels waging a one-man war. But the notion didn't sit well with him.

Jake felt around the pockets of the dead men, searching for IDs or weapons, but found nothing. The commotion onstage continued until four sharply spoken words cut through the din.

"Get off me, David!"

That voice he recognized. It was Rafa, Andy's friend. David was probably David Townsend. Was Andy with them? The pit had a microphone to let whoever was under the stage hear the cues clearly, but it was currently turned off. No worries—Jake's earmuffs had those built-in sound amplifiers. Binoculars for the ears.

His flashlight danced around in the dark until he found the portable staircase tucked away in a far corner. They were a miniature version of the movable steps sometimes used to help passengers and crew board or disembark from an airplane. It would be easy for Jake to roll the stairs under the trapdoor, but he would have to move the bodies.

Jake went to work. He grabbed one of the dead guys by the back of the shirt and dragged him five feet or so. He was stiff, no bend to the legs or arms. His hair was matted down with dried blood. The gunshot wound had basically turned the side of his head into hamburger. Jake didn't know if this guy had been dead one hour or five, and it didn't much matter.

Sounds of fighting continued above him. Jake could hear the loudest shouts, and those were in English.

"Liar! Liar!"

"I don't have it!"

He could tell Rafa's voice from David's. *"I don't have it!"* What did that mean?

Grabbing the railings of the staircase, Jake gave a hard tug. The wheels rolled noiselessly over the concrete floor. No squeak. He maneuvered the stairs into position, climbed almost to the top step, and pressed one of the hearing protectors to the underside of the trapdoor. He adjusted the sound controls until the chatter focused into clear conversation.

The words were meaningless without context.

"Give it."

"Hit him."

"Está perdiendo."

He heard every footstep, stomp, thump, thud, and body slam. This was a fight going on, for sure. It sounded to Jake like men screaming out wagers. He thought of a dogfight or a cockfight in some smoke-filled back room.

Somebody screamed—one of the kids. It was a howl of frustration, a call to battle of sorts. The kids were fighting each other, and whoever had taken them hostage was betting on the outcome, or so Jake believed.

His mind clicked over to a new problem. How would

he reach Andy? He assumed he was outmanned, out-gunned. Jake contemplated his options when he heard a new voice, a voice he didn't recognize.

"*¡La chica se ha ido!*" The voice was angry. "*¡Vayan a buscarla, pendejos!*"

"*Chica*" was the Spanish word for "girl." Could that be Hilary? Jake had tried to call Hilary, but he couldn't reach her. Could all of Andy's friends be a part of this? If so, why?

A new voice spoke up. This kid had been at Jake and Andy's house plenty of times. He was a quiet kid, small for his size, but his voice spoke with authority. People called him Pixie. Jake had known guys like him in the minors and in The Bigs—small guys with guts and tons of heart—lions inside the bodies of cubs. Pixie roared, and what he said filled Jake with terror.

"Wake up, Andy! Andy, wake up!"

Chapter 36

Hilary took the stairs to the lower level, two at a time, threw open the bottom door, and raced down an empty corridor, pumping her arms to gain speed. The overhead lights were still on; otherwise, she'd be running blind in this windowless section of the Academy Building. Hilary was in good shape, not short of breath, and her sneakers provided decent traction.

As she turned a corner, she slowed. Somewhere down this long hallway was the classroom with a Harkness table inside, and a backpack containing an emergency glucagon kit. But which room? Hilary could not recall the specific location, so she would have to check them all.

Most of the classroom doors were open, and Hilary paused only long enough to poke her head inside and have a quick check about the room. Some classrooms had the lights off, so Hilary had to flick a switch to get a better look inside. She closed each door before moving on to the next. If they came looking for her, it might slow them down, though she feared it would buy her at most a few more seconds of life.

About halfway down the corridor, Hilary thought she should have reached Langford's classroom by now. This flash of doubt mushroomed until Hilary believed she had screwed up royally. The classroom was behind her, she was now certain, and in her rush she had somehow missed it. Hilary contemplated backtracking. She slowed and glanced over her shoulder. She wasn't going to have enough time to double back and finish checking the remaining classrooms.

Go forward, or go back: whatever choice she made had to be the right one. The corridor was empty, but Hilary imagined men rounding the corner, picking up speed, coming at her like a hungry pack of jackals. The hallway seemed to stretch on forever—a trick of the mind, she knew, but it made the choice to turn around even less appealing. Maybe it was her gut telling her to keep going forward. She listened to her gut.

Fear bubbled inside, igniting every nerve, seeping into her joints, taking over like a quick-moving fire. She had thought she understood fear. Roller coasters and scary movies and snakes made her shiver and set a clammy chill against her skin. But this was a new level, an entirely different dimension of terror. Her fuzzy mind conjured up horrors beyond anything she had ever conceived possible before today. She became the central figure in each nightmare, the object of supreme violence.

A drill into her leg.

A makeshift club bludgeoning her head.

A machete peeling her skin.

Hands pushing up the skirt of her school uniform.

Compared to those, a gunshot to the temple felt almost merciful.

Near the end of the corridor, Hilary slowed. Langford's classroom had to be nearby. Her footsteps clomped on the linoleum flooring; she might as well have been shouting, *"Hey, I'm down here. Come find me! Come get me and skin me alive."*

Hilary ached to think how close she had come to leaving this godforsaken school. By now, she would have been clear of The Quad and deep into the dark woods beyond. Maybe she'd already be with the police, safe. An angry and vengeful voice inside her head spoke up.

"Save yourself," the voice said. *"You can't help Andy or the others. The Shire was Andy's idea, not yours. Why should you get killed because of his stupid idea? Go back upstairs. Get outside. Run! Run! Run!"*

Hilary shook her head and dislodged the voice from the dark crevices of her mind. Out in the open, those thoughts became exposed for what they were: *fear.* She knew the voice was lying to her. Andy hadn't made her join The Shire. She did so under her own volition. She liked the rush, the thrill. It had made her heart flutter. Each theft had hit like a comet and left behind a void that could only be filled by another rush. Addictions could be dangerous. She knew that now.

Everything had snowballed from there, including Hilary's feelings for Andy. If she didn't love him, would she have fled the school? This question came to her not as a conscious thought, but more as a feeling. It came to her as she ran the rest of the way down the corridor, as she breathed hard as a galloping horse, as her heart leapt about her chest, and as her skirt flapped like a cape around her waist.

Not that room. Not that room. Would you have done this for Solomon? Not that room. Not that room. For David? For Pixie? Not that room. Maybe not. Maybe only for Andy. Maybe only for him, she realized.

As she approached the end of the hallway, Hilary's earlier thought returned: *Somehow I've missed Langford's classroom.* Panic clogged her thinking, but it didn't make her turn around. One more room—she'd check one more, even though she believed it wasn't this far down.

Hilary opened the classroom door on her right. Nothing there, so she shut that door and went on to the next. *One more. Just one.* This next room was on Hilary's left. The door was closed, and she pulled it open with force. Her head poked through the door frame. There was enough light for her to see the Harkness table in the center of the room. She went inside and shut the door behind her. She flicked on the room light and immediately spotted the backpack tossed into a corner.

Hilary flung herself forward, tripping over chairs on her way to that backpack. She dropped to her knees and tried the zipper, but it got caught on the fabric and she feared she might need a knife or something to cut it open. After a moment's struggle, the zipper gave way.

Hilary emptied the contents onto the floor. Folders. Papers. Junk. More junk. And then she found it— tucked inside a mesh pouch was a red plastic case containing the glucagon emergency injection. There was also a package of glucose tablets in the same pouch, along with several vials of insulin and a few hypodermic needles.

She opened the red case and examined the contents. She found a capped hypodermic needle and a small clear vial labeled *Glucagon for Injection (rDNA Origin)*. The dosage read *1 mg (1 unit)*. Andy would need the entire vial.

Andy needed the glucagon, not the insulin, but Hilary put all of his medicines into the backpack, just in case, and headed for the door. Her hand was on the knob when she heard a loud bang coming from down the hall. Someone had slammed a door. Hilary pressed her back against the wall and felt her knees go weak. Her breathing grew labored as her blood turned to ice. She thought about the light seeping out from the classroom into the hall like a homing beacon for her potential murderer to follow. She could turn it off, but that might only draw attention.

Hilary heard more doors slam shut. Heavy footsteps were coming her way. It sounded like one person to her. Whoever was out there did not spend long searching each room. He went quickly from room to room, and Hilary doubted she could make an escape while he was occupied with his search. She looked for a place to hide, but the room had no closet, no door to another room, no windows.

Hilary searched for a weapon, but what could she use? A chair would be too unwieldy. A ruler was blunt and flimsy. There was nothing here, really. She could use one of the hypodermic needles, but what damage could a thin needle inflict?

The needles made Hilary think about the backpack, and that gave her an idea. The backpack could be a weapon of sorts. Something she could swing. Working frantically, with her vision blurred by tears, Hilary transferred the diabetes paraphernalia to the pockets of her skirt. Then she stuffed the backpack full of the heaviest books she could find. Her hands trembled as she closed the zipper.

Out in the hallway, doors continued to slam shut. It wouldn't be long now. She took up a position to the right of the door. Sweat dotted her forehead as she still breathed fast. Hyperalert, her eyes were open wide, but they weren't actually seeing anything. This was all about her ears, all about those footsteps coming her way.

Hilary positioned the backpack on the floor just beyond her left foot; she gripped one of the straps in both hands. Her knees were bent and her hips engaged, ready to uncoil at a moment's notice. Another door slammed. She guessed he had three more doors to go before getting to this one. Hilary shut her eyes and gritted her teeth to keep from crying out.

The door across the hall opened and slammed shut again. Blood thundered in Hilary's ears. She tightened her grip on the strap. She heard footsteps crossing the hall. The doorknob began to turn. Hilary wound her hips a few degrees more.

The door came open and Hilary uncoiled at the waist as she lifted the backpack off the floor. She swung her makeshift weapon high and connected with something—the man's chest or head. The strike produced a powerful jolt, which momentarily numbed her arms. She heard a loud grunt, followed by a thud as a body hit the floor.

Hilary let go of the backpack and sprang from the wall. Through the open door, she saw in the hallway a heavyset man on his back, writhing in pain. This was the one called El Cortador. The man was groaning, trying to get back on his feet, and he seemed hopelessly dazed.

As Hilary stepped over him, El Cortador lunged with startling quickness and seized hold of her ankle. He squeezed hard and Hilary shrieked at the intense pressure exerted on her tendons and bones. She wriggled her ankle, but the man would not let go.

About to lose her balance, Hilary hopped forward on one foot, moving toward her attacker, and kicked with the leg clutched in his grasp. The kicks weren't damaging, but it was enough to get him to let go of the ankle. Hilary spun as she tumbled to the floor. Her knees cracked and her wrists ignited in pain when she landed. The glucagon was secured inside the hard plastic case.

The man groaned as he rolled onto his stomach. Hilary clambered back to her feet, ignoring the lingering pain in her wrists and knees, and took off running.

She sped down the hall, fear giving her wings. If El Cortador caught her, he'd climb on top of her. Pin down her arms and legs. Place his grotesque hands over her throat or, more likely, the blade of some knife. He was The Cutter, after all. And then he'd hike up her skirt. In his humiliation and rage, he would take from her something she could never get back.

At the end of the hallway, Hilary gave a quick look before she turned the corner. El Cortador had gotten to his feet and lumbered toward her. He brandished in one hand a meaty knife, big enough to carve a pumpkin. But he was too far back, and it would be impossible to catch her before she reached the stairs. The steps seemed to go on forever.

Breathless when she reached the top landing, Hilary spilled out of the stairwell and tumbled awkwardly into the upstairs corridor. Ahead of her were the double doors to the outside, but those were guarded by one of Fausto's men, the thin man Andy had called Whippet. He was outside, standing on the steps that overlooked The Quad, but Hilary could see him through the tall picture windows on either side of the door. His attention was elsewhere, scanning the wide expanse of lawn—looking for her, perhaps—and Hilary thought she could get to the auditorium without being noticed.

She crossed the hall and pressed her body against the wall, getting as flat as she could, and began to inch her way to the door.

From the stairwell, she heard a loud bang. A door had slammed shut from below. El Cortador was coming for her. It would have to be a footrace. Who could reach the auditorium first?

Hilary bounded off the wall and began her sprint. As she did, Whippet must have sensed movement inside the school and turned in time to see Hilary making a dash for it. Behind her, the door to the stairwell flew open, and Hilary caught sight of El Cortador as he stumbled out into the hallway. He staggered toward her, dazed and slightly off balance.

The real race was between Whippet and Hilary. Whippet reentered the building and started his charge. *It's fifty-fifty, at best,* Hilary thought. Whereas El Cortador moved like a tranquilized rhinoceros, the other one came at her like the wind. She could see the whites of Whippet's eyes. He never raised his gun, maybe because he had orders not to kill.

Hilary got to the auditorium door a few steps ahead of Whippet. She pushed on the door, but it wouldn't budge. From somewhere down the hall, El Cortador bellowed, *"¡Voy a matar a esa maldita puta!"* He was closing in fast.

In her panic, Hilary pushed again. Still, nothing. Whippet was close enough to reach out and grab her. A voice inside Hilary's head screamed, *"Pull, not push!"* This time, Hilary gave the door a hard yank and she threw herself inside.

Andy was slumped over in his chair. *Is he breathing?* Whippet came at her from behind, screaming something she couldn't understand. He grabbed her by the shoulders and tossed her to the floor. Hilary's feet left the air as if an invisible rug had been yanked from under her and she landed on her backside.

The auditorium door opened and El Cortador staggered in, grunting. He charged at Hilary. Hilary could hear others shouting as they, too, entered the auditorium. It sounded as if Fausto had sent everyone to look for her.

Whippet's arm wrapped around Hilary's throat, and he began to squeeze. She had gotten on her knees, basically kneeling in front of Andy, who was dying as well. Hilary gasped for air as her throat closed. She clawed at Whippet's arm, to no avail. His grip around her neck only tightened. Hilary felt as though her eyes were going to pop out of the sockets from all the pressure building up.

The faces of her family popped into Hilary's head— Mom, Dad, her sisters—right before her world went black. But somewhere on a vast, endless horizon, Hilary heard a scream, more like a war cry. In the very next moment, the breath returned to her, the pressure fell from her eyes, and air flooded her lungs. Hilary fell to the floor, gasping, rubbing at her throat. Whippet spun around in erratic circles. It took a moment for Hilary to understand what had happened.

Pixie had climbed on Whippet's back and held on with one arm secured around the man's neck. Pixie bit at Whippet's head and neck like a blood-starved vampire, while using his free hand to claw at the man's face. El Cortador rushed over to help, when a loud, piercing whistle that came from the stage told him to stop. Standing center stage, Fausto bellowed with laughter as he watched Pixie and Whippet do battle.

Despite the pain and burning in her throat, Hilary took advantage of the tumult to crawl over to Andy. She fished out the glucagon kit from her pocket. From the stage, Fausto yelled, "The little one is kicking your ass, Inigo." He unleashed another roll of laughter.

Andy looked as sick as could be: pale, listless, drenched in sweat, his whole body shaking. Blocking out the noises in the room, Fausto's hoots, Pixie's war cries, Whippet's rage, Hilary glanced at the instructions adhered to the inside cover of the emergency kit.

Put the needle into the vial. Give it a shake. Fill the plunger. Stick into exposed flesh. Hilary's hands trembled as she filled the syringe with glucagon.

Then she pushed the needle into Andy's upper arm and depressed the plunger. She held the syringe in place and counted to ten. Only then did Hilary check her surroundings, fearful that El Cortador might come for her, or Whippet, or one of the others. Nobody was moving. Everyone's eyes were on Whippet and Pixie. From the stage, Fausto shouted insults in Spanish. He laughed and whistled with delight, more animated than Hilary had ever seen.

Pixie grunted as he gouged Whippet's face with his clawed hand. Whippet spun and twirled like a rodeo bull, but could not dislodge the boy, who continued to hold on with one arm wrapped around Whippet's throat.

Hilary did not know how long it would take for the medicine to kick in or if it would.

Three loud bangs cut short Hilary's thoughts. The air reeked of gunpowder. Fausto held his pistol above his head. Whippet stopped swirling and Pixie leapt off the man's back. El Cortador turned to face Fausto. The auditorium fell into a heavy silence.

Hilary sat down beside Andy, put her arm around him, and pulled him close. David and Rafa, both battered and bruised, huddled on the stage floor next to Solomon. Those three were flanked by Armando and Efren. Three other armed men were on the stage standing behind Fausto and his smoking gun.

Eight cartel men.

Six kids.

Fausto said, "Everyone, get back in your seats, right now! I want the kids in the front row. The games, this fun, it is all over. I am going to tell you now why nobody is coming to your rescue. And why you are all about to die."

Chapter 37

Jake couldn't think, couldn't move. Hidden below the stage, he listened, in agony, and tried to visualize what might be happening inside the auditorium. Andy was slipping into a diabetic coma. His son was dying. Pixie's words replayed over and over in Jake's mind.

"Wake up, Andy! Wake up!"

Jake felt utterly helpless, paralyzed by his choices. He had the glucagon. Conceivably, he could spring up through the trapdoor in the stage like some jack-in-the-box, guns blazing, and maybe get some of the hostage takers, or maybe not. More likely, they would kill some of the kids, or all, and then kill Jake, and then it would be over.

To act out of urgency could be the worst mistake possible. While the situation was far removed from baseball, Jake knew the importance of impulse control. On the mound, urgency would cost him mechanics and control. Here it could cost lives. No other approach but patience would work. But holding still was pure torture. Jake was aggressive enough to go after these mongrels, and relentless enough to pursue them all to their graves, but what he needed right now was control.

Jake knew the stages of diabetic crisis the way he knew his guns and his pitches. His son's blood sugar level was below fifty. Maybe as low as thirty. Maybe lower. Andy was probably past the stage at which the liver released its stored glucose and various hormones started to activate.

"Wake up, Andy!"

It sounded to Jake like his son had lost consciousness only recently. Either way, Andy was in insulin shock now. His body systems were breaking down. How long could he hold on? Minutes? An hour? Jake came in here thinking there would be some way to get Andy his medicine. He had more thinking to do.

There was time, but not much time.

If Andy had anything, however, it was an indomitable spirit. What else had made his son stand up to confront the foremost survival expert? What else gave him the courage to go head-to-head with Ryan Coventry? He had demanded that Jake dismantle his bug-out location. He had made his own arrangements to meet his estranged mother. These were signs of a boy becoming a man, and Andy had a strong will. Jake knew this about his son.

Ultimately, Jake had no recourse left but to believe Andy could endure for a while longer. When the moment was right, Jake would strike. But not yet. No, it would endanger too many lives.

Hidden belowground with his camo-painted face and a headlamp strapped to his forehead, Jake looked something like a bedraggled coal miner up on those movable stairs. He took in every scream, every shout, all the garbled chatter.

A bellow rose above the other sounds, a holler of sorts, a true warrior's cry. A cacophony of noises erupted again before a man's voice cut through the din, loud and clear, chilling, almost gleeful.

"The little one is kicking your ass, Inigo," the man said.

Laughter and grunts and other noises continued for a while longer until three loud claps, short bangs, put a stop to the bedlam. Jake knew a gunshot when he heard one. His throat seized and his vision went dark. *They killed them,* he thought. *Somebody just got shot.* Jake pressed his shoulder against the underside of the trap-door, and made sure the safety on the AK-47 was off. This was it. Guns would blaze and he would do every-thing in his power to save these kids or die trying. No choice. He'd been shown his call to action, all right.

Jake took in a deep, readying breath and he counted. *Three . . . two . . . one . . .*

The man spoke again. Instead of charging, Jake held his ground.

"Everyone, get back in your seats, right now! I want the kids in the front row. The games, this fun, it is all over. I am going to tell you now why nobody is com-ing to your rescue. And why you are all about to die."

Every organ in Jake's body seemed to deflate. They were alive—the kids, everyone, even Andy. For now. Those shots were meant to get their attention and noth-ing more.

Jake slung his rifle over his shoulder to free his hands, and put his ear up against the trapdoor, not wanting to miss a word. For a few moments, all he heard were footsteps as orders were followed and people took their seats. How many people? How many good guys and how many bad? Couldn't say. Right now, he suspected that Pixie, Andy, Rafa, David, and perhaps Hilary, the *"chica"* the man had mentioned, were all captives. Jake remembered another kid in that group, a boy named Solomon. Perhaps he was in the auditorium as well. As for the captors, Jake heard only one voice clearly, the rest hard to distinguish. Could be three, could be five, could be more.

The sound of footsteps and creaking chairs gave way to a hollow silence. The familiar voice spoke. Jake believed he was the alpha.

"What did you do to that boy?" "Alpha" asked.

A girl said, "I gave him a glucagon injection. He was dying."

Relief washed over Jake. The girl who spoke had to be Hilary, he was certain. Jake didn't know how she had done it, but he suspected whatever it was had taken tremendous courage. The injection would stabilize Andy.

Jake would backtrack and alert Ellie to the location of the hostages. He could even give them the location of the kids inside the auditorium—"front row," Alpha had said. It would be valuable intel for the police and rescue teams. Jake didn't trust the police or the FBI at all, not one bit, but his options were limited. He was outmanned and heavily outgunned. The right thing to do was stand down, but he would not vacate the premises. No. Never. Jake would remain underground, and operate as an asset for the police to utilize as they saw fit. With the correct frequency and channel information, he could sneak aboveground to use his two-watt Motorola radio for communications.

Alpha spoke again. "So fine, he's not dead. Not yet. But listen. This was not how things should have gone. *Este no era el plan.* We should have been alone. This place should have been—what is the word in English—*evacuado*—"

A different voice spoke up. "Evacuated."

The first man said, "Ah, yes, 'evacuated.' Good word. We should have been alone, in this evacuated school long enough to get the money you stole, or kill you all and we get away. Then we had the little problem. A woman shows up here and she's the one who gets away." Alpha sounded incredulous, as if meeting God would be a more conceivable outcome. "I lose my temper, and then I lose some men, and, well, here we are together in this big room. And maybe you think you stay quiet long enough, you get rescued. But nobody is coming to your rescue. Now, you may want to ask me, 'Fausto, why is this? Why no rescue?'" A lengthy pause ensued, like a question posed to a classroom of students who did not know the answer. "The reason is because I have lied to them."

Jake had another new piece of information of potential importance to share with the authorities. He knew Alpha's name.

Fausto.

A thought came to Jake. These blood-soaked corpses must have been killed over some failure on their part. Somehow they had caused the master plan to go awry; and for that, they had paid a dear price. The woman

Fausto mentioned had to be Laura. Jake guessed that
Laura had seen what was happening inside the auditorium. Perhaps she came looking for Andy and somehow managed to escape. During a pursuit, they shot
her, but she had already reached the woods and they
couldn't confirm the kill.

Listening to Fausto speak at length gave Jake a bet-
ter sense of his accent, too, which he thought was from
Latin America, maybe Mexico? His native tongue was
Spanish, for sure.

"Do you not believe me?" Fausto asked. "Do you
think I lie to you?"

There was no response. This was a lecture, not a
conversation.

"I promise they will wait and not come charging
in," Fausto said. "They will try to find the dirty bomb,
but there is no dirty bomb. We will . . . *vamos a darle
atole con el dedo.*" Fausto made a frustrated noise.
"Oh, what is the meaning in English? To make them
think . . . to lead . . . to . . . to . . ."

"To string them along."

The sharp-edged voice that spoke was Hilary's.

Jake heard Fausto say, "Yes! That's good. String
them along while we torture you like Javier and kill
you, unless you give me what I want. Even if I don't
live, which is a very good chance now, you see, I get
my boss his money. I do my duty. Now you must do
yours. Give me the money you took and maybe we
come to some other arrangement. Maybe we just leave
you here alive and we try to get away. Okay? But no
money, no live. This, my young friends, is the choice
you now face." Fausto clapped his hands. "Now, who
the fuck has my money?"

The ensuing silence swallowed Jake.

"None of us," said a voice.

Jake thought it was David, but it could have been another kid. Not Pixie. Not Andy.

"None of you?" Fausto repeated.

Jake heard footsteps that grew louder until they hammered right above his head. Fausto was on the stage, pacing directly over his head.

"None of you has two hundred million dollars. Two hundred million dollars. Two *hundred* million dollars! None of you has it? Really? The drill I put in Javier's leg is nothing compared to what I'm going to do to you. You want to change that answer?"

"We would give it to you. We promise."

The voice that spoke cracked with emotion. Something told Jake it was Solomon who had spoken. Jake's head was spinning. What could Andy and his friends have to do with $200 million of missing money?

"That's the truth," Solomon said. "Somebody must have stolen it from us."

"You better hope that it's not true, piggy boy," Fausto said. "Because if so, I will kill you first and do it slowly."

"Please just make an exchange," a boy said. "Let us go, and get them to let you go." Again, the voice sounded like David's.

Fausto snorted a laugh.

"You think that will happen? No, *hijo*. No. They will—¿*Cómo se dice en inglés?* They will play with us, make us think we do this thing you say. But they will not. No. They will arrest us. Or shoot us. With or without the money, either way, we are as *chingados* as you. I've got to get something out of this mess. So it's the money or your blood."

A different set of footsteps stomped onstage. *"Debes darte prisa, Fausto,"* somebody said. *"No tenemos tiempo que perder."*

"Yes, you're right. We don't have time to waste," Fausto said. Jake heard footsteps walk off the stage and return to the auditorium floor. "I'm setting a timer starting now. I give you an hour. One hour. I'd make it less, but I understand technology can be hard. We have a laptop right here. The Internet. All that. If you can't get me the money, I'm going to start killing, starting with you, big boy. Ready. Set. Go!"

Jake heard those final words as he bounded down the rolling staircase. When he reached the pit floor, Jake set the timer on his watch to one hour. He moved the stairs back to where he found them without making a sound. Then he dragged the bodies close to their original landing spots. Valuable minutes off the clock, but he couldn't risk someone going into the pit and seeing the contents disturbed in any way. Jake opened the tunnel door and unclipped the cell phone from his belt.

Ellie had to know there wasn't much time.

Chapter 38

Jake navigated back through the tunnels and returned to the janitor's closet, where he could get a cell phone signal again. He checked his watch. The countdown on Fausto's deadline continued to tick away.

Jake made the call. Images of death came at him like wraiths in the dark.

Ellie answered on the first ring. "Jake, where are you?"

Jake noticed an edge to Ellie's voice, a tone he had never heard her use.

"I'm in the school. Listen, Ellie, there are at least six kids who have been taken hostage. I can confirm four of the hostage takers are dead, but I don't know how many are left. One called himself Fausto. They may be from Mexico, I'm really not sure."

"Jake, you need to get out of there. You need to get out of there now."

Jake's pulse spiked. "There's a deadline on their lives, Ellie," he snapped. "We've got less than an hour to rescue them before they start killing hostages."

"Jake, you should have told me."

"What? What are you talking about?"

"They don't want you anywhere near that school."

"Who are 'they'?"

"They've been to your house. They know what you do. What you believe. They think you're unstable."

"You should have told me." He understood. "We don't have time to bullshit about what I believe, Ellie."

In the background, Jake heard a gruff voice say, "Is that him?"

"Yes," Jake heard Ellie answer.

A moment later, the gruff voice barked into Jake's ear, "Listen to me, Jake. This is Special Agent Leo Haggar, with the FBI's Hostage Rescue Team. I'm ordering you to evacuate the premises immediately."

Jake's inner dialogue was rambling, but he silenced the noises in his head. His mind could work that way. Brain waves like an earthquake one second, flatlining like a corpse's the next. It was the same mind control trick he used to shake off a home run and strike out the next batter. It was imperative he sound calm and composed. He already had a three-ball count against him. They knew he was a prepper. They would be biased. He was the only inside man, and they wouldn't use him as an asset.

"Agent Haggar, there is a hostage situation here at the school," Jake said.

"No shit, *Detective*," Haggar said.

Jake ignored the rebuke. "My son and his friends. Six kids. Four armed men are dead. I engaged with one myself. He's in the second-floor boys' bathroom of the Society Building. The other three were dead when I found them. I believe all of the kids are being held in the Feldman Auditorium on the first floor of the Academy Building."

"You 'engaged'?"

"I shot him."

"Shit," Haggar muttered. "And how do you know the other information?"

"I have access to the underground-tunnel system at the school. I overheard conversation from a pit underneath the stage. That's where I also found three additional dead guys."

"You killed them?"

"No, somebody else did."

"Who did?" Haggar asked.

"Look, I don't know. I don't know how many hostage takers there are, or what they're armed with. But I think it has something to do with missing money. A lot of money. Two hundred million, I heard one of them say. I told Ellie they might be Mexican, or South American, but I don't know. One of them is called Fausto."

"That's all really helpful information, Mr. Dent. Now you need to get out of there right away and let us do our job."

"Aren't you hearing me?" Jake said. "There's a deadline. One hour."

"Yeah? And now you listen to me. You might be doing a lot more damage than you realize."

"The bomb," Jake said. He needed something to build up his damaged credibility, and this was it.

"What bomb?" Haggar asked.

"You know. A radioactive bomb of some sort. It's all bullshit. It's a lie. It's a trick. They're trying to buy more time."

"Yeah, and how do you know that?"

"I heard him say it."

"From under the stage," Haggar said.

"That's right," Jake answered.

"You know what I heard?" Haggar growled. "I heard you think the world is coming to an end. I heard that you store food somewhere, and lots of it, and guns, too, and you're just waiting for the day when all hell breaks loose."

"That has nothing to do with this," Jake said.

"How do I know that you're not just looking for any excuse to make that day happen sooner rather than later? You already shot one guy, you said. Hell, maybe you're tired of shooting things with four legs."

"I'm not crazy, if that's what you're saying," Jake said. "I don't want to hunt people."

"I'm not saying anything except you have to vacate the premises."

"They won't negotiate. They know you won't honor any exchange for immunity."

"Please, Jake," Haggar said. "Let us do our job and you do yours by getting the hell out of there."

"I'm not going anywhere until I know you're coming in."

Haggar went silent. It lasted long enough for Jake to think the phone connection had dropped.

"Okay," Haggar said at last. "Okay. We're going to take your word for it. We'll go in hard and fast. But you get out of there first."

"You got my word."

"What are you wearing? We need to make sure my teams know you're not a threat."

"I've got on full-camouflage gear, and my face and hands are camo as well." Jake also gave Haggar his size and weight measurements. He said he would exit by the Society Building.

"Easy enough. I'll mobilize our teams and we'll try to establish communications with the terrorists."

"I don't think these are terrorists," Jake said.

Haggar didn't respond to that.

"One of them is Fausto," Jake reminded him. "I think he's their leader."

"Right. Fausto."

"There's a deadline," Jake added. "Less than an hour now. You've got to go quick."

"Not a lot of time for us to work with, but we'll get it done. Thanks for your service here, Jake. I mean it. Now, please, for the sake of your son and the other kids, get out."

"Okay," Jake said. "I'm leaving now."

"Good. The school is surrounded by police, SWAT, and FBI. You see somebody with a gun or a badge—I want you to turn yourself in to them. Understood?"

"Understood," Jake said.

"We're on this, Jake," Haggar said. "We're going to trust you. Now you've got to trust us. You got it. Right?"

"Got it," Jake said. "Don't let my son or any of his friends die."

"We're going to do everything we can. But you're the danger to them right now. Just turn yourself in."

"I'm on my way," Jake said, and he ended the call.

From his belt buckle, Jake unclipped his Bearcat handheld. He powered on the device and navigated to the stored frequency for the Winston PD.

The chatter was consistent and sounded a lot like air traffic control managing a busy airport.

"Team One checking in. No change."

"Sniper Team Three. No change."

"Same here. This is Orange Team Two. We got the back of the Academy Building."

"SWAT Team One. All clear by the library."

This was all interesting and entirely expected. But Jake was waiting for word about him to come through the command vehicle. Jake had read enough police procedures involving crisis situations to know that a Mobile Command Post would coordinate all field-unit activities. These specialized vehicles contained a complement of radio and telephone communications equipment, as well as advanced audio and video surveillance technology. Haggar would relay Jake's description to the MCP, and they, in turn, would communicate it out to the field. But Jake wanted to hear something else.

"Mission command reporting a white male dressed in camouflage gear, face and hands camouflaged as well, expected to leave Pepperell Academy near the Society Building any moment. The subject is six-two, about two hundred pounds. Do not engage. If any units see him exit, try to detain, but he's not necessarily a threat."

"Any change in the plan? This is SWAT Team Four asking."

"Negative. Situation is unchanged. Hold positions and maintain surveillance. That's the order."

"Hold positions."

Jake lowered the volume on his scanner. There was nothing else for him to glean. Things were status quo.

No change in the plan. *Of course.* Jake didn't doubt that for a minute. Haggar didn't believe him, or wouldn't trust him. It was as simple as that. The implications hit Jake hard. The FBI was going to try to negotiate with a bunch of killers who intended to string them along for at least an hour. At least until Fausto's deadline, until his son and his friends were dead.

Jake tried to put himself in Haggar's shoes. Would he have done anything different? Not a chance in France. Haggar had been right to try and draw Jake out of the school. Making entry was the biggest risk during any hostage crisis. The bad guys could take cover, and shoot from the shadows. Out in the open, it was much easier and safer to engage and separate the hostiles from the friendly. Haggar had done what he could to get Jake to stand down. But it wasn't going to be enough.

Jake headed back for the tunnels, when his cell phone rang. He checked the number and saw it was Ellie.

"I'm heading out," Jake said.

"They're not coming," Ellie whispered.

"Say that again."

"Nobody is going to come into the school. They're not willing to believe you. Haggar won't take the chance. They're going to try to negotiate."

"What about you?" Jake said.

"I'm calling, aren't I?"

"I'm not crazy, Ellie," Jake said.

"I know."

"They're going to kill them all, my son included."

"I know. Sweetheart, I know. I believe you. I do. I just wish you had told me. You can trust me, Jake. All the way."

Jake was overcome with emotion, but forced his mind to clear. He remembered something, something he had forgotten to tell Haggar. Something important.

"Do some digging on someone named Javier," Jake said, recalling what Fausto had said onstage. "He may have a connection to the school or the money. I don't know. They did something to him. Something with a drill."

"Who *are* these people?" Ellie asked.

"All I know is that they're killers and they're brutal."

"Jake, please, please be careful."

"Thank you, Ellie. Thank you for not lying to me."

"What do you mean?"

"I listened to the scanners. I knew they weren't coming in. You didn't have to tell me, but I'm glad you did."

After a pause, Ellie blurted out, "I love you, Jake."

Jake kissed his fingers and put them gently to the phone. "I'll tell you how I feel when I see you," Jake said, and ended the call.

No time for good-byes. According to Jake's stopwatch, Andy and his friends now had less than forty-five minutes to live.

Chapter 39

Jake made another phone call before he descended back into darkness. He needed to speak with Lance.

"Jake! Jake, is that you?"

"Listen, Lance, I don't have a lot of time. You've got to try and convince Haggar I'm not crazy."

"What?"

"No time to explain. He'll know what it's about. Just tell him I'm not nuts. It's going to go down in here pretty soon, and I'd rather not go at it alone. Tell them to engage. If they hold back, all these kids are going to die, and that includes my son."

"Andy? Where is Andy? I'm really lost here. You're not making any sense."

"And another thing," Jake said, not wasting a second on backstory. Lance would figure it out eventually. "This is all about money. A lot of money."

"What?"

"Andy and his friends were involved in something. There was a theft. I told Ellie about someone named Javier. Does that mean anything to you? Javier?"

"No," Lance said, but then stuttered, "I—I—don't know. I'd have to think. I'm rattled."

"All right. You do that and tell Ellie what you come up with."

"What are you doing, Jake?"

"I'm doing what I do best. Surviving, big brother. I'm just surviving." Jake ended the call so he could return to the catacombs.

The call to Lance took another five minutes off the clock. Forty to go.

Jake went as quickly as he could, but not recklessly fast. The tunnels were full of obstacles that could cause serious injury from a full-speed impact. While any second could be Andy's last, Jake also believed that Fausto would honor his own deadline. Why, exactly, he couldn't say. It was a gut feeling. Fausto sounded sadistically playful in the conversations Jake had overheard, as if he would relish each minute as it ticked off the clock. The fear of death for him would be as intoxicating as any drug.

Yes, Fausto would wait the full hour, Jake felt certain of it. But, Jake reminded himself, it was no longer an hour.

He had figured on spending fifteen minutes navigating the tunnels. Ten to gather supplies. Twenty-five off the clock. The rest of his plan would take another ten minutes to execute. Thirty-five minutes total before he could engage. Jake had about a five-minute buffer, and the margin for error was wider than the Amazon. His other choice was to stand down, leave the school, get taken into custody, plead his case to Haggar, and then bury his son.

Wasn't going to happen.

The beam from Jake's headlamp bounced across the familiar walls, revealing all the places where he needed to duck, crawl, or slouch. Otherwise, he was running. He went under the Terry Science Center, the library, Gibson Hall, and the Society Building, where he had left a dead man splattered on the bathroom floor. Jake took the tunnel to the Groveland Gymnasium, and at last he returned to the section of tunnels that was home to his bug-out location.

For a few panicked seconds, Jake fumbled with the new key for the door lock on his bug-out location, cursing under his breath, and eventually got inside.

Jake turned on the lights and checked his stopwatch. The whole trip went faster than expected, leaving him an extra minute on his deadline. One minute added to his buffer. Aboveground they would be looking for him. There would be chatter on the Bearcat—*"Has anybody seen Dent? Anybody?"* Haggar would be nervous. He'd press Ellie to make Jake follow the order.

All this was happening, but none of it was of concern. If SWAT or the FBI made entry into the school, Jake would figure it out eventually. In the meantime, he'd be taking necessary action.

It didn't take long for Jake to locate the items he had come to retrieve. The flares were stored in the larder, away from the gasoline. Nearby was a case of tactical smoke grenades, with smoke output of 25,000 cubic feet. More than enough. He grabbed a handful of Cyalume Chemlights, military-grade infrared light sticks. They were just like regular glow sticks—bend, snap, crack—but the light emitted was invisible to the naked eye. With the night vision goggles, though, a few of those sticks would provide more than enough illumination.

He had seven mags of ammo for the AK-47—one loaded, three on his chest rig, three on his battle belt. Jake decided to include a few additional mags of pistol ammo inside a small backpack, along with an extra flashlight and four pieces of the rebar he had scavenged from a construction site.

He grabbed his tactical helmet and attached the night vision optical to the J-bar. He adjusted his Kevlar, inspected his guns, and paused to check his gear in the full-length, wall-mounted mirror. His face and hands were still covered in camo paint, mixed with tunnel grime. The tactical helmet fit snugly on his head. The rest of him was geared up: chest rig, battle belt, ammo, flares, glow sticks, smoke grenades, knives, two pistols, a Glock, the Ruger, and his rifle.

He was ready for war.

Chapter 40

Ellie had just hung up with Jake when Haggar whistled to her from behind. She blanched when she saw him. She had shared sensitive tactical information with a possible threat. Although Jake had obtained the same intel on his own, Ellie's actions were quite possibly criminal. Not that she regretted her choice. She believed Jake, and her goal was to convince Haggar of the same.

Haggar bounded down the trailer's front steps with purposeful strides. "Who was that?" he asked.

"Jake," Ellie said. She had no reason to lie, and Jake had every reason to call her.

"Is he leaving?" Haggar said. "We need him out of there, and that's that."

"I can't tell you what he's going to do," Ellie said. That wasn't a lie, either.

"No offense, but you two have a history, and I'm not comfortable with you talking to him without one of my agents present. Understood?"

"Understood."

"That's an order, Sergeant Barnes."

Haggar was a sharp-eyed leader, Ellie thought. "Yes, sir," Ellie said.

"Look, I appreciate all your help here. We're going to get out of this just fine. It's going to take time, that's all."

"Sir, do you really believe this is terrorism?" Ellie asked.

"Who else uses dirty bombs?"

At first, Ellie wasn't sure what to share, but she erred on the side of openness. "Jake thinks it's about money. That's what he said to me just now."

"Yeah? Jake also thinks the world is coming to an end any day now. Maybe he thinks Bigfoot somehow got his hands on all that cobalt-60."

Ellie strained to smile. "I know you're putting extra surveillance on the Academy Building," she said. "So you must not think he's completely crazy."

Haggar looked annoyed. "I take every opportunity I'm given and exploit it to my advantage," he said. "So we're looking at that building a little extra hard. Big deal. Doesn't mean Jake's on the Red Unit now. It means we have heat-detection equipment in place and it'll help us validate his claim."

"If you use every opportunity to your advantage, why not work with Jake? He's on the inside. He can help."

"He can get himself or those kids killed. That's what I'm thinking."

"What if he's right?" Ellie asked. "What if there's no bomb and we have less than an hour? We could lose the kids."

"If that's the case, I'm going to have a hard time sleeping at night for the rest of my life."

"Then believe him," Ellie said.

Haggar glanced at the trailer. For a moment, Ellie thought he was going to change his mind. "We're working on making contact with the terrorists," he said. "That's the protocol and that's the plan. I'm not about to enlist the help of a civilian under any circumstance."

Ellie backed off. She had more that Haggar needed to know. "During our call, Jake mentioned somone named Javier," she said. "He's convinced this whole thing has to do with money."

"Money?"

"That's what he said. I mean, what terrorists do anything in the name of money?"

Haggar took a breath. He looked to the sky as if the answers would come from there. "Hell, this whole damn situation is a gigantic Charlie Foxtrot, if you ask me. Look, Ellie, if you're hot on this Javier lead, then go figure out who he is and let me know what you learn."

It was as much as Haggar would budge. Ellie raced her cruiser home to get Kibo before her fishing expedition began. Where she lived was en route to her destination. Hours ago, Ellie's other two shepherds had gone to a neighbor's, but Kibo stayed behind. He didn't transition to new environments like the other dogs. Even though he wasn't a trained police dog, Ellie still wanted to take him along for the ride. At that moment, she needed the comfort of his companionship. It would help to ease her unremitting worry for Jake.

Ellie arrived home a little after sunset. The clouds were gone, and a bright crescent moon shone down like a mischievous grin against a darkening sky. It didn't take much light from town to block out the stars, but a few were twinkling off to the west. More would appear, once night settled in.

Off in the distance, SWAT helicopters, spotlights illuminated, circled over The Pep in a tight pattern. Her home was built on top of a high hill, which offered tremendous views of the valley. Far below, Ellie observed pockets of strobe light activity, patches of blue and red that appeared to burn the forest in a multicolored flame. Many of the deployed units, Ellie knew, had taken advantage of the encroaching darkness to keep well hidden. She also had a clear view of the campus buildings. Most of them still had their lights on.

From her cruiser, Ellie retrieved her binoculars and used them to pinpoint what she believed was the Academy Building, where Jake said the hostages were being held. She ignored the cold, even though the wind packed a chilly punch. Lowering the binoculars, Ellie kept her eyes locked on the Academy Building.

What are you going to do, Jake?

Her mind flooded with thoughts of the terrible things that could happen inside that school. The images went away, but the ache lingered. Ellie knew one thing for certain: Jake was Haggar's best hope for avoiding a lifetime of sleepless nights.

Kibo sensed someone coming up the driveway and barked noisily from inside the house. Soon as Ellie opened the front door, Kibo, his tongue lolling to one side of his mouth, leapt up on hind legs and slammed his front paws against Ellie's chest hard enough to knock her off balance. Then he gave her face a good licking.

"I missed you too, sweetie," Ellie said, roughing up his fur.

Kibo followed Ellie outside and relieved himself on the grass. At the same time, Ellie opened the trunk of her cruiser. A war was going on in Winston, and while she was far from the action, she needed to prepare. From the trunk, Ellie removed her body armor—POLICE emblazoned on the front pouch in bright yellow lettering—and got it fitted into place. Kibo looked wistfully at Ellie until she said, "Get in!"

Kibo barked once and got his nose under the door handle. When his head came up, the door latch disengaged. Kibo put a paw into the crack, which was enough to get the door open the rest of the way. He clambered into the front seat and sat upright and alert, like he was her partner.

Ellie gave Kibo his treat. Her dad had shown her how to train a dog to do that trick; and every time Kibo opened a door, she thought of her father. *"Failing to prepare is preparing to fail,"* her dad used to say.

She made the drive into town with her strobes flashing but siren off. The streets were quiet, and plenty of detours directed traffic away from the prep school. Five minutes later, Ellie arrived at the local high school, where she believed Lance Dent had set up a temporary headquarters.

The school parking lot was near capacity. Inside, it was noisy and chaotic. There wasn't a better place to house all the boarding kids from The Pep. Displaced students roamed the halls with drained looks on their faces. The excitement of the evacuation had given way to uncertainty and fear.

Kibo didn't seem to mind all the commotion. As long as he was with Ellie, everything was right in the world. He heeled as Ellie walked him through noisy corridors. Several students stopped to pet Kibo, and Ellie let them. She could see it gave them a few minutes of comfort. Kibo, as Ellie expected, relished every bit of attention lavished upon him.

Ellie eventually made it to the auditorium, which looked like postdisaster images she had seen on the Red Cross website. Students were splayed out on floor mats, or huddled in groups on the bleachers. Lost looks, exhausted expressions, and sagging shoulders were common. Trash barrels overflowed with food wrappers and plastic drink bottles.

Kibo didn't like the noise, or the smell, because he kept close to Ellie's side and whimpered occasionally. Several students came up to Ellie and asked what was going on. Other uniformed police officers were inside the school, and Ellie made sure the kids knew where to find them. Television reporters from various news outlets were present, but Ellie wasn't granting any interviews.

The Internet spread rumors faster than facts, and most of the stories Ellie heard were gruesome and unsettling. Kids had been killed, one girl was certain. Another boy said that some of the hostages had been beheaded and there was a video online that was being blocked. Most of what they said to Ellie was inaccurate or unconfirmed. Ellie validated only what was being reported on the news: a woman had been shot and there was an active hostage situation at The Pep.

In one of the crowded hallways, Ellie found a teacher who directed her to the principal's office on the first floor. Inside the anteroom, Ellie got nervous looks from a few parents waiting to speak to Lance. Maybe it was the uniform that scared people, or maybe it was the eighty-five-pound German shepherd.

Ellie poked her head into the principal's office and saw Lance on the phone, seated behind a large desk. Lance saw her looking at him and held up a finger to ask her to wait. Ellie thought he was puffy and pale. She had busted guys after a five-day bender who looked better. From the doorway, Ellie could hear his half of the conversation clearly.

"I want to know the same, Mrs. Eichel," Lance said into his cell phone. "And I promise we're doing everything possible to locate Hilary. Where are you now?" A beat, and then he said, "You're about an hour and a half away." Another beat. "Yes, call if you need. Anytime."

A woman in a blue suit, her hair going in more directions than a boy band, pushed her way into the office, holding a cell phone as if it were a Fabergé egg.

Into his phone, Lance said, "If you'll please just give us time, I'm in touch with the Winston Police Department every few minutes, and I'm doing what I can to help locate all of your children."

"It's William Cranston, Troy's dad," the woman with the phone said in a whispered voice. "He's demanding to speak with you."

"Yes, yes, Judy," Lance said. "Tell him I'll be right with him."

"He'll be right with you," Judy said into the phone. She pulled the phone from her ear, and Ellie could hear some angry talk.

Lance said, "Mrs. Eichel, I'm going to call you back. The police are here now."

He had been so focused on Mrs. Eichel, Lance hadn't recognized Ellie standing in his doorway. He had never met Kibo before. When Lance realized who it was, a smile came over his face. His look told her she wasn't just a cop. She was an important person to his brother.

Lance stayed in his seat. Exhaustion held him down like an anchor. "Sorry, it's crazy here, Ellie. I was going to call you. Have you heard from Jake?"

Ellie nodded.

"You know he's in the school."

Ellie nodded again. "We think he's coming out."

Lance didn't seem to believe it.

"What can I do for you?" he asked. "I'm sorry to rush, but I need to keep in contact with the parents of the missing kids."

Ellie had come to ask for Lance's help in identifying Javier. Seeing how frazzled he was, she hesitated. She could manage on her own.

"I need to see a directory with the names of every student and I need the parents' names and addresses as well. Faculty, too, even if they're part-time."

Lance wasn't bothered by the request. "Sure," he said. "I'll have Judy get it for you right away. Our records are all online, so it'll be easy to access."

"Great," Ellie said.

"Anything I can help with?"

"Nothing I can't handle on my own," Ellie said.

Chapter 41

Jake followed a branch off the main tunnel that terminated at a set of metal stairs. He took those stairs two at a time; and at the top landing, he unlocked a steel door, using his master key. He left every door he came through unlocked to facilitate a fast exit.

He made an in-and-out trip through the basement janitor's closet and sprinted to the stairwell. Then, it was up a set of stairs to the first floor of the Academy Building; he clutched the AK-47 in both hands as he went. He proceeded without extreme caution. Time wouldn't allow it. Twenty minutes had already ticked off the clock. Twenty minutes left to go. From here, Jake knew the quickest route to the Feldman Auditorium.

The end of the hallway spilled out into an open foyer with high ceilings. Jake stopped to poke his head around the corner. He could see the auditorium doors not more than thirty feet away. They weren't being guarded. Why bother? They had the FBI held at bay with a bogus bomb threat. Maybe somebody was patrolling outside, but Jake thought it unlikely. It would leave them vulnerable to snipers. The action was happening inside the auditorium. And who didn't want to be in on the action?

Jake emerged from his hiding place in a crouch, the AK-47 slung across his shoulder. His footsteps echoed softly as he inched his way toward the auditorium doors. When he got there, Jake reached over his shoulder and removed one of the steel rebar rods, which poked out the top of his backpack. The rod came free as though Jake had unsheathed a sword.

Behind the closed doors, Jake heard the voice of the man he believed to be Fausto addressing his captives. Jake did not stop to listen. He, instead, slid the rebar between the looped handle on each door with the dexterity of a bomb technician defusing a device. He released his grip and the rod dropped maybe a millimeter into place, just enough to make a small noise of metal on metal.

Jake's hand went to the butt of his Glock. He waited for an alarm to sound. Shots to be fired. Men to come for him. He exhaled when nothing happened.

Jake checked over his work. The rebar was long enough to hold firm, no matter how many pushed against the door. He snuck around to the other side of the auditorium and created the same barricade, using a second rebar rod on a different set of auditorium doors. Two additional emergency exits were at the back of the auditorium, and Jake secured those doors in the same manner. Four exits, all secured using unbendable rebar.

Jake next padded down a hallway, AK-47 at the ready. He took the stairs back to the basement and from there worked his way into the tunnels. A check of his stopwatch showed ten additional minutes off the clock. Ten left to go.

On to phase two.

Jake shot down the tunnel, headed for the pit, running as though his body were on fire. He used the headlamp to light the way, but probably could have made it there blindfolded. All his senses worked on overdrive—every sound magnified, every touch internalized, every musty odor overpowering.

Jake's heartbeat matched the pace and power of a jackhammer. He took in shallow, sharp breaths to try and slow it down, but gave up. It was impossible to control the adrenaline. The killer instinct, so natural to him on the mound, came back, but in an altered state and intensified. He in no way relished what was to come. The need to kill and a desire to do so are different beasts.

A check of the time: three more minutes gone.

Inside the pit, the headlamp lit the space well enough. He saw the three decomposing men in a heap on the floor, where he had left them—Big Red and his two mangled companions. The smell of blood hit him hard. If his stomach let go, he might give himself away. Now it was showtime. Even though he prepped like a trained soldier, Jake took inspiration from the only place where he did actual battle: the mound.

Be the aggressor. Attack and don't ever let up. Show no weakness.

Jake moved the bodies and rolled the stairs back into place. Another three minutes off the clock.

Down to four.

"You are fast running out of time, little ones. *Efren y Armando, vengan aquí.*"

Efren, Armando, Fausto. How many more were there? Didn't much matter. Jake had enough ammo to engage a small army.

With the stairs in place, Jake went to the back wall of the pit and shone his headlamp on the fuse box. He removed his backpack, opened the top, and fished out the light sticks. He had five of them. Plenty. He did the break-and-shake on each stick. They were glowing, but in infrared so that it didn't really look like any chemical reaction had taken place. He checked the smoke grenades hitched to his chest rig. Fine there as well. The flares were also within easy reach.

"Many famous Mexicans have died by firing squad," Fausto said, his voice amplified by Jake's hearing protection. "You still have a little time left."

One minute according to Jake's timer.

"Please, please, none of us has it. Believe us." That was Andy's voice. He sounded strong, alert. And that was Hilary's doing.

Jake opened the fuse box. There were circuit breakers for different sections of the auditorium, but his only interest was the red master switch. Jake held the light stick in one hand. He looked at the stairs. It would take only a few seconds to cross the pit, get up the stairs, open the trapdoor, and start shooting. Three seconds. Maybe four. Fausto could open fire on the kids during that time. It was a possibility. A serious risk. The blackout should be a big enough distraction, Jake thought. He wouldn't need them frozen for long. His other option was to listen to six gunshots.

Jake sucked down a breath and closed his eyes. He visualized exactly what was about to happen. Focused his thoughts, his intentions. This was the windup.

Now for the pitch.

Chapter 42

Jake shut off his headlamp. The pit area became a canvas of black. He lowered his night vision optical, and the dark pit was awash in a green glow. Every detail showed in high definition, including the dead bodies strewn about the concrete floor. He put his left hand on the red power switch. In his right hand, he held the IR light sticks that powered his night vision.

He hoped the kids would take cover on the floor.

He counted in his head.

One.

He heard Fausto say from the auditorium, "I'd prepare your last words."

The whimpers became sobs.

Two.

Jake bent his knees to get into a sprinter's stance.

"No? Nothing?" Fausto said. "Well, as you wish."

Three.

Jake pulled the switch down and cut the power to the auditorium. At the same instant, he bolted forward.

"¿Qué pasó?" The voice sounded angry and sur-

prised. Chatter interspersed with other commotion, like the sound of auditorium seats folding closed.

Jake bounded across the pit, navigating with the help of his optics. He got his foot on the first step, and it was easy from there to get all the way up.

Using his back, Jake forced open the trapdoor. He emerged into the dark. Nobody in the auditorium could see him on the stage. Jake gently lowered the trapdoor to the floor so it remained open. That was to be the way out. Light from cell phones waved about in the dark as if they were levitated. The chatter continued. There was movement toward the doors.

Jake rolled across the stage to get some distance from the pit opening. An accidental tumble would be disastrous. He tossed one light stick toward the back of the auditorium with the arm strength of an outfielder. The chem light bounced over several rows of seats and settled at the back of the room. He sent three more light sticks flying.

The noise they made upon landing might have given Jake away. For safety, he sank deeper into the darkness of the stage. As he did, he rolled to his left.

Sure enough, bullets came at Jake from multiple directions. Shots peppered the stage, but missed him by a wide margin. Jake peered into his night vision optical. The world was green, and well lit from the scattering of infrared glow sticks.

He could see the kids cowering on the floor. Some used their hands to shield their heads. They were still in their school uniforms. Jake counted six hostages in total, including Andy at the end of the row, hands over his head like the others. His boy. There might be additional hostages, but Jake doubted it. These six were all connected.

Flashes in the dark auditorium announced the bullets to come. They hit everywhere but where it mattered. They were firing blind, and it was highly ineffective. In the second row, Jake sighted a thin guy aiming a sizable shotgun. Even though his aim was off target, a shotgun blast covered a wide area. "Thin Man" got off a single shot that made a powerful blast and added to the overwhelming stench of gunpowder.

A fraction of a second after the shotgun blast, Jake pulled the trigger on his rifle. A quick succession of pops followed and three bullets exploded the thin guy's chest. The sticky collision caused the man to crumple over the auditorium chairs. His legs bent at an unnatural angle, and his feet pointed skyward but didn't move.

Now that he could see where to shoot and what to avoid, Jake laid down heavy suppressive fire. Bullets spit from his rifle barrel like hornets fleeing an aggravated nest. Gas-operated weapons were efficient at ejecting spent cartridges and loading another. Jake could get off about forty rounds a minute, including time to change magazines, chamber the first round, and clear any jams.

Unfortunately, so could the other guys, and they had more guns. Eventually one of them would get lucky. Then again, they didn't know how many people had infiltrated the auditorium, so they were shooting everywhere. For now, the kids were safe as long as they stayed on the floor. The bullets were going way over their heads, so the kids were in the best possible location.

Movement drew Jake's gaze to the auditorium doors on his right. Somebody was trying to get out. Through the optics, Jake targeted a heavyset man as he pushed against the doors with his substantial weight.

Jake rolled onto his stomach and took aim. He let go a burst. One bullet struck the back of the man's head, splitting it open like a watermelon dropped from a height. Two other bullets pierced him in the back near the shoulder blades. The rifle in the man's hand dropped to the floor and landed just before his lifeless body did the same.

At the back of the auditorium, Jake spotted two other targets pushing against the emergency exit doors. One had long, frizzy hair; the other guy's hair was short. Both had thin builds, a little harder to hit. But they were less than forty-five meters away. Jake was a fine shot at twice that distance. He pulled the trigger, and a fraction of a second later, there were no guys at that door.

Four hostiles down in less than thirty seconds.

"Get up here!" Jake screamed at the kids between shots. "Get up here now."

The remainder of the crew had spread out and took up cover behind different seats in different rows. Jake saw them come up from time to time like prairie dogs out to have a look around. They didn't stay up for long. Jake sighted them quickly and decorated their seats with bullets. Maybe he struck gold. Probably not. The goal wasn't annihilation. It was rescue.

Jake's constant stream of bullets pinned the hostage takers down and kept them from returning fire. This gave the kids a short window to make their move, but Jake wanted them fully concealed from view. From a prone position, he unclipped one of the four smoke grenades on his chest rig. He fired the AK-47 without aiming, using one hand. With his teeth, he pulled the pin on the grenade and gave it a toss. The projectile flew with a tall arc and a smoky tail. As soon as it hit, thick smoke billowed into the pitch-black room.

"Move! Move!" Jake shouted.

Grenade two was up and away. Bullets whizzed by Jake's head, and he returned fire with his rifle. The smoke was doing its job, but Jake launched one more grenade for good measure and went back to two-handed firing.

Pixie was the first kid to take initiative. He commando-crawled across the gap between the first row of seats and the stage. With the smoke and the dark, the flash of Jake's gun barrel would help navigate him to the stage like airport runway lights.

A thick curtain of smoke rose up behind Pixie. Only Jake could see the boy on the move. Pixie reached the front of the stage and hauled himself up. Jake never let up with the gunfire. He shifted position several times to make targeting him even harder. First he rolled right, then to the left, and back right again.

When his ammo ran low, Jake took out a new magazine from his battle belt and activated the rifle's magazine catch with his thumb. He rotated the new magazine forward to the correct angle for insertion. Total time without shooting never went more than a couple of seconds. He thought he had enough bullets with him to get all six kids through the trapdoor.

By this point, the kids' ears must have been ringing, but Jake kept his finger on the trigger. They could sustain worse injuries than hearing loss. Return fire came at Jake through the fog in spurts, and some of it splintered the stage floor, not more than five feet away. A little too close for comfort.

Jake sighted a target through his optics and fired at him through the haze. His bullets turned the auditorium chairs into Swiss cheese and flushed a shooter out of hiding. Jake tracked the man to the front door, where another man's body already lay. The smoke was still pretty thin over there and Jake had no trouble tracking him. It looked to Jake like the man at the door had a claw for a hand. He could have ten clawed hands. That door wasn't going to budge.

Jake let a burst of bullets fly that put plenty of holes into his target. Liquid exploded from the man's midsection and blended with the gathering smoke.

Jake kept up the suppressive fire. At some point, someone would shoot blindly at the front of the stage and hit one of the slow-moving kids. Jake had to hurry them along. He yelled, "Move now or you'll be shot."

Hilary had her hands over her eyes, and a scream fell from her mouth, which was mostly drowned out by gunfire. At least she was on the move. David and Rafa followed, and next came Andy, who looked a bit disoriented. Solomon brought up the rear. All of them crawled toward the stage. Ten feet felt more like ten miles. They were going too slow. Jake screamed, "Move it! Move it!"

The kids needed better protection, so Jake stood up. It put him in a vulnerable position, but he improved his vantage point. He peppered the auditorium seats with as many bullets as his gun could spit out, sweeping the barrel from right to left and back again. He changed magazines three times. This happened as more smoke poured out of the canisters and turned the visibility nearly to zero. Return gunfire came at Jake through the smog, but it was way off the mark.

One by one, the kids crawled onto the stage. He kept up the gunfire until he again ran out of ammo. This time, he changed magazines, using the new cartridge to release the old. It was a skill Ellie had taught him at the range.

"Down in the hole!" Jake yelled. "The pit door is open. Get down in it!"

Jake turned his head in time to see Pixie feel his way across the stage in the dark and drop into the pit. One by one, like lemmings on the march, they all went down into the hole. Andy said nothing as he crept along. Chances were, he didn't even know it was Jake doing the shooting.

As Jake had calculated, the return fire was nonexistent. In this environment, he had all the advantage. He could target better than they could. He had won the first round. But this wasn't over. Not by a long shot.

Whoever had taken the kids hostage would follow them into the tunnels.

Chapter 43

Three Javiers had connections to the school: one was a student and two were parents.

Ellie found the student huddled on the auditorium bleachers with a group of his friends. He was a tall and thin boy, with tousled dark hair and a handsome face. Ellie asked him some basic questions to determine whether he had any connection to Andy Dent or his missing friends.

Javier was pleasant enough, and not the least bit nervous to speak with her. He answered politely and confirmed what she initially suspected: Javier Ortega was just another displaced student from Pepperell Academy caught up in the chaos. Javier gave Kibo some much-appreciated affection, and Ellie returned to her cruiser. This time, Ellie opened the door for her dog, and Kibo climbed in the front passenger seat, where he sat patiently while Ellie got the second Javier on the phone.

Javier number two lived in Orange County, California, and was a father of a student named Willow. Naturally, he had heard all about the incident at the school where his daughter boarded and answered the phone almost as soon as it rang. Ellie introduced herself as a member of the Winston PD and asked the same questions of this Javier as she did the other. There was nothing here, either. Javier said he hadn't heard of any of the kids she mentioned, and Ellie was inclined to believe him. His biggest concern was for Willow, to whom he had spoken just moments ago. Ellie assured him the local high school was a safe environment for his daughter and ended the call after offering a few more assurances.

The last Javier on Ellie's list lived in Winston, so she decided to take a drive over there.

The neighborhood where Javier Martinez lived with his wife, Stacey, seemed a different world from Jake's little trailer home. The Martinez family, Ellie learned, had one son, Gus, who boarded at the school. Judging by the size and condition of the Martinez homestead, Gus's education was not a strain on the family finances.

Ellie pulled her cruiser to the curb and cut the engine. All the lights in the home were off, except for one in the hallway. At the high school, she had asked around for Gus Martinez, but a girl named Rebecca had told her that he and his family had gone on vacation. Ellie's radar went up right away.

A vacation before a major incident at the school? The timing was certainly a little peculiar.

She figured if this Javier had been somehow involved, he had pulled up stakes and gotten his family out of Dodge. Ellie wasn't surprised to find the house dark and no cars in the driveway. The garage had no windows, but Ellie doubted she'd find any cars inside.

The Martinez family was supposedly gone, after all. But to where?

Ellie cupped Kibo's face in her hands. "Wait here, buddy. I'll be right back."

The evening air had a bite, so Ellie zipped up her jacket to stave off the cold. The neighborhood was quiet, as most neighborhoods were at this hour. The persistent chop of helicopters overhead was the only clue that something big was going down a few miles away.

Ellie walked up the front steps and peered into a side window, using her flashlight to enhance her vision. It was dark inside except for a single light in the kitchen, a typical precaution any family might take when leaving home for a week or so. Ellie knew this same as the burglars. From what she could see, the place looked in order. No overturned furniture. Nothing to suggest a struggle. Ellie noticed an ADT sticker on the window, but the panel was out of view, so she had no way to know if the alarm was on or not. She assumed it was on.

Maybe it was just a vacation.

Ellie decided to check around back. She was going to report this to Haggar. It was worth doing even if the lead didn't pan out. He was already working on other intel that Jake had supplied, including the name Fausto. According to Haggar, the FBI had agents investigating reports of major thefts. Two hundred million dollars bought a lot of chatter. They could investigate and make inquiries all they wanted. At some point, Haggar would realize Jake wasn't unstable—that he was, in fact, their best hope for a positive outcome. She only hoped that realization did not come too late.

After Ellie scoped out the backyard, she'd see what she could do to get Jake some support. She hadn't heard any reports on the radio, but the FBI was using secured channels to communicate and Ellie wasn't privy to most of those conversations. Jake could be up to his eyeballs in bullets. She had no way of knowing.

Do what you can do. Focus on making a difference.

That was what her father would have advised. Maybe this jaunt would help. Maybe she could find a clue that would help locate the Martinez clan, and, assuming they were involved somehow, make a difference.

Ellie kept her flashlight on, even though the moonlight sufficed. The side yard was nicely manicured, Ellie observed. The trees were pruned, the hedges trimmed, and Ellie saw nothing out of the ordinary. She shone her light into the small hopper windows and saw a finished basement with all the accoutrements of wealth: foosball table, pool table, comfy couch, and that was just what she could make out. A closed door probably opened into an unfinished side. Nothing unusual.

The backyard was broad and flat. Flower gardens looked lovingly maintained. Things didn't have to be in shambles for something to be going on, but Ellie was scoping out the scene. Doing what she could do.

Ellie stuffed her hands in her jacket pocket and gazed up at the sky. The stars winked down on her and the vastness of it all was a reminder of her distance from Jake. What was happening with him? Ellie couldn't waste another second chasing down this lead. She needed to be back in the action.

As she turned to go, something in a tall row of juniper trees at the far end of the backyard caught her eye. A glowing reddish ember hovered inexplicably in the dark. It took Ellie a moment to realize what it was: a cigarette. Somebody was in the yard, concealed in those trees, smoking a butt.

Ellie undid the snap on her gun holster. Her hand went to the handle of her Glock 19. She took a step toward the smoker.

"This is the police. Come out where I can see you."

The ember glowed brighter. The smoker took a drag.

"Come out from the bushes now."

Ellie's heart began to race. Her nerves tingled. She pulled the gun from its holster, trained the weapon on the ember and shone her flashlight on the bushes as she took another step toward the smoker.

"Come out now."

Ellie saw the bright flash, heard the pop, and an instant later felt pain in her leg. She went to the ground as her injured leg folded in on her. She felt an excruciating burning sensation, and hot blood pumped through a hole in her thigh. The ground seemed to sprout hands that held her down. She couldn't move, couldn't get up.

Another flash came from the dark. This bullet struck the ground near Ellie's head. She found strength to lift her body maybe a few inches off the ground. It was enough to squeeze the trigger in the direction of the shooter.

Ellie got five shots off in rapid succession. She aimed just to the right of the glowing ember. She saw the cigarette fall from the shooter's mouth and heard him cry out. Then she heard nothing.

Ellie put her finger on the bullet wound to her thigh.

The blood flowed steadily, but she didn't think the bullet had hit a major artery.

The basement door flew open, and Ellie cocked her head in the direction of the sound. Sensors on the door detected movement and turned on a powerful set of floodlights. Ellie saw a tall, shadowy figure come lumbering toward her. Fear was something foreign to Ellie, but now it wrapped around her like a straitjacket. The man came fast. She saw the flash when he was maybe fifteen feet away. The gunshot echoed into the night.

Ellie heard Kibo bark in distress. The bullet struck Ellie in the chest. The pain was instant and intense. She puffed out her cheeks and tried to make the burn go away. The shadowy figure approached and put three more bullets into her body—another one in the chest, one in the stomach, and a third in her other leg. With each bullet, Ellie's body jolted in shock. She came up off the ground a few inches and fell back down with a thud.

The fourth shot, a head shot, landed in the dirt.

She heard the man say, *"Hijo de puta."*

Through slits in her eyes, Ellie watched the man continue his approach until he now loomed over her. Blood seeped out of the hole in her other leg in steady hot spurts. The chest and stomach wounds were nothing; those bullets had struck her body armor and would leave nasty bruises. But her legs burned. The hot lead was like a blowtorch to her muscles.

Ellie felt the ground for her Glock. She brushed against the metal with the tips of her fingers. If she stretched, she might be able to reach it. But the pain in her chest and stomach made the slightest movement impossible.

The man came over to her and laughed as he put a boot on her chest. *"Adios,"* he said. He took aim with his gun.

Her next move was pure reflex. Ellie latched onto the man's ankle and gave it a hard yank. His surprised eyes widened until the whites became the size of cue balls. As he fell backward, Ellie reached for her gun. The man quickly rolled on top of her and moved his arm to get the gun in front of her face. Ellie seized his right wrist with her left hand and applied counterforce. She pushed across her body while her right hand continued to search for her weapon.

Her attacker was at least six feet tall and outweighed her by fifty pounds. His square face was frozen in an expression of rage. He pushed hard against Ellie's arm and gained an inch. Another few inches would put the barrel of his gun in front of her face.

Ellie's fingers brushed against something metal. She stretched them until it felt like her knuckles would separate from the joints. The man snarled and pushed even harder, his gun inching ever closer to her face. With one final stretch, Ellie's fingers grazed her gun once more. At that very moment, her attacker put a hand around her throat and began to squeeze. Bile raced up Ellie's esophagus, collecting there and choking her more. Ellie kicked frantically as her right hand finally got a good grip on her gun.

With one final effort, as her world turned dark, Ellie lifted the gun off the ground and moved it under the man's body. She fired several shots in rapid succession into his gut and chest.

The intense pressure on her throat released as the man tumbled back and off her body. His legs kicked spastically; then they went still.

Ellie rolled over onto her stomach, coughing, spitting, fighting the burn in her throat, her legs, her body. She started to crawl toward her car. She had bitten her tongue in the struggle and spat gobs of blood onto the grass. Her stomach and chest felt as if they had been torn apart by some animal, but she knew it was just bruising from the gunshots.

Ellie reached for her radio during her crawl. She had just pulled it off her belt, when the basement door flew open again. She cocked her head once more in that direction and saw a man charging at an angle that didn't give her a clear shot. He came fast. No letup in his stride. He dove on top of her, tackling her while she was already on the ground. Ellie tried to fend him off, but he was wiry and far stronger. He had little trouble wrenching the radio and gun from her hands.

He stood and used his boot to flip Ellie onto her back. "You just killed my friends, bitch." He pointed what appeared to be a miniature cannon at Ellie's head.

Kibo's barks echoed like gunshots.

Chapter 44

Everyone was in the pit. It was crowded, and Jake almost landed on one of the kids. It was too dark to see which one. Whoever it was scurried off into a corner like a terrified animal.

The blackness had to go. Jake flicked on his headlamp and whirled in the direction of the mewling teens. All the color had drained from their faces. David and Rafa put fingers in their ears, as if that could fix their damaged hearing. Their uniforms were in shambles—dirty, torn, stained. They stared vacantly, each one looking utterly lost and wholly terrified. They huddled together in a corner of the pit as far from the three corpses as possible.

"Through the door," Jake said. "It's unlocked. Hurry!"

Nobody moved, paralyzed possibly by hearing loss, but more likely by fear.

Jake lunged at the door and pulled it open with force. He grabbed the closest person to him, David, and stuffed him through the compact opening.

"Go and run!"

One by one, the kids stooped to get low enough.

Like Alice crawling through the small door to enter Wonderland, they vanished into the dark tunnel beyond. As they departed, Jake stood below the pit opening and fired round after round from his AK-47 into the air. Shell casings plunked down like metallic raindrops. Bullets fired from his gun hit the ceiling and probably nothing else. Jake's only goal was to deter the others from trying to follow. Eventually somebody would, though. It was the only way out of the auditorium, unless they somehow managed to break down one of the exit doors.

Jake went through two more magazines while keeping anybody from attempting to enter the pit. He was down to just two magazines of ammo. Sixty more shots, plus his pistols.

Jake looked back in time to see the last kid enter the tunnel. It was Andy, and Jake wasn't at all surprised that his son waited for the others.

Jake stopped shooting, secured his weapon, and dove through the door to the tunnel like a base runner sliding headfirst into second. From a pocket on his chest rig, Jake retrieved the key and spent precious seconds getting the tunnel entrance locked.

The kids had not ventured far. They huddled together for comfort, for contact. They were safe, but that could change in a heartbeat. Jake heard footsteps descend the metal stairs. Death was coming.

Jake said, "Go. Go. Hurry!"

Jake's headlamp fell on Andy. He could see his son's puzzled and awed expression.

"Dad?" Andy said.

"No time," Jake answered.

More footsteps bounded down the stairs. How many

sets Jake couldn't say. He had made a body count in his head: one in the bathroom, three down in the pit, and five confirmed kills in the auditorium mêlée. How many did that leave? He would find out from Andy later, but not now. Now they had to run.

"Go! Go! Go!" Jake yelled to the pack of teens.

"It's dark down there," Hilary said.

"Start running!" Jake ordered.

A gunshot blast came from behind the closed metal door. They were going to shoot it open. Handguns would be underpowered. But these men had high-caliber weapons at their disposal that could blow the hinges off the door. Jake had killed a guy with a shotgun, and that was an ideal weapon for the task.

The gunshot sent Rafa running like a starter pistol had gone off. *Smart kid.* He squeezed past the others and, soon enough, Hilary fell into step behind him. The pack became a line. But it was dark, as Hilary noted, and there were pipes and wires and other things to trip over.

Jake heard a smack that sounded like bone on concrete. David cried out in the darkness. Jake heard another loud bang; this time, it was Pixie who yelled. These kids were literally running blind, Jake realized.

Rather than waste time fishing a flashlight from his backpack, Jake took out one of the flares he'd stored in a pocket on his chest rig. He undid the top and it became a torch. He passed it up to Andy, who passed it along to Hilary, who got it to Rafa. Then Jake sent another flare up the human chain. All this happened as they ran.

The tunnel glowed ruby red and sparkled like a mobile fireworks display. Smoke from the burning flares fanned back and filled Jake's mouth with the metallic taste of potassium and magnesium. Smoke began to fill the tunnel as well, ironically making it more difficult to see. But no one wanted to abandon the light for the alternative.

There were grunts but no words spoken, and footfalls, and lots of heavy breathing, but nothing close to conversation. This was all about escape. They were a line of seven people hunched over, weaving down the Stygian tunnel.

Behind them, Jake heard another blast. If they got the door open now, they'd be dead. Just like that. This place offered no cover. They would fire high-capacity weapons blindly down the tunnel and hit something. Guaranteed. Jake could return fire, but he was last in line, so he'd be shot first. Then what? One by one, they would gun down these kids. Simple as that.

Another blast hit the door.

Up ahead, Rafa was first to reach the branch off the main tunnel. He stopped there and yelled back, "Which way?"

Jake paused to think. They could take that branch to the staircase, then spill out into the janitor's closet. From there, it would be a trek up to the first floor; if they crossed The Quad without getting shot, maybe they could reach the forest. Jake processed that scenario in a flash. There would be congestion getting up the stairs and through the closet. Delays.

Farther ahead was a crawl space. It would act as a shield. If they could get through that crawl space, they could take the exit by the Terry Science Center. Up and out, and then into the woods from the basement exit. If

Jake could send their pursuers off on the wrong course, it would buy even more time.

Jake yelled, "Go. Keep running straight!"

As he ran, Jake unsheathed the knife strapped to his ankle and used it to cut a long swath of fabric from his shirt. At the tunnel branch, he stopped and fixed the cloth to a jagged piece of stone that jutted out from the passageway. The cloth looked like an arrow pointing the direction to go. Jake lit another flare, carried it partway down the branch so the smell of smoke and burning magnesium would be there as well, and then he extinguished the flame with his boot. He left the flare on the ground like a discarded cigarette. His hope was that these killers would mistakenly go up the metal stairs and chase their prey into the janitor's closet.

Jake returned to the main tunnel. "Keep as quiet as possible," he called in a low voice.

A short time later, Jake could see the ragtag line of escapees up ahead. Sound carried here, and Jake heard another gunshot in the distance, followed by an excited yell and a loud bang. The pit door was open. They were coming.

Gunshots came rapid fire. Bullets sank into the darkness. Some careened off concrete pipes, while others ineffectively sprayed the tunnel floor and walls. Jake couldn't see any flashes, which meant they couldn't see any flares. The whole line found a sudden burst of speed.

Jake was running at a sprint and didn't notice a figure down on the ground in front of him. It was pure agility that allowed him to hurdle Solomon without landing on the boy's head, but Jake's right boot kicked

Solomon's leg hard. Airborne, Jake outstretched like he was making a diving catch. When he hit the ground, the tactical helmet Jake wore bounced off the concrete. He heard a horrible crunching glass sound, and Jake knew his night vision optics were no more. At least Jake still had his headlamp.

Solomon lay on the ground close by and may have tripped over a pipe or his own feet. Jake stood and helped Solomon find his footing. Behind them, the gunfire continued unrelentingly. Only the angle of the tunnel was keeping them safe.

"Get up! Get up!" Jake yelled.

Solomon staggered to his feet and Jake held on to the boy's hand, dragging him forward. Up ahead, Jake saw the kids gathered in front of what he knew was a tight crawl space into the next section of the tunnel system. They were unsure of what to do. Jake let go of Solomon's hand, but glanced back to make sure the slower boy kept pace. The flares in Hilary and Rafa's hands hissed like a snake pit, expelling pungent smoke. Jake took the flares and extinguished them with his boot. He kept his headlamp on, but the flares were more likely to give them away.

The sound of gunfire down the tunnel sputtered and then stopped altogether. The kids were covered in filth and grime, breathing hard, stooped over, hands on their knees. Jake shushed them to better hear. He was counting on his bit of misdirection to send their pursuers off course, and his plan appeared to have worked. It was impossible to hear footsteps from this far away, but the quiet was a telling indicator.

Jake removed his backpack. He took an extra flashlight from within and powered it on. He handed the flashlight to Andy, along with a couple of flares.

"Andy knows these tunnels," Jake whispered. "He takes the lead. This is it for light, so going forward hold hands. Andy, call out any obstacles, but do it quietly. Get out the Terry Science Center exit. Hit the woods and start calling for help. Understood?"

Jake shone his headlamp on six terrified faces and got confirmation from each.

"We have time," Jake said. "Don't rush. A broken bone or even a twisted ankle here could be real trouble, so use your flares if you have to and go slow. Stick together and you'll make it out alive. Now go."

Andy reached out and took his father's hand. "Dad—"

"Not now, son. You're the leader here. Get everyone to safety. That's all that matters. Here, take this." Jake pressed the Ruger into Andy's hand.

"How are you feeling?" Jake asked. "Your diabetes, I mean."

Andy said, "Better now," and he gave Hilary a look. "I'm so sorry, Dad. I'm so sorry."

Jake put his hand on Andy's shoulder "These guys, who are they?"

"Drug cartel from Mexico," David answered.

Jake gave Andy a hard look that said the explanation could wait.

"How many total?" Jake asked.

Andy said, "Twelve," without hesitating.

Jake did the math again. Nine confirmed dead left three still alive. "Don't hesitate if you have to use this," Jake said. He squeezed Andy's hand around the butt of the pistol.

Andy examined the weapon in his hand before he stashed it in the waistband of his jeans. He gave his father a quick embrace. Then Andy got low to the ground. "Follow me," he said to the others as he crawled through the opening on his stomach.

One by one, the kids wormed their way through the narrow crawl space that linked the tunnels between the Academy Building and the Terry Science Center. Jake would go last.

He removed his helmet. Sure enough, the optics were trashed; the glass was cracked and not functioning. Jake ditched the helmet and his hearing protection entirely. He stuffed his backpack through the opening, which was two feet high and not much wider. It was a tight fit for an average-sized person, but it also provided lots of thick concrete that would stop any bullets if they came this way. He hoped that wouldn't happen. By the time the cartel men realized the mistake, everyone would be long gone.

Jake checked his ammo for the rifle. One mag was already loaded in his gun, and the other he had strapped to his battle belt. He still had the Glock. With any luck, none of it would be needed.

The last in line to go through was Solomon. The boy shot Jake a frantic look.

"You got this," Jake said.

Solomon got low to examine the opening. He pulled back. Andy poked his head through.

"I'm coming," Solomon said.

"Go!" Jake said to Andy. "I'll stay with Solomon."

Andy nodded and then he was gone.

Solomon put his head into the opening, but again the narrow fit unnerved him, so he slunk out and turned himself around. He took a long time to calm down. Too long.

By now, Andy and the others were already out of earshot. Probably out of the building.

"I'll back in," Solomon said.

Jake kept his headlamp on Solomon's sweat-drenched face. He watched Solomon's feet get through, next his legs, then his hips, and then Solomon stopped moving entirely. Jake heard the boy grunt and struggle, but he didn't move another inch. Solomon began to hyper-ventilate and Jake's headlamp illuminated every crevice on the boy's panic-stricken face. The part of Solomon's body Jake could actually see squirmed in a frantic wiggle.

"Help! Help! I'm stuck!" Solomon screamed.

Jake's eyes went wide with horror. The boy's screams would give them away, for sure. Jake crouched in front of Solomon and said in a calm voice, "Take it easy, buddy. Take it easy. You've got to keep quiet."

"Help!" Solomon screamed again. "I'm stuck! I'm stuck!"

Panic. Pure, terrified panic.

Jake couldn't see through the opening; Solomon blocked the way. But he could hear just fine. He put his hands on Solomon's shoulders and gave a shove. The boy didn't budge. Next, Jake took hold of Solomon's wrists and gave a hard yank. No movement in either direction. Solomon was lodged in there good. Most of his body was through the opening. If Jake could get to the other side, he could probably pull him through. Of course he couldn't reach his legs because Solomon's body blocked the way.

Solomon kept screaming. "Please! Get me out! Get me out!"

Jake put his hand over Solomon's mouth to quiet him. "Easy there, easy," he said in the whisper he wanted Solomon to mimic. "You've got to be quiet. You don't want them to hear you."

Solomon was hearing none of it. If anything, his pleas and cries for help grew only louder. Amidst the racket, Jake heard another sound, one as terrifying as gunshots—footsteps.

They were coming.

Chapter 45

The man's eyes gazed upon Ellie like two black moons. His long hair framed a thin, angular face. Under the weight of his boot, Ellie writhed to get free, but the man's foot held her in place. Her strength weakened with each spurt of blood that shot out from the holes in her legs. The pain was all-consuming, and her thoughts were gummed with terror.

The man bared his teeth like a set of fangs and tucked his gun into the waistband of his pants. Evidently, he had something other in mind for Ellie than a final bullet. With a wicked grin, he extracted a knife from a holster latched to his belt. The massive blade looked to Ellie like a sword.

He lowered himself down onto her. Soon he had the blade pressed against Ellie's throat. She could feel him getting hard. Ellie had no weapon with which to fend him off, and little strength left to fight. Her last bit of resolve pumped out her leg and colored the green grass red. The man put his face close to Ellie's, close enough so she could smell onions and peppers on his breath.

He pressed into her, hips grinding, and she felt his excitement build. With his free hand, the attacker reached behind Ellie's head and seized a clump of her hair. He gave it a hard yank, as if pulling a rope.

Ellie cried out in pain. "Help," she whimpered. "Help me." Her voice grew in volume until Ellie finally found the scream she'd been looking for. "Help me!"

Her voice sailed into the night, catching the breeze, going nowhere and to no one. She listened for sirens. Perhaps someone had heard the gunshots and called the police. But all Ellie heard was the man's heavy breathing, Kibo's desperate barks, and the blood that thundered inside her head. The man cupped her mouth with his calloused hand. He pushed the blade harder against her throat. Hatred consumed him. Blind to the possibility that help might be on the way, he was determined to make her suffer to the greatest extent possible. It seemed that was all that mattered to him.

"Voy a hacer que dure," he said.

Ellie knew *"voy a hacer"* was Spanish for "I am going to." *Going to what? Kill me? Cut my throat? Rape me?* All of the above, she believed. Every single one of those things. Even if that wasn't exactly what the words meant, it was what he was going to do.

The man pulled Ellie's hair and breathed into her ear. *"Te va a encantar mi verga."*

Ellie knew for certain what was to come when he undid her belt. She clawed at his face. *Clawed.* The blood loss had left her completely drained. Her attack couldn't repel a fly. Ellie writhed beneath him. She kicked haplessly. Fatigue beat out resolve and Ellie began to give in. Her mind went blank and the pain went away. The brush of steel against her throat became nothing.

She felt her body rising up off the ground. Suddenly there she was, ten, maybe fifteen feet in the air, maybe higher, just floating. She looked down upon herself and the man on top of her . . . but then, it wasn't her. It was someone, somebody else thrashing beneath this stranger. How horrible it was, she thought, to see this poor woman being savaged in such a vicious manner.

Where Ellie was now, nothing hurt. She felt no pain, only peace, profound peace. But the woman, that poor woman. Something had to be done to help this woman. It was her duty, though she couldn't exactly say why. She felt nameless. She had no past. No future. She was just a presence watching over this woman in such duress.

She called out, "Somebody help!"

Her voice was a hiss of air, a whisper in the wind.

Poor woman . . . poor woman . . . I'm so sorry. . . .

With a sudden stab of horror, Ellie understood she *was* the woman. In the very next instant, Ellie returned to her body, and the pain came back sharper than ever. It flooded her eyes, her mouth. It was shards of glass against her skin. The pain sank deep into her joints and the fibers of her muscles. She wished herself back to the place where she was floating, where she was nothing and everything all at once. The blade sank into her throat and a tug on her pants pulled them to her hips.

Ellie's screams grew softer. She was thinking about that place. The place without any pain. A noise in the distance registered in her ears. What was it? Strange but familiar. She wasn't scared of this sound at all. It grew louder until it made sense to her. Until she knew what was coming. It was the sound of growls, and snarls, and snapping jaws. It was the sound of paws slapping the soft earth. It was the sharp bark of Kibo streaking at the man like a missile on target.

He had heard her. In her cruiser, he had probably barked, spun around in the front seat, pawed at the door handle, and nuzzled it with his snout until he got it open.

And then he ran.

Ellie saw little of the attack. But it was enough.

Kibo flew in the air over her head and struck the man in the chest with the full force of his eighty-five pounds. He snarled and snapped his jaws into the man's shoulder. His paws ripped long streaks down the man's face. Then Kibo sank his teeth into the fleshy part of the man's leg and shook his head from side to side. Ellie heard a ripping sound as the flesh came free. Then Kibo bit again.

Free of the man, Ellie reached for her Glock and managed with a stretch of the fingers to take hold of the weapon. From the ground, she aimed through the gauze of her vision and fired a single shot, which found the center of her attacker's head. The man fell backward. Kibo pounced on his chest and snarled in his face. When the man didn't move, and his scent changed, Kibo got off and came over to Ellie. He curled up next to her, licked her face, and whimpered.

At some point, a new voice came from the dark. "Hello? Hello? Are you hurt?"

The voice was a boy's. Kibo growled.

Ellie managed to wheeze out, "Easy, easy, Kibo. It's fine, sweetie. It's fine."

The boy held his ground. "My name is Gus. We're being held hostage, but I think you might have killed them all. I called the police. They're on the way."

Kibo growled low and menacing. The boy would not approach. He was smart to be cautious. Ellie gripped Kibo's fur to keep him close, though she knew for certain her guardian angel would never willingly leave her side.

Chapter 46

Solomon wore his terror like a gruesome mask. His mouth hung open wide, lips twisted and curled, eyes bulged from strain as he pushed futilely to get through the compact opening. Stuck in that hole, Solomon's cheeks billowed and collapsed from the effort. He kept up a steady stream of grunts, groans, and cries for help. How much time did he have before the cartel men showed up and started shooting? Fifteen seconds? Thirty? A minute. Not much more, that was for certain.

Jake focused again on those approaching footsteps, and something clicked. He could distinguish two distinct sets. Two people were coming for them. Jake flashed on his count again. Three of the cartel were still alive, assuming Andy's information had been correct, which meant one of them had taken the wrong route, while the other two had come to investigate Solomon's racket.

Jake ran toward those footsteps. Solomon watched him go. As soon as Jake vanished, the boy's panic escalated. It sounded to Jake as if Solomon was screaming in his ear.

Jake backtracked a good distance and dropped to his knees to fire his AK-47 blindly down the corridor. Without night vision, it was pitch black. He sent round after round screaming into the darkness, firing in three-shot sequences to conserve ammunition. Flashes of gunfire briefly lit him like a strobe light. In the interludes, Jake listened for footsteps. What he heard was Solomon's desperate pleas.

"Come back! Come back! Help me get out!"

Shots rang out at Jake from the darkness, sharp against his exposed eardrums. The bullets struck concrete. Jake was thankful again that this particular section of tunnel angled in such a way that kept him out of any direct lines of fire. It was a temporary sanctuary from the bullets, at best. In no time, the men would reach a point where the angles played in their favor. As long as Jake kept shooting, he could hold them at bay until Solomon freed himself.

That was his big strategy anyway.

Part two of his plan wasn't much better. Once Solomon was free, Jake would keep shooting long enough for the boy to get away. Then it would be two against one, and Jake understood his odds.

But there was a problem with this plan, which Jake reasoned as soon as his thoughts had time to gel. One former pitching coach nicknamed this interlude "the gathering," which accurately described the process Jake used to pull himself together during a game. The gathering helped him focus and visualize the task at hand. In all instances, it heightened his mental acuity;

and in this situation, it helped Jake see the obvious fault of his thinking.

He would run out of ammo long before Solomon got free.

The only way to dislodge Solomon, Jake believed, was to pull him from behind. Maybe Andy had gotten to Haggar by now. Maybe help was on its way. Maybe. But Jake's ammunition would be gone long before that theory proved out.

For the time being, Jake couldn't shoot them and they couldn't shoot him. As long as they heard gunfire, they wouldn't advance. Once he stopped shooting, they would come, guns blazing, for sure. And eventually they'd hit him or Solomon. One of them, or both, would die.

Jake settled on his best option: take out the two men at the exact same time. But how? Charge them? That seemed reckless at best. Wait for them to come to him? In these close quarters, a stray bullet had a good chance of becoming lethal.

And then it came to Jake, a plan formed during another miniature gathering episode. Jake knew how and where to set up an ambush, but it required Solomon to become invisible. For his plan to work, Jake would have to lure the cartel into this section of tunnel. That was the easy part. All he had to do was stop shooting.

The problem was Solomon. If the cartel men heard the boy, they'd shoot, even if they couldn't see their target. Jake needed it completely silent for his ambush to work.

Walking backward, taking hurried steps, Jake returned to Solomon. As he went, Jake fired at regular intervals—ineffective, he knew, but he hoped it would be enough to stave off an assault. He had to get in position. Had to get ready.

At the hole, Jake bent down and gave Solomon his headlamp—the power of light. He brushed aside the boy's tears and set a comforting hand on Solomon's flushed cheek. With his free hand, Jake fired off a couple more rounds from the rifle.

"Listen, buddy, listen. I need you to go silent now."

Solomon was having none of it. He was in the midst of a full-on panic attack.

"Can you get quiet?" Jake asked again. "We've got to be silent. Right now. Starting now. I know you're scared, but you've got to do this."

Jake had talked long enough. The men might already have advanced their position. He set off another burst of gunfire, and that made Solomon jump, but it didn't get him free from that blasted hole. Jake pulled the trigger once more, but the magazine was empty. He changed it. And that was the last one.

"I'm so scared!" Solomon hollered.

Jake gazed down into the void. Somewhere in that darkness, two men waited for their opportunity to strike.

Calm the boy. Calm him.

"Fear is in the mind," Jake said. He spoke slowly so Solomon could hear his words clearly, and he got close to reveal his serious expression. "Just get those negative thoughts out of there."

Jake shot off a few more rounds.

"I can't do it. I can't. I can't. I can't calm down."

He had to reach the boy. But he couldn't rush him, couldn't force it. Reach him. Connect with him. Jake went to the one subject he knew best besides prepping.

"You play any sports?" Jake asked in a soothing voice. "Baseball? Football? Anything like that?"

Jake fired off a couple more shots. He was down to maybe twenty bullets. With one hand, Jake undid his battle belt and let it fall to the ground.

"Bowling," Solomon whimpered.

"Bowling," Jake repeated as he worked quickly to get his chest rig removed. "Fine. Fine. That's a good one. Bowling. I like that. Okay, okay, so do you scream at the bowling alley?" Jake fired some more bullets at nothing.

"'Scream'? No," Solomon said.

"Do you get all nervous when you bowl?"

The chest rig came off and fell to the ground, near to the battle belt.

"Never," Solomon said.

It was working. Solomon needed the distraction. His breathing was already less ragged, his panic less pervasive.

"Never," Jake repeated, sounding pleased. "Well, then, imagine we're just bowling right now. I know it doesn't seem like it, but think of this corridor here as nothing but an alley. Get yourself into a quiet space. Concentrate on it. See it in your mind. The pins. The lane. The feel of the ball. The smells. The noise. Everything. Think about every detail until it's like you're there. You understand?"

"No," Solomon said in a panicky voice.

"Right, of course you don't. Of course not. You see, nervousness, that's just your worry all pent up with no place to go. That's where the anxiety comes from. You've got to have a release valve for that, get it?" Jake's voice came out breathless from a combination of dread and exertion.

He took three more shots. Jake was down to the last ten bullets in his rifle. Solomon had that many bullets left to get calm and quiet. Jake removed his shirt and revealed the Kevlar he wore underneath.

"You're feeling anxious, right?" Jake asked.

"Uh-huh."

"Well, your anxiety is making that fear happen. Like a little fear factory working overtime inside you. And that fear, it becomes a self-fulfilling prophecy," Jake said. "Do you know what I mean by that?"

Jake's last baseball coach had said something similar to him a week or so before the car crash that ended his career. Lance had said something similar as well, right before Jake agreed to take the job at Pepperell Academy.

"You can't live your life like a scared little animal," Lance had said. "You've got a son to raise. Man up, Jake, and take the damn job."

Jake had done what Lance asked of him: he "manned up" and took the job. Jake had spent a lifetime trying to overcome his fear, and poor Solomon would have to do it in just a matter of minutes.

"Do you understand what a 'self-fulfilling prophecy' is?" Jake asked. He worked to loosen straps on his Kevlar.

"I think so," Solomon replied in a shaky voice. "If I think it, I make it happen."

"That's right," Jake said, energized. "What you think, you make happen. So this is a challenge, buddy. Nothing more. A really awful challenge that you got to face, and you can't give in to the pressure." Jake fired off two more shots. Eight bullets remained. "You might be stuck in that hole, but you're still in control. You understand? You have the power. We don't want them to know they're close to you. If they do, they'll shoot. And they'll hit you."

As if to illustrate the point, Jake fired his weapon. Flashes spit out the barrel of the gun. The echo of each gunshot rattled off the walls loud enough to sting the eardrums. *Rat-tat-tat.*

Jake was down to his last five bullets.

"Think about what you want to have happen, not what might happen. What do you want to have happen, Solomon?" Jake fired off another shot and the Kevlar came free from his body.

"I want to get out," Solomon said, his voice shaky and on the verge of tears.

"What else? When those men come, what else do you want to have happen? Remember, you make it happen."

"I want you to knock 'em down like pins," Solomon said.

"Yeah. I want to do that, too. But what I need is for you to stay quiet as can be," Jake said as he fired off two more shots.

Two bullets left.

"Are you a fighter?" Jake asked.

"They called me a pig," Solomon said, sobbing. Jake could hear him sniffling. The tears were flowing again. "They pretended to cut me *like I was a pig.*"

Jake propped his Kevlar vest in front of Solomon, positioning it in such a way as to completely cover the boy's face and head. He took the headlamp from Solomon's hand. It wouldn't do him any good now.

"This Kevlar is like a shield," Jake said as he slipped his shirt back on. "It'll hide you from them and protect you if a bullet comes. You can hold on to it with your hands if you like, but don't let it fall down. Keep it in front of your head and face at all times. Understand?"

"Okay," Solomon said.

"Are you a fighter?" Jake asked again in a voice that commanded attention and respect.

"I'm a fighter," Solomon said. His voice came out softened behind the bullet-resistant fabric, but that wasn't why his words lacked conviction. "I am a fighter," he repeated.

That time, Jake believed him.

Jake cut the light from the headlamp, casting them both into an impenetrable darkness.

"I thought so," Jake said. He fired a bullet from the rifle.

His last one.

Chapter 47

Navigating the darkness like an experienced spelunker, Jake returned to the intersection where the tunnel's distinct sections converged. From his ankle holster, he removed the Glock and pulled the tang of the firing pin toward the rear of the slide to make sure the gun was ready to shoot. He holstered the Glock. The gun would come out later. Above his head, Jake was aware of the sturdy, insulated electrical and communication cables that ran along the ceiling.

The ceiling here was about eight feet high, and Jake's outstretched arms acted as an antenna of sorts that helped him to feel where to grab. His fingers were soon wrapped around a bundle of thick, industrial-strength cables from which he now dangled.

He gave a solid tug, testing to see if it could hold his body weight. Satisfied, Jake engaged his upper-body strength to hoist himself up. He swung his legs behind him, so he was facing the floor, and wrapped his ankles around the cables to secure him in place. If Solomon could see him, Jake would look like a fly caught in a monster spider's web.

To his credit, Solomon was quiet as a church mouse. Everything was perfectly still down here. The silence would eventually lure these men toward his ambush. Sure enough, Jake's ears picked up the sound of feet scuffing across the concrete floor. The pace of footsteps quickened, less cautious, more brazen. They were coming, and coming fast.

Jake retrieved the Glock from its holster. That fraction of movement was enough to cause the cables supporting his weight to go slack. He dropped maybe half a foot. He heard a groaning sound, an indication the fasteners holding the cables were starting to give.

Ahead of him, not too far away, Jake saw the first flash of light bounce off the tunnel walls. Without warning, Jake felt a second sensation of falling before the slack cables became taut again. Jake's body jolted violently at the end of his free fall.

Though he had dropped another several inches, Jake was still high off the ground and would be able to take his pursuers by surprise. But the fasteners that held him suspended in midair were one big breath away from becoming completely dislodged. The sound of footsteps rumbled in Jake's ears. For the first time, he heard a man speak.

"¡Ven! ¡Ven! ¡Por aquí!"

Two men emerged directly in front of Jake, no more than ten feet away. In one hand, they held flashlights; in the other, they carried large-caliber handguns— Glocks as well, 37s, super-advanced, big-bore technology, power-packed firearms in a compact frame. They slung rifles over their shoulders.

These men were clearly prepared to take over the school by force, so it was no surprise to Jake they came equipped and carried flashlights. Those lights illuminated a thin and muscular man, with a horribly scarred face, in the lead, followed by a tank of a man in the rear. As they approached the intersection where the tunnel angles changed, they moved with caution—the way a marine might cut through a jungle stitched with trip wire. Something had put them on guard. Those flashlights canvassed the tunnel area, the walls, but not the ceiling, and soon settled on the Kevlar some sixty feet away.

Jake took aim with his Glock, when the cables sagged again. The groan of those fasteners coming loose sent his nerves crackling. He couldn't move, certainly couldn't shoot without dislodging the cables supporting him.

"¿Qué es eso, Efren?" the scar-faced man said.

Efren.

Jake had heard the name before.

Scar Face fired an indiscriminate shot down the tunnel at the Kevlar. The blast was earsplitting at such close range. Gunpowder scented the air.

Oh, God! Jake thought. *Was Solomon hit? Did the Kevlar protect him?* Impossible to say. But Jake couldn't let them shoot again, so he fired off a single shot, which entered Scar Face's skull and never came out. The now-dead man's eyes rolled back into his head as his knees gave out. At the same instant, the already-brittle concrete holding those fasteners in place broke loose from the ceiling with a sharp crack. Entangled in cables, Jake plummeted straight to the ground and landed with a loud sound. It was the sound that flesh makes when it smacks concrete. The gun dislodged from Jake's hand upon impact.

Efren froze. Shock. Surprise. Both. Jake fought to get air into his lungs. The flashlight that had been in Scar Face's hand was now on the ground and lit the tunnel enough for Jake to see his remaining opponent.

Efren's white tank top had collected so much grime it looked like something dragged out of a fireplace, but it showed off arms with muscles that protruded like baseballs sewn under the skin. The big man had a head like an anvil, and Jake figured he'd shatter the bones of his hand if he hit him wrong. But Jake wasn't about to punch his face. This monster sweated aggression and his expression was that of a rabid dog's.

Jake's Glock had skittered out of reach; so without fully recovering, he unsheathed his knife and sprung from the ground. His swipe was aimed for Efren's gun hand. Had he got there a split second sooner, it would have found flesh. Instead, Efren yanked his hand away, and twisted at the waist as if executing some advanced dance move.

A fraction of a second later, Efren unleashed two quick strikes, which rattled Jake's kidneys and produced the kind of lightning pain that turned vision white. Close-quarters combat was not ideal for gunplay, but the butt of the Glock worked fine as a club, and Efren brought the weapon down hard against the side of Jake's head.

Jake could do little but hit the ground face-first; and thanks to the stunning blow, his arms didn't get the message from his brain to brace for impact. Jake's chin smacked against the concrete floor and snapped his jaws together with enough force to crack several teeth. At least he managed to keep hold of the knife. A heavy boot came down against Jake's ribs and something went haywire inside. The boot found his side again, and it was a repeat of the earlier earthquake to his body.

Mustering his remaining strength, Jake flipped onto his back and flung the knife at his attacker. He'd had enough knife-throwing practice to hit pay dirt, but the blade sank into the meatiest part of Efren's thigh. To Jake's dismay, the huge man's face showed not the slightest indication of pain. But the contact provided enough of a distraction for Jake to reach his Glock.

No sooner had Jake produced his weapon than the hulk fired his gun.

At first, Jake didn't know what to feel. When he tried to squeeze off a shot of his own, nothing happened. Then the pain came with the intensity of a speeding train. Warm blood oozed out a sizable hole in Jake's hand, where a bullet had gone through.

Efren fired again, but Jake rolled to his right, just in time, and that bullet missed by inches. Jake's Glock didn't roll with him. No way to hold on to the gun with most of the bones in his hand shattered.

Jake was on his back, scrambling to get away. Efren lurched forward and took aim with his weapon. He straddled Jake, but he didn't shoot. Instead, he set his boot down hard on Jake's bloodied hand and applied tremendous pressure. The screams that blew out of Jake's throat were hardly human. Efren grinned.

With his right hand still pinned under Efren's boot, Jake ignored the pain as he lifted part of his body off the ground. Reaching with his left hand, he seized the handle of the knife protruding from the Goliath's leg and gave a hard yank. The razor-sharp blade sliced through muscle and tendon as if cutting air. Jake opened a gash that extended the length of the thigh. Efren fired his weapon, but the discharge went toward the ceiling as his big body fell toward the ground.

With his hand freed from the boot, Jake scrambled to his feet and jumped onto Efren's back to try and pin him down. The monster bucked and thrashed beneath him, but could not get Jake dislodged. Reaching with his left hand, his good hand, Jake yanked down a slack portion of cable and wrapped it like a noose around the man's beefy neck. With the cable secured, Jake pushed his knees into Efren's back as he pulled with his arm.

Underneath him, the hulking man went wild. His enormous body thrashed in every conceivable direction. With each thrust, each twist, Jake tightened his grip on the cable, and through gritted teeth pulled on it like a horse's reins. Maybe it was thirty seconds. Maybe a minute. But at some point, all that bucking, and thrashing, and moving about just stopped.

Breathless, Jake slid off the dead man, clutching at his bleeding hand. He retrieved the flashlight from nearby and examined his wound, a nasty red hole ringed black with gunpowder. The bullet had passed clean through, but the hand was useless to him now.

Jake took off his shirt and used the fabric to stanch the blood flow. He staggered over to Solomon and, with the flashlight, saw where a bullet had struck the Kevlar. Jake pulled the makeshift shield away to reveal Solomon's panic-stricken face.

"I did it," Solomon said. "I kept quiet. I kept quiet."

The boy's cheek was red and bruised, marking the spot on the Kevlar where the bullet had struck.

"Yeah, you did it," Jake said in a shaky voice.

Jake's body was covered in blood, dirt, grime, and smeared greasepaint from his camouflage, but Solomon took no notice. Relief radiated off the boy like light from a star. The good vibes didn't last long. Jake's ears filled with sounds of footsteps and gunshots. The third man was coming, and fast. Light from one of the dropped flashlights revealed the location of Jake's Glock. He took a wobbly step toward the gun. It seemed so far away. Jake felt completely enervated, and his breathing bordered on hyperventilation. Pain commanded every nerve in his body. Even if he reached the gun, Jake hadn't trained at weak-hand shooting.

"Get that shield back up," Jake said to Solomon. His voice came out lacking authority. Solomon got his protection back in place.

Jake assessed the probability of his getting to the gun before this armed man appeared and started shooting. It was somewhere between zero and none. The shirt wrapped around Jake's injured hand was already heavy with his blood. His vision came in and out of focus. He was going to lose consciousness at some point, he could feel it, and those footsteps were getting louder. But Solomon's body blocked the only way out.

Jake swallowed hard and took another uneven step toward his weapon. From behind, Solomon shouted, "Hey! Hey!"

Jake spun around just as Solomon vanished into the hole. Somebody must have grabbed his legs and used tremendous force to yank him through. A second later, Andy, flashlight in hand, poked his head through the opening where Solomon had been stuck.

"Dad!" Andy yelled. "Let's get out of here. It's go time."

Jake didn't need a second invitation. He spun around and slid through the narrow opening just as a hail of bullets came screaming from the darkness.

Chapter 48

Fausto Garza stepped over the lifeless bodies of Efren and Armando so he could take aim at the man at the end of the hall. Rage owned him. The mission was gone; he had nothing left to salvage.

Fausto did not know how many fighters his team had gone up against. Five? Had to be that number, at least. His entire team was dead, that much he knew. He also knew that he had followed the wrong path. While Efren and Armando went to investigate the commotion they heard, Fausto followed the other trail, thinking they could have split up. He wasn't sure what had made him turn around. Instinct, perhaps. At some point, he knew he had fallen for a trick and so he returned.

As this played out, Fausto contemplated his options. They were limited. He could hide in the tunnels, but eventually he'd be found. They'd bring dogs down that would sniff him out like a fox in the hunt. He could try to escape into the woods, but he could be caught. The response from law enforcement would be intense, massive. The game was over, but there remained one thing for Fausto to accomplish.

Revenge.

Efren's and Armando's bodies meant nothing to him. They were just carcasses, pieces of meat. What mattered to Fausto was whoever had put them down. He would shoot at anybody he found down here. Though bullets to the body would not provide much satisfaction. He'd prefer to flay those responsible alive. No matter what happened, Fausto would not be taken into custody. Oh, no, he wouldn't. He would go out in a fiery blaze of bullets, like the outlaw he believed himself to be. He was born into a world of violence and death, and he refused to leave it any other way.

But a question burned in his mind, one he did not know would ever be answered: *What happened to Soto's money?*

The kids would have given it up if they had it, Fausto believed. He had guns to their heads. The countdown was no joke. The money really *was* gone. Soto would take over from here. He would keep up the hunt and never rest. Money was like air to that man—it kept him alive.

Fausto leveled his assault rifle and uncorked a flurry of bullets that would have taken out the knees, had the man up ahead not vanished through a narrow opening. Fausto screamed with rage and sent a volley of gunfire into the concrete. Some of them might have flown through that hole, but Fausto had a feeling his bullets hadn't killed anybody.

And so the chase was on.

"Go! Go! Go!" Jake screamed as he shoved Solomon hard from behind to hurry the boy along.

He had no weapon and no plan but to flee from his pursuer as fast as possible. Jake was well aware his son had just saved their lives. But that was seconds in the past, and irrelevant now. They were sprinting once again; this time, Andy, with flashlight in hand, was taking the lead. The blood-soaked shirt functioned as a pretty decent makeshift bandage, but the pain in Jake's hand was brutal and throbbing. It pulsed with its own beating heart.

From behind, Jake heard the crack of gunfire and felt a burning sensation tear up the back of his leg. A sharp, stinging pain followed. The force of the bullet's impact knocked him down as if a baseball bat had struck him from behind. Lurching as he fell, Jake skidded on the ground, jarring his shoulder painfully on impact.

Andy whirled and saw his father splayed on the ground behind Solomon.

As he stumbled back to his feet, Jake screamed, "Run! Run!"

From the dark, Jake heard a taunting voice call, "Did I hit you? I hope so! I have plenty more where that came from!"

Andy came toward his father, but Solomon went the opposite direction and vanished into darkness. Jake understood why. Somebody was coming up behind them.

Andy aimed the Ruger at the hole they'd just crawled through and fired enough times to empty the magazine. The hole was a good twenty meters away, but it looked like Andy shot with tremendous accuracy. The ringing in Jake's ears was now as persistent as the throbbing in his hand. Andy helped his father to his feet. The bullet had just grazed the back of Jake's leg. He was hobbled, but could walk.

Making their way in the darkness, Jake and Andy caught up with Solomon just before they came to a tunnel branch on the left, which led to the exit under the Terry Science Center. Andy was first to go that way. For a moment, no bullets came at them. Whoever was in pursuit had slowed. Even if someone did fire at them, they were safe unless the ammunition happened to be smart enough to make a sharp left turn.

Shirtless, sweating, covered in filth, blood, and violent-looking scratches, Jake's chest heaved as he fought to take in as much air as possible.

"The others?" Jake asked as he removed his belt. He quickly secured the belt around his injured leg as a second makeshift tourniquet.

"Safe," Andy said. "They went into the woods, and I came back to look for you."

"You and Solomon get out of here, take the exit," Jake said.

"No, I'm staying with you."

"No, you're not."

"That's Fausto," Andy said in a shaky voice. "I heard his voice. He's the worst of them all, Dad. Please don't stay. You can't fight. You can't shoot. Let's get out of here."

"He'll follow you. All of us. We can't risk it. You've done enough, son. Get going. Now!" Jake barked the command.

Andy flinched a little. They had no time for arguing. This was about survival, and Andy listened and understood. He and Solomon took the exit, but they left Jake with the flashlight. Jake used that light to watch them go. When they were out of sight, he emerged from the relative safety of the branch and returned to the main tunnel. Only one target remained.

Fausto.

Jake would not leave this final job to the government or to law enforcement. He trusted no one but himself. Nobody from the cartel could leave this place alive. The only way to safeguard his son, and the others, was to protect their identities. If Fausto had yet to pass that information along to his boss, then the last man who knew them by name was coming this way.

Jake slipped out from the tunnel branch and was on the move again. He walked loudly, and as he went, he smeared on the walls the blood that seeped from his injured hand. There would be no question which path to follow.

Fausto wasn't going to waste ammunition. He could fire at that opening until all his bullets were gone, but it would accomplish nothing. No, he had to go through the hole in the wall, same as the others. If anybody waited in ambush, he would make an easy target, but retreat was not an option. Caution was tempered somewhat by blind fury. He went in headfirst, shooting rounds from his rifle to provide some cover, and emerged from the hole into a section of tunnel dark as the others. His flashlight allowed him to see somewhat, but the rifle was useless to him. He couldn't fire effectively one-handed. His pistol would have to do. Fausto's prized gun was his Glock 37, with gold accents and mother-of-pearl grips. The gun was a totem to the pistol Carlos lent him back in Ciudad Juárez many years ago—the one that Fausto had used to commit his first murder.

Fausto paused and took stock of his surroundings. Nothing ahead looked unusual. No sounds. No signs of life. He proceeded at a cautious pace. At one point, he checked the pistol's magazine and saw only six shots left, plus one chambered round. He was down to one magazine for his assault rifle, and seven shots in the Glock.

Fausto heard footsteps; sound carried well down here and he discharged two bullets in what surely was a wasted effort. He set off at a quick pace, and it was not long before he came upon the blood smeared along the tunnel wall. He saw a branch to his right, but he followed the blood, expecting the trail to vanish. It did not. It continued. It wasn't like the fabric or crushed flare that had tricked him before. Something human had left this stain. Fausto imagined an injured man using the wall to keep himself propped up, and the notion pleased him.

He followed the trail of blood like a shark tracking an injured fish.

Chapter 49

Jake made frequent checks behind him as he went. Fausto was coming, that much was certain. He could hear him, but not see him, which was fine. More than enough blood pooled from Jake's injured hand to coat the walls, but at some point he wouldn't have enough left in his body to keep him upright. Still, Jake knew where he needed to go. Having a destination kept him motivated and moving. The leg was bothersome, but not crippling. The tourniquet seemed to be working well, another positive Jake used to spur himself on.

As for his thoughts, Jake kept those task-oriented. Return to his bug-out location. Get to his weapons cache, where he had plenty of ammunition. This became a mantra of sorts. He had used mantras in baseball on plenty of occasions, and it proved valuable here as well. *"One step at a time"* replaced *"One pitch at a time."* Repetition kept Jake alert and in the moment as he traveled through different sections of tunnel, while leaving behind enough of a bloody trail for Fausto to follow.

When necessary, Jake crawled on his belly to clear

the low ceilings. He navigated successfully through crumbling archways and over-corroded pipes without incident. His injured hand produced mind-numbing pain at times and required special protection. He favored his good hand when forced to clear a particularly difficult obstacle.

Despite his extensive injuries, Jake moved briskly, somewhere between a walk and run. Markers spray-painted on the walls revealed his position as he journeyed underneath the Terry Science Center, the library, Gibson Hall, and the Society Building, where he'd shot a man dead. Soon enough, Jake was back in the section of tunnel that hid his bug-out location.

It was here Jake retrieved a Smith & Wesson .22 LR—rimfire pistol, good for target shooting, maybe a little recreational fun, but not ideal for gunning down drug cartels armed with assault rifles. It was all that Jake could shoot. He held the gun in his left hand and gazed at the black barrel, noticing now how his vision came in and out of focus. He did not have long.

Jake aimed the weapon. It was shaky in his weak hand. He would need his target perfectly still to make a kill shot. In this condition, Jake was all but guaranteed to lose a gunfight—or, for that matter, any other type of hand-to-hand combat.

But like any good prepper, Jake had a solution.

In his storage room, Jake kept plenty of .22 long-rifle ammo sealed inside military 50-caliber BMG ammo-storage cans. The cans were made of metal, with handles on top that made them easy to stack. A latch closed the cans tightly, and a rubber seal inside helped keep moisture out. He could store ammo for years this way, and it was just as good as a vacuum seal, Jake would say. He kept his bullets inside Ziploc bags, with a packet of silica gel thrown in for good measure to suck up any excess moisture. Each can held six Ziploc bags with 150 rounds. Jake didn't want that much ammo going off. He wanted fifty bullets at most. Enough to do the job.

Jake checked the ammo in the Smith & Wesson before he slipped the pistol into the waistband of his pants. He next opened a can of ammo, using his good hand, and returned to the larder with a Ziploc full of bullets. He formed a pile of ammunition, fifty rounds give or take, in the center of the room, which he soaked with gasoline from one of the many canisters stored down there. Working quickly, Jake made a trail of gas from the pile of bullets to the wall just to the right of the door, where he took up position. He checked that his Zippo lighter worked, which it did just fine.

Soon enough, he heard footsteps approaching. Fausto had followed the blood trail to the bug-out location. Cast-off light from a flashlight grew brighter. Jake had been wrong. Sometimes death did schedule an appointment.

A smile came to his bruised and battered face. For some reason, "The Star-Spangled Banner" had popped into his head, a song that he cherished for the many fond memories it evoked. It was game time—that was why it had come to him so suddenly, so out of the blue.

When the moment felt right, Jake lit the Zippo and let it fall from his grasp. Easiest pitch he'd ever thrown. Straight down. The flame caught the gas and, with a *whoosh,* a trail of fire lit up. It soon engulfed the pile of ammunition inside a contained ball of flame.

Jake knew what happened when ammo caught fire.

Bullets didn't go whizzing around like they've been discharged from a gun. Cartridge cases burst open, sure, and bits of brass might go flying about, but not with any velocity. Wouldn't even puncture the skin if it struck. The bullets wouldn't explode in one big simultaneous burst, either, but rather piece by piece.

A cartridge case confined to a chamber of a gun was a different matter. A gun caught in a fire would shoot a bullet at full velocity, and that risked injuring or killing Jake. But this was a show—The Show, as the big leagues were called—and Fausto was part of the game, though he didn't know it just yet.

Soon the bullets had started popping, one by one. It sounded a hell of a lot like gunfire. Jake observed the position of the flashlight beam and knew right away that Fausto had taken cover against a tunnel wall. He inched closer toward the door until he could poke his pistol into the larder. Fausto proceeded to fire blindly into the room. It was a bit imprudent to shoot without a target, but there was some logic. He could shoot at the sound without exposing his body to return fire.

The bullets from Fausto's weapon smacked against the walls of the larder, damaging only sacks of rice. The popping sounds continued, and so did Fausto's dispensing of bullets. This time, he poked the barrel of an assault rifle into the room and let off fifteen rounds. He covered most of the room, except for the wall where Jake waited. Soon enough, though, Jake heard a click, followed by another. Fausto had shot all his ammo at nothing but a diversion.

In that next instant, Jake's arm shot out. He snatched with his left hand, giving the barrel of Fausto's rifle a hard yank. The gun came free of Fausto's grasp, and

Fausto came stumbling into the larder, off balance, with his long hair rising up behind him like a silky wave.

With a snap of his wrist, Jake pulled the pistol from the waistband of his pants and fired off a single shot, which hit Fausto's arm, but missed the head. *Damn left hand!* The bullet's impact sent Fausto to the ground, but he was quick with the leg and used it to sweep Jake off his feet.

Jake went down on his back, hard. Before he could react, he felt weight on top of him, and a hand clawing for the Smith & Wesson. Jake resisted as best he could, but soon enough Fausto pulled the weapon from his weakened grasp.

Panting, Fausto stood to take aim. His mistake. Jake sent his leg skyward, right into Fausto's unguarded testicles.

Jake heard the air hiss out of Fausto's lungs, along with an agonized cry. Fausto doubled over in pain and staggered backward into the adjacent storage room as Jake struggled to his feet. In a way, Fausto had stumbled into a more advantageous position. He had gained some distance, and still had Jake in his direct line of fire. But Fausto was in too much pain to aim his weapon, so the gun in his hand hung useless at his side.

Frozen where he stood, Jake briefly contemplated running. Maybe he could get out of the larder, maybe down another corridor, but he would not get very far. He would eventually be gunned down. Those deep-set eyes of Fausto shadowed a rage Jake could feel in his bones.

Jake's opponent wasn't moving very quickly. The pain in Fausto's groin had turned his movements into molasses; but Jake, shot in both the leg and hand, wasn't in much better condition. He couldn't quite catch his breath. Fausto looked away as he got steady on his feet.

During this brief interlude, Jake reached behind with his left hand, his good hand. Without taking his eyes off Fausto, he grabbed a can of beans, which was stored on a low shelf within arm's reach. Jake brought his arm to his side and held his hand in such a way as to hide the object he had taken.

Fausto's pain finally settled, or so it seemed, since he managed a satisfied grin. For the first time, Jake got a good look at the horrific metal mouth, which contrasted sharply against his dirt-covered face. The pile of ammunition positioned between Jake and Fausto continued to burn, and produced tiny explosions of gunpowder, which sounded like a mash-up of firecrackers and popcorn popping.

"How many more are down here?" Fausto asked. His chest heaved from fatigue. He spoke with an accent, but Jake had no trouble understanding him.

"None," Jake said.

"None?" Fausto could not contain his utter disbelief. "It's just you?"

Jake smiled. "Yeah. Just me."

"Well, then, *váyase al diablo, pendejo,*" Fausto said.

Jake stood with his feet shoulder-width apart, the left-handed grip on the can of beans mimicking a four-seam grip on a baseball—the best grip for accuracy. He took a small rocker step forward with his right leg, and pivoted his left foot at the same instant Fausto raised the gun to take aim. Fausto lifted the gun higher, but he didn't have it targeted yet.

Jake's right leg came forward as his left arm went

back, producing enough separation to generate velocity. Jake was perfectly balanced, right in the middle of his feet, not too much over the front leg or back leg. His hands were equal and opposite. Jake's trigger foot—his left, not the usual one—turned in, and that brought him to the release point. He drove his shoulder toward Fausto's head, which he visualized as a catcher's mitt, and brought his right arm into his side. His feet were perfectly aligned so that his hips could open up. He stayed up and over the front leg as he released the can of beans way out in front of his body.

For not being a southpaw, Jake generated tremendous thrust. The can shot forward at incredible velocity at the same instant Fausto's gun went off. If Jake hadn't been in his follow-through, the bullet would have hit him in the head. Instead, it struck Jake's shoulder.

The impact knocked Jake off his feet and backward into the shelf with all those cans. The shelf shattered on impact and sent a hailstorm of tin raining down on Jake's head.

The bullet and the can of beans passed each other, but never made contact. Instead, the can sailed right through the open door of the adjacent storage room and connected in the middle of Fausto's head. Maybe it was going forty miles an hour, maybe faster. Either way, it was fast enough to put a dent in Fausto's skull and knock him to the ground.

Jake groaned and rolled on the floor of his larder, while Fausto did the same in the storage room. Expending what felt like his last bit of energy, Jake forced himself onto his knees. The hole in his shoulder was just another place for the blood to leak out. Jake's world was going dark, but he could see the nearby can of gasoline, the same canister he'd used to ignite the pile of ammunition.

Jake went for the Zippo first. He stretched his arm like a ballplayer going for an errant throw to cut down the distance he had to travel, before he slid his way over to the can of gas. The cap was still off, with plenty of fluid inside. In the other room, Fausto, even more dazed than Jake, somehow got to his knees and took aim with the gun again. A river of blood poured out from the jagged gash that had opened up the middle of Fausto's forehead and had bathed much of his face and eyes. Even on his knees, Fausto was wobbly, off balance. He fired two shots, which went in two completely different directions, both ineffective.

Jake tipped the can of gasoline over, spilling pungent liquid onto the floor. Using his legs, he shoved the whole thing into the storage room as if he had launched a shuffleboard piece. The open canister left in its wake a long trail of gasoline that continued until the container of gas came to a stop against Fausto's knees.

Jake wasted no time getting his Zippo out. He hit the flint and dropped the lighter at the start of the gasoline trail.

The flame traveled faster than Jake's pitch. In a blink, it vanished inside the open container of gas. An enormous fireball soon erupted. The explosion lit every crevice of the storage room and expansive larder in a bright yellow and orange light.

A wave of heat shot out, so intense it singed the hair on Jake's arms and face. Biting odors of gasoline and smoke failed to mask the odor of Fausto's burning hair and flesh as he vanished inside a swirl of flame. Fausto's skin blistered and peeled. Soon he wasn't *in* the flames, he *was* the flames; he was part of this entity that licked and spit and thrashed in all directions.

The pain had to be unbearable. Sounded that way, at least. In a matter of seconds, the flames melted another canister of gas in the storage room, and a second fireball erupted.

Jake shielded his face and turned away from the intense blast of heat. He crawled toward the door as another blast shook the room. By the time Jake reached the corridor, he heard the popping sounds of ammunition going off, followed by an explosion big enough to send a column of flames shooting out the larder door. Those flames licked the wall near Jake and then sank back into the larder as if the flaming beast had uncoiled and retracted its burning tongue.

When Jake finally reached the ladder that would bring him to the field house, his bug-out location was completely engulfed in flames. Gunpowder ignited, and chambered rounds went off as though someone had pulled the trigger. Food on the many shelves, in sacks, cooked until it was charred. Stored water boiled before it evaporated. Sacks of rice burned, as did the salt, the sugar, and the honey. Wood shelving fueled the flames and the heat melted the cans of fruit, vegetables, and beans it had scorched. The larder was seldom above sixty-five degrees, but now it was sixteen hundred degrees Fahrenheit, on its way up to two thousand.

Jake pulled himself up the ladder, rung by rung. His shoulder and leg begged for him to stop, but he went up anyway, one-handed, one rung at a time. He pushed open the trapdoor and was outside the field house, stumbling in the grass as if his legs were new and walk-ing was something still to learn. His blackened body was invisible against the night sky. Eventually voices came at him from all directions, shouting orders, call-ing for medical attention. Figures approached carrying lights.

So many lights.

From darkness, at last, Jake stepped into the light.

Chapter 50

The preoperative holding area at St. Mary's Hospital, in the same town where Jake and Ellie had once dined at a cozy Italian restaurant with checkered tablecloths, was an open-floor plan that used movable curtains on tracks to create the illusion of individual rooms. Jake was resting on a stretcher—his shoulder was immobilized in body wrap, his hand mummified in gauze dressing, and his leg suspended in traction. He had several IVs and a catheter in him, and he was hooked up to an array of equipment that monitored his vital signs with rhythmic beeps and hums.

In addition to the anesthesiologist, a trauma specialist and orthopedic and vascular surgeons had already consulted on Jake's condition. As a team, they decided to operate on the hand first. Amazingly enough, considering the number of shell casings that would be recovered at the scene, none of Jake's wounds had been deemed as life-threatening.

Jake was feeling logy from the pain medication, but he was alert enough to inquire about Ellie. According to the duty nurse, she was still in surgery. One of Ellie's leg wounds was more severe than any of Jake's injuries due to the proximity of a major artery, and she'd been rushed into surgery soon after her arrival and initial evaluation. Police and FBI were swarming about the hospital, purportedly there to keep an eye on Jake in case some cartel operatives were still on the loose and aware of his location, and because Jake's involvement in the mêlée was part of an ongoing investigation.

At some point during an especially medicated fuzzy period for Jake, the curtain to his makeshift room parted. A broad-shouldered man with short-cropped hair entered, escorting Andy. The man had eyes as hard as a steel girder and his mouth seemed forged into a permanent grimace. He came right to Jake's bedside with purposeful steps, and gripped one of the steel side rails in his sizable hands. He leaned over the bed, his hard-scrabble visage looming large before Jake's eyes.

"Jake, I'm Leo Haggar, the FBI agent you disregarded and disobeyed." The man had a voice gritty and coarse as Jake's favorite manager in the minors. "That said, from the statements the kids gave, I think I owe you a debt of gratitude."

Jake's mouth felt cottony dry, his throat achy and raw, but he managed to croak, "If I were you, I wouldn't have listened to me, either."

Haggar formed a half smile, which Jake matched.

"Listen, we've got a lot to chat about, me and you, but it can wait. In the meantime, I brought somebody with me who really wants to talk to his dad. I'll leave you two alone."

Haggar took a few steps toward the exit, but then turned around.

"Jake, before today I never would have said a hero could be a renegade. Heal quick, son. We'll talk soon."

Andy hung back for some time, until Jake encouraged him forward with a slight wave of his left hand, his good hand. Andy took a few tentative steps, his eyes taking it all in—the tubes, the monitors, the bandages.

"I'm . . . I'm so sorry, Dad. I'm so sorry for everything."

Jake noticed the quiver in Andy's lower lip, but somehow his son held those threatening tears at bay.

"Tell me everything," Jake said.

When Andy finished, a story that took considerable time and effort to tell, his eyes were red, and his face looked drawn.

"It's all my fault," Andy said.

"You didn't know how this was going to go down," Jake said.

"But a woman died because of what we did, Dad," Andy said. His voice carried the full weight of his regret.

Jake's facial muscles tensed. With it, an unpleasant jolt of pain ripped into his hand before it shot down his wounded leg.

"A woman died . . ."

"Andy, there's something you need to know about that woman."

Maybe it was the timbre of Jake's voice, or his phrasing, but something struck Andy as alarming. He went a little pale.

How will he take it? Jake didn't know, but he had to

be the one to tell him. Andy had to hear it from his father first.

"What about her?" Andy blinked rapidly and drew in several short, sharp breaths, as if he knew the news would be devastating on many levels.

Jake could feel himself getting choked up. His throat closed in silent protest.

"It was Laura. It was your mom, son."

Andy made a noise, a breath that swallowed a cry, and he had to lean on the bed rails for support. Jake covered Andy's hand with his own to make contact and to help keep his son upright.

Andy was having a hard time getting out any words. He pulled away and shook his head as if that show of denial, his protest, could somehow alter this new reality.

"What—what—was she doing there? Why was she even there, Dad?" The warble of Andy's voice, close to a stutter, punctuated each word.

Jake remained quiet for fear of implying any blame, but Andy seemed to focus on his father's silence. It gave him enough information to put the pieces of the puzzle together on his own.

"We were supposed to meet up," Andy whispered to himself. "Oh no, Dad. Did she come looking for me? Did she?"

Jake reached out his hand. "Come here, son," he said.

Andy squinted hard as he could, but those tears leaked out anyway. He gritted his teeth, but a sob broke free. Next, Andy covered his face with his hand and began to cry, full on, taking heaving breaths to get air down his lungs. It was raw, honest, and gut-wrenching for Jake to hear, to watch, but it was also very much needed. Like a sliver on the verge of causing an infection, those pent-up emotions had to come out for the healing process to begin.

"She wouldn't have come looking for you if she didn't honestly care. Her feelings for you, everything she said to you—that was genuine. I can attest to it."

Andy might have heard the words, but his head rested on Jake's chest and his tears continued unabated for a time. Jake caressed the back of Andy's head, and felt so sorrowful for his son that it actually took away his pain.

After some time, Andy looked at his dad through eyes that were red and raw. "I killed her," he said.

"No, son, those men did. They shot her. She saved you."

Andy stood up fully and took a step back from Jake's bed. "*Saved me?* How?"

"We might not have known there were hostages inside the school without her warning. They would have tortured you to get what they were after, and eventually killed you, leaving your bodies for us to find as they slipped away, undetected. That was their plan anyway. She sacrificed herself for you. She stayed alive long enough to tell somebody what she saw. I knew your mother pretty well, and the old Laura would never have gone to look for you in the first place. But the new Laura . . . well, I think she would have exchanged her life for yours if that had been a choice."

Andy hung his head in sorrow and shame.

"The best way to honor her death," Jake continued, "the only way, is to find it in your heart to forgive yourself. I do, son, I forgive you. I love you, Andy, more than anything. You're my boy—" Jake got emotional and the words stuck, but he found his voice soon enough. "I would do anything to keep you from harm. Anything. In that way, your mom and I are a whole lot alike."

Andy stayed with Lance while Jake recovered at the hospital. Jake hadn't seen Ellie yet, but she was there, recovering too. Today was going to be the first day since he climbed out of that hole in the field house's floor that he saw the woman he loved. It was also the first day he ate solid food—some Jell-O and toast. Not bad.

Jake's hand surgery was deemed a complete success, but more surgeries were to come. They had used arthroscopic intervention to remove bullet fragments from the shoulder joint, but a follow-up procedure would evacuate more debris to protect against infection and inflammation. His leg wound had healed some without surgery, but not enough to walk on, even with the aid of a cane—he had tested it. Instead, Jake wheeled himself to Ellie's room, with a bouquet of flowers resting on his lap. The flowers weren't spectacular by any stretch, the blue and purple hues didn't look like anything that grew in the wild, but the hospital gift shop offered a limited supply.

Ellie was sitting up in bed, leafing through a magazine, when Jake arrived. Both her legs were in traction. Bandaged. Healing. She was hooked to monitors and such, but not to an alarming array of apparatuses. She was clearly on the mend. When Ellie saw Jake, her whole face lit up.

"Officer Barnes," Jake said, cocking a half smile. "I heard you were looking for someone to go running with."

"Only if I can sit on your lap and you wheel me around."

Jake picked up the flowers to make room for her. "Hop on," he said.

Jake wheeled over to the bed and tossed the flowers onto a side table crowded with other floral arrangements and a sea of get well cards. He leaned far enough forward to kiss Ellie tenderly on the forehead, then a kiss on her cheek, and then one on the lips.

"How are you feeling?" he asked.

"Like a woman who got shot twice in the leg. Actually, the surgery went really well. I'll be on my feet before long, or so the doctors say. How about you?"

"For human Swiss cheese, I think I'm doing all right. Who's been looking after your dogs?"

"My neighbor is on it. What about Andy?"

"He's with Lance."

They fell into a brief silence, during which Jake took hold of Ellie's hand. Tears came to Ellie's eyes, and she laughed and cried at the same time.

"I'm sorry," she said. "I'm really happy to see you. Honestly, from what I've heard, I can't believe you made it out of there alive."

"Yeah, well, that makes two of us."

Ellie got quiet again, but then said, "Why didn't you tell me, Jake?"

"Tell you what? That I think you're beautiful, that I love you? I do, and I do."

Ellie blushed a little as a smile brightened her face. "Yeah, well, I love you, too. And I should have said it sooner. I should have told you how I felt about you when I knew what those feelings actually were. But what I'm talking about is your lifestyle. Why did you keep it a secret from me all this time?"

Jake gripped Ellie's hand tighter as he looked deeply in her eyes. "Because I didn't want to lose you, I guess," Jake said. "Look, when there's a reality-TV show dedicated to your lifestyle, you know what you do isn't exactly mainstream. I was going to tell you at some point, but I just kept putting it off."

"Well, in case you were wondering, I wouldn't have broken up with you," Ellie said.

"But you would have had doubts about me. About my mental makeup. Come on, let's be honest here."

"I have a big guard dog to look out for me. I wouldn't have been scared." Ellie laughed a little in a way that Jake found so endearing.

"Well, my choices might have raised a question or two in your mind. But I guess it was something more than just you thinking I was a nut that kept me from telling you."

"Yeah? What more reason could there be?"

"I think I was holding on, Ellie . . . to my past, to Laura, to a time in my life when everything made the most sense. I was stuck there, which was probably why our relationship couldn't get beyond a certain level. I didn't really want to move forward."

"And now you do?"

Jake touched Ellie's face with much tenderness. Ellie pressed his hand against her even more strongly, and held him close.

"More than anything," Jake said.

A visitor was waiting for Jake when he wheeled back into his hospital room. Pixie sat on a cushioned chair tucked in a corner of the room, Beats by Dre headphones locked over his ears, eyes glued to his phone, thumbs moving at a blistering pace.

Somehow, despite the multitasking and sensory overload, Pixie sensed Jake's arrival and looked up. The headphones came off and the boy stood, seemingly with some trepidation. He remained quiet for a time—no greeting, no hello. While Pixie's purpose might have been guarded, his anxiety was evident. The boy's feet tapped out a rhythm, even though the music was off, and he massaged his interlocked fingers vigorously.

"Hey, good to see you, buddy. What brings you here? Is Andy with you?"

Jake wheeled over to Andy's friend, who shook his proffered hand a bit timidly.

Something was up with this kid, Jake thought. Something had him unsettled.

"Hello, Mr. Dent, and no, to answer your question Andy's not here. I came alone."

"Please call me Jake. We've been through a lot together, so I think we can skip the formalities. What brings you to 'The Pleasure Pit'?"

Pixie went silent, eyes to the floor, hands in his pocket, feet shuffling.

"Talk to me, Troy." Most everyone called Troy by his nickname, but Jake wasn't big on joining the crowd.

"I've been doing some work," Pixie said, keeping his voice soft.

"Work?"

"Trying to figure out who stole the bitcoins from us."

"Yeah? How'd it go?"

"I wasn't getting anywhere. The public key was still there, but the amounts had changed, meaning somebody had transferred or sold some of the coins to a different public key that I didn't know about."

"How?"

"Well, that's the thing. I figured the thief—well, the other thief, not us—might use Bitcoin Fog to try and hide the transaction."

"'Bitcoin fog'?" Jake needed clarification.

"It's a bit complicated, Mr. Dent—Jake—but let's say, you can use the service to sell the coins anonymously. Anyway, I had set up a monitor because I thought David was the thief, and I wrote a program that would alert me if he ever accessed that service from his school computer."

"And?"

"And he didn't," Pixie said.

Jake contained his disappointment.

"But I realized something about my program. I was actually logging a lot more data than I was looking at. I was scanning the IP address of everyone at the school."

Jake's expression came alive. "Let me guess. You got a hit, right?"

"I did."

"Whose computer was it?" Jake asked.

Pixie did something on his smartphone and held up the device so that Jake could see the display.

Jake's mouth fell open wide. "Are you sure about this, Troy? Are you sure?"

"Only a thousand percent."

Chapter 51

One month later

Jake and Ellie hovered by the closed door of the large conference room adjacent to Lance's expansive office. In addition to Lance, six members of The Shire waited inside for Jake and Ellie's arrival. Jake was dressed in a gray suit and no tie, and Ellie wore a cream-colored top accented by a silver necklace, dark pants, and no gun. She was on medical leave, which was fine by her. It gave her more time with Kibo and her other dogs.

Jake was still using his cane, an oak shaft with a brass-embossed collar and classic derby-style handle. While the surgery on his shoulder and hand had been a success, he'd never be the same again. The fingers didn't move quite as dexterously, and the pain never completely went away.

Jake was about to step inside, but paused at the door to take Ellie in his arms. She was not in much better condition: hours of surgery followed by extensive rehab, which was still ongoing. But her hands were fine, and on one finger was the diamond ring Jake had put there while she was still in the hospital.

Jake touched her face with his injured hand. She reached up and clutched it to her cheek, unable to get him close enough.

"Are you ready for this?" Jake asked.

Ellie's expression implied the concern was misplaced. "Are you?" she asked.

"What choice do I have?"

"We always have choices, Jake."

Jake gave Ellie a gentle kiss. "Then I choose to love you," he said.

He opened the conference room door. Ellie went inside and Jake followed.

Lance, dressed in a crisp blue suit and striking red tie, rose from his seat at the head of a long mahogany table and came over to give Jake and Ellie each a hug. He might not have endured the tunnels, but the experience had an aging effect on Lance as well.

The kids, wearing new school uniforms, remained seated. Andy and Hilary sat next to each other, holding hands. They were an official couple, though from the Facebook messages Beth MacDonald had been sending Andy, not everyone was pleased. David, Rafa, and Pixie were to the left of Andy and Hilary. Solomon was to the right. The six former members of The Shire sat glum-faced, deeply solemn, and quiet in an uncomfortable way.

Jake had just returned from a long meeting with Leo Haggar and the FBI, and he had news to share. To this day, nobody knew for certain the identities of who'd been held hostage inside the school. Everyone in The

Shire denied they were involved and provided credible alibis for their whereabouts. It was intentional, given they could still be targets for retribution. Jake had been treated for his injuries, which he explained away as a camping accident—a knife to the hand followed by a tumble off a trail. Rumors swirled, of course; but like the tunnel maps that cropped up from time to time, some of those were close, while others were way off base.

From his hospital room, until today, Jake had functioned as the group's ambassador, a spokesperson for leniency. It was a necessary role, too. The six students were technically criminals. They were computer hackers, and bank robbers, and while their actions might have been well-intentioned, their methods could hardly be condoned or go unpunished. There had been extensive conversations, with the threat of arrest hovering over the students' heads, but so far no formal charges had been filed. No public records existed, which also helped safeguard the identities of the hostages.

The FBI still had their hands full. Bodies had long been removed, statements taken, forensics done, and evidence gathered. The FBI initially had been quite harsh with Jake, threatening to press charges, but it was all bark and no bite. For all their bravado, the FBI was profoundly grateful and pleased with the outcome. In total, fifteen murdering cartel operatives were dead, opening cracks into Arturo Soto's seemingly impenetrable criminal empire. Still, the threat of retaliation from Soto remained a constant worry, a scar left behind that might never fade.

Consequences.

Now it was time for a different moment of truth. Had Jake and Ellie worked their magic with Haggar and the other higher-ups at the Bureau? Could an immunity deal be struck?

Lance returned to his seat, with Jake to his right and Ellie to his left.

Jake's expression remained grim when he said, "We cut the deal. Nobody is getting charged."

It was good news, what everyone wanted, but that didn't make it cause for celebration. "I have the paperwork with me," Jake said. "You'll have to sign it with your attorneys and your parents present. Speaking of parents, the ones you stole from don't want the money returned. In fact, many of them have given to the same organizations you donated to on their behalf. So that's done.

"But here's the thing. And I mean it, too. No more hacking. Not once. Not ever. You do it and get caught, you're going to jail and they'll charge you as adults. It's in the paperwork, but I wanted you to hear it from me as well. *No hacking.* Is that understood?"

Heads nodded, but nobody spoke. The mood was too intense for words.

David broke the heavy silence. "What about school?"

Jake looked over at Lance. "Not my department," he said.

Lance spoke up. "Business as usual," he said. "We don't want to draw any attention to your identities. Go about your lives. It's the best for everyone involved. But know this—I'm deeply disappointed in your choices and your actions, but I'm far more grateful that you're all here at this table."

"So I can still run track?" Rafa asked.

"Yeah, Rafa, you can still run track. You're lucky kids. In so many ways."

There was a bit of chatter and dialogue while Jake showed everyone the paperwork prepared by the U.S. Attorney's Office.

Later, Jake said, "I have to speak with Lance alone. Andy, I'll drive you home after school, as usual."

The kids stood. Andy locked eyes briefly with his father. There had been a number of difficult conversations at home, but Jake continued to make it clear that he forgave his son. The therapist they'd hired believed Andy was making good progress at forgiving himself. Nobody had imagined what would come of Andy's secret club. Nobody could have foreseen the terrible events that followed. What mattered was moving forward. That was what Jake focused on. He couldn't change yesterday, and the future would always have uncertainties, but Jake could live for today. He chose to live in the light—after all, he no longer had a tunnel hideaway to retreat into. All windows to his past were closed up tight.

Hilary paused at the doorway and looked to Ellie. "What about the money?" she asked.

"The drug money?" Ellie asked.

"Yeah. Two hundred million in missing bitcoins," Hilary said. "We didn't have it. We never did. What happened to the money?"

"I guess that's for the FBI to figure out," Jake said.

Jake and Pixie locked eyes for a moment.

"Go on to class now," Lance said.

The kids all left.

"Can I get you something to drink?" Lance asked, once everyone was gone.

"No, I'm fine," Jake said, taking a seat at the table.

"So, how did the meeting go?"

"It went fine," Jake said. His voice had changed, more somber.

"What's going on?" Lance asked. "You look strange, Jake."

Jake hefted his cane, lowering it in front of Lance like a barricade going down.

"What gives?" Lance asked.

Without a word, Jake sprang to a standing position and pressed his cane under Lance's chin. He used the shaft to coax Lance out of his seat; then he applied enough pressure to the throat to force Lance to move backward until he came to an abrupt stop against the wall.

"You son of a bitch," Jake said, his face turning crimson. The cane stayed flush against Lance's throat. "How could you do it, Lance? How? To Andy, to his friends, to Ellie? You could have gotten everyone killed!"

"What? What are you talking about?" The pressure on Lance's throat made it difficult to talk, but not hard to breathe.

"Don't," Jake said through gritted teeth. "Don't lie to me!"

"Jake, please . . . please . . ."

Ellie came forward and put a hand on Jake's shoulder. "Jake, don't make it worse," she said.

Adrenaline turned Jake's breathing shallow. He hesitated before he lowered his cane. Lance sank to the floor with a grim expression.

"I've been thinking about this moment for so long," Jake said, still breathing hard. "What was I going to say to you? How would I react? Just be grateful Ellie's here, Lance. Just be grateful Andy wasn't hurt."

Lance looked as if he was about to get physically sick.

Jake went on. He used the cane for balance now, not as a weapon. "You can thank Pixie for figuring it out," he continued. "Guess you tried to sell some of the bit-coins and he was watching for it. What? One Patek Philippe isn't enough for you?"

"The Lion is already in jail and you're next, Lance," Ellie said. "The FBI knows you helped The Lion steal the money from Andy and his friends. For all his skill, Javier's computer expert still needed a person on the inside to breach the network. You were that person."

"Javier didn't know The Lion's identity, but once Pixie nailed you, it wasn't hard to find him," Jake added. "The FBI has been building a case against you for a while, keeping you under surveillance, so I had to keep quiet and keep my anger in check. Believe me, that was harder than the toughest game I ever pitched."

Lance said, "Jake, I—I—don't know what to say."

Jake kept his calm, but inside he was seething.

"I can understand why you did it. You got tired of being the poorest guy at the party. But you should have come forward when Andy was in danger. You knew, but you didn't do anything to help."

"What did you want me to do, Jake?"

Jake let the cane fall from his grasp. Then he bent at the waist and seized Lance by his shirt. In a fluid motion, Jake hoisted Lance to his feet as though his brother were weightless. A second after that, Lance was back up against the wall, with Jake holding him in place.

Jake's eyes were wide and wild. He'd been in plenty of bench-clearing brawls in his day. Throwing a punch was never something he shied from, but somehow he found the restraint to keep his hands from becoming fists. Even so, Jake got right in Lance's face.

"What you should have done is told the FBI!"

"I d-didn't know what—what was happening," Lance stuttered out the words.

Jake was incredulous. "What? Did you think a hostage situation at The Pep and your two-hundred-million-dollar heist weren't connected? When Andy and his friends couldn't be found, the kids you stole from, did you not think to be concerned? They all could have died because of your greed. All of them, including me!"

Jake cocked a fist and Lance flinched. Twice Jake went to make the punch, but he couldn't bring himself to do it. Instead, Jake let go and Lance sank to the floor. Lance kept his head bowed, hands covering his face. Jake turned his back to his brother, stood there a second with his hands at his sides, shaking, and then he, too, sank to the floor, resting against the same wall Lance used to stay upright. The brothers' shoulders were touching.

"You don't have long before the FBI gets here, Jake," Ellie said.

"Long for what?" Lance asked.

In a soft voice, Jake said, "I wanted to get you alone beforehand so I could tell you something."

"Please, Jake," Lance said, his bottom lip trembling.

Jake returned a sympathetic look. "I've got a lot of

conflicted emotions here, brother, so hear me out," Jake said. "When I was at my lowest, you were there for me. I'll never forget that. I love you, Lance. You're my brother. And I won't turn my back on you. Not ever. But you did the crime. Stealing from anybody, even if the money originally came from a drug cartel, is still illegal. There's a whole host of charges coming your way. Javier is going to jail for a long time for money laundering, tax evasion, and probably wire fraud. They might try to get you on similar charges. Either way, you're going to be criminally punished for what you've done—that's for certain. I don't know how many years you'll get. First offense. Who knows? But I'll help you make bail, no matter what."

"Jake, I can't go to jail," Lance said. "This school is my life. How can I just leave it and the kids?"

"Yeah, well, that's all in the past now. Trust me, you're going to have to move on. And you'll adjust eventually. What matters most is that you have a choice to make."

"Choice?"

"In the closet of your bedroom, I've prepared a GOOD pack for you. It has everything you'll need to survive on the run. If you don't think you can do the time, then I've given you a way out. It's the best I can come up with. My way of taking away some of the sting of your mistake, just like you helped take away some of the sting of mine. I've spent weeks writing a detailed handbook for you to follow. It's everything I know about survival, about prepping. It'll teach you to live off the grid. Follow the rules. Don't break them. Don't even bend them a little, and you'll have a chance. There's a map for you to use. It shows how you can get to New York by foot. Buy some disguises. It's all in that handbook."

Jake stood and Ellie came to his side. They held hands while Lance hid his face once more.

"I'm so sorry," Lance said, blubbering the words as the tears came out.

"Yeah, I know you are," Jake said.

Jake helped Lance to his feet eventually, and all three were soon seated in silence at the conference-room table, waiting. At some point, the doors to the conference room burst open, and in came a swarm of FBI agents. Seconds after that, Lance was in handcuffs. Jake came over to his brother while he was being read his rights.

"I swung for the fences, little brother," Lance said. "But you got to understand, I had to take the swing."

Jake set a hand on Lance's shoulder. "If you play your life like it's a baseball game, then someone has to lose," Jake said. "Those are the rules."

The FBI escorted Lance in handcuffs to the door, where he paused and looked back at Jake.

"Please tell Andy I'm sorry," Lance said, "and tell him I love him." With those parting words, he was gone.

Jake and Ellie stayed awhile, but it was too painful to watch Lance's life get dismantled. They walked to The Quad and sat on a stone bench and listened to the leaves rustling in the trees. The Pep was in full bloom, and school was just about done for the year. In September, a new crop of students would arrive, and they'd hear stories about what had happened in those tunnels. The Feldman Auditorium would be reopened by then, with all new seating. Pixie's dad would see to that.

Ellie gazed up at a cloudless sky and took in a breath of fresh air. "What if Soto comes looking for you, Jake? What if Javier talks? What if Soto finds out who you are and what you did?"

Jake looked to the sky as well, put an arm around Ellie, and pulled her in close. "Don't worry," he said. "I'll be prepared."

ACKNOWLEDGMENTS

I love reading the acknowledgments in novels, as much as I like writing them. As a reader, it gives me a greater appreciation for what the author went through, and as a writer, I can reflect on those who helped me along the way. *Constant Fear* was hardly a solo effort. Many people lent their time, expertise, and considerable knowledge to the telling of this tale. I'd like to start by thanking my editor, John Scognamiglio, who believed in the story concept from the start and encouraged me to bring it to the page. Equally important is the team at the Jane Rotrosen Agency, especially my fabulous agent, Meg Ruley and fellow agent Rebecca Scherer, who offered keen insights and encouragement along the way.

My amazing mom, Judy Palmer, dedicated innumerable hours to reading various drafts and providing exceptional feedback. I would also like to thank Clair Lamb for her help in shaping this novel into its final form. All things bitcoin came courtesy of Johnny Dilly from Pantera Capital. What I wrote about guns, ammo, and such I learned from Ben Beauchemin and Brian Noe of Wicked Weaponry in Hooksett, New Hampshire. Ali Karim, friend to the mystery/thriller writer community, educated me on hazardous chemicals. Susanna Cummings translated all of the Spanish, and if you're looking for help in that regard I suggest you send her a message at keynotesinc.com. Dr. Richard Dugas educated me about diabetes, and a lot of what I learned about pitching comes from the incomparable book, *The Mental ABC's of Pitching* by H.A. Dorfman. I have a newfound appreciation for the art of pitching thanks to this book. All baseball pitchers, regardless of their level, should give it a read.

There is a big back office operation that makes possible the book's production and distribution. I would like to thank everyone at Kensington: the sales force, the production and art teams, and the marketers and publicists who make it happen. A special thank you goes out to the publisher, Steven Zacharius. His passion for this business is truly infectious.

As always, my family played a pivotal role in this endeavor. So thank you Jessie, Benny, Sophie, and now Monte (our new puppy) for bringing Jake's motivation to life for me. I'd battle for you guys any day of the week. Thanks also to Matthew, Ethan, and Luke—better brothers a guy couldn't have.

Every book of mine I've acknowledged the contributions of my father, Michael Palmer. This time, however, my dad wasn't here in person to play a part, but his spirit was with me throughout, and I'll forever be indebted to his teachings on the craft. Miss you and love you, pop.

And lastly, I want to acknowledge you, my dear readers. Without you, none of this is possible. As for me, well, I have to admit I started canning vegetables after I finished writing this book.

Better to be prepared, I guess.

New Hampshire, 2015

In a heart-pounding thriller from one of the most innovative voices in contemporary suspense, a woman unravels the shocking truth about her parents, her past, and a life built upon an unthinkable lie.

At DeRose & Associates Private Investigators in Virginia, Angie DeRose strives to find and rescue endangered runaways—work that stands in stark contrast to her own safe, idyllic childhood. But in the wake of her mother's sudden death, Angie makes a life-altering discovery. Hidden among the mementos in her parents' attic is a photograph of a little girl, with a code and a hand-written message on the back: "May God forgive me."

Angie has no idea what it means or how to explain other questionable items among her mother's possessions. Her father claims to know nothing. Could Angie have a sister or other relative she was never told about? Bryce Taggart, the U.S. Marshal working with her agency, agrees to help Angie learn the fate of the girl in the photograph. But the lies she and Bryce unearth will bring her past and present together with terrifying force. And everything she cherishes will be threatened by the repercussions of one long-ago choice—and an enemy who will kill to keep a secret hidden forever.

Please turn the page for an exciting sneak peek of Daniel Palmer's

FORGIVE ME

coming in June 2016 wherever print and e-books are sold!

Prologue

She sat at her writing desk in her home's spacious first-floor office, dreading this moment that came every year on this date. The dainty desk was a replica of a *bonheur-du-jour*, a piece of furniture from the eighteenth century made specifically with a woman in mind. The name, "good hour of the day," referred to the time of day when women took pleasure from opening, reading, and writing letters. She was there for that purpose, but took no pleasure in the task.

Gazing out a bank of windows, she saw the empty garden beds. They would blossom beautifully in springtime, as they always did. But spring was several weeks away. The grass around the beds was brown, and her mood was somber and gray as the overcast sky.

From one of the desk's lacquered panels, she removed her checkbook, then fished a ballpoint pen from the desk's main compartment. Out of habit, she checked the balance in the check register—plenty of money in the account, as there always was. The simple observation summoned a familiar feeling of guilt, followed by profound sadness.

She wrote out the check for the same amount as always. Her handwriting was impeccable. The loops, curves, and lines formed perfect, beautiful letters, properly spaced, neat and elegant, almost like calligraphy. She'd loved writing in school, and dreamed of one day writing a novel. She felt she had so much to say about love and relationships, the big questions of life. But that was a long time ago, a different lifetime, and she had since become an entirely different person.

From the living room next to the office she could hear the television. The sound of some sporting event in progress—basketball, she thought. What did she know? Watching sports on TV was her husband's pastime, not hers. And yet, this was her dream—a husband resting on his lazy chair; a child reared and off on her own; a fine house kept tidy and organized, thanks to her fastidious nature; gardens in need of tending—everything as it should be.

But some dreams come at a price.

She knew that now.

From one of the little drawers across the back of the desk, she removed an envelope and addressed it from memory. Her tears began to fall. The words turned to smudges. She crumpled up the envelope, took another, and started anew. From the same drawer, she got a blank piece of paper and wrote *With gratitude for your efforts*. She signed her name and folded the paper around the check. Then, she slipped both items into the envelope and licked it closed. The glue tasted extra bitter on her tongue. She slipped the envelope into her purse. She would drive to a mailbox tonight, so it would go out first thing in the morning. She closed her eyes and took inventory of all she had, all her good fortune.

In a whispered voice, she uttered the same phrase she spoke every year on this day, at this exact moment. "May God forgive me."

Chapter 1

Nadine had thought about running away for years. She lived in a nice colonial house in Potomac, Maryland, but home was hell. She was supposed to be the child, so why was she the one taking care of her mother? It wasn't fair. No, not right at all. Her mother had always loved to drink, but it was different after Dad left. Wine used to make her giddy, but now it just made her slur her words.

Nadine had begged her father to let her come live with him, but he was too busy with work to look after her, or so he'd said. She'd be better at home with Mom, he'd said. Ha! He should come and see what Mom had become since he'd left them for that bitch.

She tried to tell her father what it was like living with Mom. Weekends spent in bed. Often there was no food in the refrigerator, and Nadine would have to do all the shopping (driving illegally, but always carefully, on her learner's permit) and the cooking, not to mention the cleaning. Mom walked into walls, tripped over her own feet.

Somehow her mother still had a job. She worked for Verizon, doing something in customer service. How she got to work each day, given her evening's alcohol consumption, was nothing short of a miracle. Her get-ready ritual involved a lot more than a shower, some makeup, and breakfast. Her mother needed half the Visine bottle to get the red out. She often turned on bathroom faucets full strength to mask the sound of retching.

She'd come downstairs, cupping what looked like a handful of aspirin in her palm, and bark something unpleasant at Nadine. "Turn down that TV. I have a headache."

Of course you do, Nadine would think.

"Is that what you're wearing? You look like a tramp." It never failed. Mom's mouth would open and something cruel, something cutting, would spill out.

"I made the honors list," Nadine announced on the fifteenth day of March, the day she finally ran away.

Her mother rubbed at her pounding temples as she poured a cup of coffee flavored with Kahlúa. Something to take the edge off, she would say.

"You better, for what we pay that private school," was her mother's reply.

Nadine's chest felt heavy, throat dry, while her eyes watered. She would not give her mother the satisfaction of seeing her cry again. Her mother would pounce if a single tear leaked out.

"Toughen up, Nadine," she'd say. "The world is a brutal place, and you'd best have a thicker skin."

Her mother's jabs always held a hint of truth, which

made them hurt even more. Nadine's school was expensive, that was a fact. But her father paid most of the tuition.

Money, it seemed, was the only thing that wasn't a problem in Nadine's life. Dad sent them plenty. He said he was happy to support them, but Nadine knew the truth. He was assuaging (an SAT word she'd recently learned) his guilt.

He didn't want her in his life. He wanted his new, young wife and no kids to hassle them. He wanted to travel and go to all the fancy restaurants he posted on his Facebook feed. One look at her dad's profile page and it was obvious a kid didn't fit into the picture. After the divorce, her father had moved to Philadelphia—Bryn Mawr East, to be exact—with a new executive position at an insurance company and a new woman in his life. He posted a few photos of Nadine, but those were all recent. No "Throwback Thursday" posts (#tbt in Facebook parlance) on her dad's page. No pictures of Nadine aged infant to tween; no evidence of his former life, aka his great mistake as he'd called his marriage during an epic pre-divorce blowout.

That was how he viewed his family. That was all Nadine was to him—a great mistake.

Apparently her mother felt the same way.

Nadine's last meal at home was chicken casserole, which she prepared using a recipe she got off the Internet. Her mother downed a bottle of wine with the meal. In her drunken stupor, she failed to notice the shoes Nadine had left in front of the closet door. Her mother tripped over the shoes and fell to the floor, twisting her ankle on the way down.

Nadine apologized. She had meant to put the shoes where they belonged, but was preoccupied with school, and dinner, and her too many responsibilities.

Her mother was hearing none of it. She went to the couch and applied ice to the injury, then poured herself another glass of wine, allegedly because it helped with the pain.

"Sorry again, Mom," Nadine said. "Are you okay?"

Her mother's eyes were red as her nail polish. "You're so thoughtless, Nadine," she slurred. "How am I going to go to work now? I can't even walk. Sometimes I wish your father would let you go live with him. I know that's what you want."

That was it. That did it. Enough was enough. Her father didn't want her. Neither did her mother. The choice was made not *by her*, but *for her*. Nobody wanted Nadine, so nobody had to have her.

After her mother slipped into drunken sleep, Nadine took all of the money they kept in the house—$400-some dollars—and her mother's jewelry and walked out the door with a school knapsack filled with clothes instead of books. She walked to Montgomery Mall, about four and a half miles, then took a Metrobus downtown. She had plenty of money to spend, plus whatever a pawnshop would give her for the jewelry.

Pretending to be her mother, Nadine had called in sick to school. It was that easy. Her mother would take the day off to nurse her injured ankle—she'd already sent the e-mail to her boss. She'd wake up late and hung over, and think Nadine was at school. She'd think that until five o'clock rolled around.

Then she'd wonder. Maybe she'd call some of Nadine's friends. It would be seven . . . and then eight . . .

and then panic. Maybe panic. Or maybe not. She'd probably be happy. Relieved to be rid of Nadine once and for all.

Nadine didn't know what her mother was thinking. She'd been gone for three days without calling home. She'd found a motel on the far side of the city that didn't bother to check ID, didn't care that she was a sixteen-year-old girl out on her own.

The question was what to do with all the time on her hands. She enjoyed school and did her homework diligently. She loved English especially, loved to escape into other people's happy or miserable lives and forget about her own for a while. She found a used bookstore off Dupont Circle and bought several books, including the entire Testing Trilogy by Joelle Charbonneau. She devoured all three volumes in the span of two days. But something was missing. Idle time to read had in some ways diminished the pleasure.

She was wandering aimlessly in Union Station, admiring the shops and all the things she had no money to buy, wondering how to pass the day, when a man approached.

He was tall and good-looking for an older man, with a nicely round head sporting a buzz cut like Jason Statham's, and a clean-shaven face. His most notable feature was a pair of piercing blue eyes. He carried a bag from Heydari Design, which Nadine knew sold women's clothing and accessories.

"Can I ask you something?" he said to her.

He had a foreign accent, Nadine thought. But it was subtle. Something distinct—*sophisticated* was the word that came to mind—something like a count would use. He was dressed sharply in a tailored navy suit, blue oxford underneath, no tie. His shoes were polished black loafers.

Nadine gazed at the man, unable to speak before finding her voice. "Yes," was all she said.

Why is he talking to me? What could he want? Did Mom put out a missing persons report? Does he recognize me? Am I in trouble? Will he call the police? Will they take me to jail? Worse, will they take me back home?

"I just bought something for my daughter. She's about your age. But after I left the store, I was hit with doubt. I could use a second opinion. She likes the color blue, if that helps any."

From inside the Heydari bag, he removed a twilight blue linen-blend scarf, fringed at the ends for a touch of sophistication. It was lovely, something Nadine would have bought for herself if she had money to spend on such purchases. Books and food were all she could afford to buy. Plus she needed money for her motel room. Where else was she going to sleep? There was a lot more to running away from home than she had contemplated.

"I think she'll love it." Nadine meant it, too. To her surprise, her chest suddenly felt heavy. Here was a dad doing something lovely and thoughtful for his daughter. Her father gave her birthday presents, but always mailed them. It was never anything she wanted because he didn't take the time to get to know her tastes, her color palette.

Her father was nothing like this one, she decided.

"Thank you. I feel a bit more confident now."

That accent, where was it from? European? "You're welcome," Nadine said.

The man nodded his thanks, turned to leave, but stopped. He seemed to be appraising her in a way that made her feel vulnerable. "This is going to sound odd," he said as he took out his wallet.

Does he think I need a handout? Nadine was mortified to think she looked so bedraggled (another SAT word) that he suspected she was homeless and in need.

To her great relief, he took out a business card instead of cash. "I run an entertainment agency, and I'm always on the lookout for new talent. If you don't mind my saying, you have a great look. Almost like a Jennifer Lawrence type."

Nadine had to suppress a laugh. JLaw? Her? *Come on.* Nadine didn't think herself exceptional in any way. She was average at everything—height, weight, academics, sports. Name it, and she fit smack dab in the middle, undistinguished and undistinguishable from her peers. Her hair color was brown, eyes brown, and that's what it would say on the missing person posters if her mother bothered to file a report. Weight 118, height 5'3". Average. Perfectly average.

She blushed.

"I'm not saying you look like her exactly," the man explained. "But there's something about you that's very compelling. I'm not kidding. I find talent for TV, movies, reality shows. It's a booming business these days with so many places for content."

Nadine shrugged. She didn't know what to say. She looked down at the card. STEPHEN J. MACAN. MACAN ENTERTAINMENT. No address, no phone number, no website or e-mail. It felt secretive, which made the business seem more exclusive. He had to find you; you couldn't find him.

"Have you ever had headshots done?"

Before Nadine could answer, the man's cell phone rang. A smile came to his face as he answered the call. "Hi honey. I'm still at the mall shopping for Megan." He pulled the phone away and mouthed the words *my wife* for Nadine's benefit. He held up his finger, an indication he wanted her to stay.

For some reason, she did.

"I'll be home soon. Want me to pick up something for dinner? I could grill up salmon, if you'd like."

A pause while his wife said something in response.

"Great. Oh, and I got the opinion of a girl about Megan's age, so I think I did well with my gift. We shall see." He gave a little laugh.

Some inside joke about how difficult Megan could be to shop for, Nadine supposed. The joke was made with love, not malice. It was so obvious Megan's dad adored her.

Nadine's heart turned. *Why can't I have the same sort of relationship with my father?*

"I'll be home soon. Love you. Bye." The man's attention went back to Nadine. "So are you interested in becoming famous?" His smile was warm, genuine.

Nadine wondered if his daughter Megan had the right look. The man, this Stephen Macan, seemed so certain *Nadine* did.

He wouldn't lie about something like this.

It was all happening too fast for her to process. A little tickle in the gut told her to be cautious. She handed the man back his card. "I don't think so."

The man looked resigned and a little disappointed, but offered no hard sell. "Just so you know, there's no second chances. This business is too hard for any self-doubters. We look for people who think they were meant for something more. I thought I had it right with you." He shrugged. "Maybe all this shopping has dulled my instincts. Anyway, I wish you the best of luck." He stuck out his hand.

As soon as she shook it, Nadine felt numb all over her body. She wasn't sure what she was feeling. Ashamed? Disappointed in herself? What were his words exactly?

People who think they were meant for something more.

That struck a chord. Despite her parents, she thought she was worth something more. She could make something out of her life and show them all. That's right. Become somebody and get on *Ellen* or *Good Morning America* and have a tear-filled reunion on live TV while her parents apologized to their celebrity daughter for years of mistreatment. Wouldn't that show them!

She watched Stephen Macan walk away, swinging the bag that contained a beautiful scarf for his daughter, who wasn't pretty enough for a movie career of her own. He wasn't creepy at all. She got no vibes like that from him. He had a wife to whom he spoke sweetly and a kid about her age. It was happenstance that he saw her and asked a very reasonable question about the gift, and then luck that he saw something *in her*.

It was the real deal, Nadine decided, a genuine opportunity that she let pass by. And think! The next time her mother might see her could be on TV or in the movies. She tried to imagine her expression. It would be priceless!

The man was a good distance away, almost out of sight.

Nadine took a determined breath and went running after him.